Battlefield of Deceit

Faith in the Parks, Book 5

J. Carol Nemeth

Written by: J. Carol Nemeth
Published by: Forget Me Not Romances, a division of Winged Publications

Cover Design: Cynthia Hickey

This book is a work of fiction. Names, characters, places, and incidents are the product of the author's imagination and are used fictitiously. Any resemblance to actual events, locales, or persons, living or dead, is coincidental.

ISBN: 978-1-956654-50-9

Dedication

I would like to dedicate this book to the memory of my father, the Rev. James W. Pruitt and to the memory of my mother, Mary Sue Amick Pruitt. My parents instilled in my siblings and me the love of camping and the outdoors at an early age. I still remember our first camping trip in an old canvas army tent that closed by tying long strings at the door, and it had no floor. We slept on old army cots. I must have been three or four years old. We soon graduated to one with a floor and a zippered door where creepy crawlies were encouraged to stay out. My parents introduced us to the national parks and monuments as well as state parks, and we traveled from the mountains to the coast as often as we could. We climbed lighthouses, descended into caves, swam in the ocean, visited presidents (homes), and saw where man took flight to name only a few places. Thank you, Mama and Daddy, for spreading our wings and giving us the love of travel!

I would also like to dedicate this book to my father-in-law, Robert S. Nemeth, Jr, who passed away on March 1, 2020 and my mother-in-law, Charlene K. Nemeth, who a character in this book is named after. I love you both and am blessed to have you as my in-laws. The best in-laws ever. Thanks for raising your son to be the strong Christian man he is, so when I came along, he'd be the perfect husband for me. The Lord knew what He was doing when He sent us both in the Army to Italy from Ohio and NC.

And we know that all things work together for good to them that love God, to them who are called according to his purpose. Romans 8:28 KJV

Acknowledgement

Without my Lord and Savior there would be no books to read from this author. I depend on His guidance and help to give me the stories He wants me to write. Due to some of the topics in this story, I second-guessed myself at the end and as I waited for my beta reader to get back to me. I should have known better and simply trusted what He gave me. When she responded with her critique, I was blown away. God is good. Not sometimes or when He feels like tossing a few crumbs our way. He's good. All. The. Time. Period. I praise Him for His wonderful direction in my life and how he directs me when I write. I wouldn't be anywhere without Him.

Thank you, Sherri Stewart, for stepping up and filling in as my editor when my usual editor was unable to work with me this go-round. It was short notice, and yet you worked hard to get the job done so we could get the manuscript in before deadline. You're a blessing.

Janice Bittner, you're always a blessing to me. Your willing heart and giving spirit to spend time no matter what are amazing. This time the shortened timeline you had to beta read and the time you put in made it tight for you, yet you gave it your all. Thank you for the prayers, especially when you realized the discouragement I was undergoing at the end. You stormed heaven for me. Thank you just doesn't seem like enough.

Jan Tomalis is one of my faithful readers. She won a contest a couple of months ago in which she won the chance to have her name used for one of the characters in this book. Congratulations again, Jan!

Mark, my awesome husband, you always come last on the list, but besides my Savior, you're first in my heart. You're always willing to take me anywhere for research and drive that big ol' RV to do it. You encourage me and love me, and are my biggest cheerleader (minus the pompoms, of course.) I love you, sweetheart. No more national parks to research for now. We'll have to see where we go from here.

Cellar of an abandoned home
Gettysburg Battlefield
Gettysburg, PA
July 1, 1863

Prologue

"You've gotta add your name to the list, Corporal." Sergeant Edwards tapped the wrinkled paper he'd tugged from inside his royal blue uniform jacket and laid on the small, wooden drop-leaf table. "Stand with the rest of the men whose names are on this list and tell the truth."

The younger man yanked his uniform cap from his head and wiped sweat from his brow with his sleeve. Shaking his head, he reseated the cap and swallowed hard. "I don't know, Sarge. I just ain't sure."

"What do you mean, you're not sure?" Incredulity imprinted itself on Sergeant Edwards' face. "You were there, and you saw what happened. How can you even hesitate?"

Corporal Peterson's gaze shifted around the dank, dark cellar. Only an oil lantern on the table lit the space. The young man had agreed to meet him here after the rest of the company settled in for the night. The cellar lay beneath an old, abandoned home near the battlefield. Since the battle had begun that day, most of the homes stood empty as families fled the area, especially those nearest the battlefield on the outskirts of town.

This battle wasn't over. If tomorrows were anything like today's, it would be a long, brutal day. Likely none of them would go home. However, in the off chance they did, Sergeant Edwards intended to see his commander brought up on charges for what he'd done. Even court-martialed, if possible.

"I don't think I want to sign that there paper, Sarge." Corporal Peterson shook his head again. "I just can't do it."

Sergeant Edwards slammed his hand on top of the paper. "But you have to. He has to be stopped. The truth has to be told, Corporal."

A dark figure slowly emerged from the shadows startling both men. A deep voice accompanying his appearance. "Sergeant Edwards, I do believe the man refused to sign your paper. Short of forcing him at gunpoint, you can't make him, you know."

The muscles in Sergeant Edwards body wound tighter than a metal spring as he withdrew his hand from the paper and straightened. "Colonel Mayfield. What are you doing here?"

The colonel, with his royal blue wide-brimmed calvary hat still covering his graying head, allowed a faint grin to lift one corner of his thin lips beneath a long, narrow gray mustache. "Well now, I could ask you the same thing, Sergeant. What are you doing here in this dank cellar antagonizing one of my troops?"

Sergeant Edwards swallowed and remained silent. How could he pick up the paper and stuff it in his shirt without drawing attention to it? Before he could decide what to do, Col. Edgar William Mayfield stepped closer and picked it up, his gaze scanning the page, then returned it to the Sergeant's face.

"Do you have a sweetheart, Sergeant Edwards? Someone who is waiting back home for you?" With precision, he folded the paper in half, then in half again. After a third fold, he reached over and tucked it into the sergeant's inner coat pocket.

Sergeant Edward's nodded, the metal spring deep inside him coiling tighter. "Yes, Colonel, I do."

The colonel turned to Corporal Peterson. "And you, son? Do

you have a sweetheart back home?"

The corporal blinked, swallowed nervously, then nodded. "Yes, sir."

Colonel Mayfield clasped his hands behind his back and screwed up his lips for a moment, his gaze narrowing. Then he nodded. "Wonderful. It's a lucky man who has a good woman in his life." He turned to the corporal. "Peterson, you're dismissed. Head back to the company and tend to your evening duties."

Corporal Peterson stood at attention and saluted the colonel. When he received a salute in return, he scooted out of the cellar as fast as he could, never looking back.

Colonel Mayfield turned to Sergeant Edwards and nodded toward him. "You know that piece of paper you have isn't worth the ink that's written on it. While you may think you have the upper hand and know what you're doing, you do not. As far as I'm concerned, you and all those men on that list have committed insubordination, and I deal with that *my* way." He pulled his saber from its hilt and before Sergeant Edwards knew what was happening, the colonel ran it through his heart.

The sergeant gasped as pain seared through his chest. The colonel pulled the saber from his body and stabbed him again and again, sending waves of excruciating pain over and through him. Gasping for air and unable to breath, Edwards fell against the stone wall and the dirt floor of the cellar. His life's blood flowed from him and into the dirt beneath him.

His vision grew dim as a smirk formed on the colonel's face.

"I'm sure your sweetheart won't mourn for long, dear boy. She'll move on and find some other dandy to wed and live life with." The colonel bent and tapped the sergeant's chest with the point of the bloody saber. "The truth will die with you, just as your squad will, Sergeant."

The dimness of Sergeant Edward's vision faded into blackness as the spring inside him uncoiled and his life ebbed away.

Gettysburg National Military Park
Gettysburg, PA
Early May, Current Year

Chapter One

Blake Hunter sat at the stop sign waiting to turn his park police cruiser when a cobalt blue Mini Cooper flashed past doing far more than the assigned speed limit. He caught a glimpse of a blond ponytail on the driver before the miniature vehicle vanished over a rise in the road. Releasing a heavy sigh, Blake flipped on his overhead flashing blue lights and made sure there was no oncoming traffic then took off after the Mini Cooper.

As he caught up with it, he registered the speed then waited for the driver to pull over. The woman glanced back in her side mirror, but she continued on.

"Really? You've got to be kidding me!"

The driver slowed to the legal limit but continued on, then turned into the Gettysburg National Military Park Visitors Center. She didn't stop at the visitors parking lot but went around to the employees parking and pulled into a marked spot. Blake followed and stopped behind her car leaving his blue lights flashing.

Before she could climb out, Blake was out of his cruiser and beside her door, hands on his hips.

She rolled her window down, but before she could speak, Blake did. "Do you have any idea what it means when a police car is following you with his lights on?"

In spite of Blake's irritation, a part of his mind registered one word: gorgeous. If only her sunglasses weren't covering her eyes. He'd love to see their color. But he wasn't the only one irritated. Her shapely lips clamped tight, and her brow creased between honey-blond feathered eyebrows, but neither detracted from her delicate beauty. Nope. Not one iota. Whoever this young woman was, she was delectable.

Blake mentally head slapped himself. *What in the world? Get your head in the game, dummy.*

"Of course, I know what a police car following me with lights on means." She huffed. "Can I go now? I'm late for work."

Blake eyed her park uniform. What audacity. "You think because you work here that'll get you out of a ticket? I don't think so." He pulled out his ticket book. "Are you aware you were going twenty over the speed limit?"

The young woman's gaze shifted away. "Twenty, huh?"

"Yep. Driver's license and registration, please."

Digging through her purse on the passenger seat, she withdrew the first then took the second from the glove compartment. Blake noticed it was well organized and not cram packed with junk. Nice. She handed both to him.

"Thanks." Blake accepted the documents. "Hang tight. I'll be right back." He returned to his cruiser and climbed in. Glancing at the young woman's driver's license, he noted her name as Chloe Rogers. He typed the information from the license as well as the vehicle registration into the laptop positioned above the console to the right of his steering wheel. As he waited for the information to come back, Blake glanced at the window of Chloe Roger's vehicle. Her arm rested on the windowsill, her fingertips tapping an impatient rhythm.

I just bet she's anxious. Too bad. This is what she gets for driving twenty over the speed limit. Blake eyed the computer screen. Hmm. No record. This was her first speed stop. He released a heavy sigh. Why did it have to be him to issue her first ticket? Firming his jaw, he grabbed his ticket book and headed back to Miss Rogers' car.

A frosty glare behind those sunglasses met him as he approached. Those luscious lips were pursed tightly before she spoke. "You're going to spoil my perfect driving record, aren't you?'

Blake didn't even attempt to prevent his humorless chuckle. "I'm afraid you did that all by yourself, Miss Rogers. I didn't force you to drive twenty over. You did that."

He completed the information on the ticket and ripped it from the tablet. "Here you go. The information you need to know is on the back. Have a good day." Blake tipped his Smokey-Bear hat and turned, striding back to his cruiser. He couldn't wait for this traffic stop to end. Since Chloe Rogers was a park employee, he'd likely see her again. No matter how beautiful she was, he hoped it wasn't anytime soon.

~

As the park police cruiser drove away, Chloe dropped her head against the headrest and closed her eyes. She wanted nothing more than to scrunch the ticket in a ball and toss it out the window, but Mr. Park Police would likely return and give her another one for littering. Recalling the man, she couldn't help but notice how tall and good looking he was *and* how well his park uniform fit. What woman wouldn't, she supposed. Such broad shoulders. Trim dark brown hair peeked from beneath his flat-brimmed, Smokey-Bear hat, which fit perfectly on his head. She should know. She had to wear hers the same way. At one point he'd removed his aviator sunglasses, and she'd noticed his dark gray eyes surrounded by long lashes any woman would kill for.

Chloe huffed a frustrated sigh and frowned at the pink paper in her hand. Enough. She wasn't interested and hadn't been for a long time. As for the ticket, she glanced at the date. There was plenty of time to take care of it, and she certainly didn't have to deal with it right now.

Rolling up her window, Chloe grabbed her purse and messenger bag and headed into headquarters. Already a half hour late, she had work to do. Thankful she'd worn flats with her uniform today, she hurried in the back door of the building and upstairs to the office she shared with her fellow historian, Clifford Weston.

Chloe shoved the office door open to find Clifford standing by the long wall full of bookshelves, his face and one finger buried in a book. He didn't glance up as Chloe strode to her desk and dropped onto her chair. She shoved her purse into the bottom drawer of her desk, dropped her bag beneath, and booted her computer.

"Morning, Chloe. Car trouble?" Clifford's dark gaze behind tortoise-shell framed glasses eventually peered over the top edge of the book, then disappeared within its pages once again. His curly dark mop that passed for hair was disheveled as usual. It had the perpetual appearance of him having run his hand through it from frustration. Chloe wasn't sure if he ever combed it, and she didn't care. Clifford Weston was the most knowledgeable historian she'd even met, and Gettysburg National Military Park was fortunate to employ him.

Chloe cast Clifford a quick glance then returned it to her computer. "Car trouble? Something like that. Anything important going on this morning, Cliff? Your text indicated you had some interesting news." She swiveled her chair toward him. "It didn't give any clues. What's going on?"

Clifford snapped the book shut and strode toward his desk, dropping it on top of a stack of other books. Chloe never understood how Clifford could work at his desk with the piles of books, papers and files covering every inch of it, but he seemed to have a method to the chaos that reigned there.

"Oh, yes, the text I sent. I have amazing news." He approached the front of Chloe's desk and shoved his hands into the pockets of his rumpled, olive uniform slacks, the shirttail of his gray uniform shirt slipping out on one side. “We received a call from a Mrs. Maureen White-Smith. She’s in possession of the diary of her great-great-grandfather. He was a Union colonel in the Civil War right here at Gettysburg and a hero to boot. Apparently, he performed some feat that saved the lives of many of his men, and she has a letter from that era that goes along with his diary. Mrs. White-Smith would like to loan them to the museum here at the national military park. Isn’t that fantastic?”

Chloe stood from her chair and circled to lean against the side of her desk. “Seriously?”

Clifford’s features quirked. “Of course, I’m serious. Why wouldn’t I be?”

“That’s fantastic. This is one of the best things to happen to the museum in a long time.” Chloe clapped her hands together and brought them to her lips. “Hey, we could have a ceremony and invite the important people in the community. You know, the mayor, council members, the park superintendent—”

“Of course, *he’ll* be there.” Clifford aimed an incredulous look at her.

“—maybe even the governor.” Chloe ticked off the titles on her fingers. “We could have a dinner and make a big deal of this.”

Clifford chuckled, crossing his arms over his wrinkled shirt. “You’re really getting into this. Give you a little history and you’ll turn it into a social event.”

Chloe spun around toward him. “And why not? Some of these people are the park’s biggest donors. It won’t hurt for them to see where their money goes and perhaps encourage them to donate a little more. With this new loan from Mrs. White-Smith, it’s going to need its own display spot in the museum, and that’s going to take money. How do we get that if we don’t invite the right people?”

“There’s a reason they have us working together, Mrs. Rogers.”

Chloe's gaze fell to her bare left ring finger. A faint tan line could still be seen there. Pain speared through her, and she blinked back the stinging behind her eyes. She dropped back onto her computer chair. "Yes, I'm sure there is."

"Awe, Chloe, I'm sorry." Clifford leaned his hands on the front of her desk. "That slipped out. I haven't called you Mrs. Rogers in…well, a long time."

Chloe smiled up at him and sighed. "It's okay, Cliff. It's who I was, and now I'm not anymore. It's taking time, but…."

Clifford walked around the desk and placed a kind hand on her shoulder. "For a historian you'd think I'd remember who said 'Time heals all wounds,' but I don't, so just take the sentiment for what it's worth."

Chloe patted his hand and gave him a faint smile. "Thanks. Sometimes it takes a long time to heal wounds."

"Yeah." Clifford pulled out his cell phone. "Now, here's the number for Mrs. White-Smith. You're better with living people than I am. I do better with the past and those who are no longer living. You call her."

~

Blake pulled away from the traffic stop and drove out of the visitors parking lot. He headed back out on patrol hoping things would remain quite for the rest of the morning. Hopefully he wouldn't run into any more beautiful, young women like Chloe Rogers. Beautiful? More like exquisite. At least the parts of her face he'd seen. Her sunglasses covered what were sure to be lovely eyes. Wonder what color they were? With honey-blond hair like hers, could they be blue or gray perhaps? Maybe hazel?

He glanced down at the thermal coffee mug he'd filled up that morning. He'd nearly drained it before pulling over the beautiful blonde, and he wanted more. Moira's Coffee Shop was the place.

Having only been in Gettysburg two weeks, he had a lot to learn about the historic town, but he'd discovered Moira's his first day on duty. With the early morning shift and in need of coffee, he'd spotted the neon sign on a corner in town and pointed his cruiser in that direction. He'd done the same every morning since, even on his days off. The owner, Moira Campbell, not only served the best coffee, but she made the best Scottish scones imaginable. With a selection of delectable pastries made by the cheery and slightly rotund owner, Blake didn't mind giving them all a try. Why not? He worked out and ran five miles every other morning.

Blake parked on the street outside of Moira's and, grabbing his thermal mug, headed inside.

"Well, now, if it isna me most favorite new customer." A voice with a slight Scottish brogue called from the counter at the rear of the shop as the door squeaked closed behind Blake. "Come in and pick yer pastry. I'll fill yer mug for ya."

Blake set his mug on the counter, and Moira picked it up and placed it by the coffee maker.

She cast him a glance through narrowed eyes, her brows lowered. "Well, me laddie. What's got ya in a stew this fine spring morn? Ya lookin' s'if someone stole yer tartan, ya do."

Blake crossed his arms on the high counter and leaned forward. He shook his head. "Nothing really. Why?"

Moira capped the mug and set it in front of Blake along with creamer and sweetener. A sly smile lifted a corner of her lips and filled her wizened eyes. She leaned toward him. "Ol' Moira's been around, me lad. She can tell when a man's been touched by a woman."

Blake doctored his coffee and reached for a stir stick. He stirred too vigorously and slopped onto the counter. "I haven't been 'touched by a woman', Moira. That's ridiculous."

The wizened grin grew. "Are ya sure, laddie? Did ya meet a young woman that might 'o affected ya this mornin'? Ya sort o' have that look about ya, ya know."

Blake cut her as stern a look as he could muster, then glanced over at the plexiglass pastry box on the counter. "I don't see any of your Scottish scones. You didn't make any today?"

"Not today. But the lemon curd bars are to die for. They've almonds and coconut in 'em."

"I'll take two." Blake pulled out his wallet. It was time to get out of here. How in the world had Moira detected he'd met a beautiful, young woman? Was Chloe Rogers still on his mind? Well, maybe. But how had Moira known? Surely, she wasn't a mind reader. He didn't believe in such things.

"Here ya go, me lad." Moira handed him the receipt, his change and his bag of pastries. "Now, go get her."

Blake met Moira's gaze as he pocketed his change. The older woman gave him a wink.

Back in his cruiser, Blake set his coffee in the cupholder and dropped the pastry bag on the passenger seat. He sat in silence for a moment, Chloe Roger's face taking shape in his mind's eye. "*Go get her*," Moira had said. Blake had no intentions of starting a relationship when he'd come to Gettysburg. Thoughts of Michelle slipped into his mind, and pain surged through him. No. He closed his eyes and shoved the thoughts away. That had all been too devastating, and he had no desire to relive the past. Never again.

Opening his eyes, Blake stared across the street as Chloe's face once again slipped before his mind's eye. He was likely to run into her again and again here at the battlefield. From her uniform, it was obvious she worked here, but that's where things would end. He'd make sure of it.

~

Chloe waved at the park superintendent's secretary, Margaret Miller, as she and Clifford slipped through her office and knocked on Superintendent Dan Fielding's door. Margaret waved back and grinned as they waited for the superintendent to call for them to enter. When he did, Chloe opened the door and Clifford followed her in, closing the door behind him.

"You wanted to see us, sir?" Chloe stopped before his desk and straightened her cordovan leather messenger bag on her shoulder. Clifford stood beside her, his arms at his sides. At least he'd tucked his shirttail in before their appointment with the superintendent.

The broad-shouldered, white-haired man behind the desk glanced up. His salt and pepper mustache twitched as he grinned and indicated the chairs in front of his desk. "Chloe. Clifford. Please, have a seat. I have some news I think you'll find both interesting and welcome. As our park historians, I'm sure you're always eager to get your hands on more historical...hmm...how shall I put it?" He tapped a finger against his chin for a moment, then his grin grew. "Well, in simplest terms I suppose you could say historical artifacts."

Chloe leaned forward in her chair. "Are you saying the military park has acquired more historical artifacts?"

The superintendent's smile broadened. "You could say that. And I think you'll like these."

Chloe turned to Clifford whose round eyes were as filled with eager anticipation as a kid at his first birthday party. She half expected him to rub his hands together in glee. Her own heart beat with expectation. First, the diary from Mrs. White-Smith's ancestor. Now more artifacts? It had been a while since something truly interesting had come into the park's history department. Her mind buzzed with questions as to what they could be.

Superintendent Fielding leaned back in his desk chair and rocked back and forth for a few minutes, silence filling the room.

Her eyes darted from him to Clifford and back. Her historian partner looked like a spring was about to jettison him from his chair. She couldn't allow the poor guy to be tortured this way. Chloe cleared her throat. "Sir, about these historical items. Could you tell us about them, or is there a reason you're delaying in sharing the details?"

Superintendent Fielding leaned forward resting his arms on his desk. "Oh, I'm sorry. Once I told you you'd like them, you didn't seem all that interested."

Chloe spotted the sparkle in his eyes and sent a glare his

direction. She would have to have a talk with him later. Clifford was likely on the verge of heart failure this moment. Any item of historical value meant the world to the historian, and any practical joke was lost on him.

Clifford's hands clamped together in his lap and his knuckles were bone white. Yep, it was time for their boss to reveal the news before he passed out or experienced some other bodily failure.

"Oh, we're more than interested, superintendent. We're ecstatic to know the military park has acquired something of historical value, and we're eager to get started on it." She tilted her head in Clifford's direction. "If you don't believe me, take a look at my colleague. He's going to pop a valve."

The superintendent's gaze moved to Clifford and his eyebrows lifted. "Indeed. Well, the first item the park has acquired is the property you may be familiar with out on Emmitsburg Road. You know, the old Bryant place? It was actually sold to the park recently by Mrs. Karen Bryant Montague. It was her family home until she was about ten years old, then they moved away. They never sold it, and Mrs. Montague inherited the house and property. She's now in her late sixties and has decided to get rid of it, thinking the park would benefit from it more than she could."

"An old house?" Clifford spoke for the first time since entering the room, his voice squeaking. "An old Civil War house?"

The superintendent nodded. "Yes. And no one has lived there in over fifty-five years, Clifford. I'm not sure what you'll find, seeing as how the Bryants may have changed things completely, but I do have Mrs. Montague's phone number. She said you're welcome to call her if you have questions." He slid a slip of paper across the desk. "I highly recommend you call and speak with her. She's sure to be a wealth of information for you. Even though she was a child when the family left the home, I'm sure she can tell you things."

Clifford glanced at the slip of paper then at Chloe.

She caught his message and reached for the paper. "I'll

definitely give her a call."

Superintendent Fielding opened a drawer at the side of his desk and reached inside. "There are a couple of other things." He retrieved an old skeleton key and slid it across to Chloe. "Believe it or not, this is the key to the front door. Apparently, the Bryants never had a modern lock installed."

Chloe picked up the key and examined it. "Amazing. I hope we don't find any squatters on the property. With this kind of lock, it wouldn't be hard for someone to break in."

"True. It might not be a bad idea to have park police check it out before you go in. Let me know when you plan to arrive, and I'll have an officer meet you there." Fielding reached into the drawer and pulled out a small package, sliding it across to Chloe. "Here's the last item. I opened it but didn't look inside. It's a diary found by Mrs. Montague when she was a child. I suggest once you take a look at it, you talk with her to find out more about where she found it."

Chloe tucked the small package into her messenger bag. She'd delve into the diary when she had more time.

The superintendent continued. "Clifford, have a go at the house. Do your research and find out what you can. If the two of you find that it's feasible, I'd like to restore the house and eventually open it to the public as a Civil War home. I know that kind of project will take a lot of time and money. Do an assessment and let me know your thoughts. If you find it feasible, I'll have a contractor go through, and then we'll talk about the restoration process."

"I'll be more than happy to, sir." Clifford rubbed his hands together. "This is the kind of project I've wanted to sink my teeth into for a long time."

The superintendent grinned. "I'm sure you have, son. We're not making any promises, but the two of you will determine if it's even possible. That house has been sitting empty for a long time. No telling how much damage has been done with no one living there for so long."

"Yes, sir. We'll find out for you." Chloe stood and turned to Clifford as he stood to his feet beside her. "If you wouldn't mind waiting outside, I'll be right there, Cliff."

"Sure, no problem." He turned to his boss. "Thank you, sir. I appreciate the trust you're putting in me with this project." Clifford stretched a hand toward the superintendent. "I'll do my best."

Superintendent Fielding shook Clifford's hand. "I know you will, son. I look forward to your findings."

Clifford stepped out of the office, and Chloe turned toward the superintendent.

"Dad, why do you have to tease Cliff like that? You know he takes every bit of historical research in this park seriously, and when you dangle a new artifact under his nose, it's like bees to honey. He was almost salivating."

Fielding chuckled. "I know. I couldn't help myself. It didn't escape my notice that he took the house over the diary."

"What did you expect? He'll be like a kid in an amusement park." Chloe smiled. "Don't worry. I'll be there to keep him on task. And I'll go through the diary and see what I can find." She started to turn toward the door, then stopped. "By the way, are you aware of the diary and letter being donated by Mrs. Maureen White-Smite?"

Fielding came around and sat on the edge of his desk. He shook his head. "No. When did this happen?"

"Clifford told me about it yesterday." Chloe sat on the edge of the desk beside her father. "Apparently, her great-great-grandfather was a hero here at Gettysburg during the battle, and it's documented in the letter and in his diary. She'd like to put those documents on loan here at the museum."

"Well, now. If the historical department hasn't had a windfall of artifacts, huh?" He gave her arm a gentle bump.

"We don't actually have the diary and letter from her yet. She's going to bring it by. I thought we'd arrange a pay-per-plate dinner or a fancy shindig of some kind and invite donors to donate toward a new display in the museum. It's going to take a lot of money to set up a display for the diary and letter for our hero."

"That's a great idea, honey. Are you going to head it up?"

Chloe gave him a sideways glance. "If I'm going to help Cliff with the Bryant property and research the diaries, how can I dedicate time to a big shindig too?"

"Then who?" Her dad's brow furrowed.

"Who else?" Chloe shrugged. "Jan has worked magic on all the other events she's coordinated in the past." Chloe stood then planted a kiss on her dad's cheek. "I'll even fill her in on some of the details after *you* give her the job." She backed toward the door with a wave of her fingers. "I have to go. I love you dad. I'll see you tonight."

"Bye, honey. See you."

Chapter Two

Blake pulled his cruiser to a stop on the grass beside the only other vehicle near the old, abandoned house. Now why did that cobalt blue Mini Cooper look familiar? Hmm. He'd seen it recently, but it didn't ring any bells. His eyes roamed over the front of the old house. It hadn't seen paint in many a decade, and some of the shutters were either in sore need of repair or were missing altogether. A wide roofed porch with simple columns ran the full length of the house. If some boards were replaced, a generous amount of paint were applied and a few well-placed rockers and a swing were installed, the porch might almost be welcoming.

As he climbed from his vehicle and strolled across the tall grass, Blake noticed the lower half of a slim, feminine, figure clad in blue jeans bent over before the peeling and scuffed front door. Tilting his head, he planted his hands on his hips. What was she doing? Advancing a few steps, he crossed his arms over his chest and watched.

Her only movements were the slight shifting of her shapely rear and her feet. She emitted sounds of frustration as she shifted, then a low, "Oh, for goodness sake." The words sounded as if they were ground out between clamped teeth.

"Excuse me. Can I be of assistance?" Blake stepped forward as the woman straightened, her blond ponytail swinging wildly as she whipped around toward his voice. Her eyes were saucers.

A bubble of laughter surge upward, but Blake shoved it down. From the morphed expression of surprise to irritation on Chloe Rogers' features, Blake doubted she'd see humor at the moment. This was great. Just great. He'd hoped not to run into this woman again anytime soon, and here it was only a few days later. *That's* why he recognized the cobalt blue Mini Cooper.

"What are *you* doing here?" If words could scorch, he'd be a pile of ashes. Blake chose not to take offense, and instead decided whatever she'd been doing had gotten her in a foul mood.

Inhaling a cleansing breath, Blake climbed the seven or so rickety steps to the porch. The boards here didn't look any safer than the steps. How had *he* drawn the short straw this morning? Funny how the superintendent had called him directly requesting *he* come out to the Bryant house to check for squatters. Why him, for Pete's sake?

Blake gave a cursory glance down the front of the house then around the front property before peering at Chloe. "Superintendent Fielding called and asked me to come. Something about checking for squatters. Since you arrived first, have you seen any indication of anyone living here?"

He doubted Chloe's furrowed brows could furrow any further, but they did. "Are you serious? He actually sent you for that?" She released a huff then shook her head in disbelief.

"Yep, he sure did." Blake tilted his head, then grinned. "So please don't shoot the messenger. By the way, my name's Blake. Blake Hunter." He held out his hand.

Chloe eyed it for a moment, then with a frown, she gave his hand a shake then tugged hers away. "You may or may not remember mine from the ticket you wrote me the other morning." Her gorgeous blue eyes narrowed slightly as she tilted her head.

Ouch. The acid in her voice indicated she still held a grudge. Of course, Blake remembered her name, but he wouldn't give her the satisfaction of knowing that.

He schooled his features to exude skepticism. "Do you have any idea how many people I give tickets to in a week?"

It must've worked because Chloe Rogers had the grace to drop her gaze, and when she looked up, her expression was a bit sheepish.

"Chloe Rogers. I'm one of the park historians."

"Oh yes. Nice to meet you again, Miss Rogers. At least this time it's under better circumstances." Blake caught her dropped brow and pinched lips as he turned his gaze to the door where she'd been working then looked at what was in her hand. "Is that a skeleton key? May I give it a try?"

"Please, by all means. I've tried for fifteen minutes, and it hasn't budged." She dropped the key into his outstretched hand then stepped back.

Blake moved to the old door and slid the key into the keyhole in the rusted rectangular metal rim lock plate, feeling for the mechanism inside. He'd had his share of these old locks and keys when he was growing up at his grandparents' house in Montana. They rarely locked doors on their old ranch, especially to the house, but there were a few his grandpa kept locked. In the end, the property had been left to Blake when his grandparents had passed. They'd never changed those pesky old skeleton-key locks.

The mechanism inside this lock gave a rusty, grinding sound then gave way as the key did its job. Blake turned the old steel doorknob and turned his gaze on Chloe. "I'll take a look around. It would be best if you wait out here until I come back and tell you it's safe."

Chloe opened her mouth, but Blake didn't give her a chance to argue. "It's what the superintendent sent me here to do, Miss Rogers, and that's what I'm going to do. Wait here."

~

Chloe released an exasperated sigh as Officer Hunter disappeared inside the creepy old Bryant house. As eager as she was to check out the old place, she was secretly glad he'd come along. Clifford was late in arriving, and she wasn't excited about going in alone for the first time. She hadn't thought dad would actually send someone to check for squatters, but now that the park cop was here, she was glad. Not this particular cop, necessarily, but a cop.

She turned at the sound of a car door slamming and watched as Clifford strode through the tall grass. Why hadn't she heard the park cop's approach? Maybe she'd been too engrossed in trying to unlock that silly door.

"What are you waiting on?" Clifford climbed the rickety steps, his hand grabbing the railing. It nearly gave way, wobbling beneath his weight, but he caught himself and let go.

"Goodness. Be careful. There's a park policeman inside checking things out." Chloe waved an airy hand toward the door. "Dad sent him. Apparently, he was serious about checking for squatters."

Clifford's eyebrows shot upward as he stepped onto the porch. He turned to gaze at the police cruiser then back at Chloe. "Really? Well, okay then. Better we didn't go in and find a bad situation, I suppose."

Chloe shook her head. "I doubt he's going to find anything."

Officer Hunter stepped through the front door, holding it open. "It looks safe, but I found something…interesting."

Chloe spotted the furrow between his brows. "What is it? You didn't find anyone in there, did you?"

He gave her a strange look, glanced at Clifford then back at Chloe. "Just come with me." The officer reentered the house, holding the door open for Chloe and Clifford then closed it behind them. The old wooden floorboards creaked beneath their feet as they stepped further inside.

Chloe's gaze swept the wide musty entrance hallway they'd entered. It was hard to see with the little light streaming from the grimy windows in the rooms on either side of the hall. Dingy wallpaper lined the walls leaving the impression of nondescript print or color. An old five-bulb chandelier hung from the high ceiling giving evidence the house had been converted to electricity at some point.

Chloe turned toward the front door and spotted an old two-button light switch beside it. The top button was pressed to turn on the light, the bottom button pressed to turn it off. Wires ran up the wall and across the ceiling to the chandelier. Her gaze moved up the staircase on the left of the hallway. Without a light, it was simply too dark up there to see anything. She glanced into the rooms on either side of the entrance. From the placement of the fireplaces and the smallish, drooping chandeliers, she could imagine the room to her right had been the parlor and the one to the left had been the dining room.

Chloe moved through a wide archway into the parlor and stared at the wallpaper. Once it must have been the latest fashion of green and gold with curlicues and floral patterns. Now it was faded from time and neglect. Dampness caused edges to come loose and droop in places. Velvet drapes hung from the windows, dusty and covered with cobwebs. What must they have looked like in all their glory? Now faded to a brownish gray, they once likely matched the green in the wallpaper. With a careful hand, Chloe separated a fold to find a vibrant green buried deep within. What a shame. Allowing the heavy fabric to drop back, she made a visual sweep of the room. There was no furniture, all likely removed eons ago, either by the original owners or the Bryant's. In a room like this, there would have been some beautiful pieces. The fireplace mantel and surround would have been lovely. The carved wood had long since lost its luster to age and dampness.

Clifford stepped over to it and ran a hand along the mantle. "What a shame there's so much damage here, but unless I miss my guess, the house seems to be pretty solid. We'll take a further look around to be sure. Of course, a restoration contractor will know a lot more, but I think—."

What sounded like footsteps walking across the floor above

their heads halted Cliff's words. All three pairs of eyes shot to the ceiling as they listened.

Chloe's wide eyes met Officer Hunter's. "I thought you said there was no one in the house. Is someone up there?"

"That's the interesting part." He shifted his feet, hands resting on his hips. "I went up and looked around. There's no one in the house. Up there. Down here. I found no one."

~

Chloe insisted on going upstairs to check things out so Blake went with her. Cliff was less than eager to join them and said he'd wait outside. "Umm, let me have that skeleton key. Just in case I find any more interesting locks outside."

Blake handed it over before he led Chloe back into the hallway and up the rickety stairs. "Be careful. I don't like the condition of some of these steps. The railing is pretty solid though, so hang onto it."

Most of the stairs creaked beneath their feet, the sound sending a chill up his spine. It sounded like something straight from a horror movie. Now why did that thought creep into his mind? The lighting on the stairs was almost non-existent, especially the closer to the top they went. Blake tugged his flashlight from his utility belt, sending it's beam over the steps so Chloe could see as well.

At the landing he turned to wait for her, but found her right behind him. Minimal light reached the wide, dingy corridor, and Blake shined the flashlight beam around. Doors to the rooms stood open, filthy windows inside allowing a modicum of daylight in between dark curtains. Blake stepped to the door of the nearest room, Chloe on his heels. He glanced around, flashing his beam.

"Nothing or no one in this one."

They proceeded to each room, five bedrooms and a storage room in all, only to find each one empty. No one on this floor, as Blake had said, and no one had passed them to escape down the stairs. It was the only staircase in the house.

They returned to the front hallway below, and Chloe turned to Blake. "I don't understand. What did we hear?"

Blake shrugged. "I have no idea, but I can tell you there's no squatters here. If you'd like to take a further look around downstairs before we leave, I'd be happy to walk through with you."

She glanced around and nodded, sending that blond ponytail into a bouncy-dance. A grin tugged at his lips then he suppressed it as she turned back to him.

"Yes, if you don't mind taking the time. We only went into the parlor before going upstairs to...well...investigate. Anyway, let's take a further look around."

After completing their walk-through, they went outside to search for Clifford who was nowhere to be found. His car was still parked beside theirs.

"Cliff?" Chloe called. "Clifford! Where are you?"

A muffled sound came from the rear of the house.

She stopped walking. "Did you hear that?" Her head tilted, brows scrunching together.

He nodded. "Yeah. I think it's coming from the back of the house."

They hurried around the back corner to find an old wooden cellar door standing open, a dank, musty odor escaping with cool air.

Blake stepped inside and once again tugged his flashlight from his utility belt. He switched on the light and stopped a few feet inside the door. Chloe waited beside him as they allowed their eyes to adjust to the darkness from the bright sunshine outside.

"There's a lot of cobwebs down here." Chloe's voice was little more than a whisper.

"Yeah, but the plus here is we can stand up straight." Blake pointed his flashlight overhead. "We don't have to worry about cracking our heads on the rafters." He glanced at Chloe's shorter height. "Well, at least I don't. But you're right, there are cobwebs everywhere." Blake shined his light on the floor. "I suppose dirt floors in a cellar were the norm back in the day?"

"Yes. Wood was impractical because sometimes there was dampness from the ground. Unless you had lots of money, dirt was the best option."

Blake turned the flashlight against the wall on his left, panning it slowly across the stone masonry.

"I wonder where Cliff is." Chloe peered into the darkness on her right. "How did he know to investigate down here?"

"He had the skeleton key and he found a lock. Cliff's a historian, right?"

Chloe chuckled. "That's true."

All of a sudden Cliff was at her side. "There you guys are. What took you so long?"

Chloe jumped, releasing a soft yelp. She swatted his arm. "Clifford Weston! Don't do that."

Blake turned the flashlight in his direction when Clifford appeared.

"Do what?" Clifford's brows furrowed as he shifted his gaze darted between Chloe and Blake. "What did I do?"

"You startled me, that's what. You can't just jump out at person from the darkness like that."

Blake couldn't withhold the bubble of laughter that slipped out. Chloe's face had turned white when Clifford appeared beside her, and she'd grabbed Blake's arm without realizing it. He wouldn't say a word, and he attempted to reign in his mirth.

She spun toward him, her lips drawn in single line. "What are you laughing about?"

Blake raised the hand that wasn't holding the flashlight and shook his head. "Not a thing."

"It was pretty comical the way you jumped, screeched and grabbed Officer Hunter's arm, Chloe." Clifford crossed his arms over his chest, rolled his eyes and chuckled. "Your face turned as white as your shirt. What gives?"

Chloe turned a deadpan expression first on one, then the other. "Comedians. That's what I'm dealing with here. Can we return to why you called us into this dark, cobwebby cellar in the first place? You obviously had something you wanted to show us, right?"

Clifford motioned with his forefinger. "Right. Follow me."

~

Clifford pulled a flashlight from his pocket and led the way into the darkness. Chloe followed him, and Officer Hunter took up the rear with his flashlight lighting Chloe's way. The handsome officer may be annoying, but at the moment she was thankful for his thoughtfulness. Between the beams from the two men's lights, she was able to see where she was going, and she caught a glimpse of her surroundings in the dark cellar. Cliff led them about halfway under the house to a squared-off room with a solid wooden door standing half-way open. From her estimations, the room appeared to have been built on the front mid-section of the house.

"Is that a root cellar, Cliff?" Chloe stepped beside him as he stopped in front of the door. "Did you go inside? With all the cobwebs out here, I can only imagine what's inside."

"Yes, and not exactly." Clifford pointed his flashlight toward the door. "It is a root cellar, and no, I didn't go inside, but I did take a peek. There's not as many webs as you'd think, but there are a lot of shelves full of items in there. Even some old stoneware crocks. I dread to think what might be in them."

Chloe caught his shudder and smiled. "Exactly. Can I borrow your flashlight for a second?"

He handed it to her, and Chloe stepped to the door shining the beam around to catch a glimpse of the shelves and what sat on them. A movement in the corner caught her eye. A mouse. Better than a spider. Not that she cared much for mice either. "Interesting. Apparently, the Bryant family didn't use the root cellar. At first glance, I'd say those crocks are early to mid-1800's." Chloe stepped back from the door and turned to her fellow historian.

"What do you think, Cliff?"

He and Officer Hunter had moved away from the door and were examining a wall beside the root cellar.

"Cliff?" Chloe spoke in a soft voice. For goodness sake. Who was she afraid of disturbing? She stepped over to where they stood.

"What I find interesting—" Cliff was saying, "is this wall isn't original to the building of the house."

"What do you mean?" Blake shined his flashlight along the edges of the brick-and-mortar wall.

Chloe stepped forward and ran a finger along the mortar holding the brick in place. It was crumbly and pieces flecked off easily at her touch.

"That's interesting." Clifford did the same thing, rubbing his forefinger along the mortar causing small chunks to fall off.

"Do you think you should be doing that?" Blake asked.

Clifford stepped back, seeming to ignore his question. "What's interesting is this wall was put up in a hurry with inferior mortar. It shouldn't be sloughing off like that. And that's not all. The placement is all wrong. If you step back and look at it—" He took several steps back from the wall, "—it's built from the front edge of the root cellar on the left to the outside wall of the house on the right. No way would it have been put there when they built the house. The original foundation is made of stone and mortar. Follow me."

Chloe and Blake followed Clifford to the stone and mortar foundation wall on the other side of the root cellar. He shoved aside cobwebs and aimed his flashlight at the foundation where he ran a fingernail along the mortar.

"See? Nothing flecks off. This was made from good solid mortar that was meant to last. It was made before the Civil War when the house was built." He returned to the brick wall followed by Chloe and Blake. "I took a walk around the rest of the cellar and didn't see anywhere else where this kind of brick and mortar were used."

Chloe ran her fingers over the rough surface of the dark bricks in the light from the flashlights. “I agree with you, Cliff, and these aren’t new bricks. These were made prior to or during the Civil War. They’re from the early to mid-1800’s.”

“Agreed.” Clifford shifted from one foot to the other. “I would say this wall was built, as you say, prior to or during the Civil War. However, due to the state of the mortar, it was built in a hurry, and I’d like to know why.”

Chapter Three

The next morning, a knock sounded on Chloe's office door just seconds before it swung open and Jan Miller floated in, her smile bringing a ray of sunshine with it.

"Good morning." Chloe's closest friend propped onto the corner of her desk and shoved her wire-framed glasses up onto her pert, freckled nose. Her mousey-brown hair slipped from the clip, now framing her heart-shaped face. Her perfect teeth shone in a smile that was perpetually sent in anyone's direction. She clasped a clipboard to her uniformed chest, her tights-clad legs swinging along the side of the desk. "The superintendent said he wants me to work on a project that you'll tell me all about." Jan scrunched her shoulders like a wee girl waiting for a puppy. "I'm all ears. What are we working on?"

Chloe leaned back in her office chair. "Thank goodness. I have a big event coming up, and you know how awful I am at events. Not to mention I have another project I'm working on with Cliff that's going to take up most of my time. I pretty much need to dump this one in your lap. You're amazing at event planning. That's why Dad called you."

Jan waved her words away. "I don't know about that, but I do enjoy planning them. Tell me what we have going on, and let's see what we can do."

"Someone has loaned some items to the museum, and we're

going to need to raise funds to put a display together. But, the items aren't just any old items. They're a diary and a letter that belonged to the donor's ancestor. He supposedly fought right here during the Battle of Gettysburg. The donor says he performed some deed of heroism during the battle. I'll research that part to verify, of course, but we'd like to start planning this donor event. I'd like to invite the Pennsylvania governor, state senators, the mayor, and some other local bigwigs. You get the idea. In a few words, I want it to be a fundraiser for the display. Perhaps the donor can do a reading from the diary or something like that."

Jan jotted down notes then she stopped, pointing her pen in Chloe's direction. "That's a fantastic idea."

A knock sounded on Chloe's office door.

"Come in," she called.

The door opened a crack then a little wider. A thin woman with stylish white hair stood in the doorway. "Pardon me. I'm not sure I'm in the right place, but I'm looking for Chloe Rogers."

Chloe plastered a smile on her face and stood from her desk. "You're in the right place. I'm Chloe Rogers. Please come in. How can I help you?"

The woman opened the door further and stepped inside, closing it behind her. She approached Chloe's desk and held out a hand. A thin smile stretched her red lips. Her makeup had been applied with care and her hair was professionally done. The style of her clothes and high heels bespoke Fifth Avenue. Certainly not where Chloe shopped.

"My name is Maureen White-Smith. We spoke on the phone several days ago."

Chloe shook the older woman's hand then indicated the chair in front of her desk. "Yes, of course. It's a pleasure to meet you, Mrs. White-Smith. Won't you have a seat?"

Jan had hopped from the desk when the woman had entered the room and stood to the side.

Chloe retook her own seat. "On behalf of the Gettysburg

National Military Park, we appreciate you loaning your family diary and letter to us and placing it in our care. We look forward to displaying it in the museum."

The woman gave a brief nod, then released an almost bored sigh. "Yes, well, I'm sure you do." She opened her rather large handbag and withdrew a small manilla envelope. Leaning forward she laid it on Chloe's desk. "Here's the diary and the letter I spoke of. I'll leave it in your capable hands, Miss. Rogers."

Chloe reached into her desk and pulled out a pair of cotton gloves then, after slipping them on, slid the envelope in front of her and opened it. She removed an acid-free bag which held the diary and the letter. With great care, Chloe slipped both out onto the desktop. The leather-bound diary showed its age. The dry leather had cracked along the edges, missing small pieces here and there. A worn and cracked leather strap wrapped around the small book holding it closed where the broken metal clasp no longer worked. The hand-written letter was made of one hundred percent rag paper, commonly used during the Civil War. Although the letter's print was legible, the edges of the page were worn, and bits were torn away.

Chloe opened one of the side drawers of her desk and took out a long, narrow booklet. "I'll be happy to write a receipt to you, Mrs. White-Smith. This receipt will list what you have loaned to the museum and how long you wish to have it on loan. If you would like, you can stipulate family members to be included in the loan and if you would like for them to be able to reclaim the pieces in the future."

"No."

Surprise filled Chloe at the vehemence in the lady's response, and it must have shone in her gaze. Mrs. White-Smith waved a hand.

"I have no one in my family I want to claim the diary or the letter. It is to stay with the museum indefinitely. I will be the *only* one to claim it if it is to be claimed."

Chloe tilted her head in acknowledgment and continued to fill out the receipt. “I understand.” Although she didn’t. Not at all. What a strange response. Still, it wasn’t her business. She ripped the receipt from the booklet and handed it to the woman. “Thank you again, Mrs. White-Smith.” Chloe waved a hand in Jan’s direction. “This is Jan Miller. We’re planning an event to draw attention to your loan and hopefully bring in some donations for an appropriate display for your items. I hope you’ll be available to join us.”

For the first time since entering Chloe’s office, what passed for a genuine smile lifted the corners of the woman’s lips. “I would be delighted. Please keep me apprised of the plans and when the event will take place.” Mrs. White-Smith stood and held out her hand. “It was a pleasure to meet you both.”

Moments later as Chloe closed the door behind her visitor, she turned to Jan. “Well, now you’ve met the illustrious donor. What do you think?”

Jan wrapped one arm across her chest, tapping a fingernail on her bottom lip with her other hand. “Interesting to be sure. I wonder, though, why she’s adamant not to include family in claiming her items? Do you think she really doesn’t have any family? That would be sad.”

Chloe moved back to her desk and dropped into her chair. “Yes, it would, but I guess she has her reasons. Oh well. I think you have enough to start on the event. I’ll leave the date up to you. Don’t make it too far off though. We need to move on this. I’ll start reading the diary and find out what her illustrious ancestor did that was so great. Then I’ll research to find any possible information to substantiate or refute it. I also have another diary to read and an old house to help Cliff evaluate.”

“No wonder you want me on this event.” Jan picked up her clipboard from the desk and edged toward the door.

“Uh huh. Now you’re catching on.”

“No worries, Chloe. I’m on it.” Jan reached for the doorknob.

"Just don't forget to have some fun in there somewhere, okay? Sometimes you forget about that, and as your friend, it's my job to remind you."

Chloe heaved a sigh then chuckled. "Fun? What's that? Kidding, I see that look in your eye. Remember, I have Evie to have fun with. She's the light of my life."

"I know she is, but maybe it's time you had some grown-up fun. Like a date. You can do that, girlfriend. It's been three years, and it's time to move on. You've already made the first step by removing your wedding rings. Now go hunt up a date and start having fun again."

Chloe looked at her wedding-ring finger. She'd taken the rings off six months ago, and the lines had faded but were still visible. "I'll get there."

Jan nodded as she opened the office door. "Sure, you will. If you let yourself."

~

Chloe opened the door from the garage and dropped her purse and messenger bag on the table by the door. She kicked off her flats and headed into the kitchen. Aunt Charlene was standing in front of the stove stirring a pot of something that emitted a delectable aroma.

"What are you cooking?" Chloe wrapped an arm around the older woman's waist and gave her a squeeze. "It smells amazing."

Aunt Charlene turned her hazel gaze on her niece and smiled, the corners of her eyes crinkling. She removed her reading glasses which hung from a colorful beaded chain around her neck. "It should. This is Grandma Minnie's old recipe for Bohemian chicken paprikash. I've already made the bread dumplings and their keeping warm in the oven."

Chloe clapped her hands softly. "Sweet. That's Dad's and my favorite meal. Wait. Is there something going on I'm not aware of? You usually only make this for special occasions."

Her aunt lifted the lid from the pot and stirred the gently

bubbling cream sauce. She shook her head. "Nope. I just had a hankering for chicken paprikash tonight and thought you and your dad would too. The little princess has already had a few tastes and given her seal of approval."

"Which begs the question, where is my little princess?" Chloe glanced around the kitchen then beyond into the expansive family room. She eyed the cushiony armchairs and the long, overstuffed couch set before the large fireplace built of river stones. A set of French doors led out to a patio and large fenced backyard.

"Your princess is having a tea party. Mrs. P has joined her today. I'm so glad she's not discriminatory when it comes to who she plays with. She's fair and plays with all of her toys." Aunt Charlene gave her niece a wink.

Chloe chuckled and padded barefoot across the carpeted family room. "That's my girl. Let me go say hello, then I'll come and give you a hand with dinner."

"Take your time. Dinner's ready. We're only waiting for your dad to show up."

Chloe pulled the French door behind her and strolled across the patio into the cool, springy grass. Beneath one of the large shade trees, her three-year-old daughter, Evie, sat at a small table with a play tea set pouring water in tiny teacups. Her companion, a pink stuffed pig, sat in the small chair opposite Evie.

Chloe bent to give her a kiss and a hug before dropping onto the grass beside the table. "How's my sweetie this afternoon?"

"Good, Mommy. I'm havin' a tea party." Evie shoved her dark bangs from her eyes. She'd gotten that dark hair from her father. Those sweet elfin features? Not so much.

"I see that, and I see you invited Mrs. P. It looks like she's having fun. I bet she likes your tea."

"She likes it lots and lots."

"How many cups has she had?"

"Sebenty-eight."

Chloe chuckled. "Wow. She must've been super thirsty."

"Yep, sure was." Evie dumped Mrs. P's cup on the ground and pouring another one.

"There you two are. Aunt Charlene said you were out here. What are you up to?"

Chloe and Evie both swiveled at the sound of her father's voice coming from the patio.

Evie's face lit up in smiles and she jumped from her chair, knocking it over. She ran across the grass to her grandfather and jumped into his arms. "Gwampa, You're home!"

"There's my girl." Although her father was still in uniform, the change from superintendent to grandfather morphed in a millisecond. The clothes made no difference to the little girl he now held in his arms. Chloe might be her mother, but Evie had no father. Dan Fielding was the man in her life, and Chloe was thankful for that. If Joshua couldn't be around to help raise Evie, then Chloe's dad was an awesome substitute.

"We're havin' a tea party, Gwampa." Evie held his cheeks between her chubby hands. "Wanna have some tea wif me?"

"I would love to, princess, but your Aunt Char sent me out here to get my girls to come to dinner. She said it's time to eat. I hope you didn't spoil your dinner with too much tea." He poked his finger under her armpit, tickling her.

She giggled and shook her head. "Nope, I didn', Gwampa. I'm starvin'."

"You're starvin'?"

"Uh huh." She gave an emphatic nod.

"Then let's go eat. Tell Mommy, 'Let's go eat.'" He took Evie's hand and waved it toward Chloe.

"Let's go eat, Mommy." Evie repeated after her grandpa.

Chloe joined them. "I'm right behind you two."

After everyone said grace, the dumplings were passed and then the sour cream-and-mushroom gravy filled with chicken and spices. The first few minutes passed in silence as everyone savored the delectable family recipe. As their stomachs filled, they sat back, taking it more slowly.

"How goes the diary reading?" her dad turned to Chloe. "Find anything interesting from it yet?"

"Haven't even started it yet." Chloe took a drink of water. "I've been busy working with Jan Miller on the event-planning. I handed it over to her, but she needed a kick start to get going. While we were working on that, Mrs. White-Smith arrived and gave me the other diary and the letter that goes with it. Now I need to get busy and read that one first. Yesterday I spent the day with Cliff and Officer Hunter at the Old Bryant house. You came home late from your meetings, so I didn't have the chance to tell you about it. We went through and found some…interesting things."

Dan laid down his fork and folded his hands together, his forearms against the edge of the table. "Really? Like what?"

"Well, first off, the house seems solid, and I would recommend having a restoration contractor take a look at it. The house is a great example of pre-Civil War architecture. It has its issues, but I'm amazed it's held up considering no one's lived there for so long. There's still Civil War era wallpaper hanging in many of the rooms. The Bryants took great care of the place. I'll research to find out who the original owners were."

Her dad's eyes lit up. "I surmise there's more to the story."

She nodded. "Back to your question, there's a wall in the cellar alongside the root cellar that we don't think should be there. It's built of Civil War era brick and cheaply and hastily made mortar that wasn't used in the foundation of the house. Our question is why is that wall there? The root cellar is built in the middle on the front center of the house. There's no wall on the other side of it. Clifford wants to break through the wall and see if there's anything behind it. You know, find out if there's a purpose for it."

Dan steepled his forefingers against his lips for a few moments, then shrugged. "I trust both my historians, or I wouldn't have them on my staff. You folks have a way of taking things out methodically and documenting them so you can put them back if necessary. I say go for it. Find out why that wall is there and what's behind it."

Chloe couldn't have prevented the grin that stretched her lips. "I'll let Cliff know in the morning."

"I've been listening to all this with great curiosity." Aunt Charlene wiped her lips with her napkin. "What's it all about?"

Dan picked up his fork and paused. "A lady who owned a house on the battlefield near the edge of town just sold it to the park. I asked Chloe and Clifford to go through and access whether it's worth restoring."

"The woman also sent us a diary she found in the house when she was a child," Chloe added. "I'm going to read through it and find out what era the diary is from and what significance it might have, say, with the Civil War—"

"*And,*" went on Dan, "we now have on loan a diary and a letter from a lady whose great-great-grandfather was a colonel who fought in the Battle of Gettysburg. According to her his diary, along with the letter which she says substantiates the diary, states that he performed some feat of heroism during the battle."

"We're planning an event to raise funds for a display of the letter and diary in the museum," Chloe said. "We want to invite illustrious donors—the governor, state senators, the mayor, etc."

Aunt Charlene's head ping-ponged between them as they took turns explaining. When they finished, she shook her head. "My goodness. You have your hands full, Chloe, dear. I'd love to know what's in those diaries." Aunt Charlene finished the last bite on her plate and set her fork down.

Chloe dabbed at Evie's mouth with her cloth napkin. "After I get this little one to bed in a while, I'm going to start reading the colonel's diary. It should make for a fascinating read, don't you think?"

"I do." Aunt Charlene sat back in her chair and laid her hands in her lap. "You told your dad at the beginning of this conversation that you and Clifford found some interesting things at the house. What else did you find besides that fascinating wall?"

Chloe glanced at her daughter whose plate was clean. "Are you finished, princess?"

Evie gave an exaggerated nod.

"Why don't you ask to be excused, then go bring in Mrs. P and your tea set. It's supposed to rain later, and I would hate for poor Mrs. P. to get wet. Her stuffing would get all soggy, you know."

A frown tugged the little girl's brows down. "Oh no. M's. P. won't be happy wif soggy insides, Mommy."

Chloe tweaked Evie's nose. "You're right, sweetie. Now excuse yourself."

"Gwampa, 'scuse me, pwease."

"Why of course, Evie. You're excused." Dan gave her a wink.

She climbed down from her booster seat and hurried from the dining room to do Chloe's biding.

"It must be something you don't want Evie to hear." Dan raised a brow at his daughter as he leaned back in his chair and finished his iced tea.

"You would be right about that." Chloe watched through the opened French doors as her daughter took her time packing up her tea set. "While we were in the house, we heard something. Something...we couldn't explain." She peered at her father and aunt. "We were standing in the parlor looking around when distinct footsteps sounded on the floor above our heads. All three of us heard them. Cliff refused to go upstairs and took the skeleton key to go outside and explore. Officer Hunter and I went upstairs to look around. Someone had to be up there, but...there was no one. We searched the whole house. Nobody."

Dan's brows lowered as he set down his empty glass then leaned his elbows on the edge of the table, clasping his hands beneath his chin. "What are your thoughts? What did Officer Hunter think?"

"He had no idea, and neither do I."

"Hmm." Aunt Charlene tapped her chin with a thoughtful finger. "Perhaps it was a ghost."

Chloe cast a reproachful glance in her aunt's direction. "Aunt Char, don't be ridiculous. There's no such thing."

"Says who?" Aunt Charlene lifted her shoulders and brows at the same time.

Chloe shook her head. "I won't even entertain that suggestion. It's an old house and old houses make noises all the time."

With a cocked brow, Aunt Charlene gave her niece a skeptical glance. "Noises that sound specifically like footsteps crossing above your heads?"

Chloe peered at her dad.

He shrugged. "Gettysburg is renowned for being one of most haunted towns in the US. I can neither confirm nor deny that. All I can say is there was a huge three-day battle here. There were more than seven thousand men who died during those three days, both Union and Confederate. Many thousands more were wounded and left behind in Gettysburg to be tended by the townsfolk when the armies moved on. Countless wounded soldiers left behind died later. There was a lot of death and anguish in and around this town, and I'm sure it left its imprint."

"You don't believe in ghosts do you, Dad?"

"If you're asking if I've ever seen or experienced one, then the answer is no, I haven't." Dan shrugged. "Having said that, some of the rangers have reported experiences around the area—in some of the buildings around town as well as on the battlefield. Do I believe them? They were sincere when they told me about their experiences. I have no reason to disbelieve them."

"And there you have it." Aunt Charlene stood and began gathering the dishes.

"Well, until I have proof, there isn't a ghost in that house." Chloe also stood and helped clear the table. There had to be a better explanation for the sounds they'd heard. Besides, she had too many other projects to worry about that. Interesting? Perhaps. It certainly wasn't important.

Chapter Four

Diary of Col. Edgar William Mayfield
Gettysburg Battlefield
Gettysburg, PA
July 1, 1863

Today was a harrowing day for the 5th Connecticut Infantry Division. I'm sure it was for other Union states' divisions and regiments as well. Amongst the many battles and skirmishes that took place today, we didn't make any headway with the enemy. The leader of those fractious Confederate troops, Gen. Robert E. Lee, fought and led with passion and skill. It was that passion and skill that won the battle this day. Our own brave Gen. George G. Meade did the best he could but was outmaneuvered by a southern gentleman. Let us hope that tomorrow, on the second day of this fierce battle, General Meade will lead us to victory.

My own great triumph today gives me pride in my abilities as a leader and hopes that if we make it through this horrible battle, perhaps I'll gain a field promotion and advancement in the ranks. As first squad was surrounded by a large group of Confederate troops in an entrenchment on the eastern side of the battlefield, I was able to come to their aid and singlehandedly rescue them. Their ammunition was depleted, and there was no way out for them. I came upon this scene along with three of my men who were riding with me through the battle. As we rode, all three of my fellow riders were shot by the large group of enemy soldiers. We were far outnumbered, but I jumped from my horse, fired on the group, killing several of the enemy in the process.

I gathered the calvary pistols of the fallen riders and continued firing until all the enemy were dead. I then joined my first squad. They were all safe. After collecting the firearms of the fallen enemy, we took a circuitous route back to our division. The battle was waning as the northern regimental lines had collapsed. Our esteemed Union troops retreated through the streets of Gettysburg into the hills to the south of town.

A rumble of thunder tugged Chloe's attention from the diary. She lay stretched out on the couch in the family room, a throw pillow tucked behind her head. The lights were out except for the lamp on the end table behind her. A flash of lightning lit the back yard a few seconds before a louder rumble of thunder sounded. After the third rumble caused the house to shake, soft hurried footsteps padded down the hardwood floor in the hallway then became muffled as they tread across the family room carpet.

Chloe glanced up in time to see Evie before she launched herself on top of her. She raised the antique diary in time to prevent a catastrophe. Laying it on the end table next to the couch, Chloe gathered her young daughter in her arms. "What's up, princess? You're supposed to be asleep."

Her daughter wiggled between Chloe and the couch back, still wrapped in Chloe's arms. "I heard woud booms, Mommy. A storm's comin'."

With gentle fingers, Chloe wiped Evie's bangs from her forehead and tweaked her nose. "I think you're right. Those booms are thunder. Just the noise that comes after the lightening. They won't hurt you, you know."

"That's what you always say, but they sound wike they will."

Chloe chuckled. "They do, but they won't. Trust me. I'm your mom, and I know what I'm talking about." She tickled Evie's ribs, and the little girl giggled.

"I know."

"Good. As long as you do."

"What's going on here?" Dan came out of his study at the side of the family room. "I hear giggles. What's the princess doing out of bed?"

Lightening flashed and thunder rumbled causing the house to shake again. Rain slashed across the doors and the windows.

Evie covered her eyes and buried her face against Chloe.

"Want to tell Grandpa what woke you?" Chloe tugged at her hands.

"The booms, Gwampa. The booms waked me."

"The booms, huh? Well, they are a little loud, but I bet your mommy told you they won't hurt you. Am I right?" Dan sat in one of the armchairs.

She nodded then covered her eyes at another flash and boom.

"Come here, sweetie." Dan crooked a finger.

Evie climbed over Chloe and ran into her grandpa's waiting arms. She wrapped hers around his neck and held on. "Come on, I'll read you a story and tuck you back into bed. Then I'll sit with you for a bit. Blow Mommy a kiss and tell her goodnight."

Evie blew Chloe a kiss. "Night, Mommy. Love you."

Chloe blew one back. "I love you too, princess. Sleep well."

As they drifted down the dim hallway, Chloe picked up the diary and began reading again.

Diary of Col. Edgar William Mayfield
Gettysburg Battlefield
Gettysburg, PA
July 2, 1863

Today one my most dedicated sergeants, Sgt. Timothy Edwards, first squad leader, was killed in battle. Sergeant Edwards was one of the soldiers I rescued yesterday when a large group of enemy troops surrounded first squad. I'm saddened this fine example of a young military leader is gone. Not only did he lead his squad with aplomb, but he fought well and shall be remembered as a hero. He told me he had a young lady back home. I'm sure he will be greatly missed.

The soldiers in first squad are to be commended for

their efforts in holding their own in the battle today. Our illustrious leader Gen. George G. Meade led us in holding the lines. Although there was not a resounding victory, the enemy, led by Confederate Gen. Robert E. Lee, surrounded our lines and held their own. We lost many brave men today, and it's with great sadness I report the soldiers of first squad were all killed in battle. If I make it through tomorrow and we win this battle, I will write letters to the families of those brave men.

Chloe was glad the good colonel bragged on his men, but he sure didn't mind bragging on himself either. Mrs. White-Smith no doubt was proud of her great-great-grandfather and certainly had a right to be.

Chloe knew all about the Battle of Gettysburg, she didn't know the name of every colonel and officer in the battle, but she knew many of them. She wasn't familiar with Colonel Mayfield of Connecticut. It had been a colossal battle with two huge armies. As a result, it was impossible to keep track of every officer without sitting down and pulling every record from every regiment. Which they had, by the way. She would look up the colonel and see what she could find out about him.

"Evie's asleep." Dan returned to the family room. "The thunder has rumbled off into the distance, and the rain has settled to a steady patter. She'll be fine."

Chloe kept her finger in the diary and lowered it to her lap. "Thanks for putting Evie back to bed, Dad. I appreciate you. And I appreciate you being the solid man in her life. I don't know what I'd do if you weren't here."

Dan dropped into the armchair once again and crossed his legs onto the hassock in front of him. "Honey, it's been a rough few years for you, and I wouldn't want to be anywhere else. I'll be here for you and Evie as long as the good Lord allows me to be. And you know as well as I do, God's grace is sufficient for whatever we have to face."

Chloe stared out the French door but barely noticed the lightning flashes in the distance. "Perhaps." She used to think that way. Since Joshua's death, she wasn't so sure. Yeah, she still went to church with Dad and Aunt Charlene, but she wasn't convinced

God really cared anymore. If He did, why had He ripped Joshua from her and Evie?

~

"Hey, Hunter."

Blake stopped in his trek across the parking lot and turned at the sound of his name. His fellow park policeman, Gabe Holland, strode toward him from his cruiser.

"Oh, hey, Gabe. How's it going?" Blake held out a hand and Gabe reached for it as he halted in from of him.

"Well, things were pretty quiet for the day shift." He propped his hands on his hips and glanced over his shoulder toward the western sky, "But it looks like there's a storm rolling in. I hope it won't cause you too much trouble this evening."

Blake followed his gaze then peered at Gabe. "Yeah. Me too. Nothing more fun than an evening spent sitting in a car in a thunderstorm."

"Right," Gabe chuckled. "Hey, I heard you gave the boss's daughter a ticket the other day."

Blake's brows drew together. "Oh yeah? Who?"

"The boss. You know, Superintendent Fielding's daughter, Chloe Rogers." Gabe gave Blake a light punch on the shoulder. "That took some guts."

Buzzing began in Blake's ears at the same time his insides twisted. Chloe Rogers was Superintendent Fielding's daughter? "You're joking me, right?"

One of Gabe's brows quirked upward. "You mean you didn't know?"

Blake shook his head. "How did I not know that?"

Gabe shrugged. "Everybody knows that."

"Except me, apparently." Blake took off his "Smoky-Bear" hat and scratched his head. "So why is her name Rogers and the superintendent's name is Fielding?

"Easy. Chloe's a widow." Gabe clapped Blake on the shoulder and sauntered away. "Have a good shift. Be careful out in that storm. It's going to be a doozy."

Two hours later, Blake sat in his cruiser sipping steaming hot coffee from Moira's coffee shop as rain streamed down his windshield and lightening shot bolts across the night sky. Night turned to day for several seconds every few minutes. As he sipped

Moira's delicious roast, Blake was reminded of her advice to "go get her." Without knowing who "her" was, Moira advised him to go after whoever the woman was on his mind. Since the morning he'd given Chloe Rogers a ticket, he'd been unable to shake her from his thoughts. Her blue eyes and honey-blond ponytail had stuck there. Now that Gabe Holland had told him Chloe was a widow, did that make a difference? Blake wasn't sure. Probably not, but it would depend on Chloe and her journey through her grief. It couldn't be easy for her.

Another bombshell Gabe had lobbed was the fact Chloe was the superintendent's daughter. Blake shook his head. The hits just kept coming. If he was smart, he'd simply turn his interest elsewhere. Like on sightseeing and familiarizing himself with the area and *not* on another women. The only woman he'd ever thought he loved had merely brought him pain. He didn't need more of that in his life.

"Well, Lord, if You'd just take that little seed of interest I have and pluck it up, I'd sure be grateful." Blake placed his travel mug into the cup holder in the console and put his cruiser in gear. It was time to go on patrol. Sitting here gave his mind too much time to think. About Chloe Rogers and those amazing blue eyes.

A rumble of thunder shook the cruiser.

Blake heaved a heavy sigh. "I know You're listening, and I need Your help."

~

Chloe parked her Mini Cooper next to Cliff's alongside the Bryant house and climbed out. Glancing at the exterior of the old structure, she was certain she wouldn't find him inside. Striding around to the back, she found the entrance to the cellar open, cool and musty air escaping and dissipating in the bright, warm morning breeze. A generator sat beside the entrance with large extension cords feeding into the darkened doorway. Chloe turned on the small flashlight she'd brought from her car and stepped inside. Sounds of banging came from further under the house.

Following the sounds and the extension cords, she headed to the mysterious brick and mortar wall next to the root cellar. Chloe was careful not to trip on the cords that powered several halogen lights on stands facing the wall. There Clifford worked to retrieve a brick where he'd already dislodged another one. He chipped away at the flakey mortar around it.

“Good morning, Cliff. Slow progress, I see.”

Clifford, who squatted, supported only on his toes, jumped at the sound of Chloe’s voice and fell backward onto his rear.

Chloe covered her mouth and chuckled. “So sorry. Did I startle you?”

A reproachful glare said it all in the light from the halogen lamps. “Don’t sneak up on a person like that.”

Chloe couldn’t contain her smile. “What’s the matter? You don’t think this place is…haunted, do you?”

Clifford pushed up from the ground and brushed off the seat of his khakis. The lowered brows over his narrowed gaze implied he might. “It’s not easy working down here when someone’s walking around overhead, and I know there’s no one up there.”

Chloe’s own brows shot up at this. “Seriously?”

“Yes, seriously. Tomorrow I’m bringing my radio and turning it up. Loud.” Clifford bent his knees back and forth as if working out kinks. “And I’m bringing a stool to sit on.”

Chloe chuckled to herself. “Why don’t you work higher on the wall to begin with so you can stand up straight?”

Clifford muttered something.

“What was that?” Chloe stepped closer.

“I said, there’s always a critic.” Clifford’s voice was plenty loud enough this time.

“Just a suggestion, my friend. Can I help?”

“Sure. Extra tools are in the box by that lamp.” Clifford pointed them out.

“How much of the wall do you intend to take down?” Chloe found a pick that should work well on the mortar and began on a section a short distance from where Clifford started anew while standing up.

“I don’t want to take the whole thing down until we see what’s behind it. It may not be worth it if there’s nothing back there. Let’s just work on this section.” With his finger he drew an imaginary line around a section big enough for them to get a good look behind.

After they’d been working for a few minutes, Chloe said, “I started reading the good colonel’s diary.”

“Oh yeah? And?”

"Well, Mrs. White-Smith has good reason to be proud of her great-great-grandfather if what he claims is true. However, he was an arrogant fellow. He didn't mind annotating what a hero he was."

Clifford stopped his work and turned toward her. "Really? That blatant, huh?"

"Yeah. That blatant. I've only read the entries through the first two days of the battle. He firmly believed his act of courage should've secured him a field promotion at a minimum."

"What did he do that was so courageous?" Clifford removed another brick.

Chloe explained what the diary stated. "I'm going to see if I can find anything that historically backs it up."

"Good idea. Wasn't there a letter that went along with the diary?"

"Yeah, but I haven't read it yet. Evie was disturbed by the storm last night, and although Dad took her back to bed, it wasn't long before I headed there myself. Hopefully I can get through more entries this evening after she goes to bed."

The sound of footsteps walking across the old floorboards above their heads caused them both to cease their work. Chloe's eyes met Clifford's in the bright halogen lamplight. His eyes were round like saucers. Were hers? Had someone slipped into the house unnoticed?

"I'm going to see who's up there." Chloe tossed her pick back into the box and grabbed her flashlight. "This is ridiculous."

"Don't. There's no one up there." Clifford's voice was little more than a loud whisper.

She held her hand out. "I need the key, Cliff."

He hesitated then tugged the skeleton key from his pocket. "Please don't go up there. Not alone."

Chloe pinned him with one raised brow. "Are you going with me?"

After a few seconds, he shook his head then dropped the key in her hand.

"I didn't think so." Switching on her flashlight, she made her way through the darkness of the cellar until she reached the sunlight and warmth of the outside fresh air. Was someone trying to play tricks on them? If so, why? For what purpose? It made no sense.

Chloe strode around to the rickety front steps and, with care, climbed to the porch where she slipped the key into the old lock. Now if she could open it. It had taken Officer Hunter to open it the last time.

With much finagling and a good dose of patience, Chloe finally snicked the lock open then twisted the knob until the door swung wide. Switching her flashlight on again, she stepped inside and closed the door behind her. Of its own volition, her stomach lodged in her throat and her hair stood on end. Now why, for goodness' sake? She hadn't seen or heard anything since she was in the cellar. Because it was a creepy old house and she was going in by herself, *that* was why. What had made her think this was a good idea?

Chloe peered around the hallway, listening for footsteps but heard nothing. The silence alone sent gooseflesh down her body. What would happen if she heard something? Having Officer Hunter with her the last time *had* been nice. Stepping over to the parlor door and with the help of the flashlight, she peered into the room. Nothing. She walked across the hallway to the dining room and did the same. Again, nothing. After checking out the whole first floor, she climbed the staircase to the second floor where she checked every room to find nothing there as well. It was the same as when she and Officer Hunter had gone through the house.

She stood at the top of the old staircase and glanced around the hallway. The walls were devoid of pictures, and the antique wallpaper drooped in places. Long before the Bryants had come to live here, this home had been bright and new and full of life. Who was the family who'd lived here? Had they been happy here? Had laughter rung through these rooms long before the sadness of war had come? Was there beauty and love here before time and age had stolen it away? Who were those people? Chloe wanted—no, needed—to find out who lived here before and during the Civil War and particularly the Battle of Gettysburg?

With one last glance around, she descended the stairs and headed out the door, locking it behind her.

Chloe would give Cliff another hour to work on the wall, then she needed to return to the office and do some research. Something told her to start with the family. She would not put off making that call to Mrs. Montague. It would be interesting to find out where that lady had found her diary in the house when she was a child. Then Chloe would go back into the house and check it out.

Chapter Five

"Mrs. Montague, this is Chloe Rogers from the history department at Gettysburg National Military Park. How are you?" Chloe held the receiver from her desk phone between her ear and her shoulder as she pulled up information on her computer.

"Oh my, yes. It's a pleasure to hear from you, Miss Rogers. Superintendent Fielding said you would be calling me sometime soon." The older woman sounded genuinely pleased. "I've been eager to talk with you about my diary."

"Wonderful." Chloe opened the file with the information she was looking for. "I'm eager to listen to what you have to tell me."

"Have you been able to read any of the diary yet?"

"I have not yet, ma'am. We received two diaries at the same time. One on loan and the one you gave us as well as the house we purchased from you. So, we have a lot of material to go over. I'm also planning my research concerning the house and the diaries and am eager to read the one you gave us, but I have to read the other diary first. We have a huge donor event we're preparing in connection with that one."

"I understand. It's not a problem. I've had it most of my life and haven't read it either except to know that it belonged to one of the daughters of a family that lived in the house prior to the Civil War. Her name was Cecelia Langston, and the first entries were from her birthday party. That's all I know. You'll find her name is written in the front of the diary. Until you have a chance to read it, perhaps her name will help you in your research concerning the house."

"Langston." Chloe repeated the name as she jotted it onto the notepad on her desk. "Yes, that will help immensely. Thank you.

The superintendent mentioned you'd found the diary in the house when you were a child. Can you tell me where?"

"Oh certainly. When you're standing at the top of the staircase, my room was on the left back of the house. The gold room, I used to call it. The wallpaper was sort of a gold color with tiny flowers. I loved it. Anyway, there's a built-in corner cupboard, and on the bottom shelf, there's a hidden sliding panel. If you don't know it's there, you might never find it. I stumbled on it one day when my mother asked me to dust my room. The panel actually slides behind the wall and had somehow become partially opened. I'd dusted those shelves countless times, and it had never opened before. I was so surprised."

"How did you find it?"

"Well, I took all my books off the shelf and was dusting when I noticed a space in the wall behind the shelf about an inch wide. I put my finger into the space and pulled on the back wall of the shelf. It slid open and there was the diary in a narrow space behind where the wall had been. There was a small porcelain doll as well, but I kept that."

"How intriguing." Chloe made notes as Mrs. Montague spoke. "I'm even more eager to find out what this mystery daughter wrote in her diary. Would you send me a picture of the doll? I'd love to see what it looks like just so I have a picture in my mind when I start reading the diary."

"Of course, I'd be happy to."

"Thank you, Mrs. Montague, and thank you for taking the time to speak with me this afternoon. I'm going to check out the cupboard for myself. How exciting it must have been for you as a child to find it."

"Oh yes, indeed. I was a Nancy Drew fan as a child, and any little mystery I found was like being the teen detective herself." The older woman's hearty laugh came over the phone and filled Chloe's ear.

Chloe couldn't help but laugh too. "I'm sure. I was a fan as well. Like every other kid, I used to hide under the covers with a flashlight to read late at night, then my parents would wonder why they couldn't get me up in the mornings."

"Oh, dear me. I used the flashlight my father had when he was in WWII." Mrs. Montague laughed again. "I must let you go, dear.

If I can help in any other way, don't hesitate to call. I'm not sure how, mind you, but you can always ask."

"Thank you. I appreciate that. Have a good afternoon." Chloe hung up the phone and scanned her notes. She only wished she could delve into Cecelia Langston's diary now, but unfortunately, Colonel Mayfield's took precedence. Glancing at her watch. She had a meeting with Jan Miller in half an hour to go over a couple things. Jan was doing fine on her own, but she wanted Chloe's opinion. At least Chloe wasn't dealing with the planning herself. Thank goodness for Jan.

~

Chloe pulled the covers under Evie's chin and dropped a kiss on her cheek. "Goodnight, Princess. I love you."

"I love you more, Mommy." Evie giggled.

"Oh, no." Chloe shook her head and sat on the side of Evie's bed. "I don't think so. I love you more."

"Uh uh." Evie shook her dark head, those silky, dark bangs swishing back and forth.

"No?" Chloe dropped another kiss on Evie's cheek. "Well, I'm bigger than you so that must mean I love you more."

Evie stared at her mom for several moments, a pucker between her brows. Chloe could almost see the gears turning in the little girl's head as she attempted to figure that one out.

"Good night, Princess." Chloe pulled the door nearly closed behind her, leaving it cracked a few inches.

"'Night, Mommy."

In the family room, Chloe picked up Colonel Mayfield's diary from the end table by the couch and lay down, her head propped on the throw pillow. Thankful there wasn't a forecast for storms this evening, she opened the stiff leather cover of the diary with care and pulled out the torn piece of paper she'd used to save her place. Now, where was she? Ah yes.

Diary of Col. Edgar William Mayfield
5th Connecticut Infantry Regiment
Gettysburg Battlefield
Gettysburg, PA
July 3, 1863

It is with great pride that I sit at my writing desk inside my tent after the final battle this evening and write this entry in my diary. Our illustrious leader, Gen. George G. Meade, led us to victory today against a worthy opponent, Confederate Gen. Robert E. Lee. That Virginia gentleman took a chance by sending Brig. Gen. George Pickett to face our troops undermanned. His daring strategy did not pay off in the end, and tomorrow morn, Gen. Robert E. Lee, along with his much-decreased ranks, will retreat, defeated, back to Virginia.

As the Confederate army retreats, our army celebrates. I have put myself in for a field promotion. Considering the lives I rescued two days ago from the enemy, I feel it is my due.

Chloe shook her head. No matter what this man had done to rescue others, she simply couldn't overlook his arrogance.

Diary of Col. Edgar William Mayfield
5th Connecticut Infantry Regiment
Gettysburg Battlefield
Gettysburg, PA
July 5, 1863

It seems General Meade hesitates for some reason in pursuing General Lee and his ragtag army and finishing them off. This order came directly from President Lincoln himself. However, General Meade is leading the Army of the Potomac back to Washington. It is very much unlike our leader not to follow a direct order, especially from the president. In the meantime, General Lee's army puts more and more distance between us.

Chloe skimmed through the next entries, many of which were on the trail after the Battle of Gettysburg and then the Battle of Williamsport, MD, which was another indecisive and long, drawn-out battle between General Meade and General Lee that lasted from July 6th through the 16th. Chloe had read a little about that battle, but not as much as the Battle of

Gettysburg. Apparently, Colonel Mayfield and his dwindling division went where they were told to fight just as the Confederate regiments did. Each side gave all for what they believed in.

Battle after battle with few moments of rest. A skirmish that occurred ahead of the battles. Soldiers always on the march. Colonel Mayfield wrote lots of letters to families who lost their loved ones on the field of battle. It seemed that took most of his evenings in camp.

Diary of Col. Edgar William Mayfield
5th Connecticut Infantry Regiment
Battle of Bristoe Station
Bristoe Station, Northern Virginia
October 14, 1863

Once again, our illustrious leader, General Meade, has led us to a decisive victory over our enemy, Gen. Robert E. Lee. It was a hard battle and we lost too many, but he lost many more. I can rest my head upon my pillow this night knowing our troops gave their lives for a worthy cause.

On a much dourer and more disappointing note, I received an answer to my request for a field promotion today, and, I must admit, I gave into a spat of temper. I've waited these many months for an answer only to find they've denied my request on the justification there were no witnesses to my feat of rescue. @#$%& It would seem the single letter of recommendation from Major General Archibald McAdams did nothing to persuade them I am deserving of the promotion. If only someone had been there to witness...but of course how could there have been? I left no...In the heat of battle? Of course...*

Oh, my goodness. Chloe stopped reading and closed the diary, her finger stuck between the pages. Yes, indeed. The good colonel certainly had a temper, but what did he expect? There had been no witnesses to corroborate his act of heroism. Not even the Major

General who recommended him. Was the general his commanding officer? If so, he must have trusted his word sight unseen as the commanding officer of the men beneath him. Was he that extraordinary of a leader? She couldn't blame those who denied the promotion, if there had been no witnesses. Too bad, but cursing in a fit of temper certainly never solved anything. Chloe noted the entry had been left unfinished, and the wording was odd. What did it mean?

Chloe carefully thumbed through the remaining pages of the diary, skimming the words as she went. Nothing stood out or grabbed her attention. She thought she'd gleaned about all she needed from Col. Edgar William Mayfield. At least for the time being. She'd research the colonel when she was in the office. Good. Perhaps she could move on to Cecilia Langston's diary soon. The young girl wouldn't show the arrogance that the colonel had.

Chloe went to the back door where her messenger bag was, wrapped up the diary in the acid free bag Mrs. White-Smith had given her, then placed it into the messenger bag. Something grabbed her attention and she tugged it out. Uh oh. The ticket Officer Hunter had given her. She hadn't taken care of it yet. Chloe heaved a huge sigh. Yet another thing to deal with. Tomorrow. She'd take care of it tomorrow.

She reached into her purse and tugged out her wallet. Placing the ticket inside, she dropped it back into the purse and did an about face and headed for bed.

Officer Hunter's face with his lopsided grin materialized before her mind's eye. Why? Okay, maybe because of the ticket. No other reason. It had nothing to do with her going into the Bryant house by herself today and, maybe...sort of...wishing he'd been there too. Well, of course not. She hadn't, had she?

Once in her room, Chloe kicked off her slippers and slid between the cool sheets and a light blanket, tugging them under her chin. It *had* been a little unnerving going into the house alone today. Easy to be brave when she was with Clifford in the cellar. Not so easy when she'd actually stepped into the house alone. Yeah, it was nice having Officer Hunter there to check out the house the first time, but she'd managed today. There hadn't been anyone there. Simply old house noises again. Nothing more.

Chloe shooed away Officer Hunter's image and rolled onto her side, pulling the blanket closer.

It was so easy for the park policeman's features to skate before her mind's eye and yet more and more as time went on, Josh's face seemed to fade. The sudden desire to talk to the Lord filled Chloe only to be followed with the usual anger and frustration she'd felt for the last three years. Why should she talk with Him when He'd failed her? He'd allowed Josh to be taken from her. And now? The image of his features had begun to fade. It took physically looking at his picture on her dresser in order to remember. It shouldn't be. His face should be stamped in her memory.

Shame swept through Chloe as tears dripped down her cheeks and into her pillow followed by a sob before she could prevent it. She'd spent many a night crying herself to sleep since the day the Army officers had come knocking on her door to inform her Josh wouldn't be coming home. Tonight would be no different.

~

"Excuse me." Blake reached out to steady the woman who raced around the corner of the hallway and plowed right into him.

"Oh, I'm terribly sorry."

He stared into the gorgeous blue eyes he'd been unable to wipe from his thoughts since he'd given their owner a ticket. Chloe Rogers. "Mrs. Rogers, I'm sorry. I hope I didn't injure you."

"No. No, not at all, Officer Hunter. I'm fine." She ran her hands down the sides of her olive uniform skirt then glance at the floor. "Oops, we've both dropped our hats."

Blake peered down to their Smokey-Bear hats lying upside down on the gray tile floor. He reached down and retrieved them, handing her one and putting the other under his arm.

"Well, I'm sorry for bumping into you like that. Again, I hope I didn't injure you." With a nod, he said, "Have a good day."

She was staring at him beneath the pucker of her brows, her mouth slightly open as if perplexed. Now what had he done? He headed down the hallway toward park police headquarters when her voice stopped him.

"Officer Hunter, wait."

Blake turned to find Chloe following him, her "Smoky-Bear" hat on her head, only he doubted it was hers. She had to tilt her head back to see from beneath the wide brim.

Chloe stopped before him. “I think you might have my hat.”

Blake chuckled as she peeked from beneath the brim of *his* hat, and he placed the one in his hand on his head. It sat on top not even reaching his ears. Chloe’s chest began to rise and fall as she attempted to hold in her laughter. Then her lips split in a wide smile as laughter spilled out.

“Do I look that ridiculous?” Blake grinned at her.

Chloe nodded, sending the brim of his hat over her eyes and down her nose. She shoved it back. “Yep. Probably about as much as I do. Want to swap?”

“Most definitely.” Blake removed her hat and held it out.

Chloe still chuckled as she removed the overlarge hat and handed it to him. Blake had never seen her laugh or even really smile. He was enchanted.

She placed her hat on her head, the brim parallel with the floor, the fit perfect. “Better?”

“Beautiful.” Did his voice sound as husky to her as it did to him?

Warm color flooded her cheeks and Chloe dropped her gaze then removed her hat, letting it dangle from her fingers at her side. “Thanks.”

Oh boy. Too much too soon? Yeah, probably, but she *was* beautiful, and the thought had slipped out before he could stop it. Blake snapped his fingers. “Hey, I know this great little coffee shop in town. I’m leaving work now. How about you? Want to go get some coffee? That is, if you like coffee.” He shrugged, feeling less and less confident in his invitation the more he talked. “Are…are you a coffee drinker?”

One side of Chloe’s lips lifted in a slight grin. “Yes, I love coffee. And yes, I can leave work now, and yes, I’d love to go get a cup.”

Before he could speak again, her eyes narrowed. “However, it depends on the coffee shop. It wouldn’t by any chance be Moira’s, would it?”

Blake crossed his arms over his chest and snorted. “Is there any other?”

Chloe shook her head, sending her ponytail dancing. She flashed him a full-on smile causing Blake’s breath to catch. “Not in my book. Moira’s is the best.”

Blake nodded and cleared his throat. “Great. Then let me drop something off in the patrol office, and I’ll be ready to go.”

~

Chloe parked her car on the street outside Moira’s as Officer Hunter parked a few cars down. Had she really flirted with him after he called her “Beautiful?” She supposed most folks wouldn’t think twice about that kind of thing, but she hadn’t acted like that with a man in a long time. What would Josh think of her acting this way and going out with another man for coffee? Jan and Aunt Char had both been trying to persuade her to go out for a couple of years. When Chloe had called her aunt as she’d left work to let her know she’d be late coming home, Aunt Char wanted to know why. Chloe hesitated to respond, but simply told her she was meeting a friend for coffee. If she’d told her she was meeting a *man* for coffee, Chloe would never hear the end of it. Besides, this was a one-off thing, right?

Chloe exited her car and met Officer Hunter at the entrance to Moira’s. He held the door for her. Nice. His mama taught him right.

Inside the cool interior they waited for their eyes to adjust from the bright afternoon sunshine to the dimmer interior, then approached the counter at the rear of the shop.

“Well, well, me dearies.” Moira folded her arms along the countertop. “I’ve never seen the two of ye in here together. Some special occasion?”

“Oh no, no.” Chloe shook her head.

“No, not at all.” Officer Hunter echoed.

Moira’s gaze swept from one to the other then back again. Her raised brow indicated she doubted their denials, but said nothing about it. “Well then. How can I help ye?”

“We’d like coffee and dessert.” Blake announced, stepping over to the dessert box. “What do you have good today?”

“Ach, well I have bonnie delicious banoffee tarts and coconut macaroons to begin with.” Moira peered at Blake through the plexiglass dessert box. “And of course, there’s always me iced caramel shortbread and Scotch scones. What will it be, laddie?” The older woman winked at Chloe. “I’ll get yer coffee whilst he’s thinkin’. What will ye have, lass?”

“I’ll have a coconut latte and one of your banoffee tarts.”

Chloe pointed at the scrumptious-looking pastries.

Officer Hunter turned toward her. "How can you make up your mind that fast?"

She shrugged. "I just try something different every time I come. Everything Moira makes is delicious. You can't go wrong with anything you choose."

"True." Blake pivoted back and pointed toward the box. "I'll have your iced caramel shortbread and my usual coffee. We'll sit over here."

He pointed at a table and strode toward it. Chloe caught Moira's expression of interest before she turned to follow Officer Hunter. He held out her chair as she sat, then took the seat across from her.

"Thank you. This was a nice idea." Chloe hung her purse on the back of the chair then clasped her fingers under her chin. "I don't do this kind of thing often."

"What do you mean, 'this kind of thing'?" Officer Hunter leaned his arms on the edge of the table.

"I have a little girl so I usually head straight home from work, unless I have to stop for groceries or run another errand." Chloe gave a gentle smile. "My aunt watches her during the day while I work, but my evenings are at home with her."

"Here ye go." Moira stopped by the table with a tray of their coffee and desserts in her hands. "These are for ye, and these are for ye. Enjoy them, dearies. If ye need anything else, jest let me know."

"Thanks, Moira." Chloe put sugar in her coffee then noticed Officer Hunter hadn't moved. He appeared to be deep in thought. "Officer Hunter? Are you all right?"

His eyes met hers, and he reached for his fork. "Yes, I'm fine. This looks great, doesn't it? Moira is some baker."

~

Boy, the hits just kept coming. First to find Chloe Rogers was the daughter of the park superintendent and then a widow. Now to find out she's the mother of a little girl. This beautiful woman had piqued his interest, but how much? Enough to invest in someone dealing with the loss of a husband and the mother of a young child? *Lord,* am *I that interested?* No, he'd already decided he wasn't interested in another relationship. What was he thinking?

Blake's gaze met Chloe's blue eyes and a jolt pierced through him. Who was he kidding? He was more than a little interested. But how much of that was physical attraction and how much was genuine desire to know more about the woman herself? *I need some clarity here, Lord. We need to talk later.*

"How goes the old Bryant house investigation?" *Yeah, that's a safe topic.*

Chloe sipped her coffee then set the cup down. "Oh, we're making pretty good progress. Cliff is working on the mysterious wall in the cellar. It really is an odd wall, but he's having to remove each brick, one at a time, then place them in order on a tarp so that, if necessary, they can be replaced once he discovers what's behind the wall. He let me help him, but it's tedious work. I have to split my time between helping him, my research and diary reading. Which reminds me, I went back into the house yesterday. Alone."

"What? Alone? Why?" Blake didn't like the sound of that. "Where was Cliff?"

"Oh, he was in the cellar. We were working on the wall when we heard those strange footsteps again. Or what sounded like footsteps." Chloe waved a dismissive hand. "I acted all brave-like and took off to see what was going on. That is, until I got the front door open, which I managed to unlock on my own. Once inside I wasn't so brave. I could've used your company as I checked it out, but I didn't find anything. Exactly the same as when you and I went through."

Blake hoped the frown he cast her way conveyed his apprehension. "You shouldn't be going in there alone. We've been concerned about squatters already, and there's no guarantee they aren't going to move in at any time."

Chloe waved her hand again. "I doubt it, especially now that we're working there and spending more time in the building. Soon, we'll have a contractor coming in to assess the structure for restoration purposes. Not a chance squatters will move in."

Blake heaved a heavy sigh. "I still don't want you going in alone. Call me if you need to go inside."

Chloe tapped a fingernail on the table's shiny surface. After a few moments, she nodded. "All right. I have to go back in tomorrow and check out something in one of the rooms.

Something the lady who sold the house to the park told me about. I would appreciate it if you would go with me. Truth be told, I'm not eager to go in that place alone again."

"Do you believe it's haunted?" Blake took a sip of his coffee then ate some of his dessert.

Chloe shook her head. "No. It's just creepy. Old houses make noises, but to hear my Aunt Char, she believes it's haunted. And she's never even been there."

Blake chuckled and shrugged. "Some of the patrolmen tell tales all the time of things they've seen around town and around the battlefield. Who knows?"

"You're new here, aren't you, Officer Hunter?" Chloe asked.

"Now, hold on a second. Can't we dispense with the formalities? You don't have to keep calling me Officer Hunter. Call me Blake. We're going to be working together and bumping into one another. Maybe even literally on occasion." Blake tossed her a grin he hoped was disarming. "What do you say?"

Chloe shrugged. "I suppose so, as long as you stop calling me Mrs. Rogers and call me Chloe. I'm a widow and have been for three years. Most people refer to me as Miss Roger because they simply don't know what to call me."

"I heard that the other day so that's why I was calling you Mrs. Rogers. I'm sorry for your loss."

"Thank you." Chloe dipped her head, took a deep breath then gave Blake a tight smile. "Now back to my question. You're new here, aren't you...Blake? Where did you work before you came here?"

Blake wanted to respect her change of subject. Even after three years, it couldn't be easy to get over losing her husband and raising her daughter without him, even with family helping. "Yes, I worked at the Grand Canyon for several years and loved it."

"Then this must seem so different for you." Chloe reached for her coffee and finished it,

"Oh, believe me, it is. Have you ever been to the Grand Canyon?"

Chloe shook her head. "Never."

"You'd love it. We had a big archeological find a couple years back that was amazing. Unfortunately, there were a couple murders that took place because of the artifacts the archeologists dug up." Blake shook his head. "Some of my friends and co-workers were almost killed because of it."

"Wow, that's terrible."

"Yeah, it was. I miss the Grand Canyon, though. I'm from Arizona."

"I guess you do miss it then." After a lull in the conversation, Chloe said, "Thanks for the coffee and the dessert, Blake, but I should get going. Evie's going to wonder where I am."

"Is that your little girl's name?"

"Yeah. She's a precocious three-year-old who loves tea parties with Mrs. P. in the backyard beneath the old maple tree." Chloe's smile was broad. The more he was with this woman, the more his interest grew.

"Should I ask who Mrs. P is?"

"She's a stuffed pink pig. Evie's favorite companion. At least for now. That's subject to change on a whim." Chloe laughed, gathered her purse strap onto her shoulder and stood. "Thanks again for the coffee and dessert. I enjoyed our conversation too. It was nice to have adult conversation with someone other than my father or my aunt. Cliff tends to stick to historical exchange because that's what he eats, sleeps and breathes, so this was nice."

"My pleasure."

They waved at Moira as they headed out the door.

"Evenin', dearies. See ya soon." Moira called behind them.

Blake walked Chloe to her car. "What time do you plan to head to the Bryant house tomorrow? I'll meet you there."

Chloe named a time in the morning. "That too early for you?"

"Not at all. I'll be on patrol. I can head over and help as long as you need then head back out again."

"Great, I'll see you then." Chloe climbed into her car and waved as she drove away.

Blake stood by the curb for a few seconds before heading to his car. *Lord, this woman is both beautiful and fascinating, but I've already had one bad experience. What am I doing?*

Chapter Six

"Well, Cliff's already here working." Chloe grasped the rickety wooden handrail by the steps to the porch and began her ascent. The railing gave way several steps up, and she almost fell over the edge. Blake reached out with quick hands and grasped her waist, hauling her back from what was sure to be a nasty tumble.

"Whoa, there. I'd say that's something park maintenance needs to show some immediate attention to."

Panting, Chloe glanced over her shoulder at him. Why was she panting—from fear or his touch? Perhaps both? "I'll call and—uh, put in a work order this afternoon." She had to get her breathing under control. It had to be the near fall, right? Couldn't be because Blake's hands still held onto her waist.

"Are you all right?" Blake lifted her with ease and stood her on the ground, turning her to face him before stepping away. Yeah, facing him was *so* much better. NOT.

Chloe forced a deep breath as warmth rolled over her. "Yes, that was a close call, but I'm fine. Thanks for preventing what could've been a bad fall." Refusing to meet his gaze, she studied the rotten railing then the other end of the steps. "Let's hope that handrail doesn't give way." She turned and held onto the other railing, climbing with deliberate care. At the top she turned to smile down at him. "Ta da. I made it. So can you. Now, we're wasting time. Let's go." Chloe turned toward the door and retrieved the skeleton key from her pocket, shoving it into the old lock. "I managed to open this thing by myself last time. Think I can do it again?"

"Sure, why not?" Blake's voice sounded so close. Chloe jumped and whipped around to find him standing right behind her, hands on his hips. He'd maneuvered those steps quicker than she'd anticipated.

"Okay, give me a sec." She twisted the key feeling for the mechanism inside. It caught, and the lock snicked open. Chloe gave Blake a grin. "It's easier every time I open it."

"You're probably working the rust loose." He reached for the doorknob. "Maybe it would be a good idea to have maintenance replace that with a more secure lock. Here, allow me." Blake opened the door and waved her in. "Ladies first."

Chloe gazed into the darkened hallway then back at Blake. She gave him a hesitant smile. "Thanks. You're such a gentleman."

"Would you like for me to go first?"

Chloe waved the flashlight in her hand then pointed at his holster. "I'm armed with only a flashlight. You have a gun."

"You did go in by yourself, remember?

"Yes, but it wasn't fun. It was creepy."

"No problem. Follow me." Blake stepped inside the door and waited for her to follow before closing it. "So where did you want to search?" He withdrew his flashlight from his utility belt and switched it on, directing the beam around the dim hallway.

"Upstairs in the back bedroom on the left. I need to check out a cupboard in there." Chloe turned on her own flashlight and headed upstairs.

"What's so special about this cupboard?" Blake followed her.

"Mrs. Karen Bryant Montague, the lady who sold this house to the park, found a diary in a hidden compartment in the cupboard when she lived here as a little girl."

"Really? Interesting."

At the top of the stairs, Chloe entered the back left bedroom and shined her flashlight around. "Isn't it though? Ah, that must be it."

The beam of her flashlight illuminated a built-in corner cupboard, the top half of which were bookshelves, the bottom half a two-door cabinet. Chloe strode across to the cupboard and examined it. "Mrs. Montague said the bottom shelf has a hidden compartment behind the back wall." She bent over and laid her flashlight on the bottom shelf, then ran her fingers along the back wall.

"Did she say how it opened?" Blake bent next to Chloe, bringing his head near, his aftershave wafting around the close space.

Chloe inhaled. Spiced and woodsy. Similar to one Josh used to wear. Nice. *Back to work, Chloe. No time for aftershave, no matter how nice it smells.* "Um, yeah. Mrs. Montague said it slides to the side when you push…here, I think." She pushed toward the left and the back wall of the shelf slid in that direction revealing a narrow compartment.

"Were you expecting to find something?" Blake guided the beam of his flashlight around the interior of the space. "It looks pretty empty to me."

"I don't think so. She found the diary and a small porcelain doll. She gave us the diary but kept the doll." Chloe ran her fingers around inside all the edges to ensure nothing had been missed. "Guess I just wanted to see it for myself."

"I can see why. As a child, she must've been excited to make that find. Did she read the diary?" Blake straightened.

Chloe picked up her flashlight and straightened too. "No, she said she never got around to it. She thought we might find a better use for it, especially now that we have the house." Chloe's cell phone rang, and she tugged it from her pants pocket and glanced at the caller. "It's Cliff. Excuse me while I answer this." She clicked the answer button. "Hi Cliff. What's up?"

"Where are you? You have to come to the cellar. Like now. I found something. You need to come see it. *Now*. Hurry!"

"Okay, okay. Calm down. I'm here in the house with Officer Hunter. Be right down…Hello, Cliff?"

"Something wrong?" Blake asked.

Chloe shrugged and shoved her phone back into her pocket. "I have no idea what's up except Cliff is so super excited he forgot to say goodbye. Simply hung up on me. He wants me to come down to the cellar."

"Then let's go."

~

Blake led the way toward the area of the cellar where Clifford was working. He hadn't been there since they discovered the wall and wasn't prepared for the two-foot hole Clifford had made. As they approached, the historian's face and a bright flashlight we aimed inside the hole.

"What's up? You made it sound like an emergency." Chloe stepped around the tarp with the removed bricks from the wall and made her way to Clifford's side. Blake followed and waited for Clifford's explanation.

Clifford stepped back, his face pale, his eyebrows shifting up and down. What in the world was behind that wall that would elicit such a reaction?

"Cliff? What's wrong?" Chloe placed a hand on his arm. "You're pale."

Clifford pointed toward the hole. "There's a body. In there."

"A body!" Chloe stepped to the hole in the wall and focused her flashlight inside. "Oh, my goodness. He's right. It's a soldier. A…a union soldier. Blake, come look at this." Chloe stepped aside to allow Blake to take a look.

He swept the interior of the space with his flashlight beam until it illuminated the body of a union soldier. The musculature of the face and hands had long disappeared, leaving the skeletal remains. The union field cap had slipped to the side, bits of dried skin and hair still clinging to the skull, but both dark, empty eye sockets gaped. A wide skeletal smile with missing teeth belied the serious fact that this individual was walled up in a solitary tomb. He probably wasn't smiling when he died. Why was he here? Blake's law enforcement background kicked in, and he needed to determine if miscarriage of justice had occurred or if this man had died of natural causes. If the latter was the case, why was he behind this wall? Blake shook his head. His investigative mind couldn't wrap itself around this scene. It made no since. He stepped back, lowering his flashlight.

"Well, what do you think?" Clifford asked.

Blake gave him a humorless grin. "It's a bit early to be asking me that. I can hardly investigate from seven feet away through a hole in the wall. Besides, this is going to be a cooperative investigation."

"What do you mean?" Chloe shifted at his side.

"Well, it's obvious this man was walled up inside that area for a reason." Blake glanced from one historian to the other. "We have no idea what that was, but I'm sure he didn't go in there willingly. Who would? Either he was forced in or killed first then put in there. It's your job to get in there and start doing whatever you historians do. When you come across anything that indicates how he died, then I can help you."

Chloe nodded and circled a finger toward the wall. "There was a motive behind this. If a Confederate soldier came in and killed him, that would've been it. He'd have simply killed him and left. He'd have no need to wall him in. There's more to this story."

"True." Clifford folded his arms over his chest and leaned his chin on one hand. "Someone had a reason for hiding this man."

"Cliff, we need to get you some help down here to bring this wall down quicker, but we don't want word leaking about this discovery. Not yet." Chloe toed the ground with her tennis shoe. "I'm going to call Ian O'Brian and see how busy he is. Perhaps he can leave things with his assistant for a while and come over to give you a hand."

Clifford turned bright eyes and a grin toward Chloe. "That's a great idea. Ian would be perfect if he's not too busy."

Blake lowered a brow. "Who's Ian O'Brian?"

Chloe smiled. "Ian is the head historian at Antietam National Battlefield in Sharpsburg, Maryland. He's a great guy. Easy going, a hard worker and a terrific historian with a wealth of knowledge."

"Okay. He sounds like he would be just who you need." Blake glanced at the illuminated dial of his wristwatch. "I need to head back out on patrol, so I'll leave you two to this. Believe me, some days, this is more interesting, and some days, well…it can be more interesting on patrol. Until you can get in there and find out more about that body, I'll be on patrol." He met Chloe's gaze and grinned. "I'll see you two later."

~

The next afternoon Chloe sat at her desk in her office working on research when a knock sounded at her door. It immediately opened and a head stuck in.

"Hey, Chloe. You busy? Or do you have a minute for an old pal?"

Chloe glanced up to see Ian O'Brian's grinning face. "Ian? Hi. Come on in." She waved him inside. "It's good to see you. I didn't think you'd arrive until tomorrow."

Ian stepped inside and closed the door. He strode over and took a seat on the corner of her desk, the brim of his "Smoky-

Bear" hat between his fingers. "You said you needed help fast, so here I am."

"Well, Cliff will be tickled pink. He's been picking away at the wall in the cellar of the Civil War house the park acquired, pulling out bricks one at a time with such patience, but he's eager to climb inside and get to work."

"Picking away at walls and bricks is my specialty, you know." Ian shoved a lock of dark blond hair from his forehead. His blue eyes shone bright against his tan. Chloe had forgotten how attractive he was. "I'm eager to get to work and help him. It sounds like a great project. This military park hasn't had a discovery like this in…well…in who knows how long."

"Certainly not since I've been here." Chloe filled him in on the house and the diaries.

Ian shook his head. "That's quite the windfall for the park and the museum. Phenomenal actually."

"It is, but it's going to take a lot of work and research. And a lot of donations. We have a donor event coming up soon. Jan Miller, one of our staff, is working on it." Chloe glanced at her watch. "I actually have a meeting with her in a few minutes. I hate to run, but why don't you take a drive out to the house. Cliff would love to show you the project."

Ian stood. "I'll do that."

Chloe gave him directions to the house. "I'll catch up with you later. It's good to see you again."

He waved from the door. "You too. Maybe we'll grab dinner soon."

"I'd like that. Take care."

~

Chloe stepped through Jan Miller's open office door and sat in the chair beside her desk. "How goes the event planning, Jan? Please give me some good news."

Jan shoved her wire-framed glasses up her freckled nose, and a smile spread across her face. "Well, since you asked—yes, I have great news for you. While you've been off doing your historian things, I've been busy, busy, busy." She leaned back in her chair and propped her hands behind her head, elbows pointed outward, a self-satisfied smile settling on her lips.

Chloe tilted her head as she gazed at her friend. "Would you care to expand on that comment?"

Jan tapped the clipboard on her desk. "Everything for the donor event is well in hand, my friend. All the invitations have been sent, and I've been in touch with the various venders. Now all I have to do is wait for the RSVPs to roll in and a couple of the venders to get back with their estimates. The decorators will have some work to do, and there's a few other odds and ends to take care of, but, yeah, everything's looking great."

"That's fantastic. Do you need me to do anything?"

She waved a pink tipped finger in Chloe's direction as she flashed a dimpled smile at her. "All you have to do is get all dolled up in a beautiful evening dress with your hair in an up-do and, voilà, the donor event will be off to a magnificent evening. Of course, we don't have a date yet, but I'm working on that." Jan sat back in her rolling chair and swiveled it around, her hands clasped behind her head. She released a dreamy sigh, a happy smile lifting her lips.

Chloe studied her friend. Jan was far too perky. What in the world was going on? "Are you all right? What's going on with you?"

"Moi? I'm perfectly fine."

Chloe didn't trust the sparkle in her eyes. "Mm_hmm. Fess up, ol' friend. What's got you in a silly tither."

Jan drew her closed lips inward like a little girl with a secret and leaned forward. "I saw a new guy today. If I didn't know better, I'd have thought he came straight from Hollywood, but he wore a park uniform." She leaned an elbow on her desk and propped her chin in her hand, her eyes rolling heavenward before she closed them. When she opened them, her smile was dreamy. Dreamy? Really? "He was purely delectable."

Chloe ignored the sigh that slipped from Jan's lips. "Do you hear yourself? You sound like a lovesick fourteen-year-old."

"Maybe." Jan quirked her lips then grinned. "Have you seen him?"

"Seen who?"

"The new guy. Keep up, Chloe."

Could she be talking about Ian? Ian O'Brian who had just arrived from Antietam? He was the only new face she was aware of around here. Chloe had just left him. Could Jan have spotted him before he came to her office? "He wouldn't be tall with a great build and have dark blond hair, would he?" Chloe crossed her arms over her chest.

"And the most amazing blue eyes and gorgeous face this side of Hollywood." Jan nodded, releasing a long, slow sigh.

"Yeah, well that's Ian O'Brian. He's the historian from Antietam National Battlefield who's come to help Cliff and me for a while." Chloe stood and headed toward the door. She didn't want to go into details, not even with Jan at this point.

Jan stood and hurried around her desk following Chloe to the door. "You'll introduce me, won't you?"

Chloe leaned against the open doorframe and grinned. "You're pathetic, my friend. I'm sure if the occasion arises, I'll introduce you."

"Thanks, Chloe. You're a pal."

"I know. See you later, Jan. Thanks for taking care of the arrangements. Let me know how the RSVPs come in. I'd like to know who's coming."

~

Chloe spent the next morning at her desk in her office. It was time to crack open Cecelia Langston's diary. She'd grown weary of reading Colonel Mayfield's continuous self-aggrandizing and was ready for something different. Research on the good colonel revealed nothing about his heroic act in any of the records she'd found. The only thing she'd discovered was a letter from the higher echelon of officers who denied the promotion request from the colonel. It was official and backed up what the diary stated about that. It was odd that she couldn't find anything to substantiate what the colonel claimed as his act of heroism. All she had to go on was his statement and that of his commanding officer. Neither could she refute it.

Eager for a change of subject, Chloe slipped on a pair of cotton gloves to protect Cecelia's diary. Leaning back in her chair, she removed the diary from its wrappings with considerable care.

Cecelia's diary was leatherbound, yet more refined than Colonel Mayfield's had been. Where his had been a thicker, darker leather, hers combined beauty and utility. Made of burgundy tooled leather, the diary had an imprinted worn gold design that ran along the outer edge of the cover, its closed pages were edged with gold, much of which had flacked off. No locking clasp held this diary closed. It simply looked like a book. Chloe opened it to the first page. A young feminine cursive handwriting spelled out Cecelia's name and the date of August 1st, 1862. The diary had been given to the girl for her fifteenth birthday by her parents, Elijah S. and Margaret J. Langston.

Chloe reached for a notebook and jotted down the names. This was great information for her research about Cecelia's family and the house. She dropped her pen and returned to the diary.

Turning the page to the first entry, she read about the girl's birthday party. Her grandparents had come to visit from Baltimore, and they'd had a simple chocolate cake. Chloe scanned further entries, making note of sibling's names and other bits of information that might be helpful.

Chloe was fascinated to read of life before the Civil War from the eyes of the young girl. She deduced the girl's father was a lawyer, and her life wasn't difficult. From the size of the house, the type of wallpaper and velvet curtains, and other hints she'd noticed, Chloe assumed the house belonged to someone with some money rather than a laborer. The diary verified that assumption.

A knock sounded at the office door. Chloe put the diary and the wrappings away in a desk drawer then called, "Come in."

The door opened and in walked Mrs. White-Smith, a cut-glass vase of colorful hot-house flowers in her hands. The perfectly dressed and coifed lady closed the door and strode toward Chloe's desk where she set the flowers. She sat in the chair in front of Chloe's desk without waiting for an invitation.

"Good afternoon, Miss Rogers. I hope I'm not interrupting anything." The smile on her face stretched her lips in a thin line.

"Nothing I can't put on hold for a bit. Those are beautiful flowers. What's the occasion?" Chloe pinned a smile on her own face as she touched a soft, pink rose petal. This woman was hard to read, but the fact she'd brought flowers indicated something. A mere gesture of kindness? Who knew?

The woman waved an airy hand. "Oh, no occasion, my dear. I simply thought it would brighten your dreary office. You historians have so many books and old…things. The flowers will look nice in here, don't you think?"

A chuckle attempted to work its way to the surface, but Chloe jammed it back down. "It will indeed. Thank you for your thoughtfulness. Is that all you came for or is there something else I can help you with?"

The older woman crossed one knee over the other, then crossed her wrists in her lap. She looked down her patrician nose at Chloe. "Well, there is something else. I've come to find out if you've read Colonel Mayfield's diary yet, and if so, what do you think of it?"

Uh oh. Chloe had a sudden desire to rush from the room. She pasted a smile in place. Could she wing this? Why did she have the desire to pray all of a sudden when she hadn't prayed in three years? The Lord wouldn't listen to her over something like this when He hadn't brought her husband home. Now was not the time to go there.

She released a slow breath. "Yes, I have begun reading the diary, but haven't finished it yet. I have another project that's also taking my time, but I've been reading at home in the evenings."

Mrs. White-Smith didn't appear impressed.

"So what do I think of it?" Chloe leaned an elbow on her desk and propped a thoughtful finger along her cheek. "Well, Colonel Mayfield was certainly…confident in himself. He seemed to be a leader among men." *Oh brother, Chloe. Is that how you avoid describing an arrogant, self-centered man?*

Mrs. White-Smith nodded, her head tilting a bit as a self-satisfied smile lifted the corners of her red lips. "Yes, he was that. So, tell me, Miss. Rogers, how are plans for the donor event coming along? It will be in a few weeks, am I right?"

Chloe heaved a small sigh. "Well, we haven't set the date yet, but we will soon. It's going to be quite an affair. I hope you'll say something that evening about your great-great grandfather's diary. Possibly read an excerpt from it?"

Mrs. White-Smith clasped her hands together in front of her chest and breathed a happy sigh. "Oh, I would adore to, my dear."

"Wonderful." Chloe stood, hoping to end the conversation and send the woman on her way. "I'm sure we'll be in touch before then to talk more about it."

Mrs. White-Smith stood and strode toward the door. "Yes, of course. Take care, Miss. Rogers. And keep reading. There's so much more to discover about Colonel Mayfield." She waved the tips of her fingers before closing the door behind her.

Perhaps. But Chloe had learned about all she wanted to learn about the good colonel for the moment.

Chapter Seven

While out on patrol, Blake decided to ride over to the Bryant house to see how the removal of the wall was going. There was a fifty-fifty chance Chloe would be there, and he wouldn't mind one bit if she was. He'd taken a chance on asking her out to coffee, and she'd accepted. It wouldn't hurt to ask her out to dinner. It didn't mean a commitment or anything. He wasn't risking his heart. Not at this point. *It's too early to be a risk. Right, Lord?*

He was happy to see Chloe's Mini Cooper parked at the old Bryant house and parked his cruiser beside it. Blake climbed out and strode around to the cellar door. With a lit flashlight in hand, he made his way toward the work area. The hole in the wall was now big enough to step in without squeezing through. More halogen lamps illuminated not only outside the wall, but inside as well. Murmuring came from inside it.

Blake stepped closer and found three people surrounding the union soldier's body, Chloe among them. The second person was Clifford, but he didn't recognize the back of the third person. He cleared his throat, and all three heads spun in unison in response.

"Blake!" Chloe jumped to her feet and spread her arms wide. "As you can see, we're in. We started examining the body about thirty minutes ago. It's pretty tedious, but we don't want to miss anything or destroy any evidence." She waved her hand. "Come on in. Let Cliff show you what we've found so far."

Blake stepped over the rows of bricks left at the bottom of the hole and followed Chloe over to the soldier's body. A good-looking blond man stood and nodded at Blake as he stepped back out of the way.

"Take a look at this." With gentle fingers Clifford lifted the upper edge of the soldier's uniform jacket and with great care slid his hand underneath. He exposed a slash in the jacket that was nearly two inches long. "As I told Chloe and Ian, I would bet my paycheck that was made by a saber. But it doesn't end there. Take a look at this."

Clifford moved his hand beneath the jacket's delicate wool fabric in several places from above and below the wide leather belt on the body and pointed out five more slashes of the same size as the first. He peered at Blake. "When we get this body back to the examination room in our office and take a closer look, I'm sure we'll find gashes on the body to match the slashes in the jacket. And surely in the shirt underneath. I think I can guarantee this man was murdered."

~

Even before Blake showed up and Clifford demonstrated the evidence they'd found, Chloe knew it was a fact, but Clifford's statement made it seem so much more ominous. Who would do something like this? And why? What had this man done that would cause them to wall him up? And who was he? Question after question ran through Chloe's mind as she stared into the face of the long-dead soldier. Evidence indicated he was dead when he was walled up.

"So how are you going to move him out of here and back to your examination room without word leaking out?" Blake stood and brushed off his slacks. "I assume you still want to keep this quiet for now."

"Oh, for sure." Chloe stood as well and shoved a tendril of loose hair behind her ear. "Until we make our examination and find out what we have here, we can't let this leak out. The media would have a field day with this."

Clifford gathered his tools and stood beside Chloe. "Agreed. But I haven't figured out how to move him out of here without anyone seeing."

"Easy." Blake shrugged. "Do it at night after everyone's gone home."

The now familiar heavy footsteps sounded on the floorboards above their heads. Everyone glanced up then back at one another.

"I think somebody upstairs agrees." Blake smirked.

Chloe frowned. "It's an old house, remember?"

"I've heard footsteps a couple of times since I've been here." Ian peered at the ceiling again. "Someone want to explain?"

"Nope." Clifford moved toward his toolbox.

Chloe tossed a thumb in Blake's direction, completely ignoring Ian's question. "Ian, have you met Blake yet?"

Ian shook his head and held out his hand. "Can't say as I have. Hi. Ian O'Brian. Historian and anthropologist from Antietam National Battlefield in Sharpsburg, MD. These guys decided they needed my help and gave me a call."

Blake shook Ian's hand and studied his face. He may look like he should be in the movies but didn't appear to have an ounce of self-centeredness about him. His smile and hearty handshake were genuine. "Nice to meet you, Ian. Blake Hunter. Park police."

"Nice to meet you, Blake. Can you explain that sound?" Ian pointed to the cellar ceiling.

Blake propped his hands on his hips and shook his head. He gave a slight chuckle. "Nope. I can't. You work at a Civil War battlefield. All I can say is—unexplained things happen at Civil War battlefields. Or so I've been told."

Ian scratched his head and nodded. "Yeah, I've been told that too. Never experienced anything though."

"Enough weird talk, guys." Chloe huffed. "Let's figure out how to transport this poor guy out of here and back to the examination room."

Cliff moved from his toolbox to join them. "We need a back board, straps and a vehicle big enough to transport him in."

"No problem. I have a friend." Blake crossed his arms over his chest.

"But will he be discreet?" Chloe asked. "We can't involve just anyone who might let this story leak."

"I might not have been here long," Blake said, "but my friend, Paul, can be trusted. I met him the first week I started work here. There was an accident when I was on patrol involving a political family with young kids. The whole family died in the accident. We had to notify the extended family before the media got hold of the story. Paul and his partner were the epitome of discretion. I've stayed in touch with him, so it would be easy to ask a favor."

"I remember that story." Clifford snapped his fingers. "It was heart-rending."

"Yeah, it was." Chloe nodded. "So, you think he'll help us?"

"All I can do is ask." Blake held up a hand.

"If you would, we would certainly appreciate it." Clifford ran a hand through his already messy hair, then gestured in the direction of the hole. "And the sooner the better. This guy is now exposed for all and sundry to see. I mean, we can lock the cellar door, but he's not protected by the wall anymore."

"I'll give Paul a call as soon as I leave here. Until we can get this guy out of here, I can make more patrols tonight and the next couple nights," Blake said. "It's the best we can do."

"Agreed. Short of someone staying down here to guard our dead soldier—" Chloe's eyes darted from face to face, "which doesn't seem to meet with anyone's urgent desire, patrolling is the best option."

Blake chuckled. "I'm not the only one who patrols so I'll try to stay in this area and drive by more often. I'm going to go call Paul, I need to hit the road. I'll let you know what he says so we can further devise a plan of action."

"Thanks, Blake." Ian and Clifford chorused in unison.

~

"They're spending a lot of time in the cellar of that house." He sat in the back of the bar and spoke in low tones. This time of day there were few customers, and none sat near his table to overhear, but he wouldn't take any chances. His boss was particular about the information he passed on and would grow angry if he spoke in a loud voice. "What makes you think they're going to find something there?"

"Don't worry about it." Although the voice came in a whisper, it was clear and distinct. There was no mistaking the rebuff in the words. "Keep a close eye on that house. I want to know every...move...they...make. If they sneeze, I want to know about it. Understood?"

He almost laughed out loud at that but the boss would have his head, so he stuffed it down deep. "I understand."

"Good." The line went silent.

With a sigh, he held the phone away from his ear then swiped the end call button. Shaking his head, he shoved his chair back and, with a wave toward the bartender, strolled out the front door. He hoped he would get paid enough for this job.

~

Chloe followed Blake to the entrance to the cellar and paused just outside. She took a deep breath and released it slowly. “Wow. Fresh air. You don’t realize how musty it is in there until you get outside and start breathing good clean air again.”

“It’s true. I wasn’t in there nearly as long as the three of you, and even I appreciate the fresh air. How can you stand being in there so long?” Blake shook his head then donned his hat.

“I think it has something to do with the excitement of the find.” Chloe shrugged as she shoved her hands into her rear jean pockets. “You know, the search for evidence, the history and all that goes along with that. I don’t really notice until I step back outside then it hits me.” A charged moment followed, then Chloe placed a hand on Blake’s arm. “Thanks for what you’re doing to help us with all this. We really appreciate it. As a park policeman, you’ve gone above and beyond to give us a hand.”

Blake’s gaze strayed to her hand on his arm, and she jerked it away. Why had she reached out to him like that? It wasn’t necessary. She shoved her hand back in her rear pocket, still aware of the warmth from his skin. His gaze moved to hers—it held something she hadn’t seen before. It sent a skitter down her spine.

His Adam’s apple bobbed as he swallowed then he nodded, his voice husky as he spoke, “My pleasure. I’ve…I’ve enjoyed being a part of this and seeing what you and Cliff have discovered. It’s fascinating.” Blake cleared his throat. “I’d like to see where it goes and what you find out about this soldier.”

“Yeah, it is fascinating. One of the best finds we’ve had in the park in a long time.” Chloe shoved a few strands of hair behind her ear. Was he nervous? Had her touch affected him? She hadn’t expected it to, but it had affected her. Perhaps she’d think about that later.

“Well, I need to get on patrol, but before I go, I was…well, I was wondering if you’d like to go to dinner with me soon.” A corner of Blake’s mouth lifted. “Like Saturday evening?”

A bubble of joy filled Chloe’s chest like she hadn’t felt in a long time. It was totally unexpected. There was something about this guy that drew her. It wasn’t just the fact he’d asked her out, or the fact he had a cute little dimple at the corner of his mouth when he smiled. Was it the fresh uncertainty of a man unsure of himself rather than the domineering man-of-the-world expecting her to drop at his feet that was so refreshing? Perhaps. Her husband, Josh, had been a good mixture of both types of men. He was a take charge kind of guy without being domineering, but he'd had a boyishness about him that was so appealing. Was Blake like that?

Concern built on Blake's face as his brows furrowed. She'd taken too long in considering his question. She quickly answered. "I'd love to go out to dinner with you Saturday evening. How shall I dress?"

Blake rubbed his chin and shrugged. "Well, nothing too fancy, but don't wear jeans. A nice skirt or Sunday dress will do."

Chloe grinned. "Okay. I can make that work."

"I'm sure you can. I'll pick you up at five-thirty."

"Do you know where I live?" Chloe titled her head. She enjoyed the blank expression that imprinted itself on Blake's features.

"Well, no, I don't. I suppose you should let me in on that detail." His expression turned sheepish.

Chloe let out a soft chuckle. "It's not hard. I live at the superintendent's residence."

"Oh, yeah. Well, okay. Until then I'll let you know what the results of my call to my buddy, Paul, are. Hopefully we can take care of your soldier—" Blake tossed a thumb over his shoulder in the direction of the cellar, "—and move him from the walled-in area to your examination room quickly and as unobtrusively as soon as possible."

Chloe released a heavy sigh, her brow slightly furrowed. "That would be great. I'm just not comfortable with that news leaking right now. Before we release the information to the public, I want to know more about why he was in there in the first place." She tossed a glance over her shoulder toward the cellar. "I don't know why, but I think he deserves to have his story told the right way. If he truly was murdered, he deserves justice."

~

"Thanks, Paul."

Blake hung up the cell phone and dropped it into the console of the cruiser. He put the vehicle into drive, checked for traffic, and when there were no cars coming, he pulled onto the road. Paul would be more than happy to help move the union soldier to the park historian's examination room. They would do it tomorrow night after Paul got off work at ten o'clock. He promised to be the soul of discretion, and he owned the ambulance since it was his ambulance service. Blake liked how that worked out.

It was late so he'd wait and call Chloe in the morning. She would be pleased. Blake remembered her expression as they stood outside the cellar before he'd left on patrol this evening. A touch of concern etched her features. It weighed on her to keep the news of the Union soldier quiet. He could see why. This was quite a find for the park, but their information had to be spot-on before sharing it with the public. A historian didn't just find the body of a Union soldier walled up under a house on government land every day. There must be an explanation, and when evidence pointed toward murder, even an ice-cold case like this one, then that explanation needed information to back it up. History. More evidence. And Blake would do everything he could to help the historians find those things.

The touch of Chloe's hand on his arm as they stood outside the cellar had sent heat through him. Who knew a woman's touch could feel like that? Michelle's had never caused him to react that way. Had he ever really thought he'd loved her? He heaved a sigh. Perhaps he'd thought he'd been in love, but now he knew better. Blake couldn't help but compare the two women, and Michelle came up lacking. Three years ago, he'd discovered how shallow and self-centered she'd become. Thank goodness he'd seen her for who she was and come to his senses before they'd gone to the altar. Michelle had lied to him. Blatantly and repeatedly. She'd pretended to be someone she wasn't.

Blake shook his head to dispel the memories. Even three years after the events, it was hard to erase the past and his...what? Bruised ego? Yeah, what else could it be? He'd admitted he wasn't truly in love with her, but more likely in love with the idea of being in love. She'd duped him. He stared into the darkness, his headlights lighting only enough for him to see the road ahead. Monuments and Civil War cannons stood along the roadside, faint memorials to the northern and southern troops that fought here so long ago.

Shoving Michelle from his thoughts, he concentrated on Chloe. Now *she* was someone to think on. He anticipated with eagerness their dinner date Saturday evening. It was high time to take the next step. Yeah, she had a child, but if the Lord was in this, then He would work it out. Blake was ready to move past Michelle and see where things went. From what he'd seen so far, Chloe was an amazing woman with a great sense of humor and dedication to her family. He wanted to discover more about her. She intrigued him, and the fact she was gorgeous didn't hurt. Now to find out where she stood spiritually. "If this desire to know her better is from you, Lord, then lead the way."

Chapter Eight

Chloe watched the ambulance back up to the cellar door with a niggle of excitement and apprehension stirring in her mid-region. Darkness had descended and the park was closed. Visitors didn't usually use the road through the battlefield at night, but there were the occasional drive-throughs on some of the roads. More by locals nearer town. The rear of the house faced woods so it was doubtful their activities would be seen until the ambulance pulled out in the front. With traffic so scarce, it was unlikely at this late hour.

Blake walked up just as the front door of the ambulance opened and a lean young man hopped out.

"Hey, Blake. How's it going?" He spoke in low tones.

"Great. How are you, Paul?" Blake held out a hand and the ambulance driver shook it. "Come on over and let me introduce you to one of the park historians."

Chloe held out her hand. "Hi. I'm Chloe Rogers."

Paul took it. "Paul Williams. Nice to meet you, Chloe."

"Come on in." She tilted her head toward the cellar entrance. "The others are inside prepping the body for removal." She stepped inside, switched on her flashlight and led the way to the lighted work area. "Hey, Cliff, Ian. Our ride is here."

Clifford stuck his head out of the hole in the brick wall. "Cool. We're about ready. Hey, you must be Paul. I'm Cliff. Ian's in here."

"Hi Paul." A disembodied voice came from the hole. "If you've got a backboard, we've got a body."

"Oh, I have a backboard." Paul chuckled. "Want to help me with it, Blake. We'll bring the backboard and straps in here, then set up a gurney at the door of the cellar."

"I'll be happy to." Blake clapped Paul on the shoulder.

Chloe caught his wink in her direction in the glow from the halogen lights. Her breath halted even as her heart gave a skip of pleasure. Silly. It was only a wink.

Within minutes they were back with the backboard and straps. Cliff took the equipment and headed back into the hole. Chloe supervised as he and Ian gathered the union soldier into their arms and lay him onto the board, still in the half reclining position he'd been in since he'd fallen there more than 159 years ago. They propped his lower half up with pillows they'd brought for that purpose. Gently they moved him, daring not to stretch him out for fear of breaking him. Later they'd determine if there was still connective tissue and skin intact beneath the clothing. Although the head had little remaining, there was no knowing what the rest of the body's condition was.

Once the body was strapped and secured to the board, Cliff and Ian carried it through the hole and laid him on the ground.

"Wow! Now that's simply amazing." Paul propped his hands on his hips staring at the figure on the backboard. "That's the oldest, and deadest—I might add—patient I've ever transported."

"Well, I'm sure of that." Clifford ran a hand through his ever-messy hair. "Just don't log it in your books."

"I won't."

"We can't thank you enough, Paul." Chloe turned to him. "I'll be happy to compensate you for your help this evening. Believe me. It's been invaluable."

He waved a dismissive hand. "Are you kidding me? I wouldn't have missed this for anything. And don't worry. Mums the word. Blake and I already had this discussion." He ran his pinched thumb and forefinger across his lips like a zipper.

"Thank you. Your discretion is appreciated." Chloe smiled.

"Well, let's get this guy out of here and loaded on the gurney." Blake waved a hand at the body. "We still have to deliver him to your office without being seen."

"Indeed." Clifford dusted his hands together. "I'm anxious to get him tucked away into the climate-controlled examination room. He's been too long in this cellar."

"Then let's go," Paul said. "Fellows, let's each take an end and a side, and we can carry him out, no problem. We'll load him on the gurney at the cellar door where his ride awaits."

"I'll get the lights." Chloe proceeded to turn out the halogen lamps half expecting to hear the footsteps on the ceiling as usual, but only silence met her efforts. Strange.

When the last lamp was out, she made her way to the cellar door by the beam of her flashlight. As Paul secured the gurney inside the ambulance and closed the doors, Chloe locked the cellar door then tugged on the lock to ensure it was secure.

A convoy of vehicles made up of Chloe's Mini Cooper, Clifford's vehicle with Ian riding along, then the ambulance, and lastly Blake's police cruiser wound its way to park headquarters. By the time they arrived, it was almost eleven-thirty. The building was locked up and only the night security lights were on. They drove around to the door nearest to Chloe's and Clifford's office, allowing the ambulance to back up to the entrance. Blake swiped his badge at the security access reader, and the door opened.

Chloe held it while Paul and Blake disengaged the gurney from the ambulance and settled the wheels on the ground. They took the elevator up to the second floor while Chloe secured the outer door and she and the rest of the group hurried upstairs. They met Blake and Paul at the historian's office where Chloe unlocked the outer door and led them inside to the climate-controlled examination room.

With great care Clifford, Blake, Ian and Paul transferred the body to the waist high table in the center of the room, the torso still in its half reclining position. They removed the backboard from beneath the body and secured the room before returning the equipment to the ambulance.

Chloe stood at the door of the building along with the other historians and Blake. She held out her hand toward Paul. "I can't thank you enough for what you've done here tonight. You've allowed us to continue our investigation into the death of this man without the whole world finding out about it first."

Paul's expression grew sheepish as he shook her hand. "Just do me a favor and get to the bottom of why he was in that hole to begin with. Unless he was a pretty bad dude, nobody deserves to die alone like that."

Unbidden, tears pricked behind Chloe's eyes, and she blinked to prevent them from falling. She totally agreed. Her gut told her the man lying on the examination table upstairs had been murdered in cold blood, and she was determined to find out why. "We'll do our best."

As he drove the ambulance away, Clifford turned to head back upstairs.

"Where are you going?" Chloe's voice was little more than a loud whisper.

He turned to look at her and waved both arms in the air. "Why, to get to work of course."

Chloe stared at him in astonishment. "Seriously? At this hour? Cliff, it's after midnight. Go home and get some rest then we'll start fresh first thing in the morning."

Clifford took slow steps back toward them and waved an arm in the direction of their office. "Do you think I can actually sleep knowing he's lying in there waiting to be examined?"

Ian chuckled. "Cliff, he's not going anywhere. He'll be waiting for you in the morning. No one knows he's here except us. Go home. Get some sleep. Start working on the answers to your questions tomorrow."

Dejection oozed from every pore as Clifford's shoulders slumped and he heaved a huge sigh. He resembled a little boy who'd had his candy stolen, only he wasn't. Cliff was a talented and educated historian being prevented from studying a historical find of significant value. But only until morning. Poor guy. He wouldn't sleep a wink tonight. But Chloe wanted to be there when he discovered all the wonderful things he would find, and she couldn't stay up all night and work tomorrow too. He would simply have to be patient.

Blake locked up after them as they exited the building. Cliff drove Ian back to his car at the Bryant house.

Chloe was walking to her car when Blake appeared beside her.

"It was an exciting evening, don't you think?" Blake matched his steps to hers.

"I do." Chloe clutched the strap of her shoulder bag. "I feel like I can breathe easier now knowing our soldier is secure though I feel bad for Cliff. He won't sleep a wink tonight, but we'll get a fresh start examining the body in the morning. And now that the body is out of the house, I can move forward with bringing a contractor in and seeing if restoration is feasible. I hope it is. That house has character, and I think if it can be restored to its former self, it'll be beautiful."

They stopped by Chloe's car, and she unlocked it. Blake opened the door for her.

"I agree. It definitely has character. Will you rebuild the wall or tear it completely down?"

"It's not original to the house so we'll tear it completely down. It had no purpose except to hide the body. I want it gone."

Blake nodded. "If you're restoring it to how it was originally, it doesn't belong."

"Exactly." Chloe tossed her purse onto the passenger seat and climbed in. She started the car and rolled down the window. "Be safe out there on patrol."

He leaned down to see her better through the window. "I will. Sleep well. See you soon."

~

From his vantage point behind a tree in of the woods at the back of the Bryant house property, he watched and waited. They had an ambulance. From where he stood, it was hard to see exactly what they were doing, but it stood to reason they were removing something. Why bring an ambulance unless it was something big? His boss would know. One of the men slammed the ambulance doors shut, then the vehicle pulled out, followed by the rangers in their vehicles. Hurrying through the woods to where he'd parked his Toyota Camry in a parking area nearby, he climbed in and pulled out his cell phone then dialed the boss.

"Yes?" The usual clear, whispered tones crossed through cyberspace.

"Boss, they left the house with an ambulance. I think they took something big away. Got any idea what it could be?"

"Of course, I do, you imbecile. Follow them. Find out where they're taking it. Go before you lose them."

As usual the boss hung up without saying goodbye. He cranked the engine and turned his Camry in the direction the ambulance and the other vehicles went. Hopefully he could catch up with them. With a swift mental kick, he wondered why he hadn't thought of following them before calling the boss. What if he couldn't find where they'd gone? It didn't bear contemplating.

He'd be a dead man.

~

Chloe dropped her purse into her desk drawer the next morning and shoved her messenger bag under the edge of the desk, then she headed straight for the examination room. When Clifford wasn't in the office, she suspected he was likely getting started on examining the body. She opened the door and stepped inside. Yep. She was right. Busy gathering tools and his electronic tablet to record his findings, Clifford hummed per his usual MO when preparing to study or examine an artifact.

"Good morning, Cliff." Excitement filled Chloe's voice as she secured the door. She didn't want anyone walking in on them during the examination. They would have to knock to gain entry. Ian would be the only one allowed entry.

Clifford jumped at Chloe's voice. He was so involved in his preparations, and the loudness of his humming, he slapped a hand over his heart as he turned to face her. "Chloe Rogers, you have to stop sneaking up on me like that. You're making a habit of it. Do you want to give me heart failure?"

She chuckled. "Well, I think you're being a bit melodramatic, but I'm sorry. I didn't mean to startle you. Again. But you had to know I'd be in sooner than later."

He released a huge huff of air. "Of course, I did. I hope you slept well. Some of us didn't sleep at all." Clifford's last words were clipped. Then he muttered, "So much for getting rest before starting fresh this morning."

Chloe laughed. "Oh, for goodness sake. Get over it. It was way too late last night, and I wanted to be here to help with the findings. You're far too impatient."

Clifford murmured something and dropped a tray of tools on a wheeled metal cart beside the examination table then tossed a pair of rubber gloves in Chloe's direction. "Don't forget your apron."

Catching the gloves, Chloe shook her head and rolled her eyes. "Are you going to stay mad at me forever, or are we going to get past this and get on with the examination?"

Clifford didn't answer right away, but his narrowed eyes studied her for a full thirty seconds, his lips pinched to the side.

Chloe crossed her arms over her chest and tapped a toe, staring back with a grin. "Well? We'll accomplish nothing with you in a snit."

Clifford's brows furrowed momentarily then his face cleared. He shoved his glasses up the bridge of his nose. "You're right. I can't stay mad at you. Sorry. I was simply eager to get going last night. But it wouldn't have been fair of me to work without you. This is your project as much as it is mine." Clifford waved a hand at the body. "Albeit, he's still here, and we can begin work now."

"All's forgiven, my friend." Chloe patted his shoulder. "Now, let's get to work."

~

Returning to headquarters after his night on patrol, Blake drove past the Bryant place. As Chloe commented, that house had character, and something about it drew him. He hoped the contractor she hired found it worthy of restoration and would take the job. He didn't want to see it sit and rot away to nothing, or worse, torn down if the park service couldn't restore it. Chloe had indicated she was beginning to research the history of the house. There had to be a story there, and it would be interesting to find out what it was. Perhaps the diary found in the back bedroom's secret hideaway all those years ago would reveal some information.

As Blake approached the Bryant house, he spotted something out of place that sent his senses on high alert. Stepping on his breaks, he pulled off the edge of the road and into the grassy area beside the driveway. Turning off the engine, Blake pocketed his keys and climbed out, closing the door quietly. He edged around the left side of the house, opposite the cellar door entrance. The end of a pickup truck bumper peeked out from the back corner of the house. Neither Ian or Clifford had pickups, and Chloe had a Mini Cooper.

Once at the far back corner, Blake took a quick peek around then slipped back to process what he'd observed. A shiny late-model black pickup truck and a man stood by the cellar door. He wore a dark jacket with his collar pulled high and his ballcap pulled low. Apparently, he hadn't heard when Blake pulled onto the property in his cruiser. The man had the lock on the cellar door in his hand. Was he trying to break in? Blake took another quick glance around the corner. It looked like he was doing something with the lock.

Blake stepped around the corner but didn't advance. "Excuse me. What are you doing? Didn't you see the Park Service No Trespassing sign up front?"

The man's head swiveled in Blake's direction, but Blake couldn't make out his features. All of a sudden, he pulled a gun and fired two shots in Blake's direction.

Blake spotted the gun and the man's reaction in time to dive behind the corner of the house. He gulped in a huge breath. Of course, he would have a gun. Pulling his own, he prepared for the next onslaught when he heard the truck engine fire up and the motor rev as the man slammed it into gear. It was coming his way.

Blake peeked around the corner. The man had his gun out the window and fired as he came even with the corner of the house. Blake dove to the ground in time, and rolling over, aimed for the truck tires. Even with a volley of shots, he missed the tire but hit the rim and right above the wheel well. The truck bounced across the uneven ground and jumped the shallow ditch near the road, hitting the pavement. Gaining speed, it swerved then course-corrected and drove away with a screech.

Blake slammed a fist on the ground. Not only had he missed the truck's tires, but there was no license plate to get a number.

~

"Well, there's not a lot of flesh left on the bones, unfortunately." Chloe carefully lifted the fabric of the soldier's uniform shirt with cotton gloves. The front of his navy wool jacket had lifted away easily once they'd removed the stiff leather belt, but they didn't dare remove it all the way. They wanted to attempt to match the slices in the jacket and shirt with any body tissue they might find. "There may be enough body tissue to match up some of the wounds. Look at all the rust-colored blood stains on the yellowed shirt. This poor fellow bled to death. Even if there's not enough flesh to match up, it's obvious he was stabbed numerous times."

"We can count the slashes in the shirt." Clifford pointed at the body. "But look here, and here and here. There are at least three visible slash wounds in this small area that approximately match the length of those in the clothing." He laid the shirt back over the body and attempted to match up the slashes. "The flesh here and here is gone, but it's obvious from the shirt he was stabbed in both places."

Chloe stuck a probe through another slash in the shirt and hit something hard. Lifting the shirt, she nodded. "Take a look at this, Cliff. If you observe the ribs here and here, you can see there are cuts where the stabbing object, or what we're assuming was a saber, left marks on the bone. There may not be flesh, but there's still an indication of a wound."

"Great observation. Let's see what else we can find."

Hours later, after they redressed the body, Chloe gathered the personal effects they'd removed from the soldier's pockets before they began their examination of the body. They'd found a prayer book, a few letters which were folded, yellowed and delicate. A pipe and a fragile pouch of tobacco were also found along with a small framed but faded daguerreotype of a beautiful young woman. His beloved perhaps? Poor woman. She'd never known what had happened to her beau or her husband. In her eyes he'd simply fallen off the face of the earth. Missing in action, never to come home again. Even the names of many of the fallen in battle were reported home to their loved ones. No one knew what happened to this soldier. What torture had his loved ones endured at the hands of a murderer?

"She's beautiful, isn't she?" Clifford peered over her shoulder at the picture Chloe held in her hands.

"Yes, she is. I was thinking how this man's family never knew what happened to him. Most soldier's names were sent home even if their bodies weren't. His family would have gone to their graves never knowing if he was dead or alive, and this woman? I wonder if she simply moved on, or died of a broken heart?"

"Until we know who he is, we won't have any answers about anything." Clifford striped off his rubber gloves and tossed them in the trash.

"I'll preserve his personal effects and when I have some time, I'll go through them and see what I can discover." Chloe reached for a box of acid-free bags.

"Good idea, but you should probably make it sooner than later." Clifford removed his clear face guard and apron. "No telling what cool info is in those letters. Maybe even something from that sweetheart in the daguerreotype. Aren't those things the coolest?"

"Yeah, they are, and, yes, I'll add it to my growing list of research, diary reading and other things to do. I still need to find a contractor to check out the Bryant house to see if it's even feasible for restoration." Chloe finished bagging the personal effects and stored them away in a marked bin on a shelf, then she removed her gloves, clear face guard and apron.

"I can help with that when the time comes. Just let me know." Clifford started to leave the room.

"Uh, Cliff?" Chloe tossed a thumb over her shoulder. "Maybe we should store this guy? You know for safe keeping?"

Clifford's gaze moved from Chloe to the body on the table. "Oh yeah. I almost forgot."

"No, you did forget." Chloe teased, grabbing a body bag and more rubber gloves.

Chapter Nine

After spending the day on further forensic research on the union soldier, Chloe, Clifford and Ian came to the conclusion his murderer hadn't come closer to him than a saber length. Apparently once he'd stabbed his victim, he'd kept his distance. They found no evidence of other human remains. No hair. No skin. No one else's blood. The Sarge, as they'd begun calling the soldier from the insignia on his uniform, had apparently kept his uniform in tip top shape. Considering he'd been fighting in a battle that day, he still took pride in his uniform. He probably brushed the jacket and pants every evening. From his rank, he was likely a leader of a squad. Chloe admired his attention to detail. Once they'd dispensed with the dust and cobwebs from the years since the battle, they'd simply found his remains. A large amount of his own dark hair clung to his shoulders and down his back from where it had fallen out over the decades since his death.

"Well, I'm done for now." Chloe tossed her magnifying glass and tweezers into the tool bin. "This has been intense, and I'm finished for the day. What about you fellows?" She removed the paper mask worn to prevent her from blowing any evidence away unintentionally, then she removed her rubber gloves with a snap and tossed them into the trash.

Ian stretched his back and removed his mask. "Sounds like a great idea." He nudged Clifford who still leaned over the body with magnifying goggles. "Come on, Cliff. It's past time to call it quits for the day. Time to grab something to eat."

Clifford mumbled something as his stomach growled. He straightened and stared at them through the goggles, his eyes looking enormous through the thick lenses.

"See?" Chloe pointed at him. "You'd better listen to your stomach before you pass out on Sarge there and end up looking like him."

Ian chuckled, removing his apron and gloves. "So where are we eating?"

"I'm heading home." Clifford shoved the goggles up and began removing his gloves, paper mask and apron. "There's a documentary on the ten thousand neolithic standing stones of Carnac, and I don't want to miss it. I've got a frozen pizza I'll stick in the oven."

Chloe nodded and walked over to the storage bins. "Okay then. Sounds like an exciting evening to me. I'm going to take the artifacts we found on Sarge and start going through them as I get a chance. Right now, I'm still reading Cecelia Langston's diary. I thought teenage girls today wrote about the most inane things. Believe me. Nothing has changed in a hundred and sixty-two years." She took the small bin with her as she strolled out to the office and set it on her desk. Opening the bottom drawer, she removed her purse.

Ian stopped by her desk. "Well, Cliff's not interested in grabbing a bite. How about you? Want to go to Moira's? This time of day her Scottish meat pies will be fresh."

Chloe gave him a wry glance through narrowed lids. "That's not fair. I was going to head home."

"She usually has beef pies, sausage pies, shepherd pies." He ticked them off on his fingers. "Even lamb on occasion."

"And they are the best." She nodded, her lips breaking into a smile. "I can smell them now."

"I'm buying." Ian grinned.

Chloe released a heavy sigh. "I'll call Aunt Charlene and tell her I'll be bit late coming home."

~

Blake parked in front of Moira's and grabbed his travel mug. He couldn't head out on patrol without filling it up with Moira's delicious brew. She'd started making meat pies in the evenings the last couple of weeks, and they were to die for. If he let himself, he would eat them every night, but his middle would grow and that would be a bad thing. Blake hadn't had one this week and since he hadn't eaten dinner yet, why not grab one for the road?

Stepping inside the little coffee shop, he allowed his gaze to adjust from the early evening sun, only to find Chloe Rogers and Ian O'Brian sitting at a table. Their laughter carried across the room sending a stab of jealousy through Blake. As he made his way to the counter at the rear of the shop, he attempted to douse the disagreeable emotion that coursed through him.

"There's me favorite park policeman." Moira crossed her arms on the countertop as Blake set his mug down. She eyed the table across the room, then peered back at him, lowering her voice as she spoke. "Now I ask ye. Why are ye here, and she's sittin' there with another man?"

Blake's brows furrowed. "Not that I *have* to explain anything to you, but I'm working. She has every right to be there with whomever she chooses. In this case, she works with him. If they choose to make it thing, that's up to them."

"Ah, yes, dearie, but it bothers ye." Little more than a whisper, her voice held a lilt that indicated to Blake she was delighted.

"No, it doesn't." He shoved his coffee mug toward her.

"Ach, yes, it does." The smile on her face grew wider as she leaned in. "A lot."

"The usual, please." He ignored her. "And a Shepherd's Pie to go."

Moira winked at Blake and picked up the travel mug. "Anything else, laddie?"

"Yeah, one of your lemon curd pastries."

Blake heard the sour note in his voice and hated it. Moira was right, and he disliked that fact. Chloe and Ian had to have seen him come in, and it would be the polite thing to go over and say hello. Drawing in a cleansing breath, he turned. His gaze met Chloe's. A question filled hers, but as he approached, the tension that accompanied the question in her eyes eased. "Hey, you two. How's it going?" Blake forced a light tone into his voice and was proud he'd pulled it off.

"Great." Chloe nodded, clasping her hands beneath her chin, elbows on the table edge. "It's been a long day of forensic research on our soldier. It was time to stop and grab a bite."

"Forensic research sounds interesting."

"Oh, it definitely is." Ian wiped his mouth with his paper

napkin. "It was nearly impossible to pull Cliff away though. If his stomach hadn't started growling, he'd still be working."

"Sounds like Cliff." Blake forced a chuckle. Small talk. He was a third wheel, and it was time to go. "Well, I'll let you get back to your meal."

"Why don't you join us?" Chloe waved toward the other chair at the table.

Blake shook his head. "No thanks. I have to get out on patrol. Just stopped to get my coffee and a meat pie to go. Moira makes the best, you know." He pointed at their plates. "Case in point."

Chloe released a soft laugh. "She does indeed. Stay safe out there, Blake."

"I'll do my best." He waved a hand and returned to the counter.

Ian hadn't looked put out when Chloe invited him to join them. Was Ian interested in Chloe or were they just colleagues? It was hard to get a read on that relationship. But jealousy was a strong emotion. Perhaps he should put his energies toward defeating the competition rather than being jealous of him.

~

After tucking Evie into bed, Chloe returned to the family room, and found Aunt Charlene and her dad watching a show on TV. She wasn't interested and wanted to get back to Cecelia Langston's diary. She'd left her messenger bag that sat with her purse by the back door, she retrieved the diary from it. The storage tote from the examination room sat there as well. She should ask her dad to put those items in the safe until she was ready to go through them.

Gathering the small storage bin, she walked back to the family room. "Hey, Dad. Next commercial, think you can do me a favor?"

"Sure, what's up?" Relaxing in his recliner, he turned his attention toward her.

"I have some old personal effects from the Union soldier we discovered at the Bryant house that I'd like to put in the safe until I can go through them. No sense in leaving them at the office since I'll likely go through them here."

"Let's do it now." Standing, he led the way to his home office where he opened a door in the credenza behind his desk and began unlocking the safe installed there. "What do you have here?" Dan held out a hand.

Chloe opened the tote and handed him the acid-free bags holding the delicate personal effects. "There's a prayer book, a few letters, a pipe with a fragile pouch of tobacco and a small, framed daguerreotype of a beautiful young woman. I suspect she was the soldier's wife or fiancé. I hope to find out more about her from the letters."

"That does sound promising." He laid the bags gently into the safe then closed the door, spinning the dial several times to secure the tumblers. "You have an interesting job to be sure."

"It's fascinating. I hope we can get some answers for the poor soldier. To be murdered then left where no one knew where he was for 159 years? What a horrible end."

Dan shook his head and stood. "It's beyond comprehension that someone would do that to another human being."

"Yeah, it is."

Dan reached for a slip of paper from a notepad and a pen from a cup on his desk. He jotted something on it then held it toward Chloe. "Here's the combination in case you want to retrieve any of those items, if I'm not here to help you."

"Thanks. I might need to at some point. This could come in handy." Chloe led the way out of the office. "I'm going to grab a cup of hot tea and head to my room to do some reading. I'm still plugging away on the diary of this teenage girl."

"The one from the Bryant place?" Dan settled back in his recliner.

"Yep."

"Well, good luck."

~

After reading several entries where Cecelia described her daily routine of going to school, doing chores, spending time with friends. The teen shared thoughts about certain boys and the gift she was making for her mother's upcoming birthday. Yawning, Chloe felt she knew all there was to know about this young girl. Whether the girl shared these thoughts with others or not, she certainly shared her most intimate thoughts with her diary. Chloe had done the same when she was about Cecelia's age. What young girl with a diary hadn't? Had Cecelia had a brother who teased her mercilessly about her diary? Had he stolen it and read it like so many future generations of brothers had done? Chloe didn't have a brother and had never suffered that fate.

She was about to put the diary away when something in the next entry caught her eye. Something about the soldier.

Chloe glanced at the date of the entry. July 1, 1863. That was the first day of the Battle of Gettysburg. Oh, she couldn't put the diary away now. With the battle just beginning, what was going to happen to the Langston family? Their home was right on the battlefield. Cecelia must have seen it firsthand.

Diary of Cecelia Langston
Uncle Virgil Langston's Home
Gettysburg, PA
July 2, 1863

Dear Diary,

Papa watched out the dining room window most of the morning as we heard cannon fire to the west. Mr. Pritchard, the milk man, stopped by with his delivery and told Papa the Confederate troops were coming up from the south, and that the Union general had sent a lot of soldiers to try and cut him off. Papa looked awfully worried. He told us to gather only what we would need for several days and pack them in carpet bags. Julie and I had to share one.

Who was Julie? An older or younger sister perhaps? She skimmed down through the young girl's description of their preparations to leave if her papa deemed it necessary.

The gunfire and cannon booms got so close Papa said it was time to go. It was dusk, and he wanted to get to Uncle Virgil's before dark. Mama held little Charlie constantly because he was crying and wouldn't stop. He was so afraid of the noise. I was afraid, too, but I wouldn't let them see. I had to be brave for Papa's sake. He was trying to protect us, and as the oldest, I had to be brave for him and for

Mama.

We left the house and hurried toward town. We got to Uncle Virgil's house and settled in. Mama put the little ones to bed, and Papa and Uncle Virgil sat up talking about the armies that were fighting on the edge of town. Mama sent me to bed so she and Aunt Missy could talk. All the adults are so worried. I was dressing for bed when I remembered tomorrow is Mama's birthday. Oh no, I forgot that I hid her birthday present in the root cellar at our house. I didn't know what to do. I worked so hard to make her gift. Then I had an idea. I would just sneak back to the house and get it.

The battle had stopped for the night. All the soldiers would've settled into their camps, so I could sneak into our cellar and get Mama's gift.

It would be easy because I was staying on the main floor of Uncle Virgil's house, and I could just slip out the window. I redressed and did just that. I slipped out the window, taking the lantern on the dresser with me but didn't light it. As quiet as I could, I hurried down the alley beside the house and down the street to the woods that led to our house. Once there, I hurried into the cellar and lit the lantern to find my way to the root cellar where I'd hid Mama's gift.

Inside the root cellar, I reached up to the top shelf behind a crock of apples where I'd hidden it. I tucked it in my apron pocket and was just about to head out when I heard voices. Turning out the lantern, I peeked between the door and the frame to see soldiers talking. They hadn't been there when I came in. I decided to stay still and wait till they left, then I'd head back to Uncle Virgil's.

One of the soldiers raised his voice at the other one, but the second one shook his head and said something about not wanting to sign a paper. The first soldier said he had to. The truth had to be told so he could be stopped. Who was he talking about? Well, I was soon going to find out. Another man came in and told the second soldier he could leave. This man looked like he might be an officer. He had a funny looking hat and he carried a sword of some kind. But what he did next was awful. Just plain horrid. He stabbed the first soldier a bunch of times. I pulled back and couldn't watch anymore. I'd gasped when he stabbed him the first time, and I was afraid he might have heard me, but I don't think he did. The first soldier cried out, and the officer was too busy stabbing him to hear me. I still see it when I think about it, so I try not to think about it. Whatever the first soldier was trying to get the second soldier to sign that paper about was concerning that officer. Wonder whatever happened to the paper?

Chloe lowered the diary to her lap. Poor Cecelia. No young girl should witness what she'd seen. What could it all have been about? Who was the officer and why had he killed the sergeant? What was the paper about? Why had he wanted the second soldier to sign it? And as Cecelia had wondered, whatever happened to it?

Questions swirled through Chloe's mind. She hadn't expected that reading Cecelia's diary would open up a plethora of questions. And where would she begin to tackle them?

She lifted the diary and continued reading the entry.

After the officer left the cellar, I lit my lantern but kept the light low. Slipping out of the root cellar, I checked to make sure no one was still around and made my way to the cellar door and doused my lantern. I ran through the woods like lightening back to Uncle Virgil's and climbed into my window. I tried not to look at the dead soldier as I passed him, but I couldn't keep my eyes away. Poor man. He didn't deserve to die like that. I'll always carry the memory of his eyes staring unseeing as I passed by. Whenever I think of It I shudder. I doubt I'll get a wink of sleep tonight, diary. I can't tell anyone but you.

Chloe's heart broke for the young girl and the burden she carried for one so young. She read through the next six entries. They explained about the nightmares she had the following nights and how her father prepared to sell the house immediately after the Battle of Gettysburg. Cecelia's final entry touched a chord deep within Chloe.

Diary of Cecelia Langston
Langston Home
Gettysburg, PA
July 7, 1863

Dear Diary,

This is the last time I'll write in you. We're leaving our home today. Papa is moving his law practice to Baltimore to join with another lawyer and seems relieved about it. After the battle, he and Mama are both eager to leave Gettysburg. Our house just isn't the same. There's so much damage, and Papa has sold it to a local man who is willing to make repairs and fix the house up again. He's a businessman in town and can afford it, I guess.

Since I've been having nightmares and not sleeping well, I've decided to hide you away in the secret place in my room. I'm not taking you with me when we leave today. I want to forget what I saw in the cellar, and I think this is a good way to begin. By leaving behind this memory that I've written down, perhaps I can begin to heal and begin to sleep.

Papa and Mama don't understand why I can't sleep. They think it's simply the war, and I can't tell them different. But you know all.

You've been my only real friend, diary. You hold all my intimate thoughts and desires that no one knows about. Hold them and protect them until one day someone may discover them in my secret place. And if they don't, hold them forever hidden away long after I'm gone.

I place my favorite little doll, Beatrice, with you to keep you company. I don't play with dolls anymore so she'll be better off with you.

Your best friend,
Cecelia

Chloe wiped tears from her cheeks. How had this young girl who wasn't quite a child but wasn't yet a young woman dealt with having witnessed a murder? She wrote it in her diary. She struggled with sleeping but didn't feel she could share it with her parents because she'd stolen away in the night to return for her mama's birthday gift. Poor Cecelia. Chloe had no idea beyond the final entry whatever became of the young girl. Perhaps she needed to find out what happened to the troubled Cecelia Langston and her family. Was it important to the mystery of Sarge and the house? No, not really, but it was important to Chloe.

Closing the diary and laying it on her bedside table, Chloe prepared for bed, the young girl firmly ensconced in her thoughts. She'd just finished brushing her teeth when her cell phone rang. Who would be calling at this hour? Chloe retrieved the phone from the comforter on the bed where she'd settled while reading.

Clifford's name appeared on the screen. He never called this late. She swiped the answer button.

"Cliff? What's up?"

"We've got a problem. You better get over here to the office. ASAP."

~

Chloe parked in the lot behind the building and rushed inside. Before he hung up on her, Cliff said the door would be unlocked. Nothing more. What in the world could this be about? Two park police cruisers with flashing lights parked near the entrance as she'd approached the parking lot. That wasn't a good sign. Had someone been injured? Or worse?

When she arrived upstairs at the historian's office, the door stood wide open.

Park police officer Gabe Holland stood just inside the door, thumbs hooked on his utility belt. His head swiveled in her direction as she charged into the room.

"Hey, Chloe." He gave her a two fingered salute as her eyes met his. He shook his head, his expression sympathetic. "Sorry about all this."

"About what, Gabe? What's going on?"

"Didn't Cliff tell you?"

Chloe heaved a huge sigh. "Cliff didn't tell me anything except to get over here."

Gabe pointed toward the examination room. "You'd better go on in there. Blake's with Cliff. It's not pretty."

Chloe's heart faltered. What in the world…?

She hurried toward the door to the open examination room, dread stirring in her mid-section. Clifford had called her so surely he was okay. Not Ian….

She stepped inside the doorway. Blake stood with his hands on his hips, his gaze downward on something behind the examination table. His glance flicked toward her when she entered the room. He'd removed his hat, and his expression was grim. He stepped back to allow her to move into the narrow space between the table and the shelves along the wall.

Stepping around the examination table, Chloe spotted Clifford kneeling on the floor beside…she gasped, her stomach lurching at the sight before her.

Sarge's body lay all over the floor, his uniform shredded and tossed around the room. His remains had been dismembered and scattered. Bins from the shelves had been pulled out and dumped then tossed around.

Chloe's hand flew up to cover her mouth. A swirl of nausea overcame her. She swallowed in an effort to force down the bile that threatened to surface. Who would do this? And why? Who even knew Sarge was here? They'd been so careful in hiding his transferal from the Bryant house.

A warm hand rested on her shoulder, and Chloe knew it was Blake's. It was comforting, and she appreciated it. She wanted to turn into his arms and hide from this show of violence and irreverence. No. That was too weak a description for what had been perpetrated against this soldier. Why had this been done?

As a historian, Chloe had chosen a long time ago to never condemn either side in the Civil War. If she wanted to portray history as it had happened, she couldn't take sides. Both sides fought for what they believed in at the time, and they gave their lives for those beliefs. The same could be said for people today.

People may disagree, but they must agree to disagree, not condemn without discourse.

She didn't yet know why Sarge was murdered, but someone, even today, must know something about that murder. They didn't want that information to get out. What other explanation was there? Chloe leaned over and placed a hand on Clifford's shoulder as he knelt in silence. "This escalates things to a whole new level, you know."

He lifted his head, his tortured eyes meeting hers. "What do you mean?"

"Think about it. Why would someone come in here and destroy the body? How did they know it was here?"

Blake stepped around the examination table and leaned on it. "Great questions. But you have them backward, Chloe. How did they know it was here? Did someone see us take it out of the house and follow us here? If so, why would someone come in and destroy the body? For what purpose? They have to know something about the original murder and don't want that information to get out." He pointed around the room. "Look at all the bins that were emptied onto the floor. Were they looking for something? My guess is, yes."

Chloe dropped onto a rolling stool that sat nearby. She surveyed the carnage. "So many questions. I finished reading Cecelia Langston's diary this evening and she described the murder of our sergeant. The poor girl actually witnessed it."

"What?" Clifford stood and turned toward Chloe. "She was only…what? Fifteen?"

"Yeah. She'd hidden her mother's birthday gift in the root cellar, and when the family left the house in a hurry the morning of the first of July to go to her Uncle Virgil's house in town, she forgot it. Her mother's birthday was the next day. That night she snuck out of the house and went back to the root cellar to retrieve it after the battle ended. She was in the root cellar when she heard men's voices. Apparently, Sarge was trying to convince another soldier to sign a paper of some kind. He told the soldier he had to so the truth could be told and 'he' could be stopped. The soldier didn't want to sign it. Then an officer came in and sent the second soldier away. Once he was gone, the officer stabbed Sarge many times."

Chloe closed her eyes and shook her head. “Cecelia waited for the officer to leave then she lit her lantern and left but not before she glanced at the dead soldier. Over the next entries, she talked about having nightmares. Her last entry nearly tore my heart out. She thanked her diary for being her best friend and for listening to her most intimate thoughts. Cecelia hid her memory of that night away in her secret place with her favorite doll until someone might someday find it. But if they didn’t, it was okay. She wanted her diary to protect all her thoughts and memories for her. It was only a few days after the Battle of Gettysburg ended, and her family moved to Baltimore that day. She hoped that by hiding her diary away, she would be able to stop having nightmares.”

“Wow, and I suppose she never talked to her parents about the murder?” Blake scrubbed a hand down his face.

“That was the impression I got.” Chloe nodded, clasping her hands between her knees. “They left in such a hurry I doubt they ever went back to the cellar. If they did, they would’ve noticed a wall where there wasn’t one before. The new owner wouldn’t have known it wasn’t there before and wouldn’t question its presence.”

“Poor Cecelia.” Cliff propped his hands on his hips. “And now, poor Sarge. I’m glad we didn’t waste time in doing our examination. There’s not much left to examine, and it’s all contaminated now.”

“What are you going to do with him?” Blake tilted his chin in the direction of the scattered skeletal parts.

Chloe stood and inhaled, releasing the air in a huff. “We’re going to bury him in the Gettysburg National Cemetery in the section with the rest of the Union soldiers. We may have to put ‘unknown’ on his headstone since we don’t have a name.”

Clifford nodded. “I agree. I believe we’ve found all we can from this man. It’s time to lay him at rest. His body’s been desecrated. We need to give him a burial with honor.”

“I like the way you two think.” Blake picked up his Smoky-Bear hat from the examination table. “Before I head back out on patrol, do you need any help cleaning this up?”

Clifford shook his head. “No thanks. It’s going to take a while and a good bit of sorting. I’m kind of particular where I want things so I’ll take care of it. Chloe, you go home. I’ll take care of this.”

“Cliff, you can’t do all this by yourself.” Chloe waved her arms, encompassing the whole room. “Two people will get the job done quicker. I’m staying no matter what you say.”

“But—”

“No, I’m staying. I have a vested interested in the office as well as Sarge. So shut up and let’s get to work so we can both go home at some point.” Chloe turned to Blake. “Thanks for coming, Blake.”

He seated his hat on his head until the brim was level. “I wouldn’t have wanted to be anywhere else. Somehow, I feel like I’m a part of this whole process, and I, too, have a vested interest in Sarge.” He stepped toward the door to the office then stopped. “Before I head out, I’ll have Officer Holland join me in a walk-through of the building to ensure no one is still here. You never know.”

Chapter Ten

When Chloe had arrived, Gabe had secured the entrance to ensure no one else could come in. After leaving the historian's office, Blake and Gabe split up to check out the rest of the building. Blake wanted to ensure the perpetrator of the carnage in the examination room wasn't still lurking about.

It was a huge two-story building that included the museum, Cyclorama, bookstore, ticketing office, the education center, special exhibits, the refreshment area and public restrooms on the first floor. The administrative offices and the historian's rooms were all on the second floor. Park police headquarters which were always manned were located at the rear of the building. This would take a while, but at least the museum and special exhibits were locked up separately with alarms. Too many precious artifacts in those areas. The bookstore wouldn't be a problem either. It was secured at both ends of the store with a metal gate and an alarm.

Gabe headed to the lower floor while Blake remained upstairs to check the admin offices which should be locked. But locks could be picked. The memory of the unknown guy outside the cellar door at the Bryant house came to mind. While he headed down the hallway, unlocking doors with his master key, flipping on lights and checking offices, Blake pondered what the man was doing that day. Blake was glad he'd stopped him from whatever it was, but the question remained, would he return?

Who was he? What interest did he have in the Bryant house? There didn't seem to be anything else now that Sarge was gone, but maybe the unknown man didn't know that. Did he have anything to do with Sarge's destruction? So many questions.

Blake flipped off the lights in another office and relocked the door, moving on to the next. Right now, he needed to forget about that and concentrate on the present situation. If he were to—he started to insert his key in the doorknob, but it turned freely in his hand. The hair stood up on the back of his neck. Pulling his Glock 9mm from its holster, he pointed the barrel upward and plastered himself against the wall beside the door. Turning the knob quietly, Blake pushed the door open and waited for possible gunfire.

Nothing. He pointed the gun forward in the defensive posture and scanned the room then moved back behind the wall. It was too dark to see anything. Still behind the wall, he slid his arm around and flipped on the light then took another quick glance, his gun aimed forward. With a quick pan of the room, he didn't spot anyone or see any movement. With heightened senses, Blake moved into the room, head on a swivel. He checked behind the door. Nothing. Unfamiliar with this office, he had no idea if anything was out of place. Gun trained ahead, he inched toward the desk.

All of a sudden, a heavy object flew at him, and even though he reflexively moved out of the way, it landed a solid blow on the right shoulder, and he dropped his gun. He dove for it as a shadowy figure came at him. His searching fingers missed the gun as a fist slammed into his jaw leaving his teeth feeling like Jell-O and his ears ringing. With an elbow jammed in his back and a punch to his kidneys, the figure clamored from the room as Blake lay stunned and in pain.

Waves of nausea rippled through him. After a few seconds, he forced himself onto his back with a groan and reached for the radio mic clipped to his shoulder. Fortunately, it wasn't the injured one or it likely wouldn't work. He pressed the call button.

"Come in, Gabe." His voice was little more than a whisper as the radio squelched. He pressed the button again, forcing his voice louder. "Come in, Gabe."

"10-4, Blake. What's happening?"

"I have a 10-18. It's urgent. The perp attacked me. He's on the loose in the building. Call in back-up." Pain and nausea surged through Blake as he gasped for air.

"10-4. I'll call it in. I'm on my way."

"No. Send someone else. You head to Chloe and Cliff." Blake clenched his teeth against the pain. "And hurry. The perp may head straight there."

"On my way."

Blake lay still until the pain and nausea began to fade then he attempted to sit up. Nope. The pain surged again. Maybe he'd just rest here until help arrived. He thought about the guy who did this. The perp was big. A lot bigger than Blake, and he was well-built, like a body builder. Blake had the bruises to prove it. And prepare—the guy wore a black ski mask so there was no way Blake could describe what he looked like.

Lord, please protect Chloe and Cliff. Please don't let that guy reach them before Gabe does and help us apprehend whoever did this. Ow. Even praying hurt.

~

"He likes you, you know?' Clifford reached for Sarge's forearm and with great care laid it in the plastic bin next to him.

"What?" Chloe turned a questioning gaze on her co-historian. "What are you talking about?" She picked up the pieces of Sarge's clothing and laid them in a separate bin. It saddened her that his uniform had basically disintegrated, but she would save the largest pieces at least. Which wasn't saying much.

"Don't you mean who am I talking about? I'm talking about Blake Hunter. He likes you. Or hadn't you noticed?" Clifford picked up a couple more bones and placed them in the bin. "If you haven't, you're blind as the proverbial bat."

Warmth rolled upward into Chloe's cheeks, and she turned away to ensure Clifford didn't spot the colorful surge. "Hmm. Are you sure about that? What would give you that idea?"

"Oh, come on. The way he looks at you for one thing. The way he's always dropping by for another. I may generally have my nose stuck in a book or deep in research, but even *I* can see it from a mile away. And why aren't you looking at me right now? Afraid to admit I'm right?"

Chloe huffed out a breath. Now she'd *have* to turn around. She willed away the heat suffusing her cheeks before making a slow turn on her bent knees. "I'm *not* afraid to admit your right, because I don't think you are. Officer Hunter—"

"Don't you usually call him Blake?" Clifford broke in.

Chloe's annoyance grew as she narrowed her gaze at him. "Officer Hunter drops by a lot because he's been interested in

Sarge since the beginning. He was there when you discovered the wall and when you made the opening in it. He was there when you found Sarge, and he was the one who made it possible to sneak Sarge out of the cellar. He's been there all along."

"Are you sure it was Sarge that kept bringing him back?" Clifford grinned, wiggling his eyebrows. "Or was it because *you* were there every time. He was more than happy to go into the house with you every time you needed to go inside. Refute that one."

"It was his job." Chloe aimed a flat glare at him then turned back to picking up scraps of antique fabric. "Give it up, Cliff."

A knock sounded on the open door causing them both to glance up. Gabe Holland filled the doorway, a grim expression etching his features.

"Gabe? What's the matter?" Chloe stood and placed the bin she'd been filling on the examination table. Cliff joined her, leaving his heavier one on the floor.

"You both need to stay in here and secure this door. Don't come out until I or another park police officer, unlock it. Don't unlock it yourselves. The perp who did this is still in the building. I'll secure the outer office door then stand guard by it. No matter what you may hear, don't come out. Understand?"

Chloe nodded and noted Clifford's nod from the corner of her eye.

"Great. Lock it up." Gabe shut the door behind him, leaving them alone. They heard the outer office door close then the silence ensued.

Clifford followed his instructions, locking them in. "Wow, if that's not scary, what is?"

"Where's Blake?" Chloe realized too late she'd spoken her question aloud. She should've kept that one to herself.

"Ah hah. You like him too." Clifford tossed a satisfied grin in her direction before kneeling on the floor once again.

Chloe heaved a heavy sigh. "Oh, Cliff. It isn't that easy."

"Why isn't it?" Clifford turned toward her, his brows furrowed in puzzlement.

Chloe knelt and rested her hands on her knees. "Although it's been three years since Josh died in Afghanistan, I don't know if I'm ready to move on. Sometimes I have a hard time remembering what he looked like. I have to actually look at his picture on the chest of drawers in my bedroom to remember, and I don't stop and look much anymore. Yet the thought of moving on still seems so…unfaithful somehow."

"The fact you're having a hard time remembering what he looks like tells me your mind may be moving on." Cliff shrugged one shoulder. "Answer me a question, was Josh a selfish man?"

Chloe's heart lurched at the thought. "No, of course not. Never. He was the most thoughtful, the most generous, and the most giving man I ever knew. There wasn't a selfish bone in his body."

"Then why would he be selfish enough to ask you to live a lonely life and never know love again?" Clifford placed a hand on her arm. "As a selfless man, wouldn't Josh want you, a young vibrant woman to find love and be happy in that love for as long as you have it to hold onto?"

Sudden stinging pricked behind Chloe's eyes as she gave him a watery smile. "For someone who keeps his nose in a book all the time, you're pretty smart. You must've learned something there."

"I must have read about it in a book although I've never even been in love." Clifford heaved a huge sigh. "Maybe someday. But you might have a chance now."

"You seem awfully sure that Blake is that interested in me." Chloe shrugged her shoulders and shook her head. "Like is a far cry from love, Cliff."

"Yes, well—"

Bang, bang!

Gunfire sounded from the hallway outside the outer office door where Gabe stood guard. Apparently, the man who had wreaked havoc was back.

Shouts came from the hall, but she couldn't make them out. *Bang, bang, bang, bang!*

They scootched over behind the examination table and waited. Within a few minutes silence followed. They waited as the clock ticked the minutes away. More silence. Was Gabe dead? No more gunfire. No more shouts. No one came to unlock the door. Nothing. Gabe said not to open this door for anyone. A park police officer would open it. How long would that take? How long would they have to wait? Was the perp still out there? Had he shot Gabe?

Chloe's gaze met Clifford's. The same questions swirling through her mind were reflected in Clifford's eyes.

~

Blake shifted on the less-than-comfortable examination bed in the Wellspan Gettysburg hospital ER, waiting for the doctor. How long would he have to lay here? It was difficult to breathe.

Finally, after an eternity, a doctor came into his cubicle to share the results of the tests that had been run. In his late sixties with a white fringe of hair surrounding a balding pate, he wore an open white lab coat that revealed a light blue dress shirt above navy slacks. His glasses rode low on his nose as he met Blake's gaze above them. "Well, Officer Hunter," his half-smile was more grim than cheery, "I'd say someone did a number on you. Having difficulty breathing, are we?"

Are we? Of course, we are. Blake wanted to toss something at the doctor but recognized this doctor's particular bedside manner and decided it would be best to ignore it. "Yes, I am." Blake gritted his teeth, half from pain, half from irritation.

"Well, there's a reason for that."

You think?!?

The doctor didn't seem to notice Blake's irritation. Or he chose to ignore it. "You have three fractured ribs near your lumbar region with major bruising. Your attacker bruised your kidney as well. That's why you've been experiencing nausea. Your jaw isn't fractured, but you've got a humdinger of a bruise forming. And there's a contusion where he broke the skin but nothing a butterfly bandage won't take care of. As for your shoulder, it isn't fractured. Just a huge, deep bruise. Keep icing it and moving it so it doesn't stiffen up on you. All in all, I'd say you're fortunate to have come out of this as well as you did. You've got some healing to do, so don't get me wrong. This will take time. Especially those ribs."

"It hurts to breathe, Doc." Blake flinched when he tried to inhale. "See what I mean?"

"Sure. Happens to everyone who cracks a rib. We don't bind them anymore. Deep breathing will prevent our patients from contracting pneumonia, and binding prevents that. Instead, we'll give you something temporarily for the pain, so you can take those deep breaths." The doctor approached the computer attached to the cubical wall and typed something on the keyboard then glanced back at Blake. "That's all I've got. Any questions?"

"No. Except can I leave now?"

"What? You don't like our company? We try to be as hospitable in our hospital as possible."

The doctor chuckled at his own joke, but it made Blake want to toss something at him again. He hated hospitals.

"Okay. I'll write up a prescription for those pain meds then send a nurse in to get you ready for discharge. Take it easy for a while. It'll take about six weeks or so for those ribs to heal. Don't do anything strenuous and no heavy lifting. Without question. Got it?"

"Got it." Blake nodded causing his head to hurt.

"As for your other injures, the nurse will bandage your jaw. The pain meds will help with the kidneys. Limit your fluids for a while to take the load off while your kidneys are healing. Don't worry. I'll write all this down in your take home instructions."

Blake breathed a weak sigh to see Gabe in the waiting room when the nurse wheeled him out. "Boy, am I glad to see you. I'm ready to get out of this place. Like you wouldn't believe."

Both Gabe and the nurse took an arm and helped him out of the wheelchair.

"Sure, I would." Gabe chuckled. "What guy likes to be in the hospital?"

"Thanks." Blake tossed a half grin in the nurse's direction before she strolled away with the wheelchair.

Once Blake settled in the front seat of Gabe's police cruiser, he dropped his head against the headrest and closed his eyes attempting a few deep breaths.

"You okay?" Gabe glanced at him from the driver's seat.

"I will be. Eventually." Blake sighed.

"What all did that goon do to you?"

"Three cracked ribs, a bruised kidney, a bruised shoulder and a bruised jaw." Blake opened his eyes and turned toward Gabe. "Please tell me you caught him."

Gabe's brow furrowed, and his lips pursed as he shook his head. "Wish I could say we did. I locked Chloe and Cliff into the examination room behind the locked outer office door before our perp got there. He came on the run. I challenged him to stop, and when he didn't, I fired. He fired back. I dove to the ground and fired again. He escaped down the stairs. The other officers gave chase but he got away. They noted the make of the vehicle but there wasn't a tag on it. Go figure."

"Well, I'm glad you weren't hurt." Blake shifted gingerly in his seat, a hiss from the pain escaping before he could stop it. "What was the vehicle?"

"A dark late 80s model Toyota Camry." Gabe tossed a wry expression in Blake's direction.

"You're kidding, right?" Blake huffed in annoyance. "Do you know how many of those are out there?"

"Nope. But I know there are a lot of them. It's a common vehicle."

"Exactly. And he probably has a license plate for it in the trunk." Blake shook his head. "This guy is probably a professional for hire. At least that's what my gut is telling me. Joe Blow off the street would never think to take the plate off his car to prevent anyone from running it."

"Yep." Gabe drummed a soft beat on the stirring wheel.

A few minutes of silence passed, then Blake asked, "What happened to Chloe and Cliff after the shooting?"

Gabe gasped and slammed a hand against the steering wheel. "Shoot! I forgot all about them. They're probably still locked in the examination room waiting for someone to open the door. I told them not to come out until a park police officer unlocked it."

"You mean they've been locked in there for…how many hours?" Blake scrubbed a hand down the uninjured side of his face.

"Yeah, several." Gabe's features were grim. "I'll take you home then I'll go let them out."

"No, you won't. You drive over there right now and let them out. I'm fine. Take me home afterward. They're probably sitting there not knowing what the heck has happened. Go now." Blake met Gabe's glance in the ever-lightening interior of the vehicle from the brightening morning sky. "Let's go."

Gabe turned the cruiser down a side street and headed toward the park visitors center. As tired and in pain as Blake was, he wanted to see for himself that Chloe was fine. And Clifford, too, of course. Chloe had come to fill his heart, but even the quirky historian with the crazy hair had become a good friend.

Gabe parked at the rear of the building. "I'll go let them out, then be right back." He opened his door and started to climb out.

"I'm coming with you." Blake shoved his door open, but climbing out was a bit more difficult.

"You're crazy. It won't take me but a couple of minutes." Gabe stared at Blake as if he had two heads.

"Can you just help me out, please?" Blake made another attempt on his own, gasping for air in the attempt.

Gabe huffed in frustration. "Sure, but I don't understand why."

"They're my friends. I want to make sure they're okay."

Gabe came around and helped Blake out. Blake hated being so helpless. It would take him a while to get back in shape. He hoped he wasn't forced to take time off from work, but he was afraid that might be coming down the line from his supervisor once he received word.

They made their way upstairs to the locked door of the historian's office, and Gabe unlocked it. Once inside, Gabe unlocked the examination room only to find Chloe and Clifford nowhere in sight.

Blake stepped inside the room and circled around the examination table to find them leaning against the table, Chloe's head on Clifford's shoulder, his head on hers. Both were sound asleep. "Chloe. Cliff. Wake up." Blake couldn't bend down to shake them so he spoke loud enough to wake the dead in the next county.

They stirred and opened their eyes, staring unfocused for a few seconds. Then it registered who stood in from of them.

"Blake? Blake! My goodness! What happened to you?" Chloe jumped to her feet, leaving Clifford to nearly fall to the floor from leaning on her. She stepped toward Blake and started to touch his jaw but stopped and drew her hand back." "What happened, Blake? That bruise looks… awfully painful." Chloe put her fingertips over her lips.

Blake gave her a wry grin. "Well, a little, I guess. I was attacked by the guy who destroyed Sarge. I tried to fight back, but he was a lot bigger than me."

Clifford stood to his feet, stretching. "You can tell from the size of the bruise on your jaw he had a big fist."

"Yeah, well he rung my bell pretty good." Blake rubbed his

jaw.

"That's not all he did," Gabe said from the doorway, crossing his arms over his chest. "He cracked three ribs, bruised a kidney and his shoulder. I told him to stay in the car while I came up to let you all out, but he wouldn't listen. Said he had to make sure his friends were okay."

Blake's eyes met Chloe's and stalled. He swallowed hard; his breathing made even harder by the tenderness he found in her gaze. He forced his on to find Clifford yawning. Blake attempted another deep breath but flinched at the effort.

"Hurts pretty bad, huh?" Chloe's soft words drew his focus back. "Cracked ribs can be painful."

"Yeah." He gave a slight nod. He hurt all over and simply wanted to lay down and sleep for a long while.

"Time to go home and rest, buddy. You can see Chloe and Cliff are fine. Unless I miss my guess, they're going home too. Right, guys?" Gabe leaned a hip against the examination table.

"Nope. I've got work to do." Clifford bustled off toward the outer office.

Chloe released a soft laugh. "Cliff snored for the last five hours, so I have no doubt *he* got some sleep. Me on the other hand, I might have dozed a few times. Did I sleep? Not really. I'm going home to catch a few hours, then I may work from home today. I have some things I can work on there."

"Great idea." Blake took slow and careful steps toward the door. "It's doubtful the guy would come back here during the daytime, but it's better to be cautious."

"There's nothing left here for him to go through. He destroyed it all." Chloe's voice held a mixture of disgust and sadness. "We stored Sarge's clothing and bones on the shelf. After the donor event, we'll arrange for his interment in the Gettysburg National Cemetery. It's only right."

"That's a great idea." Blake reached to squeeze her hand. "A fitting end to an unknown soldier."

Chloe nodded. "At least he'll get a proper burial instead of being walled up and hidden in a cellar beneath an old house."

Gabe held up a hand. "Come on, Blake. Let me get you home before you keel over."

Blake started to walk out the door but allowed Gabe to go

ahead of him. He stopped and looked back around the doorframe. "I'll see you Saturday. Don't forget."

"But—" Chloe began.

"I'll be there." Blake winked and followed Gabe out of the office.

Chapter Eleven

He slammed his hand on the dashboard as he held his cell phone to his ear. "Boss, there was nothing in their office but a dried-up old skeleton in an old Army uniform. Nothing, I tell you, and I searched the whole place. I dumped out every bin there. I even ripped the skeleton and his uniform apart looking for something. Anything."

Silence met his tirade for several moments. Had the boss hung up on him? Had he done something wrong? Had he gone too far? What would the boss think about him beating up the park cop? Maybe he'd better not mention that right now.

A heavy sigh slipped across his ear. "I don't care about the 'dried-up old skeleton,' as you put it. I only care about the letter. You *will* find it. I don't care how. Find it." The line went dead.

He tossed the cell phone on the passenger seat and dropped his head against the head rest. If that letter wasn't in the office of those historians, then where was it? It had been buried in that cellar with that body since the Civil War. That's what the boss had told him. What was so all fired important about it to the boss?

~

Chloe went straight home. When she came in, Aunt Charlene met her at the kitchen door. She wore her fuzzy slippers and bathrobe, her hair in twisty curlers.

"What in the world? I heard the garage door open and close. Why are you coming in at five-thirty in the morning, young lady? This isn't like you to stay out all night?"

Chloe walked straight to her aunt and wrapped her arms around her, holding her tight.

"No, no it isn't, Aunt Char. But it wasn't like any night I've ever experience before either." She straightened her arms, her hands on Aunt Charlene's shoulders. "We need to sit down at the table while I tell you what happened." Chloe sat while Aunt Charlene made hot caffeine-free tea, then she sat in the chair beside her.

"I'm all ears, Chloe. What happened?"

"Remember I was here reading one of the diaries in my room last night? Well, I received a call from Cliff. He said something happened at the office. He made no sense." Chloe took her through her night, from the time she arrived and found Sarge had been desecrated until Blake and Gabe let her and Clifford out of the examination room. "The guy had done a number on poor Blake. He has a huge bruise on his jaw, three cracked ribs, and a bruised kidney and shoulder. Blake's having a hard time breathing."

"Oh, my." Aunt Charlene pressed her fingertips to her lips. "Poor Blake indeed. And you and Cliff too. You were locked up all night? Your dad and I didn't even know you were gone, for heaven's sake."

"You both had already gone to bed, and I didn't want to wake you. I was sure I'd be back soon."

Aunt Charlene picked up their empty cups and set them in the sink. "Well, you go on to bed and get some rest. Sounds like you didn't sleep much last night with Clifford's snoring. I'll keep Evie busy when she gets up. You just sleep as long as you want to, sweetie."

Chloe didn't want to sleep too late or she knew she wouldn't sleep tonight, so she set her alarm and climbed into bed. She was out as soon as her head sank into the pillow.

~

Chloe dressed in capris and a tank top and strolled down the hallway to the kitchen where she found Aunt Charlene cooking away. Evie sat at the child's table drawing and coloring with crayons. The delicious aromas of baking emanated from the oven and something tantalizing from a pot on the stove. Peaceful harmony pervaded the room. Of course, it wouldn't remain so when she stepped into Evie's view.

She grinned and tiptoed over to her daughter, halting behind her and dropping a kiss on the top of her head. Evie peered all around, up, right, left, as Chloe dodged each of her movements.

Finally, Evie turned all the way around and spotted her.

Chloe laughed. "Awe, you caught me, princess."

"Yes, Mommy. You twied to twick me." Evie giggled.

Chloe dropped another kiss on Evie's head then on each cheek. "Yes, but you're just too quick for me, Evie Rogers."

Evie gave one big nod. "Yup, I am."

"What are you doing?" Chloe knelt beside the table.

"Colowin'." Evie held up some of her crayons.

"Show me what you're coloring."

Evie held up her picture.

"Wow, it's beautiful. What is it?"

"You and me and Gwampa and Aunt Charwene."

"Oh, I can see that now. I love it. You be sure and ask Aunt Char to hang it on the fridge, okay?"

Evie nodded, her bangs swinging. "I will."

"Good. Now what is Aunt Char doing?" Chloe dropped her voice to a loud whisper. Her gaze met Aunt Charlene's.

"Bakin' bwownies." Evie's expression grew excited as she clapped.

"She is? Oh my goodness. I love brownies. Do you love brownies?"

"I love bwownies. She's makin' 'em for me."

"She is?"

Evie nodded again. "But I'll share."

"Oh, thank you. That's awfully nice of you. Will you share with Grandpa?"

"Yes." Evie's smile was broad.

"You know, because you're such a kind person who shares, you might even get two brownies. What do you think of that?"

Evie's eyes popped open wide, her lips forming an O. "I like that. It's good to share, huh, Mommy?"

Chloe chuckled. "Yes, princess. It's always good to share. Now I'm going to go see what else Aunt Char is up to." Chloe climbed to her feet and dropped another kiss on her daughter's head before striding into the kitchen. "What is that delectable smell, Aunt Char? Evie already gave away what's in the oven. What's in the pot?" Chloe reached for the lid, but Aunt Charlene blocked her hand with her arm.

"Uh uh. No peeking. I'm trying a new recipe. You'll find out at dinner tonight." Aunt Charlene scooched in-between Chloe and the stove. "Don't you have work to do?"

Chloe chuckled. "Yes, ma'am, but I would like a bite of late breakfast first. You know, food for thought." After eating a bowl of cereal, Chloe decided to give Jan a call and see how the preparations for the dinner were coming along. In all the excitement of transporting Sarge to the examination room, the forensic examination, then the whole horrible episode last night, she'd nearly forgotten about the dinner. The call was long overdue. "Jan? Hi, it's Chloe. How are things going?"

"Chloe? How *are* you?" Her friend's voice instantly filled with concern. "I heard you were locked into the historian's office all night, and there was a shootout just outside your office. Are you ok? I saw Cliff this morning, and he said you're at home. What happened? He said Officer Hunter was attacked. Are you okay, Chloe?"

Chloe shook her head at the barrage of questions, waiting for Jan to peter out.

"Chloe, answer me."

"If you're finished firing questions at me and will give me a chance, I will." Chloe chuckled.

A huge sigh echoed over cyberspace. "I'm sorry. I've just been so worried about you. Word is flying around the offices about what happened last night. I guess some goon came in and tore up your examination room. Am I right?"

Chloe drew in a patient and cleansing breath and released it. "Yes, that's right. Then Cliff and I were *intentionally* locked in for our protection by park police, but in all the excitement, they forgot to let us out. Officer Hunter was attacked and injured. His wellbeing came first."

"What about the gunfight?"

Chloe was thankful this was a phone conversation and not in person. Jan couldn't see her eyeroll. Her friend was simply too wrapped up in this story, and Chloe suspected she'd gleaned bits and pieces of office gossip about last night's occurrence.

"Yes, there was a gunfight, and to ensure you have the facts straight, no one was shot. None of our park police were shot or injured. Except for Officer Hunter, of course, and he was *not* shot. Does that clear things up for you?"

"But what about you?" Jan's voice rose. "Why are you at home and Cliff is at work?"

"Because we spent the night locked in the examination room. Cliff managed to sleep all night, snoring in the process. I didn't get any sleep except to doze a bit, so I came home and slept, and now I'm working from home. Which brings me to the reason I'm calling you. How are things going with the preparations for the dinner?" Chloe slapped a soft hand against her forehead. It shouldn't be this difficult, but her friend had a tendency to freak out when things went awry as they had last night. Bullet holes in the admin hallway had likely raised quite a few eyebrows this morning. Jan probably wasn't the only one freaking out.

"Oh, the dinner." Jan gave a soft laugh. "Oh, well, let me see here." Pages turned. "Yes, here we go. The caterer is booked for June seventeenth. If you don't like that date let me know soon and we can change it."

"Hold on a second. I have my planner right here." Chloe reached for the leather-bound book and flipped it open to that page. "That date looks good. I'll write it down now. What else do you have?"

"I've already contacted a rental company for chairs. I sort of assumed we're having the dinner in the lobby of the visitor's center. You never mentioned anywhere else, but it's so big, it would be perfect for it. Did you have another venue in mind?"

Chloe thought for a moment. "How many people are you inviting?"

"Two Hundred and fifty. The capacity is more than three hundred."

"Then, yes, let's hold it in the lobby." Chloe liked that idea. It would bring the donors to the place where the colonel's diary would be housed. "How about decorators?"

"I have bids for three different companies. All have appointments to come out next week and their ideas with me. They were supposed to have already come and looked at the lobby as a venue." Pages turned again. "I think that's all I have for you now. Since we have a solid date for the event, I can start moving things faster."

"That's great, Jan. Thank you. Let me know when you've talked to the decorators. I want to see what all three of their ideas are before you make a decision. I'd like to have some input in that."

"Sure thing. Thank you. Oh, and Chloe? I'm so glad you and Cliff are ok. And I'm glad Officer Hunter wasn't hurt more than he was."

"Yeah, me too." Chloe sighed. "Have you seen Ian? He wasn't around last night, and he's usually helping us out."

Jan giggled. "Yeah, well…um…we were on a…date last night."

Chloe pulled her phone from her ear and blinked at it. A date? Jan and Ian?

She returned the phone to her ear. "You were on a date? With Ian?"

"Yeah." Jan's voice couldn't get any dreamier. She sounded more like a fifteen-year-old.

"Since when did this happen?"

"It was our first. We went to a movie then afterward we went to Moira's for coffee and dessert." A wistful sigh filled Chloe's ear. "He is one hunky man, isn't he?"

It was all Chloe could do not to laugh out loud. "Well, yeah, he's…he's a good-looking guy. That's for sure. I'm assuming you had a nice time."

"Oh, I had a wonderful time."

A mental picture of Jan floating up around the ceiling in her office nearly had Chloe laughing aloud again.

"Ok, well I need to go. I have work, and you have things to do too. Have a great day."

"You too, Chloe. Talk soon. Bye."

Chloe shook her head as she dropped her phone on the desktop in her room. Jan and Ian? Wow! Who knew? They would make a cute couple though. She shrugged. Antietam National Battlefield at Sharpsburg, Maryland, where Ian worked wasn't that far from Gettysburg.

She booted her laptop and spent time looking for historic building restoration and preservation contractors. The park had used a couple companies in the past, and she'd start with them. She made several phone calls and set up appointments to have the contractors come out to give their expert opinions on the Bryant house and what it would take to restore it to its pre-Civil War condition.

Chloe had just leaned back in her chair when her cell phone rang. Clifford. After last night's debacle, what could be happening now? Chloe grabbed the phone and pressed the answer button. "What is it, Cliff?"

"Well, it's not an emergency. Your voice sounds a bit fearful." He chuckled.

Chloe heaved a sigh of relief. "Thank goodness."

"I know. After last night, it was the first thing you thought of, right?"

"Well, yeah."

"Breathe, my friend, then listen up. Ian and I are at the Bryant house. We decided to go back inside the wall and take a look around. You know, comb the area where Sarge lay all those years to see if we could find anything else of significance. Forensically speaking."

Chloe rolled her eyes. He could go on and on. "Ok, and did you find anything? Forensically speaking?"

Clifford chuckled. "Yes, we did. It wasn't actually where the Sarge was lying, but we found it behind one of the legs of the table against the wall."

"The table?" Chloe remembered seeing a small drop leaf table against the root cellar wall and reading about the table in Cecelia's diary. "That's the table Cecelia mentioned when Sarge wanted the other soldier to sign the paper against the officer that ended up killing Sarge."

"That's the one."

"So what did you find behind the table leg?" Chloe leaned back in her chair.

"We found a brass cap engraved with some letters. It's pretty grimy, so we're going to take it back to the office and clean it up, but I would bet it might have come off the end of one of two things."

"What do you think it came from?"

"Well, Ian's and my combined educated guesses would say the engraved cap came from the end of a walking cane."

That was a common item gentlemen in the mid-1800s would have used. "Cliff, you said it might have come from one of two things."

"Yes, I did. Our second guess, and the one most likely in this instance, would be the engraved cap from the pommel of a saber."

~

Blake stared at his supervisor, his last words ringing in his ears. *Go home and don't come back for at least four weeks.* What in the world was he going to do for a month? He wasn't good at simply hanging around the house. A sigh drifted out. No. Not at all. "Sir, won't you reconsider? I'm doing much better already." He attempted to add levity to his voice and hide his difficulty in breathing.

"Not a chance. I can't risk your life or someone else's because you're not up to par." Chief Morton, a former Marine, stared him square in the eye. Blake had the notion to shift from foot to foot like a second grader, but stood firm, not batting an eyelash.

"I understand, sir."

"Good. You're an impeccable officer, Hunter, and a great asset to this force. I'm happy to have you on board, but I want you in tiptop shape when you're on duty." The chief stood and came around the desk. He held out his hand to Blake, and Blake shook it. "Go home and heal, then come back ready to work when you are. But not before a month. I'll check in on you from time to time to see how you're doing."

Blake left his supervisor's office and headed up to check on the historians. To see Chloe and hear her voice would be balm to his weary soul right about now. Climbing the stairs to the admin office floor and down to the historian's office left him short of breath. He hated to admit his supervisor was right—he did need to heal, but it wouldn't be a fun process. Stopping in front of the historian's office door, he tried the knob and found it locked. Knocking on the solid wooden surface garnered him no response.

Hmm. Where could Chloe and Cliff be? After their long night, Blake had gone home and slept for a few hours before answering the call to his supervisor. Perhaps Chloe and Cliff had slept in as well. Should he call Chloe? It was nearly noon. Surely, she would be up by now. Maybe he'd call Cliff first. But Blake's body's signals indicated he needed to sit down. He made his way to his cruiser and climbed in. He'd have to park it at his house and start using his pickup truck for a while.

Once inside the cruiser Blake dialed Clifford's number and the historian picked up after a few rings.

"Hello?"

"Hi. It's Blake."

"Oh, hey. How are you? How are the ribs?"

"Well, they hurt."

"Yeah, I guess they would. What's up?"

"I've just been told by my supervisor not to come back for a month until I've healed, I'm at loose ends. Was just wondering what's up with you and Chloe?" More Chloe, but Blake wouldn't go there.

"Oh, that stinks, but it makes sense. Can't have a park cop who can't perform his duties." Clifford mumbled something. "Oh sorry. Was talking to Ian."

"You and Ian are working together? Where are you?"

"We're out at the Bryant place. Want to come by? We found something kind of neat."

"Yeah? Is Chloe there?" Blake almost wished he could withdraw his second question, but he wanted—no, needed—to know.

"Nope, she's not here right now. Matter of fact, she's not been out here since we removed Sarge. None of us have been. But I noticed something." His voice grew pensive.

"What's that?"

"When I attempted to open the lock to the cellar door today, it was hard to open. The lock's never been that way before. It's always been easy to open."

Blake's mind instantly went to the man examining the lock the day he came by the house. "Hmm. That's interesting. I'll drop by and take a look."

"Sure. That'd be great." Clifford paused. "Oh, by the way, we had a visitor today."

"Yeah? Who?" Blake couldn't imagine who it could be.

"You'll never guess, so I'll tell you. Mrs. White-Smith." Clifford's voice sounded less than pleased.

"What was she doing out there?"

"She told us she was out driving around the battlefield and spotted the house. Said she adores old houses, and when she saw cars here decided to stop and see if she could ask someone about it."

"You're kidding, right? She didn't see the Park Service No Trespassing sign?"

"Sure, she did." Clifford's voice dripped with sarcasm. "She's a rich old lady who thinks the world will drop at her feet and rules can be bent at her whim. I had to escort her back to her car and tell her to leave the property. She was less than happy with me and threatened to call the superintendent, and I told her to go for it."

Blake chuckled. "Good for you, Cliff. Stick to your guns."

"Oh, I will. I don't have time for that kind of nonsense." A sigh rolled across cyberspace then a short pause. "You like her, don't you?"

"Mrs. White-Smith?" From Clifford's voice, Blake knew exactly who "her" he was talking about.

"What? No, not Mrs. White-Smith. Chloe." Clifford guffawed. "You like Chloe. A lot. I can tell."

"Oh yeah? How can you tell?" Blake wasn't sure he wanted to know. Clifford almost always had his nose stuck in a book, a dried-up body, or an examination of something historically significant, so how had he noticed Blake was interested in Chloe?

"It's simple. You can't keep your eyes off of her." Clifford chuckled. "And you're always dropping by when she's around."

Mumbled words sounded in the background.

"Exactly."

"What did Ian say?" Blake asked.

"He said when I asked if you wanted to come by, you asked if Chloe was here before you even considered answering my question. Yep. We've got you pegged, man. You like Chloe."

Blake rubbed the bridge of his nose. "That's not proof of anything, except I asked if Chloe was there too. I went by your office just now, and the door was locked. Obviously, neither of you are there, so I called you first and found you. I simply asked if she was there."

After a brief silence on the phone, Cliff said, "Oh." Another silence. Then, "Well, what about the way you can't keep your eyes off of her? Deny the fact you like her, Blake."

Blake sighed. "I can't deny I like Chloe, Cliff. I like her a lot. There are you happy?"

A chuckle filled Blake's ear. "Actually, yes, I am. She needs to find love again, and you're a good guy. I approve. You've got my blessing."

Something shifted in the region of Blake's heart. Although he'd pretty much made the decision to pursue a relationship with Chloe, it was encouraging to know one of her co-workers approved.

More mumbling came from the background.

"Ian says likewise." Clifford spoke again. "He's known Chloe for several years, and there's no one he's met that he'd rather see Chloe in a relationship with."

"Really?" Blake always thought Ian was the one who was interested in Chloe. "He's genuinely okay with me pursuing her?"

"Yep. Go for it." Clifford said. "Look, why don't you come on over and see what we've found. It's pretty cool. Since you're at loose ends, what else have you got to do?"

Chapter Twelve

Chloe finished talking with another historic restoration contractor and took a drink of water from the bottle on her desk. Her phone rang and she glanced at the screen. She didn't recognize the number. Could it be one of the contractors she'd already called? "Hello?"

"Miss. Rogers? It's Maureen White-Smith. How are you today?"

Chloe attempted to switch gears from dealing with contractors to dealing with the park donor. She needed a totally different demeanor with this woman. "Oh, Mrs. White-Smith. I'm fine. How are you today?"

"I'm well, thank you. I'm calling to find out how the plans for the donor affair are coming along."

A picture of the aristocratic woman appeared before Chloe's mind's eye, her patrician nose most likely in the air as usual, but her voice held a cheery note.

"It's going quite well. I received a report today, and it's scheduled for June seventeenth. My event coordinator has everything well in hand." Chloe crossed her fingers and sent up a quick plea of *Please Lord*, then was surprised the tiny prayer slipped so easily heavenward. She'd have to think about this later when she didn't have Mrs. White-Smith on the line.

"That's wonderful. Such grand news, Miss. Rogers."

"You know, you're welcome to call me Chloe, if you like."

"Yes, of course...Chloe." The word dripped from the woman's tongue like molasses. Sticky and distasteful.

Chloe sighed and rolled her eyes. She wouldn't push the issue if it ever came up again.

There was a pause on the line so Chloe asked, "Is there anything else I can help you with?"

"Well, actually, perhaps there is. I was driving through the battlefield this morning, and I saw an old house near the outskirts of town. It looked abandoned so I stopped to take a look around. However, it seemed rather forbidding, so I didn't want to get too close. It's located on Emmitsburg Road. Do you know anything about that house?"

"If it's the one I think you're talking about, the park has recently acquired that property from a private owner, and we're contemplating a restoration. I'm locating restoration contractors now who can tell us if restoration is feasible or not."

A delicate gasp met Chloe's ears. "Oh my, but that would be fantastic, wouldn't it? I had a home restored that belonging to one of my ancestors. Actually, it was the Colonel's. You know, my great-great-grandfather Col. Edgar William Mayfield. The home is in Connecticut, and, of course, we used a restoration contractor from that state. I'm sure it would depend on their licensing, but many of those contractors have licenses for various states due to the fact they have such a narrow field of expertise. I can give you the name and number of my contractor if you're interested. He did a phenomenal restoration on the Colonel's home."

Although Chloe thought she had enough contractors to bid on the job, it wouldn't hurt to look into this one as well. "Certainly, I would appreciate that."

"Hold on a moment while I look at the contacts in my phone." A pause followed then Mrs. White-Smith gave Chloe the contractor's information. "There. Don't fail to give him a call."

"Yes, of course. Thank you."

"I'll let you go, Miss. Rogers. Have a wonderful afternoon."

The call ended before Chloe could respond. Obviously dismissed, she didn't miss the fact the woman had reverted to calling her Miss. Rogers again. Chloe supposed she preferred keeping people at arm's length. That was fine with her.

~

Blake examined the padlock from the cellar door at the Bryant house. Tiny scratches around the keyhole indicated something sharp other than the key had been used to open or attempt to open the lock. He shoved the shackle into its locked position then inserted the key into the keyhole, turning it. Definitely harder to open, as Clifford had told him. Could the tumblers have been damaged when someone inserted something other than the correct key? Blake turned harder, and with a scraping sound, the tumblers moved, and the shackle opened.

Oh, his ribs ached. With a mandate to go home and rest, here he was investigating a damaged lock on government property. His boss wouldn't be happy if he heard about this. Blake would have Clifford call maintenance to place a hidden-shackle combination lock on the door. It would be harder to break into than this one. Someone wanted in this cellar for a reason. He only wished he knew the identity of the guy he'd come across that day. Was it the same one who had nearly beat the tar out of him?

"Well, what did you find?" Clifford stepped out of the cellar. "Has it been tampered with?"

"It seems so." Blake handed the lock and key to him. "Call maintenance and have them replace it ASAP." After giving him instructions on the kind they needed to replace it with, he added, "Someone wants in this cellar. Why do you think that is?"

"I have no idea. There's nothing left in here. Oh, except what we found today. Come on in. I'll show you." Clifford showed Blake the grimy brass cap and explained what he and Ian thought it might be. "What do you think of this?"

"You think it belonged to the murderer, don't you?" Blake turned the cap over between his fingers.

"Yeah, we do, but until we clean it up, we can't read what's engraved on it. Initials were popular on sabers and walking canes back then, so if that's what it is, it could be a clue to help us find out who it belonged to." Clifford ran a hand through his unruly hair.

"True," Blake handed it back to him, "or it belonged to the man who owned the house."

Clifford's brows furrowed. "I hadn't thought of that."

"Neither did I." Ian leaned a shoulder against the brick wall. "I suppose that's why we need a level-headed cop who can see things from a different perspective."

Blake gave them a two-fingered salute. "Glad to help. Anything else you need some clarity on? If not, I'm going home. My ribs and my back are on fire. I need to lay down for a while."

"No, you go on home. Take it easy and we'll see you soon." Clifford walked with him to the door.

"See you, Blake. Take it easy." Ian called after him.

Blake raised a hand in response.

"I'll call maintenance as soon as you leave. Hopefully, they'll come out today." Clifford stepped out into the sunshine behind Blake.

"Thanks. I appreciate it."

"Thanks for taking a look at the lock and determining that someone had tampered with it. I can't understand why they would want to go into the cellar." Clifford shook his head.

Blake started to walk away then stopped and turned around. "By the way, have you heard any more footsteps since you've been working here today?"

Clifford's eyebrows rose as he shook his head. "Now that you mention it, no, I haven't. It's been quiet since we've been here, and we've been here since mid-morning."

Blake nodded. "Interesting. See you soon."

~

At four o'clock Saturday afternoon, Chloe's phone alarm went off, reminding her of the dinner date she and Blake had arranged. She turned off the alarm and watched as her daughter played in the backyard. It was a gorgeous June afternoon and sitting on the patio swing with a good book was one of her favorite things to do. Chloe had an hour and a half before Blake was scheduled to pick her up. He hadn't called to say he wouldn't be able to keep their date, so she would get ready as planned. Hopefully, he was feeling well enough to go, and it hadn't slipped his mind to call.

Aunt Charlene was in her usual haunt, the kitchen.

"Aunt Char? I'm going to get ready to go. Evie's still out playing. I don't know where she gets her energy, but I'd like to tap into the source. I could sure use it most days."

"I know what you mean, sweetie. That girl is a whirling dervish. She doesn't stop until her head hits the pillow. Then it's recharge time." Aunt Char measured ingredients into a bowl. "So where are you going again? And with whom?"

Chloe sighed, ready for the inquisition. Again. "Out to dinner with Blake Hunter, park police."

"Oh yes. And is he handsome?" Aunt Charlene's gaze met

Chloe's over the upper rim of her reading glasses sitting on the end of her nose.

"Some might think so." Chloe shrugged and quirked her lips. "I suppose he's nice looking. In a rugged Marlboro Man sort of way. Only not as old."

Aunt Charlene's mouth hung open. "Are you joshing me? The Marlboro Man was one handsome dude, no matter what his age."

Chloe chuckled and turned to leave the room. "You would say that. Not everyone remembers the cigarette commercials with the handsome cowboy. You're more his age, you know." She ducked as a balled-up kitchen towel came flying in her direction. "If the shoe fits…."

"We'll see who fits the shoe…." Aunt Charlene's voice faded as Chloe ran to her room. She loved teasing her aunt, and there was no doubt Aunt Charlene loved teasing back.

Chloe opened her closet and began sliding hangers. Blake had suggested a nice skirt and blouse or a Sunday dress for the restaurant this evening. Hmm. Which one? She pulled out a couple of favorites to view in the cheval mirror that stood in the corner beside her desk. One, a peach jersey knit with rounded neckline, tulip sleeves and a swingy skirt. It brought out the natural peach highlights in her skin and was a great foil to her blond hair. Second, a cotton powder-blue button-down dress with tiny white flowers. This sleeveless dress sported a square neckline and a narrow matching belt that set off Chloe's slim waist. She held first one then the other against her figure, examining them in the mirror.

There was no doubt about it. She returned the blue one to the closet and hung the peach dress on the closet door frame. Hurrying into the bathroom, she showered and dressed. A half hour later she stood before the bathroom mirror trying to decide what to do with her hair. A ponytail was her daily style, but she wanted something different for this evening. A grimace settled on the reflection in the mirror. What to do? She had never been good at French braids, but she loved the stylish clean lines, and she knew someone with the talent to produce them. "Oh, Aunt Char?!"

Twenty minutes later, Aunt Charlene patted Chloe's hair, tugged a few more tendrils loose in the right places, and gave it a couple more spritzes of hairspray.

"There. It's beautiful and you're gorgeous. This young

Marlboro Man of yours is going to be tongue tied, you wait and see."

"It is beautiful, Aunt Char." Chloe released a sigh and smiled, turning to give her aunt a hug. "I love you and thank you for making me feel beautiful."

"I love you, too, Sweetie." Aunt Charlene returned Chloe's hug then held her back, her hands on her upper arms. "You *are* beautiful."

Warmth flowed through Chloe. "Thanks."

Her aunt sniffed and brushed at her cheeks. "Now, go on and finish getting ready. Marlboro Man will be here shortly."

Aunt Charlene left and Chloe took out her makeup. A quick application then she slipped into a pair of low-heeled tan summer sandals. She dropped the necessities into a small tan shoulder bag, and voilà, she was ready.

The doorbell rang. Chloe took a quick final glance in the cheval mirror and hurried down the hallway. She stepped into the family room as her dad opened the front door.

"Good evening, Officer Hunter. Won't you come in?" Dan opened the door wider and Chloe spotted Blake on the front porch.

"Thank you, sir." He stepped inside, not having seen her yet.

Chloe waited by the hallway entrance.

"Won't you have a seat." Dad waved a hand toward the seating area.

"Well, I…." Blake's gaze landed on Chloe and his words ceased.

Chloe smiled, seeing the appreciation in his gaze. Another gaze drew hers, and she glanced at Aunt Charlene standing near the kitchen. *I told you so* was imprinted plainly on her features. Blake did indeed seem to be tongue tied. Her aunt's expression morphed to concern as her eyes darted back to Blake.

"Oh, good gracious, Officer Hunter! What in the world happened to you?" Aunt Charlene approached and stood in front of him, studying him as if he was a specimen in a science lab. "You look as if you went ten rounds with a boxer. And lost."

"Aunt Charlene!" Chloe gasped at her aunt's boldness.

Blake gave a half grin. "No, it's okay. She's right. I do look pretty frightful."

Chloe looked closer and had to agree with her aunt. The side of Blake's face was black and blue from his lower jawline up to his eye.

Dad stepped closer and propped his hands on his hips. "Your supervisor sent me a report that you'd been attacked and are now on paid leave. I had no idea how injured you are."

"Sir, please call me Blake."

"Dad, that's not all." Chloe piped in. "He has three cracked ribs, a bruised kidney and a bruised shoulder. The perp nailed him with a marble stature."

Aunt Char gasped, her expression distressed. She turned to Chloe. "That's terrible. Is that what happened the other night when you were locked in your office?"

Chloe nodded.

Blake shifted from one foot to the other, obviously uncomfortable with being the center of attention.

"We need to go. I believe Blake has dinner reservations for us." Chloe put her hand on the crook of Blake's elbow, and he immediately brought his arm up and escorted her toward the front door. "We'll talk with you both later."

"Oh sure, honey." Dad walked behind them and held the door as they exited. "Have a great evening. See you later."

Blake held the truck door for Chloe as she climbed in, then he walked around the front and struggled into the driver's seat. He turned the key in the ignition. "I hope you don't mind riding in a pickup truck."

Chloe laughed softly and shrugged. "I don't mind. I like trucks." She pointed at the pickup sitting in the driveway. "My dad has one, and I ride with him on occasion. Evie rides with him a lot."

"Evie? Your little girl. I didn't see her." Blake backed the truck out of the driveway and pointed it in the direction of town.

Chloe smiled. "No, she was in the backyard. That child would live outside if she could, but we coax her to do inside activities sometimes too. You can meet her next time."

Blake turned his half grin on her. "Will there be a next time?"

Warmth flowed over Chloe and upward into her face. She turned toward her window hoping Blake wouldn't notice. "We'll see."

~

Was that a tinge of red coloring Chloe's cheeks at Blake's question? Or was it just a reflection of the late afternoon sun? Blake hoped her slip of the tongue about a next date was a sign she was ready for a relationship. Now that his decision to move on had been made, perhaps she'd make the same one. *Please, Lord, let it be.*

The restaurant Blake had chosen was only minutes away. He parked the truck and came around to open her door and help her out.

"Thank you." Chloe smiled as he took her hand and placed it in the crook of his arm. "Such a gentleman."

"What can I say? My mama taught me right." He winked.

"I'll say." Chloe winked back, exaggerating the movement. She released a giggle that tiptoed down his spine.

Blake's breath caught. A sudden desire to catch her close and drop a kiss on those tempting lips nearly overwhelmed him. Chloe never ceased to surprise him. One minute she didn't seem to like him much, and the next she was a tease. At this moment, he felt off-kilter. Like he was toeing the edge of a wall, ready to fall off into a blissful sea of joy. Was this love? What he'd thought was love for Michelle was nothing like this. Not even close.

Chloe chattered something about the restaurant, but he missed most of it. He needed to pay attention before he made a fool of himself.

"You know what I mean?" She turned to him as he opened the door of the restaurant for her.

Uh oh. Blake's heart pounded. Yep. He was going to make a fool of himself.

It must have been evident on his face because her brows furrowed. "You didn't catch that, did you?"

Blake opened his mouth to speak, but before he could utter a word, she continued. "It's all right. I understand. You've had a lot on your mind with the attack, and I know you're probably still in pain."

As the door closed behind them, she whipped around, placing a hand on his chest, the other over her lips, concern etching her features. She dropped her hand from her lips. "Oh, I'm so sorry, I should've thought to offer to drive. You're probably still in pain and on pain meds. Or, you probably skipped your pain meds so you *could* drive. What was I thinking?"

Blake swallowed hard. Her hand on his chest seemed to burn a hole right through his shirt. He found breathing nearly impossible. How was he ever going to answer her questions? Licking his lips, he inhaled. "Well, I—"

"Excuse me, sir. Do you have a reservation?" a cultured voice interrupted.

Blake's gaze slid from Chloe to the tuxedoed man behind a wooden podium. He stared at them down a long, slim nose beneath a bald pate surrounded by a slicked back graying fringe. His pursed lips indicated growing impatience.

Blake clasped Chloe's hand and drew her over to the podium. "Yes, we do. The last name is Hunter. First name is Blake."

The man ran a bony finger down a list. "Ah yes, here we are." He snapped his fingers, and a younger man in burgundy suit and tie with a snowy white shirt made an instant appearance. His hair was slicked back without a hair out of place.

The maître d' passed the young man two leather-bound menus, then the young man bowed and asked them to follow him. He led them to a lovely table for two in a garden beside a tinkling brook. As the sun began to lower in the west, strings of lights cast a gentle and beautiful glow along with discreetly hidden lights that lit the flowerbeds.

"Oh, my goodness, this is delightful. I love the atmosphere." Chloe tucked her hands in her lap and leaned toward Blake. "Even though you can see other diners nearby, there's a sense you're dining privately out here. What a beautiful idea. Have you been here before?"

Blake shook his head. "No, but one of the guys at work brings his wife here on special occasions."

Chloe glanced at the stream, colorful flowers and greenery along its banks. "I can see why. It's a special place."

Blake's gaze trailed along the curved line of Chloe's neck from her delicate ear down to her neckline and across to her shoulder. He lifted it back to follow along her jawline, chin and the features of her face. Chloe was a beautiful woman. He closed his eyes for a moment. *Breathe, man, breathe. Deep breaths. And stop staring or she'll catch you.*

Chloe's eyes met his. "Thanks for bringing me here."

He tossed her his half grin, then turned to examine his surroundings. "My pleasure. It is pretty special. I haven't been to many restaurants in town. I usually stop at Moira's and grab something, or I fix something at home."

Interest sparked in Chloe's blue gaze. "Are you a cook?"

Blake shrugged. "I've been known to cook on occasion. I'm not an all-out chef, if that's what you're asking, but I don't mind preparing a good dish if the need arises."

Chloe met his gaze before opening her menu. "Blake, are you sure you're okay to be here? We don't have to stay if you're in a lot of pain, and we can—"

Blake reached across and took her hand from the menu. "Chloe, I'm fine. Really, I am. I appreciate your concern, but I don't want to be anywhere else right now. Right here in this beautiful place with you is where I want to be. Now, let's enjoy our evening. Okay?"

Chloe gave him a smile that made him catch his breath, then she opened her menu and began perusing it. "Hmm. There are some wonderful dishes on the menu."

Blake opened his own menu and began to search down the lists. "Do you cook?"

"Well, I can, but I don't get much opportunity." Chloe flipped a page. "Aunt Char does most of the cooking at home. She spends a lot of time in the kitchen, and that's okay with me. I stay pretty busy, and when I'm home, I'd rather spend my free time with Evie."

The waiter appeared to take their orders then left them alone to continue their discussion.

"Has your aunt been with you long?" Blake picked up his water glass and took a drink.

"My mom died six years ago from leukemia." Chloe clasped her hands in her lap. "Aunt Char is Dad's only sister and was a travel photographer and author. When my mom died, she decided it was a good time to retire and moved in to help my dad out. Three years ago, my husband, Josh, died in Afghanistan. A roadside IED blew up his vehicle. He survived the explosion, although he was severely injured."

A shadow cross Chloe's face. "You don't have to tell me this. I'm sorry I brought up a discussion that led to bad memories."

Chloe lifted tortured eyes to his but smiled, her lips curving softly. She shook her head. "I'm okay. It's important that I talk about it. I used to wall it up inside and refused to talk. Now it's becoming much easier than it used to be." Her hands rested on the tabletop, one on the other. "Josh was drawn into a fight along with his fellow soldiers in spite of his injures. He had no choice. They defeated the enemy, but there were casualties. Josh was shot and killed in the fight."

"I'm so sorry, Chloe." Blake's throat threatened to close up. How could he help this hurting woman that meant so much to him?

She reached across and gave his hand a squeeze, releasing it immediately. "Thanks, but as I said, I'm fine. It's true what they say, you know. Time does heal all wounds. I'm not there yet, but I can tell I'm going to get there. Anyway, Evie and I moved in with Dad and Aunt Char after Josh's death. We've been one happy, healing family since. Dad still misses mom, but he's actually had a few dates. None that continue to the next step, but at least he's making the effort. Aunt Char was widowed early in life, and she's dated off and on throughout her life, but I've come to the conclusion she's happy being single."

"And you? Are you ready to move on?" Blake was surprised the softly worded question popped out. *Was that You, Lord? I didn't plan to ask that now. What if she says no?*

~

Blake's question took Chloe by surprise. She'd been asking herself that question recently when she'd seen the interest in his gaze, but to hear him ask it out loud brought the topic to a whole new level. Her heart pounded. What could she say? She didn't want to be alone forever, and Evie needed a dad.

Her head seemed to nod of its own volition, and a smile lifted the corners of Blake's lips, even the injured side. Chloe blinked as her heartbeat slowed. Peace settled over her. A desire to talk to the Lord washed over her. It had been so long, and it wasn't the first time. Perhaps it was time.

"So let me just clarify here." Blake leaned forward. "From your nod you're telling me you're ready to move on and perhaps move into a relationship. That is, should you find someone who you'd like to have a relationship with."

Chloe nodded again, this time with more assurance. "Yes, I

believe I would. That is, if I found the right person. I would have to take a lot into consideration, you know."

Blake narrowed his gaze. "Like what?"

"Well, I'm not going to get into any relationship just for the fun of it. It's going to be with the goal of forever in mind. I have a young daughter to think about. She needs a father, and if the guy isn't ready for that—" Chloe shrugged and spread her hands wide, "—he can hit the road."

Blake nodded. "Understood. That's a serious responsibility for any man to take on, and if he's not ready for that, he shouldn't even try. But you and your daughter are worth having, Chloe. Any man would be blessed to build a family with you two."

Chloe's heart lifted with joy at his words. What a thoughtful thing to say. It made her decision to put the past in the past and move forward a little easier.

Their food came and they remained silent for a time as they ate, then their conversation delved into the matter that concerned them both.

"Cliff told me the lock on the cellar door at the Bryant house was tampered with." Chloe wiped her mouth with her napkin. "He said you took a look at it. What are your thoughts?"

"Looks to me like someone attempted to break in. It's a decent lock, but I suggested Cliff call maintenance to replace it with a better one. I don't understand why anyone would want into the cellar. There's nothing there."

Chloe shook her head and picked up her water glass. "If they broke into our office and destroyed the Sarge's body, perhaps they think there's evidence of something more in the cellar. When I read Cecelia Langston's diary, she mentioned Sarge wanted another soldier to sign a paper on that table inside the walled area. I wish I knew what happened to that paper. It's possible the murderer took it with him."

Blake heaved a heavy sigh. "Then it could be gone forever."

~

Chloe accepted Blake's hand as he helped her out of the truck. What an amazing evening. When had she changed from not wanting to ever consider another relationship to being okay with going out with a guy?

Blake closed the truck door but didn't release her hand as they strolled along the sidewalk toward the front door. He twined his fingers with hers and slowed his steps. The light from the front lamppost lit the way, and someone had left the porchlight on. Chloe smiled to herself. Dad.

"I had a wonderful time this evening, Blake. Thanks for taking me. It's been a while, and to be honest, I haven't wanted to go out, but I'm glad I did."

Blake gave her hand a gentle squeeze. "I'm glad you did, too, because I enjoy your company."

They stepped onto the porch, Blake still holding Chloe's hand. He turned to face her. "Chloe, I would like to kiss you, but I don't want to do anything you're not ready for." He lifted her hand and pressed a gentle kiss on her knuckles. "I'll settle for that unless you tell me you're okay with a real kiss." His eyes traveled to her lips, and Chloe's heartbeat quickened.

She smiled. "Well, it's been a while since I've been kissed except on the cheek. You know what I mean. As you say, not a real kiss." Her voice dropped to a whisper on the last words. "I suppose it wouldn't hurt to try one." Chloe's heartbeat fluttered at the expression that settled on Blake's features. A smile grew as he lowered his head.

"I'll be happy to oblige," he whispered before pressing his lips to hers.

Oh, the sweet sensations that swept over Chloe as his arms gathered her close. Then he pulled away, his gaze searching hers.

"Are you all right?" Blake leaned his forehead against Chloe's.

"Did I say to try *only* one?" She smiled.

The light in his eyes grew brighter as he lowered his head once again.

Chapter Thirteen

Monday morning, Chloe spotted the restoration contractor's phone number that Mrs. White-Smith had given her still waiting on her desk. She already had a few appointments set up to meet with local contractors, and once they visited the house, they would put in bids to do the job. But what would it hurt to get one more if they were licensed to work in Pennsylvania? Northeast Antique Homes Restoration Specialists had come highly recommended by Mrs. White-Smith, and only by calling and talking with them would she find out if they could work on the Bryant house.

Chloe made the call and was pleasantly surprised to find they indeed were licensed to restore homes in Pennsylvania. She set up an appointment for their contractor to come and look at the house on Wednesday. With all the appointments she'd made, she would have a busy week.

After she'd hung up, Chloe dressed to go into the office. Dad had already left for work, but Aunt Charlene handed her a note from him when she walked into the kitchen to grab a bite for breakfast.

"What's this?" Chloe aimed a curious glance at her aunt and fingered the folded slip of paper.

Aunt Charlene shrugged. "How should I know? He simply said, 'Give this to Chloe before she leaves the house,' so I did."

"What is it, Mommy?" Evie sat on a stool at the kitchen bar eating a bowl of cereal. She slurped milk from her spoon.

Chloe dropped a kiss on her daughter's head. "Morning, princess. It's a note from Grandpa."

She opened the folded page.

Good morning, Chloe. You didn't mention if you had gone into the safe and checked out the items you deposited there or not, but I might remind you they're still there. You know, out of sight, out of mind. You told me your bony body was destroyed at the office. Those are his personal effects. Perhaps there's something in them that will help. Thank goodness you brought them home.

Love,
Dad

Chloe gasped. "Oh, my goodness. How could I have forgotten?"

"Forgotten what?" Aunt Charlene removed Evie's empty cereal bowl and placed a warm buttered muffin in front of her.

Chloe dropped the note to her side and stared at her child. "Gracious. You're going to eat a bowl of cereal *and* a muffin?"

Evie bit into the crumbly goodness, butter smearing along her upper lip. She nodded happily then took a drink from her milk glass adding to the food mustache.

Chloe locked eyes with her aunt as the older woman leaned a hip against the counter.

"Another growth spurt?" Chloe asked.

"Yep." Aunt Charlene shrugged. "Seems to happen about once a month now. So, what did you forget?"

Chloe sighed and lifted the note again. "I forgot all about putting those personal effects from the soldier we found into Dad's safe. There are some letters and a photo as well as some smoking tobacco and a pipe."

"Hmm. How interesting. You have a fascinating job, Chloe. Lucky girl. Some of the things you come across are simply amazing."

"I'm blessed." Chloe turned to head back to her room. "I have to get the combination to the safe." In a short time, she had the safe open and the items sitting on her dad's desk. Chloe closed the safe door and spun the combination wheel to the right and then back to the left several times. She closed the door on the credenza to hide the safe and swiveled to find Aunt Charlene observing the items in the clear bag.

"Amazing. To think that poor man used to smoke that tobacco in that pipe. I bet he used to sit and ponder life. I wonder if he had a wife?"

Chloe opened the bag and pulled out the old daguerreotype of the beautiful young woman. "I would love to know her name as much as I would Sarge's. I don't know if she was his wife or a fiancé. Unless I can find something in those letters, we may never know."

Aunt Charlene took the picture. "What a shame. This lovely young lady probably had a broken heart, never knowing what happened to her young man. What a sad story." She handed the picture back to Chloe. "Someone is going to answer before God one day for that man's murder. He may have thought he got away Scot free, and maybe no one knows who it was, but God knows."

Chloe returned the picture to the bag. "Yes, he will. And yes, He does." When Chloe had finished her breakfast, she slipped Sarge's personal effects into her messenger bag, said her goodbyes to Evie and Aunt Charlene and stepped outside to a gentle summer rain.

~

"What are you working on there?" Chloe entered the examination room and leaned over the table to observe as Clifford worked on a delicate brass knob. About an inch by an inch in diameter, the knob looked to be mottled and dirty. Clifford examined his work through a large, lighted magnifying glass. "Is that what you found in the Bryant cellar?"

Clifford took another careful swipe with a long damp swab then straightened. "The very same. It's so encrusted, I've had to soak it, and it's still been difficult to clean. As you can see, the brass cleans in some areas, but not so much in others. I think there's something on the surface preventing the cleaner from reaching the brass. There's definitely an engraving on the end cap, and I can make out a partial initial, but the rest simply isn't clean enough yet. I'm frustrated but determined."

"That's the spirit." Chloe patted his shoulder. "What's Ian up to today?"

Clifford picked up another swab and dipped it into the cleaning solution before applying it. "He's helping one of the maintenance men take down the wall. Since we determined it's not original to the house, we're taking it down. Or rather, they are. I offered to help, but Ian said this was more important and only one of us could work on it."

"Great. That wall represents the hiding of an unholy act and the sooner it's gone the better." Chloe watched Clifford work, willing the dirt away to reveal the engraving.

"Agreed."

"I have several appointments this week with restoration contractors to look at the house. Hopefully we'll get some bids soon so we can move forward on the restoration."

"Cool." Clifford's voice rose with excitement but his gaze never left his work. "I'm looking forward to that."

"Me too." Chloe straightened. "I have Sarge's personal effects from home. While I have a few minutes, I'm going to take a gander at them. If you need anything, I'll be at my desk."

"No problem."

Settling in, Chloe booted her computer and pulled out the bags with Sarge's personal effects. She had opened one of the bags when her phone rang. "Hello?"

"Chloe? It's Jan. Are you in your office today or still working from home?"

"Oh, hi. I'm in the office. What's up?" Chloe leaned back in her chair.

"Well, you wanted me to let you know when the decorators all had their ideas and bids in. I have them."

Chloe sat up straight and leaned an elbow on the edge of the desk. "But you said they wouldn't send those in until sometime this week."

Jan's tinkling laugh filled her ear. "It's crazy, isn't it. They all showed up Friday and sent me their electronic décor photos, their color sketches and job bids this morning. Guess they knew this was a big government contract and there'd be competition."

Chloe gazed longingly at Sarge's effects and released an inaudible sigh. "Okay, I'll be right over."

"Thanks, Chloe. There are some amazing sketches here. It's going to be tough to choose."

Chloe hung up and slipped the bag of effects back into her messenger bag. She hesitated to leave it here unattended, so she carried it with her. Somehow leaving it in the examination room didn't even feel safe anymore. At least not until the guy who destroyed Sarge was caught.

Chloe spent an hour and a half in Jan's office looking at the photos and sketches. Jan was right. The three decorator companies knew their stuff. They were comparable to one another in ability and skill, and their bids were similar.

"What do you think?" Jan chewed on the end of her pen. "Aren't these amazing? Their color schemes are gorgeous and well-suited to the park service."

Chloe nodded and scrolled through the photos from one decorator again. "I'm drawn to this one more than the others. The décor seems to go better in the lobby and their bid is reasonable."

"That's why I called you, my friend." Jan smiled and scrunched her pert nose. "I hate making decisions like this by myself."

Chloe grabbed her messenger bag and headed for the door. "No problem. Glad to help." She halted in the open doorway. "Oh, by the way. Any more dates with our Antietam historian?"

"Who? Oh, Ian?" Jan's cheeks reddened.

Chloe rolled her eyes and chuckled. "Well, I don't know of any other historian working with us from Antietam, do you?"

A coy expression crossed Jan's features. "Well, we've had maybe one more. Or two."

"Seriously? Girl, who are you? Are you the same Jan I know and love?""

"Well, when you haven't dated in a long time, and a great guy comes along…." Jan shrugged.

Chloe shook her head and smiled. "He's a keeper, Jan. If you can hang on to him, then I would. See you later." Back in her office, Chloe settled back at her desk and slipped on a pair of cotton gloves before taking out Sarge's effects once again. Hopefully there'd be no more interruptions. She removed the picture of Sarge's female companion, whoever she was, and the letters they'd found on him. There were several, so she set the letters aside for the moment. All had been tied together with a dirty string except one they'd found in a separate pocket. She retrieved a small metal tray from a cabinet against the wall and placed the fragile pouch of tobacco in it. The pipe went in alongside it. She had just picked up the picture to begin examining it when Clifford walked out of the examination room.

"Chloe, I need to step away and take a break for a few minutes." He halted in front of her desk stretching his arms over his head. "While the brass knob is soaking in a different solution, I'm going down to the snack bar by the lobby to grab a cup of coffee. Can I bring you something?"

Chloe glanced up from the picture. "Thanks for the offer. I'd love a cup of coffee. You know how I like it."

"Sure do. I'll be back shortly."

He disappeared out the door, and Chloe returned her attention to the daguerreotype. It was encased in what once was a burgundy-colored leather frame with a glass front about three inches by four inches in size. A touch of worn and faded, gold thin cord filigree edged the glass along with a thin line of faded burgundy velvet.

The picture within the frame had also faded but was still clear enough to display the young woman's beauty. As was the style of photography in the 1800s, subjects of photos did not smile. A shame for sure since Chloe thought a smile would've lit this woman's face. Did Sarge always remember her with a smile in spite of the absence of one in the picture? Most likely. Chloe couldn't help but wonder about these people as she did about everyone she came across in her research. What kind of people were they? What were their personalities like? What were their families like? Where were they from? What did they do every day? And most of all, what were their names?

Bump, bump!

The sound coming from the examination room startled Chloe so she nearly dropped the small frame. She sat frozen in her seat for several seconds. *What in the world...?*

Laying the daguerreotype on her desk, Chloe stood and walked to the open doorway into the examination room. Had something fallen? Stepping inside, her gaze swept the room for anything out of place. Circling the area, she checked from ceiling to floor. She stood at the end of the examination table, hands on her hips, listening, her gaze sweeping the room. Nothing but silence.

The hair stood up on the back of her neck. *What* had that noise been? There was nothing out of place. Clifford hadn't left anything lying around except the few items on the table where he was working. Nothing that would make that loud noise.

"What are you doing?" Clifford's voice came from behind her.

Chloe jumped and gasped, slamming her hand over her heart. "Oh Cliff. Don't startle me like that."

"Um, sorry, but all I did was walk into the room. You're the one acting strange. You're just standing there...well, yeah, just standing there." He set two cups of coffee on the examination table. "What's wrong? Why *are* you just standing there?"

Chloe pointed at the cups of coffee. "Which one's mine?"

"That one." Clifford shoved one in her direction.

"Thanks." She took a drink. "Well, I was at my desk working when I heard two loud bumps in here. You were gone, so it obviously wasn't you. I came in to see if something fell. There's nothing out of place. Nothing. I see no explanation for the sound I heard."

Clifford's eyebrows furrowed. "Seriously?"

"No, Cliff, I just made it up and came in here to simply stand and do nothing until you came back." She propped her hands on her hips and gave him a sour look. "I ask you, 'seriously?'"

A sheepish expression moved over Clifford's features. "Okay, I'm sorry. I believe you heard something. I mean, why not? We heard all those noises over at the Bryant house, didn't we?" He chuckled then the grin on his face faded. "Wait a minute. Blake asked me the other day if we heard any more noises over at the house. I told him we hadn't been back since we moved Sarge. Until Ian and I were there looking around and found the brass knob." Clifford pointed at the knob soaking in a container on the table.

"What did you tell Blake about hearing noises?"

He shrugged. "I told him that while Ian and I were there, we hadn't heard a thing."

"You said Ian's there today." Chloe paced the floor. "Why don't you give him a call and casually ask if they've heard anything today? It was an ongoing sound while we were there, you know."

"Don't I know it." Clifford pulled out his cell phone and called Ian. He relayed the question and after receiving a reply hung up.

"Well?" Chloe leaned against the examination table.

"Ian said they've been busy removing the bricks since this morning, but they haven't heard the sounds. He said he has no doubt he would've if they'd occurred." Clifford picked up his coffee cup and took a sip.

Chloe studied the bin where Sarge's bones still lay.

"You don't think…," Clifford began.

"I'm trying hard not to." Chloe jammed her eyes closed and scrubbed her fingers across them. "I don't want to go there because I've never believed in that kind of thing before. I always thought those were old-house noises. But the noises at the house seem to have stopped."

Clifford huffed. "Oh wow, no I… uh. No, me either."

Chloe turned to walk out of the room, then stopped at the door and turned back. "When the donor dinner is over, we're having an official burial for Sarge in the Union section at the Gettysburg National Cemetery. Once and for all."

~

Chloe picked up the leather-bound frame. She turned it over and found a tiny metal lever that allowed her to open the back. Once opened, she used a pair of tweezers to remove the daguerreotype. Adjusting the desk lamp to see better, she picked up her magnifying glass. Something was written on the back of the picture.

It was difficult to read at best and some letters and numbers were so faded they seemed to be missing altogether. Chloe wrote down what she could make out.

M gar t D lene Holm s
J ne 2, 1 61

The first word was easy. Margaret. The second was just as simple. Darlene. The last name was Holmes. Now for the date. June was obvious, but Chloe wouldn't be able to decipher the day because it could either be the 12th or the 22nd. No matter. It wasn't really of any consequence. The year would be 1861. There. Simple.

The war began April 12, 1861. This young woman had her picture taken two months after the war started then must have sent it to her love. He carried it with him until the day he died. At least they now had her name. Margaret Darlene Holmes. If only they could find Sarge's name.

Chloe's phone rang again, startling her. She really had to stop jumping at every loud, unexpected noise. Laying down the photo, she reached for the handset on her desk. "Hello?"

"Hi, Chloe? This is Mikayla down at the information desk in the lobby. There's a visitor here to see you. He says he had an appointment with you on Wednesday but was in the Baltimore area and finished up early. Says if you have time, he can meet with you now."

It took Chloe a moment to switch gears mentally. "Wait a sec. What's his name?"

A muffled conversation took place then Mikayla returned on the line. "His name is Brad Wiseman. He's with Northeast Antique Homes Restoration Specialists."

Good gracious. She'd just called them this morning to make an appointment. They were based in Connecticut. But if they had a representative in Baltimore, and he arrived that quickly, well, okay then. Eagerness was a good thing.

"Okay. Thanks, I'll be right down." Chloe packed up Sarge's effects and placed everything in her bag once more. She grabbed her purse, messenger bag and her coffee, which she tasted. Nope. The coffee stayed. It was cold, and there was no time to nuke it in the microwave.

She stepped to the examination room door. "Cliff, one of the restoration contractors is here unexpectedly. I have to take him out to the house so he can see the place. It may take a while. I'll check on Ian while I'm out there."

"No problem." Clifford didn't look up from his work. "Good luck."

"Thanks. It should be interesting to see what he has to say."

"Indeed, it should."

Down in the lobby, Chloe wove through the meandering visitors and remembered why she was happy to be a research historian for the park service and not an interpreter who worked with the public. Way too many people on this level of the building. She approached the information desk where the brunette Mikayla in her park service uniform was talking with a large shaved-headed guy in a sage green shirt and khaki cargos. When Chloe stopped next to them, he turned to cast a pleasant smile above a dark goatee.

His dark brown eyes lit up as Mikayla introduced Chloe to him. He held out a large hand that engulfed Chloe's when he shook it, but he released it immediately. "It's a pleasure to meet you, Miss Rogers."

"And you, Mr. Wiseman." Chloe noted the embroidered label, Northeast Antique Homes Restoration Specialists, above his left breast pocket.

"Please call Brad."

"Okay then, Brad. Why don't you follow me to the Bryant house, so you can get started on your assessment?"

They discussed where each was parked and how he would follow her. Once they were underway, Chloe led him to the Bryant property where they parked alongside Ian's and a maintenance vehicle. She climbed out waited for Brad to catch up, and they headed toward the house.

"Well, from first impressions, what do you think?" Chloe waved a hand in the direction of the house.

Brad removed his sunglasses and shoved them into his breast pocket. "Believe me, I've seen worse on the outside, but I'll wait until I've seen the whole house. There's a lot that goes into a decision whether or not a house can be restored. Can we take a look at the foundation first?"

"Certainly." Chloe led him toward the cellar door. She expected him to ask about the wall that was being torn down and had already come up with an answer. Without lying, she would have to omit information for the sake of keeping Sarge out of the conversation. Until the mystery was solved, they still wanted to keep Sarge's presence a secret.

"Here we go. We have some park personnel working down here removing a wall that wasn't original to the house. If it isn't original, per park service protocol, it has to go."

Thuds and chipping sounds came from deeper under the house. Chloe turned on the flashlight she'd brought from her car, and Brad pulled a small light from his back pocket and switched it on.

"Where would you like to start?" Chloe pointed her light toward the rafters above the doorway.

"Here's good. I'll make my way around then head toward the center. Is there a root cellar under here somewhere?" Brad pointed his light into the corner nearest the door.

"Yes, it's near the front middle of the house. That's where the men are working. Someone built that strange wall years later. I'll show it to you when we get there."

Chloe followed Brad all around the cellar as he surveyed the place, then jotted notes into an electronic tablet he'd brought from his truck. Once the perimeter had been noted, he made his way toward the middle, then to the area where Ian and the maintenance man worked. Brad watched for a few moments.

"What was the purpose of the wall?" He leaned toward Chloe.

Chloe was ready for this question. "We're not exactly sure. When we broke through, we found some small items we're in the process of studying. We haven't discovered much from them yet." Chloe turned to Brad. "What do you think of that wall?"

He stepped closer and picked up a brick from the stack on the floor. "The bricks are Civil War era. My first impression of the house is its pre-Civil War."

"And the mortar?"

Brad knelt and picked up a smattering of scrap mortar that lay on top of the dirt floor. He moved it around on his palm with the finger of his other hand, then he pinched a bit between his finger and thumb.

"It's poorly made. Probably hastily constructed. Why do you ask?" Brad dropped the dusty mortar and stood, wiping his hands together.

Chloe shook her head and shrugged. "That's sort of what I thought, but I'm not an expert. You are. I simply wanted an expert opinion as to why whoever built this wall would use inferior mortar."

Brad shrugged and said no more, his gaze sweeping the work area.

She held out her hand toward the exit. "Shall we head into the house?"

Chapter Fourteen

Chloe allowed Brad to step out onto the porch first then she pulled the door closed and locked the old door. She stepped with care down the rickety steps. "Don't forget to stay to the right side." She grabbed ahold of the shacky handrail. "The other railing gave way on me when I was coming up one day. Fortunately, someone was there to catch me before I fell."

"Well, if we get the job, we'll make sure that's taken care of." Brad chuckled as he waved his tablet. "I've got pretty much everything I need to make my calculations before coming up with my bid. Give me a couple of days, and I'll get back with you."

"So, you think restoration is feasible?" Chloe cheered on the inside.

"It'll take a lot of work, time and money, obviously, but, yes, I believe so." Brad smiled.

Chloe opened her mouth to respond as her cell phone rang. "Excuse me a moment." She stepped away and took the call, then returned to where Brad waited. Chloe dropped the phone into her pocket. "Sorry about that. It was one of the other restoration contractors asking to move his appointment up too."

"So, I have competition, huh?" Brad strolled toward his truck and tossed his tablet onto the passenger seat.

"Well, I actually had them scheduled before Mrs. White-Smith recommended you." Chloe shrugged. "Besides, the park service will always look for the cheapest bidder to do the best job. Ever heard of the US government?"

"But of course." Brad tilted his head and smiled. "Hasn't everyone?" He opened his truck door and climbed in. "I'll be in touch soon."

"Thank you." Chloe stepped back as he put the truck in reverse and backed out of the driveway. She watched as he drove out of sight.

What an interesting afternoon. Brad had pointed out several weak points in the house but reassured her they could be overcome. He thought the house would make a great restoration project but would take time to accomplish. His confidence that his company could find the materials to restore it to its original appearance, both inside and out, was encouraging—at least with what they had to work with. Chloe would research for possible old photographs of the property and house. If she could locate decedents of the Langston family, if there were any left, they may have some. This would be a great reason to do the research she wanted to do on this family. Even if Northeast Antique Homes Restoration Specialists didn't win the bid, whichever restoration contractor did, the family photos would be an asset.

For now, it was time to get back to the office and read some old letters.

~

Blake pressed the off button on the remote and the TV went silent, the screen blank. He wasn't into gaming, and after only a few days of nothing else to do, he was tired of watching TV. He wanted to be out on patrol, but he still had a few more weeks to go before that would be allowed.

Dropping the remote on the coffee table, he scrubbed a hand down his face and heaved a heavy sigh. His ribs immediately let him know they weren't happy. Funny that, because neither was he.

Too bad he hadn't taken up a hobby. Maybe now was a good time to do that. For the next few minutes he thought about it, but nothing crossed his mind except the face of Chloe Rogers. Now *she* was worth spending time thinking about.

Saturday evening flowed back through his mind. It had been an amazing time spent in the company of a special woman. A woman he could not shake from his thoughts. Chloe managed to entrench herself there, and she probably wasn't even aware. "Lord, help me. I do believe I'm in love with Chloe. When she's not around, I want her to be, and when she is, happy doesn't describe how I feel to be in her presence. She brings me joy, Lord. Like I've never known apart from You. Other than that, I can't describe what she does to my insides."

Blake swiped a hand through his hair and heaved a huge sigh. "Yeah, that sounded weird, huh, Lord? But, it's true. I simply feel…confused…scared…happy…and a whole lot of other emotions I can't put into words. Not to mention I can barely breathe when she's around. Please lead me. Show me what you want me to do. If this is your will—a relationship with Chloe, a future with her—then please work it out, Abba Father. Show me the way. Help me."

Blake sat for a long moment in an attitude of prayer, waiting—he didn't know what he was waiting for—but he waited for something. Then peace settled over him. The peace that passes all understanding. The peace that promised things would work out one way or the other. Whether or not Chloe chose to love him, Blake could rest assured the Lord had his best interests at heart. "Okay, Lord. It's all in Your hands. Chloe is in Your hands. And so am I."

~

By the time Chloe returned to her office and settled behind her desk, she only had a few minutes to sit and read. It would be time to head home soon. She completely missed lunch today because of her visit out to the Bryant house with Brad Wiseman. Her stomach rumbled as if in rebuke for her not getting around to that all important midday meal. She slid open the bottom drawer of her desk where her purse resided and withdrew a granola bar from a box which she kept on hand for such occasions.

"This will have to do until I get home." She tore open the wrapper. "Hopefully, Aunt Char will have something scrumptious for dinner."

After downing the bar, Chloe donned a pair of white cotton gloves, then tugged the acid-free bag with the letters from her messenger bag. She removed a couple and carefully spread one open. It addressed the reader as *Dear Son* and was written in clear feminine, cursive handwriting. Chloe read down the page to find what appeared to be family news with a few names mentioned.

Son, your father works late into the evenings to ensure the foundry produces enough cannonballs to provide for the Union soldiers to fight this war. As the executive and owner of the company, he should be home with his feet up and resting each evening. Instead, he's there in that smelly, smoky, hot inferno making sure the workers finish the government orders and send them out on time. He's obsessed with it. I cannot reason with him no matter how much I beg. Perhaps you can send him a letter. He'll listen to you.

Chloe read to the end where the simple closing stated,

Come home safe and sound, my dear son,

Your loving mother.

A pang sliced through Chloe as she understood to some degree the heartache this woman must have endured when her son hadn't returned home. No, it wasn't quite the same, but Chloe's husband hadn't come home from war alive. It was still a devastating lose that a wife simply didn't recover from completely. She was learning to live without him in her life, and sometimes guilt riddled her because of it.

Blake's handsome features slipped before her mind's eye, his half-grin on his lips. Her own lips tilted at the memory of him Saturday night. His kiss had been sweet and…exquisite. The thought of Josh returned. Was she being untrue to him? What a tug-of-war. Josh on one side and Blake on the other. In the middle, Chloe still sensed Josh's tug, but was it truly Josh? Or was it Chloe's loyalty to a man who was long gone that was tugging at her.

That old desire to talk to the Lord about things resurfaced once again. Chloe had so many things she wanted to share with Him. To seek His guidance like she used to. But He'd taken Josh…. Perhaps she should start with a conversation with Dad. It had been a long time since they'd had a talk. Maybe it was time.

Chloe picked up the next letter and carefully spread it open. It began with the same greeting and was written in the same handwriting.

Dear son,

Thank you for writing to your father. Your words were

wonderful and most encouraging to him. I know you did your best. However, it is with a broken heart that I must tell you your father has died. The doctor told your older brother, George, your sisters, Susan and Mary, your younger brother, Isaac, and me that he died of a heart attack. I believe he worked himself to death in an attempt to transport ammunition to the troops. If there was ever a war hero, it was my husband and your father.

I understand that you will likely not be able to come home for your father's funeral. The whole family understands. You are fighting for your country, my son. I pray for you daily and sometimes hourly.

Please come home safe and sound.

Your loving mother

Chloe folded the letter and returned it to the bag with the others. How heartbreaking to read of the outcome of the situation with Sarge's father, but he was a man who did all he could to help in the war effort for his side of the war. In her research, she'd found story after story like this on both sides of the war, each certain they were doing what was right. If there was one thing she disliked about her job, it was when she discovered sad, personal stories in history like this one.

Unfortunately, Chloe still hadn't discovered Sarge's name through his mother's letters. There were several more to read, but not today. She glanced at her wristwatch. It was past time to go home. She carefully laid the personal effects in her messenger bag and shut down her computer. As she stood to gather her things, she heard a sound in the examination room.

Chloe spun in that direction. Odd. Clifford had gone to the Bryant house to work. Was he in the examination room after all? The door was closed, but she'd clearly heard a noise. She set her things on the desk and moved toward the door, her eyes narrowed. "Cliff? Are you in there? I thought you left."

She placed her ear near the door. Silence. The hair stood up on the back of her neck as she straightened. She had heard a noise, *hadn't she*?

A soft bump inside the room made Chloe jump, her stomach lodging in her throat. After several seconds, she swallowed. Hard.

This was ridiculous. She grabbed the doorknob and yanked the door open, stepping inside. "Okay, Cliff. What's going…?" Chloe halted just inside the door and stared.

There was no Clifford. There was no one. She inched around the room and found nothing out of place. Only the brass knob in Clifford's soaking solution still sat on the examination table waiting for him to continue his cleaning project. Everything else was as it should be.

Chloe huffed an agitated breath and stomped her foot, but her words were a mere whisper, "I refuse to believe."

She turned and left the room, slamming the door behind her and locking it.

~

When the dinner dishes were washed and put away, Chloe allowed Evie to return outside to play for a bit. Aunt Char settled on the swing on the patio to read and keep an eye on Evie.

Chloe said she'd join her shortly and went in search of her dad. She found him in the usual place, his office. She leaned on the doorframe and tapped on the door. "Do you have a couple minutes?"

Dad glanced up from some paperwork he was mulling over on his desk. He dropped his pen on the papers and leaned back in his leather chair. "For you, kiddo, I've got more than a couple. Take all you need."

Chloe smiled and dropped into the chair against the wall near his desk. "In truth, it might take more than a couple."

Her father propped his hands behind his head. "Go for it. What's up?"

Chloe wove her fingers together in her lap and scrutinized them. "Well, I have to be honest with you, Dad, I haven't exactly been talking to the Lord lately. More like in…three years since Josh died."

Dad leaned forward and clasped his hands together on his desk. "I know."

Chloe met his gaze. "You do? How?"

He shrugged. "Every time there's a discussion about spiritual things, you clam up. You pass on saying the blessing at the table. You go to church with us, but you don't seem happy to be there. Want me to go on?"

Chloe stared at her hands. "No."

"What's the problem? Do you blame God for taking Josh?"

"How did you know?"

"It wasn't hard to figure out. All these things started after Josh died, as you said. Guess you didn't realize I was watching and praying for you. I hurt because you hurt. There wasn't much I could do to make things better except pray for you and be here when you were ready to talk. Which you weren't until now. Honey, I understand what you've been through because I lost your mom. Just like you, I had a daughter, but I was fortunate that she was a lot older than Evie is. Sadly, she won't remember her dad. You'll have to help her know the man he was and the hero he was to his country. Even if you remarry, which I hope you'll do, it's your responsibility to do that."

Chloe shoved a tendril of hair behind her ear. "I will, Dad. I'll make sure she knows both sides of her dad."

Dad nodded. "Good. Now what about your spiritual needs, Chloe? What are you going to do about those?"

"I suppose it's time to talk to the Lord again, huh?"

"He didn't take Josh from you, sweetheart. Evil men in Afghanistan killed Josh. Did God allow it to happen? Well, yes, I suppose so. We don't understand God's perfect will. We can't understand why He allows a child to die of cancer, or someone to be murdered. But He has a purpose for everything. In Romans 8:28 it says, 'And we know that all things work together for good to them that love God, to them who are called according to his purpose.' I seem to remember you learned that in Vacation Bible School one year when you were growing up. Did you forget it?"

Chloe gave him a sheepish grin. "I still have it memorized, but I suppose I forgot to remember it when I needed it most."

"Well, we do that, don't we? Talk to the Lord. Lay it all out there for Him. Don't leave anything out, sweetheart. He's been waiting all this time for you to come back to Him. He wants to be there for you, to help you through everything you face. I hate to be an 'I told you so' kind of dad, but He could have been there to help you through the last three years if you would have been talking to Him instead of turning your back on Him."

The tender words bore straight to Chloe's heart, and she took the gentle rebuke as it was intended. "Thanks. I'll start repairing my relationship with Him."

"I'm glad to hear that. I'll keep praying for you like I've been doing for the last three years."

She met his grin with one of her own. He picked up his pen and started to return to his paperwork, but Chloe remained in her chair, her hands clasped between her knees.

Dad glanced back up. "Is there something else you wanted to talk about?"

Chloe cleared her throat and nodded.

Dad laid his pen down again. "Shoot."

"Well, I'm struggling with something else, too, and I haven't been praying, of course, so I'm not sure how to handle things."

A corner of his mouth quirked in a grin. "Confused? Uncertain? Guilt-ridden? Feeling disloyal to Josh?"

Chloe stared at her dad. "Don't tell me. You went through that too?"

"Of course, I did. I loved your mom so much, and I couldn't imagine another woman taking her place."

"But you dated a few women here and there."

Dad nodded, leaning back in his chair again. It squeaked with the shift in his weight. "Yes, I did. Found a couple I liked rather well I might say, but none I fell in love with."

"Is that why you've never remarried.?" Chloe leaned her chin on her fist and her elbow on her knee, crossing one knee over the other.

"Yep. Besides, I don't think your Aunt Char would be willing to give up the kitchen to another woman." He chuckled.

"No, probably not." Chloe laughed. "Well, if her big brother were to find love again, I bet she would."

"Perhaps, but we're not discussing my love life. We're discussing yours. Remember?"

Chloe sat up straight. "We're not discussing my love life, dad. We're discussing my—"

"We're discussing your hang-ups, and why you can't realize that you can have a love life again, sweetheart. Don't you understand that's what confusion, uncertainty, guilt and disloyalty to Josh is all about? Without trying to sound harsh, I remind you that Josh is no longer here. He has no hold on you any longer. Whatever you're feeling is due to clinging to the past. It's been three years, sweetheart. You have a young daughter who needs a father, and you're a young, vibrant woman who needs to love again and be loved. You need to move on."

Chloe swallowed and leaned back in her chair. "It's pretty cool having a dad who's been there and done that, you know?"

Dan smiled. "I suppose so. I was fortunate to have my sister sit and listen to me talk sometimes. Char was a godsend to me after your mom died. She would listen and we would pray. Our pastor was there for me as well as the deacons of our church."

Stinging began behind Chloe's eyes, and she blinked to ward off tears. "I missed a lot of support, didn't I?"

"Yeah, you did, but there were still a lot of folks praying for you, believe me." He winked. "So, tell me more about this Blake Hunter. He's park police, and you've dated him how many times?"

~

Chloe spent the next few days meeting with all but one of the restoration contractors, going over incoming bids, and finalizing plans for the donor dinner with Jan. An appointment with the last restoration contractor was scheduled for this afternoon.

She spent two whole days researching the Langston family and found a Langston descendant in Hanover, Maryland, named Meredith Cecelia Langston Harding. Ecstatic, Chloe made a phone call to arrange a visit. From the woman's voice, she sounded elderly but eager for Chloe to come when Chloe explained who she was and why she wanted to visit. The only thing Chloe wasn't looking forward to was the Baltimore area traffic. At least she wasn't going downtown Baltimore. She shuddered at the thought.

Chloe's phone rang no sooner than she'd dropped the receiver into the cradle. She picked it up again.

"Hello?"

"Chloe. Come on out to the Bryant place. I think you're going to want to see what we've found." The excitement in Clifford's voice echoed across cyberspace. What? This house kept revealing it's secrets.

She hugged the receiver to her ear. "You've found something else concerning Sarge?"

"Uh, well, not exactly, but it's pretty cool."

Chloe glanced at her watch. "I have an appointment with the last contractor in forty-five minutes. Can it wait until then?"

"Oh, no. We don't want a stranger to see this. And we certainly want it out before a contractor gets here." Clifford's voice rose with agitation.

Chloe sighed. "All right. I'm on my way." Her visit to Hanover was scheduled for tomorrow. It would be a great way to round out the week. She'd be gone most of the day, so whatever all this was about, they needed to deal with it now.

Several minutes later, Chloe entered the cellar. Clifford hadn't said that's where they were, but she had no doubt she'd find them there. They'd spent all their time working in the cellar and none in the house. "What's up, guys?" Chloe called out when she didn't immediately see either Clifford or Ian in the lit area near the torn down wall. She hurried over and observed where the wall had once been. They'd done an excellent job on removing all evidence of it except for the stack of bricks that still stood to the side. Even the remains of the mortar had been disposed of.

"Chloe?" A muffled disembodied voice echoed from…somewhere in the cellar.

"Cliff? Where are you?" Chloe took a slow spin of the area.

"In the root cellar."

"Right. That was my next guess." She made her way to the half-open door only to realize it was a little more open than before. They had dug out the dirt floor making it possible for the door to swing open further.

Chloe leaned her head into the open doorway to find another halogen light set up inside. All cobwebs had been cleaned out. Several of the canning crocks had been taken down from the shelves and were lined up on the floor near the door. A few were open, and disgusting odors emanated from them. She pinched her hand over her nose and exhaled through her mouth. "How in the world can you two work with that…that awful smell in here with you? It smells like something died."

Clifford turned to face Chloe wearing a full-face mold and vapor respirator. Ian turned with a matching one on his face.

"Oh, that's how." Chloe slumped against the doorframe.

"There's one on the toolbox out there for you." Clifford gave her a thumbs up and turned back to what he was doing.

Chloe returned to the lit work area and found two respirators on the toolbox. She fit one over her head, adjusted the straps and turned to walk back to the root cellar. A voice behind her startled her. She whipped around, hand over her heart.

"I don't know. It's not really your style. I prefer to see your beautiful face." Blake stood, arms crossed over his chest, a half-grin forming on his handsome features. Chloe's heartrate picked up a few beats.

She slipped the respirator up to the top of her head. "Well, they're all the rage these days. I think you should try one. You never know what one might do for your image."

His grin deepened. "Think so?"

"Sure. Here's one." She picked the second one up from the tool box and tossed it to him. "What do you say? Want to give it a try?"

Catching it, he turned it over and over in his hands. "Cliff told me I would need one when he called me to come over. He thought I might be interested in seeing what they found since he knew I have some time on my hands."

"Really?" Chloe grew miffed. Cliff hadn't told *her* that. "Come on. He's this way." She slipped the respirator back down and readjusted the straps, but she couldn't stay irritated. It was like Clifford, and she had to admit she'd missed seeing Blake over the last several days. Since he was on leave from work, and she'd been super busy their paths hadn't crossed. What was he doing to keep himself occupied?

Chloe and Blake stepped into the tight space of the root cellar.

"Cliff, what's so exciting that you called me down early to see?" Chloe stepped around the offending crocks on the floor near the door.

Clifford pivoted and pointed at the crocks Chloe had stepped around. "Those crocks are obviously spoiled foods. We checked them to make sure there wasn't anything underneath, but we'll check them again as we dispose of them. These—" Clifford indicated a row of various sized salt glazed crocks, "—are the ones that are interesting. We found money in them. 1800s pre-Civil War money, that is. Apparently, Mr. Langston…what was his name again?"

"Elijah." Chloe provided.

"That's right. Mr. Elijah Langston, who I remember you telling me was a lawyer. Apparently, Mr. Elijah Langston didn't trust banks. Take a gander at this."

Clifford and Ian stepped back allowing Chloe and Blake to move closer to the shelves. Chloe counted six crocks. She turned to ask Clifford for a pair of cotton gloves and found him holding a pair out to her.

She smiled. "Only a historian would read another historian's mind."

"I know." He returned her smile.

Donning the gloves, she reached into the widest mouthed crock and withdrew several coins, holding them in the light for her and Blake to see. She flipped them all over to read the dates.

"Cliff, I suppose you noted some of these are gold, right?" Excitement built in Chloe's mid-section.

"Oh, I noticed all right. Take a look at those dates. Mr. Langston hoarded for a long time. You know I'm a dabbler in numismatics and certainly no expert, but I've looked up a few of these coins already. They can range anywhere from $550 to $53,550 each. That's only a couple I looked up. There are six jars there."

"Cliff, you know these will never get sold. They'll go into our museum and other museums everywhere or be studied. This is about as rare a collection as you can find."

"Agreed." Clifford held out a few coins in his gloved hand. "Apparently, in his haste to sell the house and skedaddle to Baltimore, Mr. Elijah Langston forgot to take his wealth of coins with him. I wonder how long it took him to remember then regret that decision."

Chloe dropped the coins back into the crock and glanced at her watch. "We'll never know. I hate to end this, but I have to meet the contractor in a few minutes. Would you please hide these? He's going to want to look in here just as all the other contractors have. Hide the crocks in plain sight like before, but get rid of the stinky stuff."

Blake followed her out of the root cellar as Chloe removed her respirator. "Mind if I hang around?"

"Why?" She cast him a puzzled glance as she headed for the exit. "It'll take the contractor a while to go through the house. The rest of them have been extremely thorough."

They stopped outside the cellar door, and she turned to him.

Blake shrugged and jammed his hands into his jean pockets. "What else do I have to do?"

Chloe tilted her head as she read a mix of boredom and discontent stamped on his handsome features. She placed a hand on his arm. "I'm sorry this happened to you. You don't strike me as the kind of man who does well with idleness."

His gaze slid down to her fingers on his arm and, pulling his hand from his pocket, he took her hand in his, his eyes returning to hers. "You're right. I'm bored out of my silly gourd. Think you can help me out?"

A tingle danced up Chloe's arm right to her heart. What was this handsome guy doing to her? If he was attempting to draw her in, perhaps make her fall in love with him, he was going about it the right way. Had she genuinely thought the 'love' word? In connection with Blake? Goodness.

The slam of a vehicle door in the distance drew her attention. Chloe pulled her hand from Blake's. "I'm sure that's the contractor. I need to go, but I'll talk with you… afterward? You know, since you'll be hanging around." Why all of a sudden did she feel like a fifteen-year-old with her first crush?

"I'll be here." Blake winked before Chloe turned and fled around the corner of the building.

~

Blake couldn't hold back the grin as Chloe disappeared around the corner. He looked forward to her finishing with the restoration contractor. It would likely take a couple hours for them to go through the house, then he'd ask Chloe out for an early dinner. He hadn't seen her in several days, and he'd missed her. A lot. A few moments ago, when she'd laid her hand on his arm, warmth had spread through him at her touch. Oh, what this woman did to him. How he longed to make their relationship a permanent one, but he had to be patient. Chloe had to be ready. *I'm trusting You, Lord. Help her to be ready in Your time. Your will be done.*

Two shots rang out from the front of the house, and Blake's heart nearly stalled. He flew around the corner. Chloe and an unknown man lay on the ground. Was she alive? A flurry of images passed as he dashed toward her stilled body. A nearby pickup truck. A clipboard laying inches from the man's hand. Papers fluttering in the afternoon breeze. A sedan speeding away—

a dark, late 80s model, Toyota Camry with no license plate.

Chapter Sixteen

"Chloe! Chloe, sweetheart, can you hear me?" Blake ran his hand over her head and back but found no bullet-entry wounds. He did the same down her legs but found nothing. "Chloe, are you all right?"

She turned her head toward him. "Blake? Yes, I'm fine. What about Mr. Waters? Check on him. Was he injured?"

Blake helped Chloe to her knees then turned to the man who began to stir. "Mr. Waters. Are you all right? Are you injured, sir?"

The man pushed himself onto his knees then into a sitting position. He ran his hands over his torso. "No, I…I think I'm uninjured. How is Miss Rogers?"

"I'm fine." Chloe stood. "When shots were fired, I simply dropped to the ground."

"As did I." Mr. Waters brushed a hand across his head.

Blake offered him a hand up.

"Blake, you shouldn't attempt to do that alone. He has broken ribs and internal injuries, Mr. Waters."

"Oh, well, I can get up by myself. Let's not injure you further, sir." Mr. Waters climbed to his feet with Chloe's assistance. "What, may I ask, was that all about?" He turned to Chloe and planted his hands on his hips. "I've never been shot at while looking at a possible contract job before. Is there something dangerous in particular about this house that I should know about?"

Blake bent over with care and retrieved Mr. Waters' clipboard and handed it to him.

The man accepted it with a quiet thank you and returned his focus to Chloe.

"I can't say what it is, sir, but we discovered something of historical value in the house. We're not ready to disclose it to the public yet since we're still in the research phase." Chloe crossed her arms over her middle. "It's been removed to a government location, so I have no idea why that incident happened. Just know I'm terribly sorry you were involved."

Mr. Waters heaved an indignant huff. "As am I. I'm reluctant to even consider this restoration contract. If my company did, indeed, consider it, there would have to be security involved, and that would add to the cost making it more than I'm sure the government is willing to pay." He whipped around and headed for his truck.

Chloe followed him. "Aren't you even going to look at the house?"

"Why? I'll think about the situation for a few days then make my decision whether to look at it or not, but as I said, security would have to be involved." Opening the driver's door, he climbed in. "I can't risk my worker's lives. I'm sure you can understand that."

"Yes, sir. I can." Chloe held out her hand to him. "Please accept my apology again for this incident."

He shook her hand. "I do, but I hope you're going to notify the police."

"I am the park police, sir." Blake stepped forward. "I'll see this incident is reported, and someone will be in touch with you to get your statement."

"Wonderful." Mr. Waters started the pickup truck and slipped it into reverse. "I'll be happy to give it."

Chloe and Blake watched as the contractor drove away. Blake slipped his arm around Chloe's shoulders.

"Are you sure you're all right?"

"Yeah. I'm fine. Shook up and disappointed but fine."

"How about some coffee and dessert at Moira's? After that adrenaline rush, I could use some. What about you?"

Chloe patted the hand on her shoulder. "Sounds relaxing and delicious. Let's go talk to the guys and tell them they need to get those coins out of the cellar and someplace safe."

"While you do that, I'll report the shooting. I won't be permitted to obtain Mr. Waters' statement, but the park police need to jump on this." Blake reached for Chloe's hand as she started walking toward the cellar. He twined his fingers with hers. "I read Gabe's report from the night the guy broke into your office and…did a number on me. Unless I don't remember it correctly, and, I'm sure I do, that was the same vehicle the guy got away in."

"Why do you think he's doing all this?"

"I have no idea, but we'll find out. Somehow."

"Before someone gets hurt? Or worse?"

Blake didn't have the answers to those questions; however, he knew Someone who did.

~

"Ach, two of me favorite folk." Moira leaned her arms on the counter as Chloe and Blake stepped inside the coffee shop. A few customers sat at tables. "I'm happy to see ya together again. At least ye're with the right laddie this time, lass." The woman winked sending waves of warmth from Chloe's uniform collar right up to her hairline.

Chloe ignored Blake's grin as she made a deliberate study of the treats in the plexiglass box on the counter. "What's good today, Moira?" Why was her voice pitched so high?

"Ah, lass, everything's good the same as every day. Ye know that."

"Of course, it is." Blake chuckled.

She cast him a sideways smirk out of the corner of her eye. "One of your meat pies, an apple hand pie and a hot caramel latte, please."

"Hmm. That sounds good. Make it a double." Blake straightened and tugged out his wallet.

"Comin' right up. Go on. Have a seat. I'll be bringing it out shortly." Moira shooed them toward the tables and set about making their orders.

Blake led Chloe to a table in the corner by the front window and held out a chair for her.

"Thank you." Chloe sat and slid the chair forward. "Moira is incorrigible. You know that, don't you?"

"Of course, I do." Blake sat opposite her. "I also know she's right."

Chloe clasped her hands on the table in front of her. "Is that so?"

"Sure. I don't have anything against Ian. He's a great guy and all-around great historian, but he's just not the guy for you."

Chloe loved his grin and was beginning to revel in the delight it stirred within her. Certainly not boyish, it still held an amusing quirk. Aunt Charlene's Marlboro Man description came to mind, and Chloe forced down the chuckle that almost escaped. She didn't want to have to explain why she was laughing in the middle of him telling her why Ian wasn't the man for her. "No? I bet you know someone who is, huh?" She sent him a grin of her own.

His turned into a full smile. "Actually, I do."

"Imagine that. Describe him to me."

Moira set their lattes and food on the table. "Easy. He's handsome—charmin', kind, carin' and serves his community. The lad for you, dearie, impresses me as a man who'd make a wonderful husband and father."

Chloe's glance switched from Moira's knowing smile to Blake's tint of red surging beneath his tan. His glimpse met hers before both looked back at Moira.

"Oh, you know the guy he's talking about?" Chloe suppressed her grin.

Moira placed a hand on Blake shoulder. "Why, yes, I do. Ye might be surprised to find ye know him too." Slipping her tray beneath her arm, she grinned at Chloe then walked away.

Chloe reached for her latte. "Perhaps you'll introduce me to this paragon sometime?"

Blake's grin faded, his gorgeous gray eyes locking with hers. "I'll do that."

All of a sudden Chloe found it difficult to breath. Something flamed in the intensity of his gaze that made her heart beat faster. She averted her eyes and sipped her latte. "I think our food is getting cold," she murmured.

"Want to say grace with me?" Blake held out a hand across the table.

She eyed it for a moment then laid hers within it.

After he said a quick blessing, he released her hand and reached for his fork. "Since Mr. Waters has withdrawn his bid for the restoration job, what now?" Blake took a bite of his meat pie.

Chloe shrugged. "I have three more bids to consider. I'm waiting on the last one."

He nodded. "So, until then, what do you have planned?"

"I have a road trip tomorrow that I'm pretty excited about it." Chloe took a nibble of her pie.

"Where are you going? How long will you be gone?"

"Just for the day. I'm going to Hanover, Maryland, over near Baltimore. I don't look forward to the drive because I hate driving in traffic, but I'm excited about my visit." She leaned forward. "Remember Cecelia Langston? The daughter of the original owner of the Bryant house? She's the one whose diary was given to us by the woman who sold the house to the park. She found it in the secret compartment you and I looked at in the back bedroom upstairs in the house?"

"Yeah, I remember." Blake furrowed his brows. "She witnessed Sarge's murder, right?"

"Yep, that's her. Well, I found her granddaughter in Hanover."

"Seriously? That's cool."

"Yes, it is. I contacted her yesterday and asked if I could come for an official visit from the park. She was delighted and told me she has all kinds of information to share with me."

"No wonder you're excited." Blake chuckled. "Need a driver to take you?"

Chloe stared at him. "Really? You would drive me there?"

"Why not? I'm not doing anything. I'd be happy to drive you. If you don't want me to go inside, I can sit in the car and wait, or I can wait at a fast-food place until you're ready to go, then you can call me. I'll come back and pick you up." Blake shrugged. "Whatever works best."

Chloe gave a slow nod. "I'd like that. I'd like not having to drive, and I'd love the company. Although, I may do some work on my laptop while you're driving, if you don't mind."

"Whatever you need to do." Leaning forward, he flashed his most winning smile. The warmth from it wrapped around Chloe's heart.

Blake may only be doing this because he was bored silly, but that was okay. She didn't blame him. She doubted she'd last long twiddling her thumbs either. If it got him out of his house and away for a short time, she was glad to help. As she was realizing more and more, she enjoyed Blake's company. She hoped upon hope the man Blake intended to introduce her to wasn't someone else. More than anything she hoped he was teasing her, and it was actually him. He'd shown too much interest for it not to be. The flame in his gaze, his touch, his desire for her company. Why would he bring in someone else? Surely it was Blake himself. And in her heart, Chloe was coming to understand she'd be okay with that.

~

The next morning Blake knocked on the superintendent's front door only to have it opened by the superintendent himself.

Dan Fielding smiled and opened the door wider. "Good morning, Blake. Come on in and have a cup of coffee. Chloe's finishing breakfast and will be ready to go shortly."

"Good morning, sir." Blake stepped inside and followed the superintendent into the kitchen where the rest of the family sat eating breakfast. He hated not being in uniform when the superintendent and Chloe both were. Being on paid leave may pay the bills but working as a park cop brought fulfillment. His time away from work couldn't end soon enough. But if his boss found him in his uniform, he'd have a conniption.

"Good morning, Blake. How about some breakfast?" Aunt Charlene laid a plate filled with waffles and bacon on the breakfast bar then set a cup of coffee beside it. "Come, have a seat. You haven't eaten already, have you?"

"Well, I had a cup of coffee." Blake sat on the high stool next to a little girl who sat beside Chloe.

"That was all you were going to have? Coffee?" Aunt Charlene's disapproving voice and stare pinned Blake.

"I didn't want to be late." He shrugged.

Chloe chuckled from two stools down. "Take your time and eat, or Aunt Char will take a wooden spoon to you. Huh, kiddo?" She gently elbowed the little girl who gave an exaggerated nod.

"Yep. She likes to wooden spoon peoples." The little girl slurped milk from a spoonful of cereal.

Blake chuckled and poured syrup over his waffles. "She does, does she? Has she ever wooden spooned you?"

"Nope, but she did my mommy when she was wittle. Mommy

was bad, I guess." The little girl shrugged and slurped again.

Blake linked eyes with Chloe's over the little girl's head and winked. "Is that so? Good to know." He enjoyed the color flowing into Chloe's cheeks. Were her cheeks as soft and warm as they looked? A longing to find out stirred within him. "What's your name?" He addressed the little girl. "Mine's Blake."

"Evie." She dropped her spoon and held out her right hand. "Nice to meet cha."

Blake shook her hand. "Nice to meet you too, Evie."

"Are you gonna marry my mommy?" Evie's question was matter-of-fact as she picked up her spoon and slurped milk and cereal again.

Blake leaned close to her ear but kept an eye on Chloe's bright red cheeks. "That's kind of a personal question, you know."

Evie nodded and huffed out a huge sigh. "She needs a husband, and I need a daddy. You look like you would do. So ask her."

"You might be right." Blake picked up his fork, shaking his head at Evie's childish wisdom. His neck warmed at the suppressed chuckles around the room.

Avoiding his eyes, Chloe downed the rest of her coffee. "I'll grab my things while you finish up."

In ten minutes, they were on their way in the park SUV Chloe had secured from the vehicle pool. She opened her laptop immediately and began working. Blake fought the urge to address the conversation he and Evie had carried on. It was painfully obvious Chloe wouldn't bring it up. Aunt Charlene had been washing breakfast dishes and her shoulders were shaking in silent mirth. Dan sat in his armchair drinking coffee and reading the morning paper which shook from his silent laughter. Chloe's daughter was a treasure and slashed straight to Blake's heart. Her mother had done an amazing job of raising her, but she'd had the help of her dad and aunt. As the little girl so wisely stated, she needed a daddy. Would Chloe allow Blake into her life to be that husband and the father Evie was missing?

Precious little conversation took place as they followed the route toward the address Chloe entered into the vehicle's GPS. Her attention remained on whatever she found interesting on her laptop. Blake drove in silence down the highway. Glancing in her direction occasionally, he didn't want to interrupt her work. They'd been on the road about twenty minutes when Chloe's cell phone rang.

Tugging it from her purse, she swiped the answer button. "Hello?"

Blake only heard her side of the conversation.

"Oh, hi Cliff. What's up?" Chloe cradled the phone between her ear and her shoulder. "What's that?"

Silence followed as a muffled voice emanated from the phone. Chloe took the phone in her hand, her attention fully on Clifford's words.

"Seriously? But Cliff…." Chloe waited as Clifford interrupted her and continued on his end.

"No, I can't come in right now. I'm on my way to Hanover, Maryland to interview Cecelia Langston's granddaughter. What? Well, I'm sure I told you yesterday. Maybe I didn't in all the excitement of finding the coins and getting shot at, but, yes, Blake is driving me there now." Chloe cast a glance in Blake's direction. "Yes, Blake's with me. He's driving. Stop. We're on official park business."

Blake wanted to chuckle out loud at the frosty tone Chloe aimed at Clifford. He pictured Clifford as an icicle on the other end of the line.

"I'll be back home this afternoon. You can show it to me Monday morning, how about that? I'm eager to see it, and I'm happy you uncovered it. Yes. Great job. See you Monday." Chloe swiped the end call button and dropped the phone into her purse. Dropping her head back against the headrest, she closed her laptop lid and rested her hands on top of it.

Blake glanced at her. "Good news from our other favorite historian?"

Chloe's glance rolled toward his, a question there.

"Well, you're my favorite." He grinned.

"Thanks. Yes, he had some great news and some…strange news."

Blake cast her another glance before returning his gaze to the road. "Oh yeah? Want to spill?"

Chloe sat up straight. "Seems he's uncovered the engraved letters on the brass knob, but he wouldn't tell me what they were.

He wants to show it to me in person."

"Why? What's the mystery? Or is there one?"

Chloe shook her head and shrugged. "I don't know. He seems pretty excited, but he wouldn't tell me more. At least about that."

"Okay, so what's the strange news?"

Chloe didn't answer right away.

Blake picked up on her hesitation. "What is it, Chloe?"

"Cliff said when he could finally make out the letters etched into the brass, he read them softly then aloud as if they finally made sense to him. They're a monogram, and sometimes monograms are slightly harder to read at first when the last initial is larger than the other initials. It's placed in the middle of the monogram with the smaller first initial on the left and the middle initial on the right. When Cliff realized this, he called out the initials, and there was a loud noise in the examination room with him. It shook him up pretty bad at first. He couldn't find anything that would make the noise. So, he finished up and put everything away. Cliff locked the examination room, and he's heading over to the Bryant place to work with Ian. He's taking the knob with him and locking it in his car. None of the artifacts from the house are safe at the office until we can install a secure safe." Chloe turned to the window, her fingers twisting together.

"That's not all, is it?" Blake kept his voice low to encourage her to tell more. If she would. "Chloe…."

"No, there's more. Not from Cliff, but…." Chloe inhaled deeply then released it all at once. "I've had a couple of weird…occurrences at the office. You know, things I can't explain. Noises really. Bumps that made me jump when there wasn't anything to cause them. Things that have never happened until recently." She shifted toward Blake, her arm resting on the laptop. "Blake, I don't believe in…well…you know…."

"Ghosts?" Blake lifted an eyebrow in her direction. "You can say the word, Chloe. When you say the word, it won't make one appear."

Her withering stare made him chuckle.

"So, you don't believe. Okay. Not everyone does. I'm not sure if I do or not. There's an awful lot of things in this world we can't explain. One thing we do know, there's a spiritual world we can't see that's filled with angels and demons. That's straight from the

Bible. Spiritual warfare wages all around, and we can't see it, but we see it's affects everywhere. The battle between good and evil, between right and wrong, plays out right before our eyes every day. There's spiritual warfare being fought behind every situation. The Bible tells us 'For we wrestle not against flesh and blood, but against principalities, against powers, against the rulers of the darkness of this world, against spiritual wickedness in high places.' The world is Satan's realm."

"I believe all that." Chloe rubbed a hand on her arm and nodded. "But what about…ghosts? How do you explain them?"

Blake shrugged. "The Bible is a bit vague on the subject, but there's one verse where Paul states 'To be absent from the body and to be present with the Lord.' If a Christian dies, he goes to heaven into the Lord's presence. According to this verse, he, or she, doesn't hang around. I can't explain why folks see their loved ones after they die, Christian or not. I'm only stating what Paul said."

"Have you ever seen…one?" Chloe swiped a tendril of hair behind her ear.

Blake shook his head, his focus on traffic. As they drew nearer their destination, traffic had grown busier. "Nope. My grandfather used to talk about one on his ranch, but I never saw or heard it." After maneuvering through a patch of heavy traffic, Blake asked, "You mentioned hearing something you've never heard in your office before. When did it start?"

"Right after we moved Sarge to the examination room and the sounds at the Bryant house stopped."

Chapter Seventeen

When Blake parked in front of the old Victorian home, Chloe convinced him to come inside with her. “There’s no need for you to wait in the car or drive somewhere else and wait. You’ve been nearly as much a part of this research into the Bryant/Langston house as I have. You should come in and meet Cecelia’s granddaughter.”

A wide front porch adorned the old Victorian home with a circular sitting area at the side of the porch, then it continued on around one side of the house. Gables, peaks and a turret above the circular sitting area on the porch gave the second story the fairytale appearance most Victorian homes possessed. Gingerbread woodwork adorned the upper edge of the porch and above the gables. The house was painted cream, white and hunter green. Chloe adored it. Sitting on the wide porch swing amongst all those pillows in the summertime with a good book would be a dream.

Now as they stood at the huge front door, Blake lifted the brass knocker in the shape of a hand with a ball in it and lowered it to the brass strike beneath, knocking it a few times.

“Interesting door knocker.” He ran his finger over the brass fingers of the hand. “Can’t say I’ve ever seen one like that before.”

“A Victorian design.” Chloe whispered as the sound of the door lock turning on the inside.

The door opened a narrow bit and a wrinkled, feminine face peaked out. “May I help you?” Her voice warbled in an elderly way.

“Mrs. Harding? I’m Chloe Rogers from Gettysburg National Military Park. I spoke with you yesterday, and you invited me to visit today to discuss your grandmother, Cecelia Langston.” Chloe hoped there wasn't an issue with her memory, and they'd be turned away.

"Oh yes, my dear. Why of course. Just a moment." She closed the door.

Chloe turned puzzled eyes on Blake.

The door opened wide. Mrs. Meredith Harding held out an arm to welcome them. With her white hair coiffed in a neat bun, she wore a lavender sweater set and a black skirt. A single strand of pearls graced her throat, and teardrop pearls dangled from her ears. She held a curved bamboo cane in her right hand. "Please, please, do come in. And who, may I ask, is this handsome young man, Miss Rogers?" Mrs. Harding closed the door behind them. "Is he your intended?"

"No, he's not." Chloe gave her head a vigorous shake and avoided Blake's gaze. "He's a…a co-worker. Mrs. Harding, this is Blake Hunter. Blake, Mrs. Meredith Harding. She's the granddaughter of Cecelia Langston."

"It's a pleasure to meet you, Mrs. Harding." Blake held out his hand.

She shook it and held on. "The pleasure is all mine." Mrs. Harding poked Chloe in the side with her elbow. "That is too bad. He's such a good-looking young man. You could do worse, you know."

Chloe's neck heated up, and she was quite sure red splotches adorned it. He was enjoying himself. She yanked her focus back to her hostess.

"Yes, well, shall we get on with the reason for our visit?"

Mrs. Harding turned to Chloe. "What is your hurry?" The old woman waved away Chloe's words. "Please come have a seat. I'll have my girl, Julia, bring us a pot of tea and some cookies. Come, come. Let's go into the parlor. I've collected all my photographs and letters there. We'll be much more comfortable, you know."

Once seated in the old parlor, Chloe peered around to see old photos and paintings on the walls. A grand piano sat in one corner polished to a shine. A fireplace stood in the middle of the wall opposite the windows. Bookshelves were filled with books and knickknacks. The burgundy velvet-covered sofa matched the armchairs on either end. Blake made a beeline for one of those while Chloe and Mrs. Harding made themselves comfortable on the sofa. Chloe didn't miss the carved woodwork surrounding the button-tucked velvet or the carved wooden feet. The room was truly Victorian in style just as the house was. It would be interesting to see the rest of the house, but that wasn't why she was here. She could only imagine Victorian four-poster beds and porcelain washstands in the bedrooms.

The coffee table in front of the couch held stacks of framed photos, albums and a covered box a little larger than a shoebox. A young woman rolled in an old tea cart and moved a few things aside to make room for teacups and cookie plates.

Mrs. Harding poured the tea, and Chloe was surprised how steady her hand was considering her advanced age. They enjoyed the tea and cookies even as Blake looked a little out of place drinking from a China teacup and eating cookies from a gilded plate. Chloe admired how sporting he was to play tea party with his hostess. His flattering attention had the elder woman tittering like a teenager.

"My, my." She fanned herself. "If I were sixty years younger, I'd give some of these young women a run for their money. You'd be in my sights, Mr. Hunter. That you would." She tittered again and sipped her tea.

Chloe had the feeling she simply enjoyed the company because she might not get it often. She glanced at Blake. A crimson tinge flowed beneath his tan.

"Thanks for the compliment, Mrs. Harding." He bit into a cookie then sat back in his seat looking as if he wanted it to swallow him.

Chloe leaned forward and picked up a framed picture of an elderly woman who resembled Mrs. Harding. "This wouldn't by any chance be your grandmother Cecelia, would it?" Chloe placed her empty teacup on the saucer on the coffee table.

Mrs. Harding leaned over for a better view. "Why, yes, it is. I remember her just like that. My husband, Ronald, and I had recently started our family about that time. My grandmother Cecelia loved meeting her great-grandson. Sadly. she died before our other children were born."

"Hello, Cecelia." Chloe lowered her voice as she fingered the edge of the metal and glass frame. "I've wanted to meet you for a while now."

"Oh, my dear, I have other pictures. Let me pull them out so you can see them."

Julia returned and removed the China tea service as they dug into the old photographs.

"Here's Grandmother when she was a young woman." Mrs. Harding handed Chloe an unframed photograph. It was amber tinged and faded. "It would've been taken when she was about eighteen, if my memory recalls correctly. It was, of course, after the Civil War had ended and a few years after her father brought the family to Baltimore. They lived downtown, but sadly, the house they lived in is no longer there. It was torn down to make way for the big buildings they built many years ago. You know. Progress."

Chloe nodded as she examined the photograph. "She was a lovely young woman. I feel like I've gotten to know her a bit in reading her diary. Remember I told you her diary was given to the park?"

"Yes, I do. I'm glad it will be in a place where she'll be remembered for a long time to come. Where visitors to the park can visit and learn about her."

Chloe nodded. "Yes, that they will. We'll make sure they do."

They continued to peruse the old photographs, Chloe passing them to Blake so he could see them too. There were pictures of Cecelia's family—her parents and her siblings. Even an old photo of the house at the battlefield before the war.

"May I take a picture of this with my phone so I can share it with the restoration contractors? It might help them to see what it looked like so long ago."

Mrs. Harding pushed the picture toward Chloe. "Keep it, dear. I would rather it would go to such a cause and help in the restoration of my grandmother's old home than sit in a box." She released a heavy sigh then continued. "My son died a couple of years ago, and he never had children. His wife couldn't, you know. I have two daughters. One is a grandmother, the other a great-grandmother. There are plenty of photographs to go around, I'm sure. And here—" She picked up the old, amber-colored photo of Cecelia at age eighteen and one of the whole Langston family. "Take these as well. The one of Cecelia is probably the closest in age to when she lived in the house."

Chloe was flabbergasted. "B…but, Mrs. Harding, are you certain? These are three special photographs."

The older woman laid a hand on Chloe's. "I'm certain. You are doing a wonderful thing at the park. You're restoring Cecelia's home and keeping her and her memories alive. That's all I can ask for. Thank you, Miss Rogers."

They spent the next hour sifting through the box to see what else they could discover. Deciding to divide and conquer, each took a pile of papers and began going through them. There were old letters, theater tickets, shopping lists, purchase receipts, even war ration coupons. At the bottom of the box lay what looked like an extremely old ledger.

Chloe pulled white cotton gloves from her tote, and, with great care, she lifted it out. The cloth cover and binding were worn, and the front cover barely hung on. Opening it, she read that it belonged to Elijah S. Langston, Attorney-At-Law.

"This belonged to your great-grandfather Elijah Langston." Chloe turned another page then another. "It looks like an accounting ledger."

"Yes, I do remember seeing that before. My husband went through it once. I believe great-grandfather was quite meticulous in his business affairs." Mrs. Harding gave a light laugh. "I was happy to know I come from honest stock."

Blake held up a letter he'd been reading. "Here's something interesting. It's a letter from a Cordelia Mahoney, whoever that is, to Cecelia, dated November 10, 1873. That's ten years after the Battle of Gettysburg. She mentions something Cecelia told her."

Chloe reached for the letter, skimmed it, then read it aloud.

Dearest Cecelia,

I've thought about the horrific thing you told me you witnessed back during the war. How have you held this to yourself so long and not shared it with your family? Why have you waited until now to share it with me alone? Oh, my sweet friend, it must have been torture to hold this knowledge to yourself these ten years. That poor man who died needlessly. Why did he need those other soldiers' signatures on that paper? And where did the paper disappear to? Do you think the murdering officer took it with him?

My dearest friend, know that I'm here for you. I only wish you would talk to your father. He would listen because he's a good man. You're now a mother yourself and need to put this behind you. Get the help and support you need from those who love you most.

I love you, my friend.
Cordelia

"Oh, poor grandmother. What, may I ask, did she see that caused her to suffer so?" Mrs. Harding tugged a dainty, floral cloth handkerchief from her sweater sleeve and dabbed at her eyes.

Chloe proceeded to tell her the whole story of finding the body of Sarge and all she'd read in Cecelia's diary. "Please, Mrs. Harding. This information is not to be released into the public yet." Chloe placed a hand on the elder woman's arm. "You can't tell a soul. I thought it was only fair to share with you because of Cecelia and this letter. We're still investigating Sarge's death. Cecelia's diary has given us good information, but we've hit a brick wall. This letter doesn't give us anything except the knowledge that Cecelia suffered for having seen the murder. Her diary indicated that, but this proves it. It was a horrible thing for a fifteen-year-old to witness. I would love to know if she ever shared with her father. At least she opened up to a friend."

Mrs. Harding shook her head. "I have no idea, my dear. There were tales passed down that something terrible had happened at the battlefield house, but my parents wouldn't tell me. They didn't want to talk about it. My older brother always said it was haunted. We visited there when I was young, but someone was living in it at the time. I heard it changed hands several times then it was abandoned."

"The daughter of the last family to live there recently sold the property to the park." Chloe closed the letter and the ledger. "Well, we've made a thorough search here, and you've been most gracious in donating these photographs to the park. I'll ensure a display is created in the house to keep the memory of your grandmother alive."

"That's all I can ask." Mrs. Harding turned to Blake. "And

you, young man. Thank you for your help. Cordelia Mahoney was my grandmother's best friend whom she met when she moved to Baltimore. They remained friends until Grandmother passed away at the age of eighty-eight. Cordelia passed away at the ripe old age of ninety-eight. I intend to outlive them both."

~

Once back on the road, Chloe and Blake discussed their visit with Mrs. Harding. They chuckled over several moments of the visit and Mrs. Harding's abundant humor.

"She was something else, wasn't she?" Chloe chuckled as she pulled out the photos their hostess had given her for the park.

"Are you kidding me?" Blake turned the vehicle onto the highway. "Ninety? She acted more like nineteen."

Chloe's cell phone rang, and she retrieved it from her purse. She'd seen the number before but couldn't place it.

"Hello? This is Chloe Rogers. How can I help you?"

"Miss Rogers, this is Margery Baker, the receptionist at Hill Restoration Specialists. I have some, well, some terrible news."

Was the woman sniffling? As in crying sniffling? Why would the receptionist at a restoration contractor be crying?

Chloe glanced at Blake. "Okay, Ms. Baker. I'm sorry to hear that. Does it have anything to do with Mr. Hill putting in a bid on the Bryant house?"

Sniff, sniff. "Yes, I'm afraid it does. Mr. Hill won't be able to put in a bid. He's dead. He was murdered. Shot through the head in his office last night." The crying increased. "Hill Restoration…Specialists withdraws our opportunity to bid." The woman hung up.

Chloe sat for a moment as the line went dead. Shot? In his office? What…? Why?

"Chloe?"

A hand rested on her arm bringing her attention back inside the car. She jerked.

"Chloe, what's wrong? What was that about?" The concern in Blake's voice grew, his head on a swivel from the road to her.

"One of the contractors who was working on a bid for the Bryant house was murdered last night."

~

Blake's stomach churned at Chloe's news. Murdered? Was it a

coincidence? Or could it be connected somehow? His gut told him it was the later but why? Who had a vested interest in killing a contractor? He'd make some phone calls when he returned. See what he could find out. That is, if he could do it without his chief catching on. Maybe Gabe would help him out.

Chloe sat in the corner of her seat, her head against the headrest. The excitement that had flowed through her before the phone call now diminished by the horrific news. Blake hoped it didn't spread to the other contractors causing them to withdraw their bids. Chloe would be back to square one, and it was doubtful there was a plethora of restoration contractors to call on.

Since tea and cookies was the closest thing to lunch they'd had, they stopped for tacos on their way home. Fortunately, the bad news hadn't stollen Chloe's appetite and she ate well.

She remained quiet on the trip home, and Blake kept his own thoughts as he mulled over the whole Bryant house mystery. Nothing came together as the mystery murderer remained just that. A mystery.

Blake turned into driveway at the superintendent's house at four-forty-five and parked beside his pickup truck. They climbed out and Chloe stretched before retrieving her purse and messenger bag.

"It might not have been that far to Hanover, but I feel like I've been on the road all day." Chloe closed the door of the SUV and took a couple steps away.

"I know what you mean." Blake flexed his shoulders. "It was a long day. But a good one."

Chloe stood with her bags in front of her. "Yes, it was until the sad news at the end. I'll let Dad know about that. Hill Restorations was one of the contractors the park has used for years. I hope Mr. Hill's son will continue the business. He's worked with his dad for a long time, but whether or not he'll take over remains to be seen."

The front door of the house flew open, and Aunt Char ran out holding Evie in her arms. The crying child rested her head on her great-aunt's shoulder.

"Oh, my goodness, Chloe? Blake? I'm so glad you're back! It's...it's awful! I...I didn't know what to do!" Aunt Charlene grabbed Chloe in a hug and squeezed.

Chloe hugged her back then held her away. "Aunt Char, what

in the world is going on? Why is Evie crying?"

She held out her arms and her daughter scrambled into them. "Mommy, I'm scared."

Chloe held her daughter close and rubbed her back. "Sh-h. It's okay, princess. Let Aunt Char tell me what's going on, okay?"

Evie nodded against Chloe's neck.

Aunt Charlene wrapped her now empty arms around herself. "I…I didn't know what to do. I still don't."

Blake put a hand on her shoulder. "Take a deep breath."

Aunt Charlene closed her eyes and inhaled then released it. She opened her eyes, pinning Blake.

He nodded. "Now tell me what happened."

"Evie and I went shopping. I bought her a couple of dresses, then we went to the grocery store with a long list, so we were gone a while. I took the cooler bags, so things would stay cool in the car. We drove by the park so she could play at the playground for a bit. She had so much fun."

Blake bit his tongue. He hadn't meant every detail, but if it got them to where they needed to be and this was how she could tell it, so be it. "Okay, so what happened after the playground?"

"We stopped for an ice cream cone."

Evie perked up and lifted her head from Chloe's shoulder. "It was yummy. I had peaches 'n cweam."

Blake nearly chuckled when she licked her lips. "And then?"

Aunt Charlene thought for a moment. "And then we came home. I grabbed my purse, a bag of groceries and Evie's hand, and we went through the garage into the kitchen. I thought I'd lose my ice cream. The house was trashed. Someone had broken in the sliding glass door and broken into the house. The door was smashed. Shattered glass all over the place. It was like they'd taken a sledgehammer to it."

"What?" Chloe's voice rose as she clutched Evie close.

"How long have you been home, and how long were you in the house?" Blake bent down and tugged his service firearm, a Glock 9mm, from an ankle holster.

"We've been home less than five minutes." Aunt Char shrugged. "I saw the condition of the house, heard your car doors and grabbed Evie. We hurried out as soon as I saw it was you two."

"I want the three of you to climb into my truck and lock the doors." He handed the keys to Chloe. "Don't get out until I give you the all clear. Understood?"

"Do you think there's still someone in there?" She lowered her voice and moved toward the truck.

"That's what I'm going to find out. Now hurry. I'm not going in until you're all locked in."

Once they were, Blake hurried toward the front door Aunt Charlene had left standing wide open. With gun pointed upward in front of him, Blake cleared the entry hall and made his way into the open kitchen/family room.

Just as Aunt Charlene had described, everything was trashed. Furniture was upturned, cushions torn open, kitchen cabinets gaped with everything strewn on the floor. Drawers were dumped. Pictures had been torn from the walls and slashed, the backs separated from the pictures. Whoever had done this was looking for something and had done a thorough job of it.

Blake avoided the broken glass near the sliding glass doors. The culprit knew the family was gone which indicated they had watched them leave. They had no way of knowing how long Aunt Charlene and Evie would be gone unless they'd heard them talking about where they were going. Or the culprit simply took a chance. Blake's blood chilled at the thought of them walking in on him. Was he or she still here? Blake would find out.

He checked out the office only to find it tossed like the family area. A safe beneath a credenza sat ajar, papers spilling from it. If there had been anything of value in there, it was likely gone. The superintendent would have to determine that.

Blake made his way down the hardwood hallway on silent tread, his gun at the ready. He was at the most vulnerable here. At any moment the culprit could spring from one of the bedrooms or the hallway bathroom. He hoped upon hope the bathroom fan didn't automatically come on when he switched on the light. He flipped the switch and held his breath. No fan. *Thank you, Lord.* And a clear shower curtain. A double blessing.

Flipping off the light, he continued down the hallway to the first bedroom. Obviously, it belonged to Evie. Decorated with every imaginable stuffed animal, the little girl's room was decorated with pink like most little girl's rooms. One sliding door on the closet remained open giving him access. Nothing to be concerned about. He bent and peeked beneath the bed, tugging up the pink unicorn comforter. Too narrow for a grown man. There were no other hiding places in here. Blake moved on down the hallway.

He checked out two feminine rooms and picked out Chloe's without a problem. Neither held an intruder. The superintendent's room was masculine and smelled of aftershave. Blake halted in the doorway. Would aftershave leave that strong of an odor? Thinking back, he didn't remember the superintendent wearing aftershave this morning. A red flag lifted as the hair stood up on the back of his neck.

He took a step back into the hall when the bedroom door shoved toward him. His shoulder took the brunt of the hit. He dropped to the floor and rolled toward the wall. Pain arced through him at the move. He fought to take a breath.

Gunfire riddled the door. Glass shattered.

He shoved the door open. A large figure dressed in black climbed onto the windowsill preparing to jump. Blake raised his gun. "Police. Halt or I'll shoot."

The figure glanced back. Dark eyes glittered from a black ski mask. A twisted smile formed in the hole for the mouth. From the bulk of the huge figure, it was likely a man. The one who did a number on Blake? Probably.

"Climb down out of that window. Now." Blake took a few steps closer, gun still aimed at the man.

A low, almost evil chuckle emanated from the figure dressed in black. In a flash he dove out.

Blake ran to the window and fired. It looked like his shot hit the man, as he reached up and leapt over the wooden fence surrounding the backyard. Woods lay beyond the fence, and he'd disappeared into them. Who knew where he'd come out?

Blake slammed a hand on the windowsill. Gasping, he held his side. It was easier than it had been a week earlier but still not as easy as it should be.

The chief probably wouldn't be happy about this, but hopefully he'd understand. Blake would call in a BOLO on the dark late 80's Toyota Camry involved in all the other crime scenes. Perhaps if they found the vehicle, they'd find the man. Surely if they spread a net far and wide enough, they'd eventually catch the guy.

Chapter Eighteen

"We found what we think is the perp's car." Chief Morton flipped a page on his notepad as he stood behind the podium in the squad room. "It matches the description from the night Officer Hunter was attacked and the day Chloe Rogers and the restoration contractor were nearly shot. Now that we have it in the possession of the park police, I can tell you it's a black 1989 Toyota Camry. It was parked a mile behind the superintendent's house. One of our patrolmen happened on it and was obviously suspicious when it had no license plate. He impounded it just as Officer Hunter called in the break in at Superintendent Fielding's house and the BOLO on the car.

"A forensic team is working the scene now for evidence. Our perp is either on foot or has called for a ride. I want every one of you out there searching for this guy. It's doubtful he'll still be wearing the ski mask, but he was dressed in black." He shrugged and heaved a heavy sigh. "With the way kids dress in black today, it may be difficult, but this guy is built big. Dark eyes. At least that cuts down on a portion of the population. Let's get out there."

Blake remained in his chair. Chief Morton had told him under no circumstances would Blake be taking part in the manhunt.

As the room cleared of patrol officers, the chief walked to the rear of the room where Blake waited. *Here it comes. I've done it now.*

Chief Morton turned a chair around and straddled it, placing his arms along the top of the back. He eyed Blake for several seconds. Blakes insides squirmed, but he forced himself to remain still. "Hunter, I don't blame you for what you did today at Superintendent Fielding's house. If you hadn't been there, no telling what that thug would've done to those ladies." Morton paused, his gaze moving above Blake's shoulder then returning after a few seconds. "He destroyed their home. Things can be replaced. I'm thankful you were there to protect them so he didn't completely destroy their lives."

"Sir—"

Chief Morton held up a hand. "I also appreciate you driving Miss Rogers to Hanover. I'm sure that was a big help to her."

"Sir—"

"However, I have to ask you, what's it going to take to keep you down?"

Was that the hint of a grin on the chief's face? Surely Blake was mistaken. Chief Morton sounded almost angry in spite of the fact he appreciated Blake taking care of Superintendent Fielding's family.

"Sir?"

Chief Morton let out a chuckle and shook his head. "You aren't going to make it a month, are you?"

Blake's shoulders slumped as he crossed his arms over his chest. "I'm trying, sir. Believe me, I am. It's just I'm not used to sitting on the sidelines. Actually, I hate sitting on the sidelines."

The chief tossed him a half grin. "Understood. I've had my own difficulties during my career that sidelined me too, so I know exactly where you're coming from and how you feel. Look, you proved yourself capable today. You've had yourself a couple of weeks' rest so I'm going to put you back on duty. I hope I'm not making a mistake, but there you go. Starting Monday, you're back on duty."

Elation welled up in Blake, but he tempered it with a simple grin. "Thank you, sir. I appreciate that more than you know."

The chief stood and waved a dismissive hand. "Oh, I know, Hunter. But remember, you don't start until Monday morning."

Blake remained in his seat, hesitating.

The chief stopped as he noticed. "Well, what is it?"

"Sir, I have to return to Superintendent Fielding's house. Tonight."

A pucker formed between Chief Morton's brows as they narrowed and dipped. "What? Why?"

"I need to be there for her, sir. Her family is going through a rough time right now."

The chief's features cleared, and a smile formed. "It's like that, is it? Then go. Be there for Miss Rogers. She's a fortunate young lady. But steer clear of the forensic team. Let them do their jobs. Yours starts Monday morning."

Blake stood and made a beeline for the door. "Yes, sir."

~

Chloe sat on the patio swing, her sleeping daughter wrapped in a light blanket in her arms. Dad and Aunt Char answered the investigator's questions inside the house. Chloe had caught a good glimpse of the destruction that once had been their home and sought the peace and quiet of the back yard. With her head against the back of the swing, she gently rocked back and forth, her gaze on the inky sky. Distant stars twinkled amidst the velvety navy-blue background, their steady presence reminding her Someone waited for her to trust Him with all this chaos. Goodness knew, she certainly had no control over any of it. She closed her eyes as tears threatened.

I've ignored You long enough, Lord. Since Josh died, I've pretended I could do life without You, but I know as well as You do, I can't. I blamed You for his death when in reality, evil men killed him. Did You let him die? Chloe thought about that for a moment, recalling her dad's words the day she discussed with him her need to return to the Lord.

> *"We don't understand God's perfect will. We can't understand why He allows a child to die of cancer, or someone to be murdered. But He has a purpose for everything. In Romans 8:28 it says 'And we know that all things work together for good to them that love God, to them who are called according to his purpose.'"*

I don't understand your will, Lord, but You have Your reasons for allowing Josh to die, don't You? You're God, after all. I should trust You to know what You're doing, huh? I don't understand what's happening lately with the shooting at the Bryant house, the chaos inside our home, and of course, Blake getting injured and the body of Sarge getting torn apart. Is the death of Mr. Hill even related? It's all so confusing. But through it all I should simply trust You. Will you forgive my anger at You these past three years? Forgive me for not speaking to You? Forgive me for not trusting You? I want my relationship with You to return to what we had before.

Peace settled over Chloe the likes of which she hadn't recognized in years. She cuddled Evie closer, dropping a kiss on her sweet-smelling head. *Thank you, Lord, for Your forgiveness. Please protect my daughter and help the park police find whoever is doing all these...these evil things. Whatever or whoever is behind them, show us, Lord.*

"Hey there." A familiar male voice brought a wide-eyed smile to her face as she turned to find Blake stepping through what once was the sliding glass door. "Hi." Chloe kept her voice soft so as not to awaken Evie. She held a finger to her lips to let him know to stay quiet then pointed at her sleeping daughter.

He nodded then sat down on the cushioned seat beside her. "How's she doing?"

"As good as any of us, I suppose." Chloe tucked the blanket higher around Evie. "Maybe better. She doesn't understand everything the adults do."

"Yeah." Blake placed an arm along the back of the swing behind Chloe's shoulders, turning to face her. "To be a kid again, huh?"

"There are days." Chloe released a sigh. "Any news about the guy who broke in?"

"They found his car. It's the same one used the night I was attacked and also the one that took off after you and Mr. Waters were shot at. There's a BOLO out on the guy, but it's going to be hard to be on the lookout for someone who's hard to describe. He was dressed all in black. His only real description is dark eyes and a huge build. He's probably already been picked up by a friend and is in hiding."

"I'm praying the Lord will show us who is behind these horrible activities." Chloe returned her gaze to the night sky.

Blake peered at Chloe. "You've started talking to the Lord again? I'm glad to hear that."

"Yeah. I had a talk with Dad. He pointed out the fact that God didn't cause Josh's death. Evil men did. Whatever God's purpose in allowing his death, I need to trust that rather than doubt it.

There's a lot of chaos going on right now, and I believe I'd rather trust the Lord to guide me through it than attempt to wade through on my own. I haven't managed well the last three years without His help. It's time to start trusting again."

He gently squeezed her shoulder then moved his hand away. Her insides warmed at his touch.

"You know I wasn't trusting at all until a couple of years ago." Blake released a soft sigh. "I didn't know the Lord until a friend of mine who was a fellow park ranger and archeologist at the Grand Canyon led me to the Lord. Another ranger named Kate Fleming, whom he was in love with, was being chased into the canyon by a killer. My friend, Ethan Wagner, and I followed to try and reach her before the killer did. The deeper into the canyon we went the more Ethan prayed. We heard gunshots several times. The sun set, darkness making the descent treacherous. By the time we reached Kate, she'd defended herself, in spite of being shot. It wasn't long after that Ethan led me to Christ. I had seen through Ethan's example and faith how much I needed the Lord."

Chloe tilted her head and gave him a sideways smile. "I'm glad you did. That sounds like an exciting time. And here you are again involved in yet another case. Perhaps you shouldn't have shown up that day to help me check the house for squatters." She chuckled then sobered as Blake ran a gentle finger down her cheek and lifted her chin. His gaze roamed her features, igniting her skin with warmth.

"I have no regrets. Not even for a second." Blake wrapped an arm around her shoulder tugging her close.

He leaned in and placed a tender kiss on her lips, sending Chloe's heartrate into double time. Oh my. What he did to the butterflies in her mid-region. They were spirally out of control. When he pulled back a few inches, Chloe released a soft sigh and slowly opened her eyes. "That was…wow." Her voice was a mere whisper.

"Yeah, my thoughts exactly." Blake lowered his head and remained longer this time.

~

Monday morning found Chloe in the superintendent's office. The last time she was here she'd received a diary and the key to an old house. Looking back, it was more like Pandora's box. Opening that house had released a plethora of bad things mixed with good. It was a wash as to which there was more of, and she was undecided at this point if it had been worth it.

Yes, they had an old house, but so far, she wasn't sure if there was a contractor who was willing to work on it. She had information about Cecelia, but that was about it. Poor Sarge had received the brunt of someone's ire, and they still didn't know who the sergeant was or who didn't like him. Someone killed him, but they didn't know why.

There had to be a connection between the murder in 1863 and why someone still didn't like him. Now that was a long-standing grudge. Could someone have passed their hatred down through their family? It wasn't unheard of. For example, the Hatfield and McCoy grudge was certainly longstanding and passed down through generations. And theirs wasn't the only one.

Her dad's secretary ushered Chloe into his office and closed the door behind her.

"Come on in, sweetheart. Have a seat." He leaned back in his chair, his hands clasped across his stomach, his elbows on the arms of the chair. "What can I do for you?" Shadows lay beneath his eyes and accentuated the lines on his features. The park was renting them a four-bedroom house while the superintendent's residence was being repaired and insurance worked on their personal-property claim. As with most claims it would take time.

"How are you doing, Dad?" Chloe set her messenger bag on the floor beside her chair as she sat in front of his desk.

"Oh, I'm doing all right. Lots of phone calls to make, but I'm okay"

"If I can help with anything, let me know." Chloe gave him a sympathetic smile. "You shouldn't have to bear all this by yourself."

"I'm not, sweetheart. I've got some bigger shoulders than mine I'm leaning on." He pointed heavenward. "God has us covered, you know."

"I know. I took your advice and had a talk with Him." Chloe glanced at her fingers in her lap then back at him again. "Things are…good. Between us, I mean."

Dad smiled. "I'm happy to hear that. As I told you, I've been praying for you for a long time, kiddo. Praise God." He gave a little sniff then swiped a finger under his eye. "Well, now, is that what you wanted to talk to me about?"

"No, I wanted to talk to you about the need for a secure safe in the history department. Considering the artifacts we've uncovered, and any possible ones in the future, and the fact someone has been after these, we need one. I've been carrying these artifacts around with me everywhere I go. That's not safe either. I'm glad I had them with me. If they were still in your safe, someone could've taken them."

"Do you think that's what they were after?"

She shrugged. "Why do you ask?"

"Because I had some silver pieces and old coins in my safe. They were tossed out but not taken." Dad rubbed a hand over his jaw. "As I discussed with the investigator Friday evening, if it was a random robbery, they would've taken those things. Also, why rip open the couch and armchair cushions? It looked more like they were looking for something specific."

"Yes, it does." Chloe leaned an elbow on her crossed knee, her chin in her palm. "Dad, that fact should concern you. Someone tore apart the examination room at the office looking for something. They tore apart the body we found at the Bryant house. Now they tore apart our home. It stands to reason they're looking for the letters we found in the body's uniform."

"Have you finished reading them? Did you find any information that was suspicious?" Her father leaned forward, his arms on the shiny surface of the desk.

Chloe tucked a loose tendril of hair behind her ear and shook her head. "No. I've read a few, but haven't found anything yet. I have a few more to read. There's just been so much going on."

"I know what you mean, but you might want to get to the rest of those letters soon."

Chloe nodded again. "It's going to be a busy week, but I have to. Saturday is the donor event. You have your tux ready to go?" She almost laughed at the foul expression that settled on his features.

"I have to rent one. It was one of the casualties from my closet in the break-in. The guy ripped some of my clothes from the closet then dumped everything from my dresser on top of it. That included a tray of plastic bottles of paint he stepped on and squished. Char is working on finding another tux for me today."

Chloe's chuckle burst out. She covered her mouth with her hand. "Sorry. I just had a mental picture...." She paused and sobered. "Wait a minute. Did you tell the investigators about the squished paint? If the guy stepped in it, maybe they can use that to help look for him. He may not realize he stepped in the paint."

His brows furrowed. "I hadn't thought of that."

He reached for the phone receiver then stopped. "Yes, I approve an extremely secure safe for the history department. I'll look into it and will take care of it, ASAP. You shouldn't be carrying artifacts around on your person. Now, why don't you head out. I'm going to make a call to the investigators taking care of the house and tell them about the paint. Hopefully it hasn't been cleaned it up yet."

~

Chloe headed to her office and found Clifford at his desk working on his computer.

"Good morning. What are you up to?" Chloe placed her messenger bag behind her desk and her purse in its usual place. Taking a seat, she booted her computer.

"Researching the brass knob. I want to see if I can pin down exactly what it goes to."

"I'm eager to see it all cleaned up and shiny. When you have time, that is."

"Can you give me a few minutes? I think I may be onto something here." Clifford never raised his eyes from the computer screen.

"Take your time. I still have letters to read." Chloe retrieved them and pulled on her cotton gloves. She opened the next one she hadn't read and spread out the pages. The ink had faded, and the pages were yellowed and brittle around the edges. Careful not to break the edges away, Chloe aimed her desk lamp directly at the paper making the area brighter and easier to read.

The letter was from Margaret Holmes, Sarge's fiancée. It wasn't a newsy letter; nor was it long. Short and sweet and to the point. Margaret simply reminded Sarge she loved and missed him. She addressed him as *My Dearest,* so unfortunately, the letter didn't name him. She reminded him that when he returned, she would hold him to his promise to marry her.

How heartbreaking. This beautiful young woman never knew the fate of the man she loved. He never returned, so they never married. What happened to Margaret Holmes? Most likely his family received a letter from his commander stating he was missing or killed in action. It would be little solace to his family or the woman who loved him so dearly.

Chloe refolded the letter and tucked it back into the bag. She began to withdraw the next one when Cliff spoke,

"Okay, if you're ready, let's take a look at the brass knob. I think I've identified what it came from." He shoved away from his desk and stood then stopped at the printer to pick some pages.

"Sure. Let's go." Chloe stripped the cotton gloves from her hands, dropping them to her desk, and followed Clifford to the examination room.

The brass knob, now bright and shiny, sat on a plastic dish on the examination table. Clifford adjusted the arm of the extension magnifying glass and lamp combination and switched on the light. He pulled it over the knob so Chloe could get a good look. "There you go. Take a gander at that."

The knob and his finger pointing at it under the lit magnifying glass looked huge. Chloe concentrated on the engraved letters.

"This is pretty classy engraving, don't you think?" Clifford reached for a sharp wooden tool and followed the fancy engraved design encircling the monogram. "Whoever commissioned this paid a pretty penny. Especially back in the day."

"I agree." Chloe turned the plastic dish to examine it from a different angle. "You think you know what it came from?"

"Yeah. A saber. I suspected that, but from my research, I'm almost certain." Clifford shoved a couple of the printed pages over for Chloe to see. "Take a look at these saber pommels. I found a few examples online that were monogrammed, and my research tells me they were likely gifts to the saber owners for some momentous occasion. A big promotion or something like that. Monogrammed caps seem few and far between. Filigree or plain caps are far more common. I'm going to take it down to the museum this afternoon and compare it to some of the pommel caps we have on the sabers there. See if I can't get a better idea about it. There are a few straight walking canes in the museum I can compare it with as well."

Chloe glanced up at him. "I know you. You won't let it go until you pin it down for certain."

"Nope. I won't." He gathered his papers and tamped them together on the table.

Chloe observed the knob through the magnifying glass again. "So the initials on the monogram are E W M. That doesn't match Elijah S. Langston's initials so it could belong to anyone." She straightened. "We know the wall was most likely constructed immediately after Sarge was killed, and the cap was inside the wall."

"My educated guess is it came off the saber that killed Sarge." Clifford shoved his hands into his olive drab slacks. "It's the only explanation."

"Agreed." Chloe bent to observe the knob through the magnifying glass once again. "But pinpointing an officer with those initials at the Battle of Gettysburg could take time we don't have."

~

He slumped into his usual seat at the back of the bar and waved away the barmaid when she stopped by. Scanning the dark interior of the bar, he noticed the usual customers, none of which sat near him. He shoved back the hood of his black jacket, gasping. It wouldn't do to call the boss and be out of breath. He had to be in control of himself before calling. The boss hated anything out of control. Well, he'd been in control when he'd left the house, laughing in the cop's face, even though the cop had winged him.

He didn't dare lift the jacket to check the damage to his side. He'd wait until after calling the boss, then he'd slip into the bathroom and take a peek. Figuring it to be a graze wound, he could take care of it himself. What upset him was losing his car. He'd arrived in time to spot a park cop impounding it. He cracked his knuckles as he always did when he was nervous. How was he going to get around without a car? Maybe the boss could send a taxi to get him back to the house. Taking another deep breath, he dialed the number and waited.

"Did you find the letter in the ranger's house? *Please* tell me you did," the whispered words insisted.

He swallowed. His euphoria at tearing the house apart in his search had dissipated and left him vulnerable to the boss's demands.

"Well, I tore the house apart. Literally, Boss. I searched everywhere. I even broke into the office safe. There were no letters anywhere. There was nowhere I left unturned. They can't even live in that house, that's how bad I destroyed it." Wouldn't that go a long way in the boss's estimation on his account?

"Then if it's not in the office or at the historian's house, where could it be?"

He cringed. How was it possible for a person to whisper and yell at the same time? "Boss, you tell me my next move, and I'll make it. Just say the word." His side was on fire. He wanted to take a look and see what the damage was.

"I'll be in touch." His cell phone went silent.

"Of course, you will." He mumbled as he slipped the cell phone into his jacket pocket and slid from the booth. Heading for the men's bathroom, he shoved the door open and checked to ensure no other customers were in the stalls. Standing before the mirror above one of the sinks, he yanked the bottom of his hoodie up. He'd felt dampness on the side of the jacket but wasn't prepared for the long red gash along his side about halfway between his armpit and his waist. That cop had winged him good. The flesh was torn, and blood trickled down his side toward his black sweatpants. He ran a hand along them and his hand came away wet with blood. A wave of nausea roiled through him. He washed his hands then used them to drink water from the sink. Grabbing several paper towels from the dispenser, he dampened them and held them to his side. Pain surged through him causing him to hiss. Gasping in longs huffs, he grabbed more towels and applied them to his side, tucked his jacket back down, then pressed his arm against it. He needed to go home.

With a nod to the bartender, he headed out the front door and into the bright sunlight. Home was only a few blocks from here. He'd take the alleyways and get there as quickly as he could. Some first aid and clean clothes then he'd be fine. The boss hadn't been in the mood to talk about the car. He'd ask the next time there were orders. If the boss wanted this job done and done right, surely, he would need wheels. He only hoped the cops didn't fingerprint the car they'd confiscated. What were the chances of that?

Chapter Nineteen

"I understand, sir. I'm sure we'll be able to work on other projects in the future. At least I hope so. Thank you. Goodbye."

Chloe dropped the phone receiver onto the cradle and her head onto her hands. A heavy sigh escaped as tears stung behind her eyelids. Another thing to add to the list. *Lord, help.*

A knock sounded on the open office door, and Chloe lifted her head to see Blake leaning against the doorway, arms folded across his chest.

"Now that's the look of a woman who's not having a good morning."

Chloe straightened and attempted a smile. "Is it that obvious?"

"It's oozing from every pore." Blake entered the room and sat on the corner of her desk. "I almost hate to ask, but—"

Chloe waved a hand in the direction of the phone. "Another restoration contractor withdrew his bid for the Bryant house. Said he'd heard about the shooting involving Mr. Waters and the death of Mr. Hill. He doesn't want to risk getting killed. Even mentioned that maybe the Bryant property is cursed." Chloe shook her head and rolled her eyes.

"Do you have anybody left to bid?"

"Yes. Wiseman is still in the running. Or rather, they're the only ones left. They've already sent in their bid. I guess I'll call and tell them they've got the job and to get started."

"Are Cliff and Ian finished with everything they need to do at the house?" Blake crossed his arms over his chest.

"I'll have to check with him. Cliff wanted to take a look in the house first before work starts. He's concentrated on the cellar and hasn't been back in the house since the day you and I were in there with him." Chloe tightened her ponytail.

"So what's your plan for the day?"

Chloe shifted in her seat. "I have to help Jan with some plans for Saturday's donor event, then I'm heading home to help Aunt Char work at the house. The insurance adjuster came and did his thing yesterday. He asked as we go through the house to write down specific items for the claim. We can start sifting through things. You know, determine what's still good to keep and what to throw away. Dad ordered a dumpster to be delivered. He's taking the afternoon off to help us."

"Need another hand?" Blake smiled.

"Really? You're not working?" She pointed at his uniform.

He shook his head. "I worked last night, and I'm off duty. After a few hours' sleep. I'll head to your place about noon if that's okay. Since I'm off tonight and tomorrow night, I can work late at your place if necessary."

"Thanks. That would be a huge help."

"My pleasure."

The wink he gave Chloe stirred the butterflies in her mid-region and sent a sensation tiptoeing down her spine. What was it about this man that drew her? His rugged Marlboro Man looks? His kindness? The way he made her feel all gooey inside? His faith? His strength? His.... well, she could go on and on, but the answer to all these questions was yes. All these things drew her to him. *Lord, is he the one? He'll never take Josh's place, but I'm beginning to see I might be able to love again.*

~

Chloe picked up the books from the floor in her room. A few had been savagely ripped apart, but most were okay. She'd bought a notebook and written down the titles of the destroyed books. It was heartbreaking. Some were older books she doubted could be replaced. Setting some aside for rebinding, she tackled the items that had been ripped from her closet. Most literally, they were ripped apart, including her clothes.

"How's it going, sweetie?"

Chloe met her aunt's concerned eyes as she stood in the doorway, hands on her hips.

"Just as you do I feel like I've been violated." Chloe tossed one of her dresses in the box of trash. "What's going on out front?"

"Well, the sofa and armchairs are in the dumpster. Your dad thinks the table and chairs are fine. The guy didn't do anything with them. No place to hide anything there, I guess. He busted up the drawers from the end tables so they're gone as well as the lamps. I don't know why he busted them up. All the pictures are gone. The desk in Dan's office should make it, but the guy slammed his office chair into his computer monitor and his laptop is smashed. He's going to see if the hard drive can be recovered."

Chloe threw her hands into the air. "I simply don't understand the reason for the violence in this break-in. If he was looking for something, that's one thing. But why go to such lengths to destroy our house? Our lives? It makes no sense." She reached over and picked up the framed photo of Josh in his uniform in Afghanistan. The glass was smashed, and the metal frame bent.

Aunt Charlene came to sit on the floor beside Chloe. She wrapped an arm around her niece's waist and rested her head against Chloe's. "Oh, darling. We don't understand the attacks of the evil one and why God allows them, but all we have to do is look to Job in the Bible to know that God will only allow so much and no more. There's a reason we may or may not ever understand, but He's always there in the midst of every trial to see us through. Keep your eyes on Him, sweetie. We have an advocate in Christ Jesus, and God the Father still sits on the throne. Never doubt that."

Chloe swallowed the lump that formed in her throat and nodded.

Aunt Charlene tapped a finger on the bent and broken frame in Chloe's hands. "We'll buy another frame for Josh's picture, sweetie. Don't worry."

"I'm not worried. Is it wrong of me to be ready to put it away? To put it into my photo album instead of leaving it sitting out?"

Aunt Charlene lifted her head and turned Chloe's head with a finger under her chin. "It's not wrong at all if you're ready to move on. Are you?"

Chloe inhaled deeply, releasing the breath slowly as she paused. "I believe I am."

Aunt Charlene gave her shoulder a gentle squeeze. "Blake's a great guy. If I were thirty years younger, you might have to fight for him."

"How did you…?" Chloe stared at her aunt.

"Please. Give me some credit. The way you two act around each other is a dead giveaway." She climbed to her feet. "Come on. It's time to order something for dinner. Those guys are going to grab a table leg and start chewing if we don't get some pizzas soon. I'm simply glad Dan sought help from a few of the rangers. With Blake's injuries, he and Dan couldn't do it all by themselves."

~

Chloe spent the next morning back in the office taking care of several things. She hadn't called Brad Wiseman the day before and needed to. Jan had more questions for her concerning final plans for Saturday's event. It was coming down to the wire and there were a few items to attend to. But she wanted to go home and help Aunt Charlene some more.

Most of the heavy work had been taken care of the afternoon before, but she and Aunt Charlene could deal with the smaller stuff. Evie had spent the day at a friend's house which was extremely helpful. For the most part her daughter's room had been left alone. Puzzling to be sure. Why hadn't the guy destroyed her room like he had all the rest? Did he have a little girl of his own?

Picking up the phone, Chloe dialed the only remaining restoration company on her list.

"Northeast Antique Homes Restoration Specialists. This is Monique speaking. How can I help you?"

"Hi, Monique. This is Chloe Rogers at Gettysburg National Battlefield Park. May I speak with Brad Wiseman please?" Chloe tapped a finger on her desktop. She didn't have patience to speak with anyone but Brad. *You don't have a choice, Chloe, so have some patience. You can't blame this woman. It's her job.*

"Oh, I am sorry. Mr. Wiseman is out of the office today and will be until further notice." The woman's sing-songy voice grated on Chloe like chalk. Groaning inwardly, she inhaled a deep breath then forced a smile in hopes it would come through in her voice. "Until further notice, huh? And you can't tell me when he'll be back in the office? Can you give me a phone number to contact him? It's about the bid he made on the restoration work on the house at the battlefield here in Gettysburg." Chloe hoped she came across as desperate enough that the woman would help her out.

"Sorry. I can't give out his personal phone number." She didn't sound sorry. "He has been calling in to get his messages, though. When he next calls, I'll let him know you've called, and I'll give him your message."

Chloe sighed. "Yes, please tell him I need him to call me. ASAP. It's concerning the bid he made on the restoration contract." Chloe gave the woman her phone number.

"Yes, ma'am. I'll do that. Thank you for calling." The line went silent.

That didn't go as well as Chloe had hoped. She picked up her cell phone and speed dialed Clifford's phone.

When he answered she asked, "Cliff, where are you?"

"In the museum. I didn't finish my research yesterday. Do you have any idea how many sabers we have on display?"

"A lot." Chloe leaned back in her swivel chair and closed her eyes. "How far did you get?"

"About thirty-five."

Chloe chuckled. "Well, you've got your work cut out for you. When are you planning to head to the Bryant house to take the before-restoration pictures? I'm trying to get hold of the contractor to give them the go-ahead."

"I can do that today, I suppose. Ian will go along to help me set up the shots."

"Good. Let me know when you're finished, will you?"

"Will do."

Chloe reached for the bag of letters to spend a few minutes reading when her phone rang. It was Brad Wiseman. "I'm so glad to hear from you. Your receptionist said you were away until further notice."

"Yeah, I've been out of town, but I've been checking my messages. She said you called. What can I do for you?"

Chloe dragged a notepad over and doodled as she spoke. "I wanted to let you know you've been awarded the contract for the Bryant house. My fellow historian wants to go through the main house to take before photos and record them. He's doing that today. You should be able to start by Monday."

"That's great. Thanks for letting me know. I appreciate the business for our company. I'll let you know as soon as we're ready to begin. First off, I'll take my own photos so we can order wallpaper, fabric, etc. Those have to be ordered early even though we won't be ready to install them until much later. They have to be special made."

"Of course, well, I'll leave all that to you. I'm looking forward to the final results, but I'll drop in occasionally to see how the work progresses." Chloe dropped her pen on the notepad.

Brad chuckled. "I'm looking forward to handing you a shiny new key to your restored house."

They hung up and Chloe reached for the messenger bag under the edge of her desk, but a knock at the open doorway had her shoving it back under.

She glanced up to find Mrs. White-Smith standing in the open doorway. Without waiting for an invitation, the woman stepped inside.

"Good morning, Miss Rogers." The older woman walked over and took a seat in front of Chloe's desk. "I trust everything is going as planned for the donor event on Saturday? In anticipation of the event, I bought an evening gown for the affair. I do hope that's appropriate."

Chloe sighed inwardly and plastered on a smile. "Hello, Mrs. White-Smith. Yes, things are going as planned for Saturday's event. It's a tuxedo and evening gown affair so I'm sure your gown will be fine. It's been a while since I've had a reason to dress up in an evening gown, so I'm a little excited about it myself. It should be a wonderful evening."

"Yes, I expect it will, what with the governor and his wife there. I understand there may be a state senator or two in attendance as well." The older woman lifted her nose in the air. "It's always nice to meet with old friends."

Chloe locked her smile in place. "Yes, isn't it."

"Well, I won't keep you. I simply wanted to ask if they've begun the work on the display for my great-great grandfather's diary yet." Mrs. White-Smith crossed her patrician hands in her lap. "I should have a picture of him that I can also loan for the display. It would look ever so nice for visitors to the museum to see what the owner of the diary looked like. Don't you think?"

Chloe nodded. "Certainly. It always gives a more human aspect to the items on display. People see they were personal effects and not just items behind a glass. We'll be sure to take a couple of the important quotes from the diary and display those as well."

Mrs. White-Smith clasped her hands in front of her flat chest, a smile lighting her face, her eyes closing as if in quiet rapture. "My dream come true, Miss Rogers. To have the words of my great-great-grandfather immortalized for the world to see. 'A hero before the masses.'" A euphoric sigh slipped from her as she sat in silence for several moments, her eyes remaining closed.

Chloe wasn't sure if she'd fallen into a trance or dozed off. Unsure if she should tiptoe away or wait until the woman came to, she leaned back in her desk chair only to have it squeak. Mrs. White-Smith's eyes sprang open, pinning her with that dark gaze.

"Yes, well, thank you for helping to secure an old woman's dream come true." She gathered her purse and stared at Chloe down that patrician nose. "Very well, I must go. I look forward to seeing you Saturday if not before."

Chloe stood before she did. This woman had a way of making Chloe wish her visits would end quickly. Disagreeable? No, the woman wasn't exactly that, but she wasn't the warmest person either. She made Chloe feel subservient to her own superiority. The woman was a true descendent of her arrogant great-great-grandfather who thought the world of himself. Chloe was a historian and not a geneticist, but she suspected there must be a dominant arrogant gene in that family.

When the woman had gone, Chloe retrieved the letter of recommendation that came with Mrs. White-Smith's great-great-grandfather's diary. She'd almost forgotten about it. She supposed the woman's visit brought it back to mind. Chloe had intended to read it after the diary but so much had happened in the time since then she'd forgotten about it.

Tugging on her white cotton gloves, she spread the rag paper onto her desk, careful of the brittle edges. The page had been folded into quarters and the center of the page had a small worn hole in it, but she could read around it.

Maj. Gen. Archibald McAdams
5th Connecticut Infantry Regiment
Gettysburg Battlefield
Gettysburg, PA

July 4th, 1863

To the Officers of the Board of Promotions,

It is with great honor that I recommend Col. Edgar William Mayfield for a field promotion to the rank of Brigadier General. This officer has shown great leadership of his division in the midst of battle. It is my belief he will lead a brigade of men with as much honor, selfless service, courage, integrity, duty and loyalty as will be expected by him from this board.

I appreciate your consideration for the promotion of this colonel under my command and look forward to your reply.

Sincerely,

Maj. Gen. Archibald McAdams

Chloe sat for a moment regarding the letter. Apparently, Colonel Mayfield's commanding officer thought highly of the man who served under him or the general wouldn't have taken his word for the deed the colonel reported to him. How could he have gone solely on his word for a promotion without verifying it? It seemed extraordinarily risky on the general's part and beyond protocol. Nothing in the letter referred to the incident found in Colonel Mayfield's diary, so the general is only recommending him for a promotion without reference to that incident. In comparing it to other military letters Chloe had read from the Civil War, it was no wonder the promotion request was denied. According to the colonel's diary, in the end he didn't get the promotion, and he was extremely upset about it.

With great care, Chloe re-folded the page and returned it to the bag of letters.

Something niggled at her brain. Something she couldn't quite put her finger on. After reading this letter, there was something she should be remembering, but she'd read so much information recently with all the letters and the diaries, it was becoming hard to compartmentalize everything. There were the letters to Sarge from his mother and his sweetheart, Cecelia's Diary and Colonel Mayfield's diary and now this letter of recommendation.

Chloe stripped the cotton gloves from her hands and dropped them in her desk drawer. She pulled her lined notebook over and made a page for each person. It continually made her sad that poor Sarge had no name, and none of his letters addressed him as anything but dearest or son. At least he was loved and would surely have been missed when he didn't come home.

She jotted notes on the pages as to what she'd learned about that person—her insights into their characters, their thoughts and feelings. Cecelia and Colonel Mayfield had plenty of information to go on from their diaries, but Sarge had precious little. Most of what the letters from his mother and sweetheart held were information they shared with him. Their love and regard for him was genuine, and it was more than obvious they longed for him to come home. His mother held his ability to persuade his father in the affairs of the family business in high esteem.

Chloe's gut instinct told her Sarge was a man of integrity. Chloe leaned back in her chair and twirled her pen between her fingers. Now how in the world would she know that?

A soft whisper came across the room before the floorboards creaked, like booted footsteps. A finger of unease tiptoed down Chloe's spine as the hair stood up on the back of her neck. What in the...? No. Impossible.

Her cell phone rang, and Chloe jumped. She grabbed it from her desktop.

"Hello?"

"Chloe? You okay?" Clifford's voice sounded in her ear.

"Umm, y...yeah. I...I'm fine." Chloe's gaze raked the room. Where had that sound come from?

"You don't sound fine. What's wrong?"

"Nothing really. I just...I just thought I heard something here in the office, that's all." Chloe ran a hand over her eyes and propped her forehead in her hand, elbow on the desk. Maybe she was overthinking all this diary and letter stuff. But the party was Saturday, and she wanted to have it all together by then.

"Really? You heard it again?" Clifford's words were conspiratorial. "Chloe, we have to address this. We never heard noises until we brought Sarge into the examination room. You have to admit that."

Chloe didn't answer at first. Instead, she changed the subject. "Why did you call? What do you need?"

"Ian and I are about finished here at the Bryant house. Is there anything you want specially as far as photos are concerned?"

"Why don't you bring the SD card back here, and we'll take a look at what you have. We'll go from there."

"Sure. We'll be there shortly."

"Thanks." Chloe started to hang up, then added, "Oh, wait a second."

"Yeah?"

"You've spent all day at the Bryant house. Have you or Ian heard any, you know, any of the…well, the sounds we heard from before?"

A pause then Clifford responded. "Before? You mean before we moved Sarge out of the cellar and to the examination room? No. We haven't heard a thing here today. All has been peaceful and quiet. Want my opinion?"

"Not really."

"Well, you asked, so I'm going to tell you. I believe when we moved Sarge from the cellar, his ghost, which we heard in the house went with him to our offices, and that's what we've been hearing there." He snorted. "But that's just my humble opinion. Which you don't want."

Chloe clicked her pen several times. That wasn't something she wanted to hear. She didn't believe in ghosts. She didn't. She refused.

"Chloe, when we heard the sounds here, you kept saying they were old-house noises. Well, guess what, the old house is still here, but the noises are gone."

Chloe swallowed. She didn't want to have this conversation. On the phone or in person. "Bring the SD card, and we'll take a look at the photos you took. I'm looking forward to seeing them. See you when you get here."

Chapter Twenty

Blake parked his cruiser behind the building and hurried up to the second floor. He hoped Chloe was in her office. His shift was over, and he was hungry. A visit to Moira's was on his agenda, but he'd love Chloe's company for that visit. He still couldn't take the stairs two at a time as he once did, but it was much easier to climb them than right after his injury. Blake had started working out again and was make progress. Being back on duty improved his outlook on life. *Thanks for working that out for me, Lord.*

He stopped a few feet from the doorway to Chloe's office when he heard voices. Pausing, he recognized Clifford then Ian talking. Blake stepped to the open doorway and waited for a few seconds. They were gathered around Chloe's desk observing her computer monitor. Blake tapped on the door.

All eyes zeroed in on him.

"Blake. Come on in." Chloe waved him into the room. "Come join the fun."

Her last word was said with air quotes.

"Fun? What kind of fun?" Blake circled around behind them to catch a glimpse of what they were looking at.

"That's a bit of an exaggeration. These are before shots of the Bryant house." Clifford leaned over the side of the desk and manned the computer mouse, changing the photos as they scrolled through. "We wanted before and after shots. I wanted to know if there was something specific Chloe wanted that I might not have photographed."

"Gotcha." Blake nodded. "Looks like you got a lot."

"Oh, I do." Clifford clicked to the next photo. "I doubt I missed much. We were there all day."

"Have all the wall bricks been removed?" Blake asked.

"Sure have." Ian placed a hand on his back, "And I have the aching muscles to prove it. We hauled them to the maintenance area. They're going to store them until it's decided if they might be used elsewhere in the park."

Blake clapped him on the shoulder. "Good job. You and Cliff both. You worked hard on that project."

"Yeah, we did, but it was worth it." Ian shrugged. "And necessary to remove it before the restoration specialists do their thing. There was a guy out there while we were busy taking pictures. I didn't think he was supposed to be there, but he was."

Chloe spun and stared at Ian. "What? They're not supposed to start until Monday. What company did he say he was with?"

Ian rubbed a hand around his neck. "Northeast Antique Homes. He was snapping pictures all over the house. Mostly inside."

Chloe heaved a sign. "Mr. Wiseman told me he understood they'd start Monday. Maybe he didn't get the message across to his photo guy."

Clifford straightened. "So, what do you say, Chloe? Do you want anything else? Or will these do?"

"These are great." She unseated the SD card and handed it to Clifford. "You even shot a photo of the secret compartment in the upstairs back bedroom. Great job."

He accepted the card and smiled. "Thanks. I'm done for the day. Anybody up for pizza?"

Ian rubbed his stomach. "I'm always up for pizza."

"Chloe? Blake? Pizza?" Clifford stepped over to his desk and locked the SD card in the top drawer.

Before Chloe could speak, Blake met her gaze. "Actually, I had a hankering for Moira's, and that's why I stopped by. To see if Chloe wanted to go with me."

The tell-tale soft color that bloomed in her cheeks sent pleasure through him.

"Oh, I see how it is." Clifford crossed his arms over his chest.

"You'd prefer an intimate little tête-à-tête rather than a rousing party among friends. Well, I'll do my best not to be offended."

Blake spotted the laughter in his eyes and the smirk growing on his lips and gave him a gentle punch on his upper arm. "I knew you'd understand, buddy."

Clifford chuckled. "If I had a woman I was pursuing, I'd do the same."

"You guys do know I'm sitting right here in front of you, don't you? I can hear everything you're saying." Chloe tapped her chest with her fingertips.

"Sure ,we do." Clifford winked.

Blake gave her his hand. "Come on, let's go to Moira's."

Clifford waved a hand to Ian. "Come on, let's go get pizza."

~

Saturday morning, Chloe and Charlene spent time at the furniture store in town picking out replacement furniture. Grandpa Dan took Evie out for the morning to give them a chance to shop. With the donor event scheduled for six that evening, no one wanted to be gone all day.

The gown Chloe had originally bought for the event had been destroyed by the guy who broke into the house. He'd shredded the beautiful blue satin gown and tossed it aside as if it were nothing more than a used mechanics rag.

Chloe and Aunt Charlene made an emergency shopping trip to the mall in York the previous Saturday. Aunt Charlene had found her dad's tux at a Bridal shop and found some gorgeous dresses for Chloe to look at. Chloe had bought a cobalt blue gown with a lace overlay more lovely than the dress she'd originally planned on wearing, and store-died high-heeled sandals to match.

Aunt Charlene arranged Chloe's hair in a lovely updo, then she did her own hair. Chloe arranged Evie's in braids and circled them around the back of her head.

"You look like a real princess now. Just wait until you put on your beautiful new dress. You'll look absolutely royal." Chloe dropped a kiss on her daughter's cheek.

Evie patted Chloe's face. "Your hair is bootiful, Mommy. You'll look like a pwincess too."

"You think so?" Chloe took Evie's hand. "Well, let's go get dressed and find out."

When Chloe had slid into her cobalt blue evening gown, she peered at herself in the mirror and patted her hair to ensure none had slipped out of place.

Aunt Charlene, who had already dressed, took Evie into her temporary room to dress her for the evening. "Come on, princess, I'll help you dress. The pink beaded bracelet your mommy gave you to wear will look wonderful with your dress."

Chloe took the opportunity to pull the last unread letter from her messenger bag and sit on the chair in her room to read it. With no idea if this was one from the Sarge's mother or his sweetheart. Margaret, she slipped on a pair of cotton gloves from her bag then opened the letter on her lap and began to read.

Maj. Gen. Archibald McAdams
5th Connecticut Infantry Division
July 1, 1863

Dear General McAdams,

It is with great distress and uneasiness that I and the following men of the First Squad of the Fourth Company of the 5th Connecticut Infantry Division come to you with our concerns about Col. Edgar William Mayfield.

Until today's event, I had considered Colonel Mayfield to be a fair officer, albeit arrogant and over-bearing, in his dealings with his men. As Sergeant of First Squad I've done my duties to the men under my command to the best of my abilities, and it pains me when an officer does less than he could and should with the men under his command.

Sir, during the heat of battle today, a group of Confederate troops surrounded first squad in an entrenchment on the eastern side of the battlefield. As we fought the southern troops, Colonel Mayfield rode toward our position along with three other Union soldiers. Before he reached our position, he turned his sidearm on them and fired, killing his own men. I was shocked at what my eyes beheld, and I fail even now to understand why he would commit such an atrocity. However, I would be negligent as a dedicated NCO in the Union Army if I did not report this. The men of First Squad witnessed Colonel Mayfield's slaughter of Union soldiers. After his betrayal, he retrieved the fallen Union soldiers' firearms and continued to our position where he aided in killing the Confederate troops surrounding our position. His distraction made it possible for us to fight our way out.

In a sense we are alive due to Colonel Mayfield's assistance; however, the fact he needlessly slaughtered Union soldiers cannot be dismissed. Sir, I leave this in your hands. The men of my squad have signed this page in witness to the cold-blooded murders of those three Union soldiers.

Please contact me or any of the below signed members of First Squad concerning this delicate issue. We have taken an oath to stand for the truth and will do so in a military court of law.

With Great Respect,
Sergeant Timothy Edwards

Chloe dropped the letter onto her lap, her heart racing to the point she could barely draw a breath. This was bad. So bad. What was she going to do? She glanced at the clock by her bedside then snapped her eyes shut. Oh, this was terrible.

Blake would arrive anytime to drive her to the donor event where…she swallowed hard. They couldn't go through with this. Col. Edgar William Mayfield was a fraud. A murderer. He'd killed…

Chloe reached down and with care lifted the age-old letter once again. Scanning to the bottom she read Sarge's name. Timothy Edwards. Sergeant Timothy Edwards. He had a name after all. Colonel Mayfield had murdered Sergeant Edwards in cold blood.

Wait a minute. Her mind spun in an attempt to tie all the loose ends. The brass cap. What was the monogram Cliff had uncovered? Wasn't it E.W.M.? Edgar William Mayfield? Cliff was sure it had come from the pommel of a saber. It stood to reason it was from the pommel of Colonel Mayfield's saber when he'd stabbed Sergeant Edwards. Then surely it was Colonel Mayfield who'd had the wall built in a rush to cover his terrible deed.

Aunt Charlene knocked on Chloe's open door. "Blake's here. He's looking pretty spiffy too. If I were thirty years younger, I'd give you a run for your money, sweetie."

Chloe shook her head and spread her hands helplessly. "We can't do this, Aunt Char. But I don't know what to do to stop it."

Aunt Charlene's brows puckered. "What do you mean? Can't do what? What's wrong?"

"I just read the last letter. Colonel Mayfield wasn't a hero. He was a murderer."

~

Blake waited in the living room of the small house the superintendent and his family occupied until their home could be puts to rights by the insurance company. He ran a finger under his collar. Wearing his park uniform every day was no big deal, but a tux was not his style. The fact the superintendent wore one didn't change a thing. The park boss likely frequented tux affairs.

"You don't look like you're happy wearing that get-up."

Was Dan Fielding a mind reader?

"No, sir. Not particularly. I don't have a reason to wear a tux often, but I think the collar on this shirt is a half-size too small."

The superintendent chuckled. "Or it feels that way."

Blake gave a shrug feeling as if the jacket was a bit snug. "Perhaps."

"It looks fine, Blake." Dan glanced at his wristwatch. "What could be keeping the ladies?"

Evie strolled into the room, the pink tulle of her princess dress bouncing around her.

"Hi, Evie." Blake tossed her a wave. "How are you this evening?"

She waved back. "Gweat. I'm going to a big party. See my pweety gown?" Evie twirled giving Blake a full view of her princess dress.

"It's beautiful. You'll be the most beautiful princess there." He gave her a wink.

She returned his wink with an exaggerated one of her own. "Thank you."

"That's a pretty bracelet, and it's beautiful with your dress.

Where did you get that?" Black pointed at the pink beaded bracelet on Evie's tiny arm. He'd noticed her wearing it before.

"Mommy gave it to me for my birthday last year. I always wear it. See the pwetty flower beads?"

"I see them. Their beautiful. Just like you." He tweaked her nose.

Chloe stepped into the living room followed by Aunt Charlene. The air around Blake became impossible to breathe. Was it the air? Or had his lungs seized? No, Chloe had stolen his breath away. He swallowed and attempted to inhale deeply.

Chloe was more gorgeous than he'd ever seen her. Her blond hair arranged in a lovely style that left tendrils kissing her cheeks. Hmm, an amazing thought, but he'd best not go there. The color of her dress highlighted the blue in her gaze, but the color on her face was from makeup. Her natural color had drained away, leaving a pallor beneath. It took several seconds to realize trouble resided in the depths of her beautiful eyes.

Blake spotted the cotton gloves on her hands and the antique letter between her fingers. He stepped closer, and her troubled eyes met his. "What's the matter? What's happened?" His heart filled with dread. Something was terribly wrong.

Chloe lifted the letter, turning to her dad then back to Blake, shaking her head. "I don't know what to do. After getting ready, I had a few minutes to read the last letter found on the Sarge. I…I wanted to make sure I'd read every letter before I went to the event tonight."

Her chin trembled as she squeezed her eyes closed and shook her head before opening them again. "I wasn't prepared for this. It's a letter from the Sarge to his commanding General telling him that Colonel Mayfield murdered three men. The letter is signed by Sgt. Timothy Edwards, who I believe is Sarge, and his First Squad witnessed the murders. He didn't know why the colonel killed those men, but Sarge felt he had to report the colonel. It's clear to me now that when Colonel Mayfield murdered Sergeant Edwards, he placed the sergeant's letter on him, never intending that letter to see the light of day."

Chloe went on to explain about the brass cap from the saber, the monogram and how it had to belong on the saber the colonel used to murder Sergeant Edwards. Afterward he had the wall built to hide his murder. She gasped.

"What is it?" Dan laid a hand on her shoulder.

She turned to her dad. "If the colonel murdered Sergeant Edwards, what did he do to the rest of the men on this list?"

She lifted the letter and pointed to the signatures of the men of First Squad who had scrawled their names on the bottom of the page. "These men stood with Sergeant Edwards, yet their bodies weren't in the cellar. That means they came, signed their names and left before the colonel came in and stopped them. But he would've known they were witnesses to the murders. He would still have wanted to silence them."

Blake tapped the page with a gentle finger. "Do you think he would remember every name?"

"He wouldn't need to." Chloe shook her head as she gave a disgusted half smile. "He already knew it was First Squad. All he had to do was send them into the heat of battle and ensure they died." She held up Blake's wrist to glance at his watch. "It's going to be close, but I have to log into my research site and take a look at something. I can see if that's what happened to First Squad."

Chloe hurried to her room and returned with her laptop, setting it on the kitchen table and booting it. Once logged in, she tapped her way into the research site. Within minutes, she'd found what she was looking for. She leaned back in her chair. "Just as I thought. The whole of First Squad was killed in battle on July 2nd, 1863. That would've been the day after Colonel Mayfield killed Sergeant Edwards."

Chloe shook her head. "It's so sad knowing Sergeant Edwards' family waited for him to come home, and he never did. His mother and his sweetheart wrote him letters longing for the day when he'd come home. His mother wanted him to return to relieve his father in the family business, and his dear Margaret anticipated a full life of marriage with him. Colonel Mayfield not only killed Sergeant Edwards, but he stole his family's dreams. How sad."

"And all for what?" Aunt Charlene's voice cracked with emotion. "I can't imagine what they must have endured when he didn't come home."

"Well—" Chloe shut down her laptop, "—in Colonel Mayfield's diary he stated he'd sent a letter asking for a promotion to the same general that Sergeant Edwards intended to send his letter to. The letter that Mrs. White-Smith loaned to the museum along with the diary is from the general approving that promotion. I would bet a month of paychecks Colonel Mayfield killed those Union soldiers to make himself look good when he rescued First Squad from the Confederate troops. He didn't anticipate First Squad witnessing his deceit. It backfired on him, and he had to further his deceit by killing more of his men."

"What a wicked, wicked man." Aunt Charlene shook her head.

"The question is—" Dan glanced at his watch, "—what do we do now? People will be gathering shortly in anticipation of the big event. They'll be expecting to donate to the museum for a display for that diary, and now there's no way we can put it or the letter that Mrs. White-Smith has loaned on display."

Chloe put a hand to her mouth. "Oh no! Mrs. White-Smith. How are we going to break this information to her?"

Dan heaved a heavy sigh and shook his head. "I suggest you pull her aside and share the letter with her while I stand before the crowd and explain the change in circumstances. We'll invite everyone to stay for refreshments and the entertainment since they're paid for."

Chloe nodded, her shoulders slumping. "Poor Jan. She's worked so hard on this event, but we can't allow a man who lied about his service to be portrayed as a hero."

"You know, there's a name for that." Blake folded his hands behind his back, his gaze on the floor. "It's called Stolen Valor. It's a term applied to the phenomenon of people falsely claiming military awards or medals they did not earn, service they did not perform, Prisoner of War experiences that never happened, and other tales of miliary actions that exist only in their minds.* In this case, the colonel was attempting to steal valor by killing in order to gain rank. If he sent the letter to the general and the general approved the promotion, did the diary say what happened next?"

Chloe stood and went to the couch where she'd left her wrap and clutch. "Yes. Fortunately, the promotion was denied, and he wasn't rewarded for his deceit. The colonel was beyond angry. The wording of his diary entry was odd and a bit vague, and now that I know what he did, I understand it better."

"Well, there is a bit of justice, I suppose." Blake reached for her wrap and laid it around her shoulders.

"How did you know about Stolen Valor?" Chloe turned to him.

He shrugged. "I was in the Army before joining the park police."

"Really?"

Blake met her beautiful gaze as it roamed his features. Was she seeing him in a new light? Did she compare him with her lost husband? What did she see?

A soft smile touched those delectable lips. "Were you an MP?"

"How'd you guess?"

Her smile broadened. "It wasn't hard."

Dan checked his watch again. "We must get going, folks. The crowd will be waiting."

Chloe sighed. "For an evening I was so looking forward to, I now dread it."

Evie slipped her tiny hand within Chloe's. "It's okay, Mommy. I'll be wif you."

Chloe bent and swung her daughter into her arms, giving her a playful squeeze. "And that's the best part, princess. Let's go."

Chapter Twenty-One

Chloe's heart sank at the crowd already gathered. Had things been different, she'd been ecstatic. Dad had his work cut out for him, and she had hers. She wanted nothing more than to find Jan and tell her what an amazing job she'd done in preparing for this evening, but that would have to wait. There was one more important task to accomplish before she could do anything else. A gentle hand at her back reassured her as her gaze roamed the room for Mrs. White-Smith.

"I'll be happy to go with you." Blake's low voice whispered close to her ear. "I'm not eager for you to meet with her on your own. No telling how Mrs. White-Smith will take the news of her great-great-grandpappy's deceit."

"Yeah, I know." Chloe sighed. "I doubt that aristocratic lady will be happy when I tell her. Believe me, I'm not looking forward to breaking the news." Choe spotted the subject of their discussion across the room talking to the mayor of Gettysburg. Great. It would be best to take her around to one of the back hallways to have this discussion. "How hard will it be to break her away from Mayor Holloway?"

Blake shrugged. "Well, it is a campaign year, you know."

"Don't remind me." Chloe glanced over to ensure Aunt Charlene had a good hold on Evie. With a nod from her aunt, she and Blake made their way toward the donor of the diary. Chloe's stomach churned. *Lord, help me. I'm not looking forward to this. Thy will be done.*

As they approached the mayor and Mrs. White-Smith, the woman turned her patrician gaze on them, her nose in the air as usual. Her hair had been coifed perfectly, not a hair out of place. A diamond clasp held one side back. Dangly diamond earrings swung nearly to her shoulders as she turned. The sleeveless silver evening gown she wore gave her a matronly appearance except for the slit to her mid-thigh. Silver hose, a silver and diamond-studded clutch and high-heeled sandals complimented the dress. A diamond necklace around her neck caught the light from the overheads and sparkled as did the earrings. If she intended to be seen tonight, mission accomplished.

Mayor Holloway talked non-stop as Chloe and Blake stopped beside them. The mayor's subtle nod included them in the conversation. Now, how to break in and extract Mrs. White-Smith.

They were saved from that problem when the lady herself did them the favor. She laid a diamond-encrusted hand on the mayor's arm and gazed adoringly into his features. "My dear Aldon, if you'll excuse me a moment, I must speak with these young people. I'll be back shortly, so don't go anywhere." Reaching up, she tweaked his nose and gave him a beatific smile. Surely, she was laying it on thick to gain a hefty donation for her great-great-grandfather's museum display. Mrs. White-Smith wasn't the warmest person Chloe had ever met. Too bad her act would go to waste since the display wouldn't come to fruition.

Chloe sighed. This wasn't going to be easy. Blake's warm hand along the back of her waist buttressed her courage. She'd almost bet he was praying for her.

The look on Mayor Holloway's face as Mrs. White-Smith silenced him was priceless. He nodded with a puppy-dog expression as the lady linked her arm with Chloe's and led her away, Blake at Chloe's other side.

"Well, my dear. This is a fabulous event you and your little friend have planned. I'm looking forward to it. The governor of Maryland is here, I see." She waved at someone across the room. "I'm sure your father will introduce us."

Chloe inhaled and plunged in. "Mrs. White-Smith, I need to speak with you about something important. If you'll come with us, we must talk now."

Mrs. White-Smith stopped walking and stared at Chloe. "Now? But the program is about to begin, my dear."

"It has to be now. And don't worry about the program." Chloe urged her toward the hallway that led toward the museum where no one would interrupt."

"But..."

"Please, Mrs. White-Smith. Come with me. There's something I must show you. It's of utmost importance."

The older woman allowed Chloe to lead her around to the quiet area by the museum, then she turned to Chloe. "What is this all about, my dear?" She lifted her nose into the air once again. "I don't understand your urgency when the program is about to begin. We'll miss the opening."

Chloe opened her clutch and pulled out her cotton gloves, tugging them on. "There won't be a program this evening, Mrs. White- Smith. Neither will there be a call for donations for the display for your great-great-grandfather's diary."

"Wh...what?" the woman gasped, her hand pressed to her breast.

Chloe retrieved the letter from her clutch, then handed the clutch to Blake. With great care she opened the letter and met Mrs. White-Smith's questioning gaze. "I'm so sorry to have to break this to you, but your ancestor was not who you think he was. We found this letter on the body of a Union soldier under a house the park recently attained. The body was hidden behind a brick wall that wasn't original to the house. When we investigated, we found the body and this letter. I'll read it to you. It's addressed to Maj. Gen. Archibald McAdams of the 5th Connecticut Infantry Division. Apparently, he was your great-great-grandfather's commanding officer."

Chloe proceeded to read Sergeant Edwards' letter aloud, the words once again ripping at her heart. She couldn't bear to see what surely would be distress in the eyes of the descendent of the traitor to the Union Army. She kept her focus on the letter and her voice even as she read.

When she reached the final signature of the Sergeant, Chloe gently folded the letter once then lifted her gaze to find Mrs. White-Smith pointing a gun at Blake.

Chloe gasped. "What...? What are you doing?" Chloe's heart raced. The twisted, evil smile on the woman's features confused Chloe. Had she known all along what her ancestor had done? But...but how? The letter had been hidden for 159 years. How could she have known?

Mrs. White-Smith gave a slow nod. "You're a smart girl. It took you a while, but you're beginning to understand, aren't you? You simply don't understand how." She waved the gun, motioning Blake closer to Chloe. When he'd stepped closer, the wizened woman gave a grim smile. "You see, my great-great-grandfather confessed his sin on his deathbed. It was the family secret that passed down from his son to his son and so forth until my mother told me. Believe me, the secret was kept to the immediate family. Not even cousins or aunts and uncles knew. We were all sworn to secrecy. We knew about the letter that Sergeant Edwards wrote and First Squad signed. Grandfather Mayfield had Edwards walled in to hide his secret sin."

Anger filled Chloe that this woman would attempt to use the park to hide her ancestor's deceit. "And were you aware your great-great-grandfather had the whole of First Squad killed in battle to cover up his deceit?"

The older woman shrugged and gave a careless grin. "But of course. When he confessed, he confessed all. How could he die with all that on his conscience?"

Blake took a step toward her. "Yet you were willing to allow the park to display his diary and portray him as a hero to cover up his deceit?"

"Why not? No one would have been the wiser if we'd acquired that letter before you read it." Mrs. White-Smith waved the gun. "Now don't take another step closer, or I'll shoot." She turned the gun, stretching her arm to her right. "And I don't care who hears. We'll be long gone before anyone hears above the hubbub in the other room."

Chloe glanced to her left to see where Mrs. White-Smith had turned her gun. There stood Brad Wiseman, one arm around Aunt Charlene who held Evie close. Brad held a gun in his other hand pointed right at them.

~

Blake slipped back beside Chloe, his heart pounding as Aunt Charlene and Evie stood in Brad Wiseman's grip. How had he become involved in all this? Wasn't he supposed to be a restoration specialist? What did he have to do with Mrs. White-Smith? They stood several feet away, but Brad moved them closer once they'd been noticed.

The little girl whimpered as she clung to Aunt Charlene. Then she spied Chloe and her arms shot out as she leaned forward. "Mommy! Mommy!" Evie's pleading voice echoed in the hallway.

Chloe took a half step but stopped, shaking her head. "I can't, princess. You stay with Aunt Char. She'll hold you and take care of you for now." Her soft words were meant to reassure, but there was a crack at the end as if they were ripped from her.

Evie spun back, wrapped her arms around Aunt Charlene's neck, and she began to cry.

"Shhh, princess." Aunt Charlene whispered as she rubbed her back.

"Ah, so all we're missing is dear old dad." Mrs. White-Smith's laughter lacked genuine humor. "Unless he comes searching for you, we'll simply have our little party without him." She held out a hand. "Give me the letter."

Chloe refolded it and tucked it back into the clutch Blake handed her. "I don't think so. Your ancestor was guilty of Stolen Valor, and you're guilty of lying and covering up the truth."

"Perhaps." The woman nodded toward Brad. He turned and directed his captives down the hallway in the opposite direction from the festivities. Evie's wails echoed down the hallway behind them. "Tell me, Miss Rogers, how is your dear superintendent father handling this situation tonight? Does he know of my great-great-grandfather's treachery?"

"Of course, he does." Chloe's eyes followed Brad, her aunt and her daughter as they disappeared from view. "Where's Brad taking my family?"

"Away. He's my nephew, you know." The older woman took a few steps in the direction he'd gone. "He doesn't know a thing about old house restoration, by the way. He's simply my heavy when it comes to 'completing things.' My nephew did a marvelous job of wrecking your home, don't you think? He certainly couldn't restore it." She laughed out loud, her laughter ringing off the walls in the hallway. "And Sergeant. Edwards? It's too bad you'd already removed the letter. We wouldn't be where we are now if you hadn't. He could've removed it and no one would've been the wiser."

"Except I would still have broken ribs and a bruised kidney," Blake snarled.

She shrugged. "Well, there is that." Waving the gun, she added, "Down on the floor. Both of you. Face down."

Blake considered rushing her, but decided living to fight another moment was better than being shot by a crazy woman. As Chloe hesitated he tugged her down beside him.

"What are you going to do with my aunt and daughter?" Chloe demanded from a kneeling position, belligerence oozing from every pore.

"Your cooperation *might* ensure they live, my dear." Mrs. White-Smith came around behind Chloe and, with her high-heeled shoe, shoved her to the floor. "Something you aren't exhibiting much of at the moment."

Chloe let out a soft cry, then clamped her lips together. Blake grabbed her hand and gave it a gentle squeeze. If he caught up with this woman.... No, *when* he caught up with this woman, he'd.... But it was time to concentrate on getting Aunt Charlene and Evie back. That was the priority right now.

Blake met Chloe's tortured stare as her face rested on the cold linoleum floor. The bright overhead lights illuminated the shimmer in her eyes. She blinked several times fighting back tears. He gave a her a reassuring wink and received a tight smile in return.

His heart froze as a diamond-encrusted hand pressed a gun to Chloe's temple. Her blue eyes widened in terror even as she released a gasp.

"Now, Mr. Park Cop, I highly recommend you and Miss Rogers remain right where you are for at least twenty minutes. Don't think for one minute I won't shoot Chloe's precious aunt. I draw the line at children, but her aunt—I won't hesitate for an instant. The little girl will go with me, and you'll never find her."

Mrs. White-Smith's lowered voice sent chills down Blake's spine. What was it doing to Chloe? They locked eyes, hers spotting the floor with tears. If only he could hold Chloe in his arms and reassure her that he would get Aunt Charlene and Evie back. If only....

Turning his head ever so slightly, he met the steely expression of the woman holding the gun against Chloe's head. Her eyes were cold, hard, dead. What an evil woman. So like her ancestor. She reached for Chloe's clutch and removed the letter then dropped the clutch to the floor and straightened. "Now stay, or I'll kill your aunt." Mrs. White-Smith turned and hurried on clicking heels down the hallway out of sight and hearing.

When he was sure she was gone, Blake stood and helped Chloe to her feet. Tears streamed down her cheeks.

"Chloe, sweetheart." Blake swiped her tears away with his thumbs. "I want nothing more than to hold you and comfort you right now, but we don't have time. We need to move fast if we want to get your loved ones back."

Chloe swallowed and nodded. "I know. It's okay. I'm ready to do whatever we have to in order to get them back too."

With tender fingers, Blake swept a tendril of her hair behind her ear. "Great. Then here's the plan. I'm going to follow them. Now. I'm not waiting twenty minutes. You run to the event and find Gabe and/or Chief Morton. Tell them what's happened so they can take action."

He bent then handed her the clutch. "I'll do my best to retrieve the letter, but your aunt and Evie are my priorities."

"And they should be."

Blake planted a quick kiss on Chloe's lips and turned to go. She grabbed his arm, and he turned back.

"Please be careful. That woman is crazy, and two of my loved ones are in her clutches."

Blake stroked a finger down her soft cheek. "Then storm heaven, sweetheart. Pray like you've never prayed before."

~

As Blake took off at a run down the hallway, Chloe pulled off her evening sandals and hooked them on her fingers. She hiked up the narrow skirt of her evening dress and ran back to the crowded room to search for Gabe. Apparently, Dad had announced his bad news to the gathering. A loud hum of conversation competed with the live band that played in the corner of the room. A few couples danced in the area arranged for that. Several people surrounded the buffet and were helping themselves to the catered fare.

Chloe's gaze probed the crowd in search of Gabe. If she couldn't find him, surely Chief Morton would be here. Perhaps she should put her heels back on to see over the crowd. As she was about to do so, she spotted both men talking to her dad near the front of the room. Hadn't she already looked there? She rushed in that direction before they could move. Excusing herself as she shoved through the crowd, she finally arrived to where the three men stood.

"Chloe. You're breathing heavy." Her dad's brows furrowed. "What's wrong?"

"Everything." Chloe took a cleansing breath before launching into an explanation into the last twenty minutes.

Her father wrapped an arm around Chloe's shoulders. "It'll be all right. Blake's gone after them, and—" he turned toward Chief Morton, "I'm sure the chief will take it from here."

"You bet we will, sir." Chief Morton clapped Gabe on the shoulder. "Let's go, Holland. I'll get in touch with Hunter, and we'll make a plan." He turned back to Chloe and the superintendent. "Sir, Miss Rogers. We'll do everything in our power to bring back your aunt and sister—your daughter and granddaughter, sir."

"Thank you, chief. I know you will." Dan shook his hand.

"Thanks." Chloe cast him a brief smile. "I know you'll do your best. Please keep us posted."

"Will do."

Chief Morton lifted his cell phone to his ear as he and Gabe hurried away. A few moments later several men and a few women in the crowd rush from the room. Apparently, dispatch had called other park police officers from the event. Good. The more on the case, the better.

Chloe leaned her head against her dad's shoulder as he wrapped his arm around her.

Oh, Father God, please protect Aunt Char and Evie. Please don't let Mrs. White-Smith or Brad hurt them in any way. Protect Blake and bring them all home safely. Help the park police to stop that evil woman and Brad. Please don't let them get away. After 159 years, justice needs to be served for the death of Sergeant Edwards.

Chapter Twenty-Two

"Get in." Brad snarled as he shoved Charlene toward the back seat of the Cadillac town car. She lost her balance and nearly tripped as she held Evie close in her arms. Throwing out a hand to prevent the child from hitting her head against the doorframe, Charlene caught herself and straightened. She turned to the huge man and glared. "You may be her bouncer or her heavy or whatever, but show a little compassion when it comes to this little one." Charlene shot the scathing words at him with a snarl. What did she have to lose, after all? "This baby doesn't deserve whatever *that* woman is up to."

Taking a step back, Brad shifted from one foot to the other, a sheepish expression imprinting itself on his features. He ran a hand over his bald head, then without a word, he waited as Charlene climbed into the backseat and settled in. She placed Evie on the seat with the shoulder strap and moved to the middle with the lap belt. This little girl needed her as close as possible.

Within minutes someone—most likely Mrs. White-Smith—climbed into the front passenger seat. Without a glance toward the back, she ignored them as Brad started the car and they drove off.

Charlene was surprised they hadn't blindfolded her, but wherever they were taking them, they wouldn't likely stay there long. Or worse. She refused to think about that right now. Her main job was to protect Evie.

What had she gleaned about this situation so far? That this woman was the descendant of that phony colonel Chloe had read the letter about, and that she'd known he was a phony all along. Also, her plan had been to not only cover it up but to capitalize on it. Sick. Genuinely sick. Now, she'd kidnapped her and Evie in order to escape with the letter that proved her ancestor was a fraud. Not good. Was anyone coming after them? Charlene stared into the darkness outside the window. If she knew Blake as well as she thought she did, he wasn't far behind them.

Lord, You're the master of the universe and in control of every situation. Including this one. Whether anyone else knows where we are or not, You know. Please get us out of this mess.

"I wanna go home, Aunt Char." Evie's whisper was so quiet, Charlene barely heard it.

She reached over and drew the little girl close then bent to whisper in her ear. "I know, sweetie, but we can't just yet. Can you pray in your heart to Jesus to send Mr. Blake to find us?"

Evie nodded then whispered. "I will."

"Good girl. Remember, Jesus knows where we are and will look after us. He loves us so much, and I love you, Evie, my sweet princess."

Evie wrapped her arms around Charlene. "I love you, Aunt Char. I love Jesus too."

Then in the dark she looked up at her great aunt and added, "But I miss Mommy."

Charlene's heart broke. This little one should be home in bed, not here going through this. Not now, not ever. What kind of woman tears a child from her mother? She held the child closer. "I know, sweetie. So do I."

~

Blake rushed after Mrs. White-Smith and hoped he'd see her climb into a car in the parking lot. He'd brought Chloe to the event in a rental sedan this evening so she wouldn't have to climb into his pickup truck in her evening dress. She'd been impressed and appreciated his thoughtfulness. As he exited the building from the same exit his culprit had escaped from, Blake spotted her slipping into a dark luxury vehicle at the far end of the parking lot. He was parked one row over. How fortunate. Keeping low, he unlocked the sedan as he ran toward it and climbed in. Keeping an eye on the direction the luxury car took, he started the car and followed them at a distance.

With no police radio available, Blake pulled out his cell phone and dialed the park police dispatch number. After identifying himself, he explained the situation and asked them to notify Chief Morton. He gave a vague description of the vehicle and said he'd call in more when he had it.

The luxury car meandered through Gettysburg proper until it came to the middle of town. As was true of most Saturday nights, town hopped with tourists and locals hitting all the restaurants and bars. The streets were packed with people and cars, and traffic grew heavier.

Catching a closer glimpse, Blake spotted the make of the vehicle as a Cadillac Town Car, and he retrieved the license plate number. As traffic halted at the stop lights, cars shifted in between Blake and the Town Car, making it impossible for him to keep up. He slammed a hand against the steering wheel. If only he had his cruiser. Calling in the vehicle description and license number to dispatch, he placed a BOLO requesting they notify local town, county and state law enforcement.

The light changed in front of him, and the Cadillac disappeared down the street amidst traffic. Blake's heart sank even as he reported the vehicle's last known location.

Dear God, only You know where they're taking Charlene and Evie. Protect them and help us relocate them.

~

"He what?" Dan Fielding leaned on Chief Morton's desk. "How could he lose them?"

"Superintendent, have you ever driven downtown Gettysburg on a Saturday night?" The chief leaned forward clasping his hands on his desktop. He'd never seen his boss this...emotional. "I'm sure you have, and I'm sure you know exactly how busy those streets are. I'll remind you, sir, Officer Hunter is in a civilian vehicle, not his cruiser. How the heck was he supposed to move through that light and pursue the perps in a civilian car?"

Dan straightened and propped a hand on his hip while scrubbing the other down his face. "I'm sorry, chief. You're right. I'm certain Blake did all he could under the circumstances."

"Yes, sir. He reported everything via cell phone as it was happening. Our other officers are out there zeroing in as we speak as well as local, county and state LEOs. We've got a lot of manpower out searching for your ladies."

Dan paced the floor in front of the chief's desk. "Yeah, I

know. I'm happy he noted the make, model, and license of the car, but it could be hiding anywhere, or it could be long gone."

"Sir, you need to go home and let us do our job." Chief Morton stood as the door to his office opened and Blake strode in, agitation marring his features. He'd stripped off his tux tie, unbuttoned the top button and removed his jacket.

"Hunter?" The chief came around his desk. "You're back."

"Yes, sir. I'm going to change into my uniform, grab my cruiser then head back out." He turned to the superintendent. "I'm sorry I lost them, sir. I…I feel like…."

The superintendent placed a hand on his shoulder. "Son, it's not your fault. You did all you could under the circumstances and sent valuable information to help in the continued search for Charlene and Evie. Now we trust God with the rest. And of course, the expertise of our men and women in uniform."

Blake shoved a frustrated hand through his hair. "Yes, sir. I'll get changed and join them."

Dan clapped his shoulder. "Good hunting. I'll be praying for all of you."

"Thank you, sir. I appreciate that." Blake turned to his boss. "Chief, I'll see you later."

"Be careful out there, Hunter."

When Blake had gone, Chief Morton turned back to the superintendent. "Where's Miss Rogers, sir?"

"She's in my office. I told her to go home and get some rest, but she refused. I suggested she at least lie on the couch in my office for a bit, and I believe she's actually napping." Dan dropped into the chair beside the chief's desk and rested his head in his hands. "If anything happens to my sister or my granddaughter, Chief, I don't know what we'll do. I just…I just don't."

Chief Morton returned to his desk chair and wheeled it a little closer to the superintendent. He'd worked with this man for several years and always found him strong and in control of every situation. But this was personal. His sister and granddaughter had been kidnapped, and they had no clue where they were. Dan Fielding had no control over *this* situation. None whatsoever.

"Sir." Morton propped his elbows on his knees and clasped his hands together, leaning forward. He kept his voice low and gentle. "I've never been a religious man like you, but I've watched you through the years, and I know how strong your faith is. Don't let it slip now. Keep your faith. You said you'd be praying for the officers as they search for your family. Might I suggest you do that now? Spend your time in prayer. By praying for them, you'll receive the strength you need to face this situation."

Dan lifted his head from his hands, sheer misery etching his features. After several seconds he gave a slow nod. "You're right, chief. Instead of sitting here having a pity party, I should spend my time petitioning the God of heaven on behalf of my sister and little Evie. I should ask for wisdom and strength for the officers searching for them. Forgive me for acting like this, chief."

Morton grinned and waved a dismissive hand. "Are you kidding me? There's nothing to forgive. Your family's been kidnapped by a crazy woman. Who wouldn't show some emotion? You're one of the strongest men I know, sir, but your family has been touched by evil. A couple times recently, in fact. Hang onto your faith, sir."

Dan stood and held out his hand. "Thanks for the pep talk, chief. I'm going to go pray."

The chief stood and shook his hand. "I'll be here if you need me, sir."

~

Charlene held Evie close as the luxury car drove down a country road in the darkness. Where in the world was this nutcase woman and her hulking minion taking them? How in the world would anyone find them way out in the middle of who knew where?

Oh Lord God, You know where we are even if none of us do. Send help. Please.

The car turned down a dirt road and bumped along for a short time through woods until the trees ended at a large open space with an old brick pre-Civil War home situated near the center. Lit gardens trailed off from the right side of the house toward the back. It would be beautiful by day or night. The front entrance was well lit, and Brad parked in front of the brick steps that led to the door.

For the first time since she'd entered into the car, Mrs. White-Smith turned to Charlene and Evie, a less than pleasant smile curved her lips. "Home again, home again, shall we dance a jig?"

Her laugh was humorless. "Welcome to my home away from home, ladies. Please do come inside. Brad, won't you help them out of the car?"

Brad climbed out and opened the door next to Evie. Charlene met his gaze with pinched lips. Hopefully he read her meaning of "don't touch" loud and clear. He waited by the open car door as Charlene unbuckled herself then the sleepy little girl.

She slipped past her and climbed out then reached in and, picking her up, held Evie close against her shoulder. The child had nodded off during the last several miles and was ready for bed. No telling what these people had in store for them, but hopefully they had the decency to allow her to sleep.

Mrs. White-Smith led the way through the front door where a hall light had been left on. Brad took up the rear ensuring Charlene went inside. She was ushered into what must have been the parlor in Civil War days. The room had been restored to the Civil War era with furniture of the day. Under different circumstances, Charlene would've spent more time appreciating the value and beauty of the pieces, but Mrs. White-Smith shoved her onto the couch.

"Sit."

"Have some care with this child." Charlene spit out the words. "She's innocent in all this and doesn't deserve your ire."

"Perhaps." The snide comment matched the snarky look Mrs. White-Smith tossed at Charlene before striding from the room. "Keep an eye on them, Brad." Her words trailed back down the hallway, and the bouncer made himself comfortable in a chair near the door.

"Do you always do her bidding?" Charlene kept her voice low for Evie's sake and to prevent her hostess for overhearing.

"What's it to you?" Brad heaved a sigh and pulled the curtain away from the front window beside his chair, peering into the darkness.

"It simply seems to me she enjoys bossing you around." Charlene rubbed Evie's back as she rocked her gently back and forth on the couch hoping to keep the child asleep. "Don't you ever think for yourself?"

His irritated expression met hers as he dropped the curtain back into place. "Of course, I do. She pays me to work for her. That's all."

"Is that so? You couldn't do better than being the heavy for the likes of her?" Charlene rolled her eyes. "Did you go to college? I mean, you look a lot smarter than you're acting."

His brows furrowed. "Thanks. I think. And yeah, I went to college."

"For what?"

Shifting in his seat, he stared to the floor. "Accounting."

"Truly? That's fantastic. So why aren't you an accountant instead of shooting at people and doing her dirty work? Accounting would be a good honest job."

He glanced up. "She…."

"It wasn't hard to convince him to work for me." Mrs. White-Smith appeared in the doorway and leaned on the doorframe. She crossed her arms over her slender frame. "You see, my nephew may have a great mind for numbers, but he had no business sense whatsoever. When I came up with the idea to place my great-great-grandfather's diary into the museum at the park, I fully intended to go even further by having him written up in all kinds of magazines and newspapers. Can't you see it?" The woman stretched out a hand before her, her gaze seeing things not in the room. "*National Geographic*, *History Magazine*, *Smithsonian*, *New York Times*. Just to name a few. My ancestor would've been famous." Her features morphed into bitterness. "But your niece had to go and mess things up, didn't she? Chloe Rogers found that ridiculous letter before we could, and she…ruined…everything." Her voice rose as she spit out the last three words, her lips twisting in rage.

Evie stirred and lifted her head, a whimper escaping as she turned to see what all the strange commotion was.

"Aunt Char? Why's she so mad?" Evie's childlike whisper rang in the room.

"Shut up, you impudent child." Mrs. White-Smith moved across the room, lifting a hand to strike her but was stopped from behind.

Brad held her hand in a tight grip. "I can't let you hit her, Aunt Maureen. She hasn't done anything."

Charlene held Evie close to her body, her hand over the side of her head as she glared at the woman standing over them. "You lay one hand on this child, and you won't know what hit you."

Mrs. White-Smith calmed somewhat as she yanked her hand

from Brad's. "Don't threaten me. I'm the one in charge here. Not you." She turned to Brad. "It's time to prepare the ransom note. If I can't make a large sum of money from my ancestor's false legacy, then I'll do so with these two. I'm sure their dear loved ones want them back. We'll simply see how much." She stormed from the room, and Brad returned to his chair.

Evie leaned away from her aunt enough to look into her face and whispered, "She's awfy bad. I don't like her. Can we go home now?"

Charlene's heart twisted. Evie had no understanding of the situation. Poor little princess. "Sweetie, we can't go home quite yet. That bad woman is making us stay here and won't let us go. Remember how we pray and ask Jesus to help us when we're in trouble? Now's a good time to pray."

Evie's eyes darted from Brad to the doorway and back to Charlene. She gave a simple nod then toyed with the tiny pink beaded bracelet Chloe had given her to wear all the time. "I'm gonna pway Jesus sends Mr. Blake and Gwampa to find us. And maybe Mommy too. I miss mommy."

Charlene gave the little girl a gentle squeeze. "I know you do, honey."

~

Chloe fell asleep on the couch in her dad's office, only to sleep fitfully. Praying between naps, she'd finally gotten up and come to Chief Morton's office to get an update. Hoping upon hope her daughter and aunt had been found, she crammed those hopes down deep in case they hadn't.

Chloe took a seat in front of his desk. "So, nothing, huh?"

The chief leaned back in his chair. "Afraid not. The patrol officers are—"

The phone rang and Morton reached for it. "Hello?"

He listened for several moments, his brow furrowing. "What? For real? How much? When?" Morton shook his head as he listened, his lips clamping tight. "Right. I understand. I'll pass it on." He hung up the receiver and clasped his hands on the desktop, hanging his head for a few moments before lifting his eyes to Chloe's.

She leaned forward in her seat. "Well, what is it? From your expression, it can't be good."

He sighed. "No, no it's not. I'm sorry, Chloe, but Mrs. White-Smith is demanding a ransom for your daughter and aunt."

"A...a ransom?" The words were little more than a whisper. "But we don't have the money for a ransom. For goodness sake, we're not celebrities or politicians. We work for the park service." Chloe stood and paced the room. This was unbelievable. She turned back to Morton.

"How did you receive this demand? How do you know it's real?"

Morton grimaced. "A rock was thrown through the Gettysburg police station window with a note attached. The demands were written on the note. It was tied to the rock with pink tulle. The note stated the tulle was from your daughter's princess party dress she wore to the event this evening." He glanced at the clock on the wall. "Okay, so the event last night. It's already three in the morning."

Chloe glanced at the clock then back at him. "How much is she demanding?"

"One million."

Chloe crossed over and dropped back into her chair. "One million! That...that...that's ludicrous. We don't have that kind of money." She leaned forward, resting her arms on the side of the desk. "How long do we have?"

"Twelve hours."

Chloe closed her eyes, nausea roiling in her stomach. How in the world would they deal with this? *Lord, help us.* She stood and headed for the door. "I need a few minutes to think. I'm going to take a walk." Chloe made a beeline for the exit and stepped outside for some fresh air. Inhaling her lungs full, she exhaled and inhaled again attempting to clear her head. How in the world had they reached to this point? How had a crazy woman taken their dear ones and now demanded a huge amount of money to get them back? Chloe never would have dreamed of being in this position. Ever. *Lord, we need You. Right now. There's no time to try and figure things out. We don't have the money. We simply need a miracle.*

Evie. Her sweet Evie had been kidnapped by a woman with nefarious plans. She'd schemed to do one thing, and when it didn't work out, she took her sweet little girl and.... Wait a minute. Her daughter had been kidnapped. Chloe had planned for such a contingency, hadn't she? Of course, she had. What took her so long to think of it?

Turning on her heels, she raced back to Chief Morton's office where she found him still at his desk, a thumb drumming a steady rhythm on his desk.

Almost slamming the door behind her, Chloe stopped in front of his desk and planted her palms firmly on the surface. "Chief, I've got it. I know how to find them.

Chapter Twenty-Three

Blake drove the streets of Gettysburg searching for the dark luxury vehicle with the license plate number he'd taken from it. It was nowhere to be found. He, along with the other patrol officers, had searched every hotel in the county. They'd driven down every street and yet the car had not been found. It had simply vanished. Mrs. White-Smith wasn't staying in town or at any of the local hotels or motels. Where could she have taken Evie and Charlene?

Blake's cell phone rang, and he picked it up from the cup holder to see Chloe calling him. He pressed the answer button and put it on speaker phone. "Chloe. What's going on?"

"I know how to find them, Blake." Jubilation filled her voice.

"Okay, I'm all ears."

"Remember the bracelet I gave Evie? The pink beaded one?"

"Yeah. She had it on for the event last night." Blake remembered commenting on it to Evie. "What about it?"

"I gave it to her for her birthday last year. It has a transponder in it for this purpose, but I almost forgot about it. Some mother I am, huh? Here I give my daughter a transponder then forget about it when needed." Her chuckle was filled with remorse.

"Hey, Chloe. Don't be so hard on yourself. How many mothers would think to put a tracking device on their child to begin with? Besides, you remembered, didn't you? Maybe not immediately, but you remembered. Now let's find her. Tell me how we do that. Do you have a tracking program of some kind?"

"There's an app on my phone that targets her device and tracks it."

"Awesome. Where are you?"

"I'm in Chief Morton's office."

"I'll be there in ten minutes. Can you be ready to go when I get there?"

Chloe laughed. "I'll be waiting outside."

~

Chloe climbed into the passenger seat of Blake's cruiser when he stopped outside park police headquarters. In the ten minutes since they'd spoken, she'd hurried to her office and swapped her evening dress and sandals for a pair of jogging pants, t-shirt and tennis shoes she kept in her desk. She'd grabbed a brush and hairband from her desk drawer then ran for their meeting spot.

"Hi." She gave Blake a smile as she settled into the passenger seat.

"Hey, gorgeous. Ditched the evening togs for something more comfortable, I see." He winked.

"Thanks. The hair's coming down though." She handed him her phone. "I'll take care of that while you follow the app. Chief Morton said to call in the location when you have it. He'll send in backup. He doesn't want you going in alone. No telling what that crazy woman and her minion will do."

"Agreed." Blake opened the app and pinpointed the location on Chloe's phone. "This is awesome. It'll take us right to them."

"Then let's get going. I want my daughter and aunt back." Chloe pulled pins from her hair and dropping them into the cup holder in the door. "Poor Dad. He's a mess."

"Yeah. I saw him earlier this evening." Blake put the car into drive and turned out of the parking lot. "He's not taking it well. We'll get them back, then he'll be relieved."

"Won't we all." Chloe brushed her hair out and slipped the hair band around her hair, making her usual ponytail. She gave it a pat and a flip. Much better. Now she could face whatever lay ahead.

"See if that can zoom in and give us a location address." Blake handed Chloe the phone. "If so, we can call in the location to the Chief now, and he can send the other officers to meet us before we arrive. That'll save time."

Chloe placed her thumb and forefinger on the phone's screen and spread them apart. The map on the screen zoomed in. She did it again and retrieved the address for the location where the dot sat.

"Got it." She read off the address, and Blake called it in to Morton who relayed it through dispatch. Backup was on the way.

"We should be there in a few minutes." Blake turned onto a country road the map on the app led him to.

"It looks like there's another road a couple miles ahead. Turn left there," Chloe said. "The roads are different from the one we're on now. Smaller. Dirt perhaps?"

"Maybe." When Blake turned onto the dirt road, he switched off his headlights.

Thankful for a cloudless night, Chloe still had difficulty seeing what lay ahead in the darkness of the wooded road. After a bit they pointed at an opening in the trees as the dirt road led into a clearing where the lights of an older home beckoned them.

Blake stopped the cruiser fifty feet from the edge of the woods and pulled to the side of the road. "We'll wait here for backup. They shouldn't be far behind us."

Chloe scooted sideways in her seat and pulled her ankle up under her other leg. "I doubt they'll leave the house. We sent a message through the police department in town telling them we're trying to collect the money for the ransom." She glanced at Blake. "Not that we really are. No way could we gather that kind of money in twelve hours like they demanded. Instead, we're pulling a rescue party together."

Blake peered at Chloe. "How much did they demand?"

She swallowed, her focus on the lit house in the distance where her loved ones were being held. "One million."

Blake gave a low whistle. "Wow. That's a lot of money. And to expect you to come up with it and deliver it in twelve hours? That's a huge demand."

Chloe turned to face him. "Where she got the idea we had that kind of money is anyone's guess."

"This whole thing has been a debacle from start to finish with a mad woman trying to control it all." Blake reached over and gave Chloe's hand a gentle squeeze. "But don't worry, sweetheart, we'll take her down."

Chloe nodded and returned his squeeze. "Yes, we will. We have to. We can't let her win, Blake. Evie's and Aunt Char's lives are riding on this."

Silence reigned as they stared at the distant house. It wasn't long before three park cruisers pull up behind Blake's.

"They're here." He turned to Chloe. "Stay put. I'll be back."

Chloe turned in her seat and watched as Blake made his way toward the other officers who left their patrol cars and met him at the rear of his cruiser. There were six officers including Blake. Hopefully that would be sufficient to take down Mrs. White-Smith and Brad, unless there were other cohorts they were unaware of.

Oh Lord, help them get Evie and Aunt Char back safely.

~

"As far as we know there are only the two of them." Blake pointed toward the lit house a hundred and fifty yards past the end of the trees. "We'll go through the woods and approach the house from different directions. Keep in close communication via radio mics."

The officers adjusted their radios for local communication.

"The first officer to spot little Evie's and Charlene's location in the house, sound off." Blake propped his hands on his hips. "If anyone locates Mrs. White-Smith or Wiseman, call it in. I want to know where everyone is at all times. If you spot another player we don't know about, let us know immediately. Check for any open doors or windows. Once we have everyone's locations, we'll move in. We've got to get the drop on them. I'm giving you the heads-up. Wiseman is a big guy. He won't be easy to take down."

"What about a tranq gun?" one of the officers suggested.

"We can all carry tasers," another said.

"Yeah. Great ideas." Blake nodded in their direction. "A tranquilizer gun would do the trick, and maybe we should have one handy. Grab your tasers."

"I've got a tranq gun in my trunk." One officer raised his hand.

"Then take it with you." Blake pointed at him. "Let's go, fellows. Times a wasting."

They separated, grabbed their equipment, and took to the woods.

Blake opened Chloe's door and bent to her level. "Stay here. You'll be safer. Understand?" Blake spotted the war in the depths of her dark blue gaze. She wanted to go with him. Her head shook from side to side.

"You have to stay here. For Evie's and Charlene's sake. It's bad enough they're in harm's way. I can't risk you being there too. Promise me you'll stay here."

Blake heard the husky edge in his voice. His gaze searched the perimeter. The other officers had all disappeared. It was time to go. He tipped her chin. "Chloe? Promise me."

"All right." Belligerence oozed from every pore of her face. If she stayed in this car, it would be a miracle.

He dropped a kiss on her lips. "I'll bring them back, but I'm depending on you to pray since I'll be a little busy."

Her lips quirked. "I'll pray. A lot."

"That's my girl." He dropped another kiss on her lips then straightened and quietly shut the car door. With a quick salute he hurried into the woods.

~

Chloe huffed a frustrated breath and dropped her head against the headrest. Hmph. She wanted nothing more than to hurry after Blake and follow him into those woods until they reached a place where they could approach the house. He might not be able to pray on the run, but she could. Why couldn't she be there when he and the other officers rescued her Evie and Aunt Charlene? Her eyes swept the darkness surrounding Blake's cruiser as silence filled her ears. She'd go nuts sitting here doing nothing.

Reaching for the door handle, she climbed out and paced beside the car. It far outweighed sitting inside, and she could still keep her promise. Chloe closed the door with a gentle push then began her prayer-laden pacing. Only God knew the location of each player in this scenario at this time, and she had to leave each one in His ever-capable hands.

Please protect those officers, Abba Father, as they move in to rescue Evie and Aunt Char. Help everything to go smoothly.

Chloe shoved a loose tendril of hair behind her ear and turned to pace back along the path she'd worn beside the car. The sound of a twig snapping nearby halted her in her tracks. Her breath clogged in her throat even as fingers of fear tiptoed up her spine to cause the hair to stand up on her neck. Could Blake be returning for some reason? Or one of the other officers?

Chloe couldn't move a muscle, but her eyes roamed the dirt road from one edge of the woods to the other. Nothing moved. Perhaps it was simply a deer or some other night creature unaware it had nearly scared her to death.

Breathing deeply, she eased her muscles into motion and took a step toward the car. Perhaps waiting inside would be better after all. As Chloe reached for the door handle, a sharp pain exploded in the back of her head then…blackness.

~

Blake hurried through the darkness in the woods deep enough under the canopy not to be seen or heard. Looking to his right, Blake spotted the house through the trees. All the officers would approach the building at the darkest locations where rooms were not lit or from the rear. He'd communicated with his fellow officers that he would approach at the rear corner. Two others met him there while the other three approach on the other side of the house.

Once alongside the brick structure, Blake crouched low beside the other two officers and pointed in the direction of the front of the house. "I'm going to move toward that lit room. It's likely a living room or parlor. It could be where the hostages are being held. Gabe, you come with me. We'll check it out. Bill, head to the front entrance and see if it's open. If it is, wait on us. We'll coordinate with the others to come in the back at the same time we enter the front."

Bill gave a mini-salute and made his way at a low crouch toward the front of the house as Blake and Gabe followed close behind him to the lit front room.

Once there, Blake and Gabe crouched on either side of two tall windows behind tall hedges. Thank goodness for the hedges. They would help hide their shadows. Curtains and sheers adorned the windows making it a little difficult to see inside, but it would also hide their presence.

Blake nodded to Gabe, and with a quick look, they ducked away. Charlene sat on a couch with a sleeping Evie in her arms. They seemed okay for the present, and until the twelve-hour deadline for the ransom was up, he supposed they would remain so. Blake waved Gabe away from the window where they could talk in low voices without fear of being overheard.

"They look okay for the moment."

"Yeah. But we need to move fast and end this." Gabe shifted as he crouched. "Too much of a risk that something could go wrong."

"Guys, something just went wrong." Bill's voice came over their radios in a low voice. "You're not going to believe this, but the big guy is entering the front door with Chloe Rogers slung over his shoulder."

Blake's heart turned into block of ice in his chest. What? How could Wiseman have known? They were so careful. He scooted back to the window and watched as Wiseman walked into the room with Chloe over his shoulder. He plopped her into an armchair, her head lolling sideways as she slumped unconscious against the cushions.

Mrs. White-Smith hurried into the room and waved her arms, yelling something Blake couldn't make out. Then she stopped flailing her arms and smiled. Blake glanced at Charlene whose worried eyes rested on her niece. He recognized the agony of her inability to go to her he shared. Blake peered at Chloe, his heart breaking as emotions roiled inside. Anger at her mistreatment rising to the top.

He ducked back to where Gabe waited. "Bill's right. They have Chloe, and she's unconscious. No telling how the big goon accomplished that."

"Then they know we're here." Gabe heaved a sigh. "They know there's four patrol cars, but they have no idea how many officers. We need to move now."

"Agreed." Blake pressed his mic button. "Ok, guys. They know we're here, and they have Chloe. I don't know how they knew we were here, but we need to move now. Gabe, Bill and I will go in the front. The rest of you go in the back. Let's move."

With guns drawn, the officers rushed the front and back doors. All rooms were cleared until they reached the parlor where Mrs. White-Smith and Brad held Charlene, Chloe and Evie hostage. Blake and Gabe stood on either side of the large arched doorway that opened into the parlor, guns drawn and pointed upward.

"Come on out with your hands in the air." Blake called. "We don't want anyone to get hurt today."

"I don't think so, Officer Hunter." Mrs. White-Smith's voice was tight and choppy. "I will kill *all* of these ladies. Believe me. Just take a little peek in here and see if I won't."

Blake glanced at Gabe across the expanse of the doorway, and

Gabe shook his head as if to say, "Don't trust her." Leaning his head against the wall, Blake sucked in a deep breath. *Lord, give me wisdom.*

With his gun trained forward in the defensive posture, he took a quick look around the doorframe then stepped back. His heart nearly seized at what he saw. Mrs. White-Smith held a sleeping Evie, a gun to her head. Would she do it? Could she kill a child in cold blood?

"Aunt Maureen! What are you doing?" Horror filled Wiseman's voice. "You can't kill an innocent child. She hasn't had anything to do with all this."

"Shut up, you moron." She ground out the words. "I'll do whatever it takes."

"Whatever it takes for what?" Wiseman asked. "Hasn't this gone on long enough? I've done every single thing you've asked me to do, but I won't be a party to you killing an innocent child."

"I said, shut up." Her voice grew wilder and more desperate as it grew in pitch. "I'll do whatever I want to do."

"No." The sounds of scuffling, then a gunshot sounded followed by a loud groan from Wiseman.

Blake rounded the doorframe with his gun forward. Mrs. White-Smith began to turn the gun back toward Evie, and without hesitation, Blake fired. His bullet hit Mrs. White-Smith in the center of the forehead. Her face went slack, and she fell backward. Charlene jumped from the couch and dove for Evie. The little girl woke from all the noise, but Charlene grabbed her before she could hit the floor.

Although sure she was dead, Blake bent to check Mrs. White-Smith's pulse while Gabe checked on Wiseman. He'd been shot in the arm, but he'd recover to face charges. Next Blake hurried to Chloe's side where she stirred.

"Hey there, sweetheart." He helped her sit up in the chair. "Are you all right?"

She started to shake her head then grabbed it. "Ow. That was not a good idea. Someone rang my bell but good."

"I'd bet on Wiseman." Blake gently tucked a tendril of hair behind her ear then, with gentle fingers, probed the back of her head until he found a lump. "Yep. There's a goose egg. Let me take a look. Hmm. No bleeding. He probably used his fist, but we can ask him. We'll have the EMT's check you out." He drew her close and dropped a quick kiss on her lips. "I'll do better when you're up to it."

"Promise?" Chloe managed a weak smile.

"Count on it."

~

"Mommy, Mommy!" Evie rushed over and launched herself into Chloe's arms. The little girl had no idea how every movement sent bolts of pain through her mother's head, but Chloe would endure anything to have her daughter back in her arms.

"Oh, my sweet princess! I missed you so much." Chloe set her on her lap, wrapping her close. "I was praying so hard for you and Aunt Char."

Evie pushed away a little so she could look into Chloe's face. "I know. So was me and Aun' Charlene. I missed you, Mommy."

She clung to Chloe's neck and squeezed, sending pain shooting through her head and down her neck. A gasp escaped before Chloe could prevent it.

Aunt Charlene eased Evie's arms from Chloe and took the little girl back into her own embrace. "Hey princess. You're Mommy is hurting pretty bad right now. While you were napping, she hurt her head, so she's got a whopping headache. Let's give her a little space for a bit, okay? When she's feeling a little better you can give her all the hugs you want."

Evie gave Chloe a sad face. "I sorry, Mommy. I not know."

Chloe gave her foot a squeeze. "Of course, you didn't. How could you?" She blew her a kiss just as the EMT's entered the room. Her eyes scanned the scene. Two park police officers stood with a handcuffed Brad as one waved an EMT over. Blood oozed from a makeshift bandage on Brad's left bicep that an officer had applied till the EMTs arrived. What had happened? Continuing her surveillance of the room, she spotted a blanket-covered figure on the floor near the couch. Who could that...Mrs. White-Smith? It had to be. She was the only one missing from the figures in the room. Her gaze met Blake's, and he nodded.

"I'll explain everything later." He clasped her cold hand in his warm one. "I'm thankful you were knocked out when it all happened. Believe me, you wouldn't have been happy."

Her brows furrowed. 'I'm not going to like how this went

down, am I?"

Blake shook his head. "No, but as you can see, Evie and your aunt are safe and sound. You, on the other hand, are safe but not quite sound. I'm thankful you're still in one piece. Please tell me you kept your promise and stayed at the cruiser."

"Well, sort of. I stayed by the cruiser." She gave him a wry smile. "I couldn't stay inside, so I paced by the door and prayed. Then I heard a noise and was getting back inside when something struck me on the head and everything went black.

"I have no idea how Wiseman found out we were here."

Chloe placed her hand on Blake's arm, then something caught her attention. "Look. Wiseman's shoe. See the colors on the black sole? I think you're looking at the guy who broke into our house and trashed it. Dad said the man dumped a set of paints onto the floor and stepped on them, breaking them open."

"I remember reading that in the report." Blake stared at Wiseman. "I believe we're looking at evidence that'll be added to his charges. The list is growing. They've already taken a firearm that may lead to a conviction for the death of Mr. Hill. If not, it could match the gun Mrs. White-Smith used."

"How about the shooting at Mr. Waters and me the day at the Bryant house?"

Blake shook his head. "We have no evidence to match to a gun, but we may get something from Wiseman in an interrogation. Also, there's the vehicle driving away from the attempted murder scene. We have the vehicle and they're dusting it for prints. Only time will tell."

"You know what this means, don't you?" Chloe gave Blake a wry smile.

Blake narrowed his gaze. "What?"

"I have to go back to the two remaining restoration contractors and convince them to place bids. Hopefully since the culprits have been caught, they'll be a bit more eager to work with us. Perhaps now we can move forward and restore the Bryant house after all."

Blake moved closer and, while on his knees, wrapped Chloe in his arms. "You know, when Bill radioed he'd seen Wiseman carrying you into the house over his shoulder unconscious, I thought I'd go nuts. It took all I could do not to rush in after you. But I had two more hostages to consider. We had to move in so none of you got killed. As it was…well, that's for later. I'm thankful it's over."

Chloe rested her forehead against Blake's. "Me too. When my head stops hurting and the bells top ringing—" she gave a light chuckle. "I'll plan a simple burial for Sergeant Edwards. Once he's at rest, we can move forward with the house restoration and our lives."

Blake straightened and reached for Chloe's hands, twining his fingers with hers. "Yeah, about that. The moving forward with our lives thing? We need to have a discussion about that sometime soon."

His gaze met hers and the warmth there sent the butterflies in her mid-region fluttering. This man had a way of making her feel beautiful, special, desired and needed all at the same time. There was no doubt in her mind. This wasn't all about the physical. Blake appreciated Chloe for who she was. The mother of a little girl who had lost a husband and was fighting her way back from a lost love. He hadn't yet told her he loved her, but she'd seen it in his eyes. He showed her in the way he looked at her, the way he touched her and the way he treated her. Was she ready to discuss moving forward with their lives? Yes, she was. Chloe had no doubt he'd tell her he loved her in time. She wanted to move forward in life with Blake Hunter. As much as she'd loved Josh, there was room in her heart to love again, and she adored this man. Chloe reached up and ran a finger down Blake's stubbly cheek. "Whenever you're ready." Then with deliberate intent, she placed a kiss on his lips. A kiss that promised a future filled with love.

Epilogue

The large number of park rangers and park personnel assembled at the Gettysburg National Cemetery surprised Chloe. She hadn't anticipated such a turnout. When word of the remains discovered in the cellar of the Bryant House came to light, it spread like wildfire. She wasn't, however, surprised to see a few local and state news reporters with their cameramen in attendance. She only hoped they'd keep the noise down and respect the ceremony for what it was. The laying to rest of a soldier long overdue.

Chloe had arranged the ceremony to be held at dusk since the date was the fourth of July. Fireworks displays would begin shortly, a fitting tribute to the end of the ceremony in honor of Sgt. Timothy Edwards of the 5th Connecticut Infantry Division.

The Battle of Gettysburg was fought on these hallowed grounds 159 years ago, ending yesterday the third of July. It was only right to bury the sergeant on the fourth to celebrate his service to his country. It didn't matter what side he fought on, only that this soldier fought for what he believed in. Just as all the soldiers did who were buried in the graves surrounding his grave all those years ago. Buried here were soldiers not only from the North and a few from the South in the Civil War, but also from the Spanish American War, World Wars I and II, the Korean War and Vietnam.

Chloe stood between Blake and her father, dressed in their dress park uniforms, their straw, flat-brimmed Smokey-Bear hats properly placed on their heads. Dad had given an amazing speech at the opening of the ceremony. It was surprising there was a dry eye present as he gave tribute to this fallen hero. Her gaze swept over the uniformed park personnel and rangers all wearing their dress uniforms and realized how much respect they showed Sergeant Edwards. A man whose life had been snuffed out far too soon and whose body was hidden away rather than buried as it should have been.

Chloe's gaze strayed to the sergeant's casket. Draped with a copy of the US flag in service in 1863 and carried by the Union troops of the day, she'd had it specifically made for this ceremony. Any other US flag just wouldn't do.

A lone bugler stepped forward several feet from the casket. As the first notes of Taps sounded through the silence, the company of park personnel and rangers came to attention and as one removed their Smokey-Bear hats with their left hands and rested them on their left forearms, straight and parallel with the ground. A few camera flashes filled the dusk, but not a sound could be heard except for the slow, even playing of Taps.

Chloe blinked away the tears that threatened. This poor soul didn't deserve what had happened to him. She only hoped he'd known the Lord.

As the final notes of Taps echoed into the silence, the company of personnel and rangers replaced their hats, and six park police officers stepped to the sides of the casket and began folding the flag. Once the last crease was tucked into place creating the symbolic tri-cornered shape, the lead casket bearer turned to a couple sitting alongside the casket.

Chloe had been ecstatic when she'd found the descendant of Sergeant Edward's youngest brother, Isaac Edwards, and invited him and his wife to the ceremony. Glen Edwards was the only living relative to Sergeant Edwards she'd been able to locate, and when she'd talked with him, a direct descendent, he'd been flabbergasted to learn of the situation and of his ancestor.

Glen's hands trembled as the park police officer stepped before him, bowed and placed the folded flag within his hands. His words rang clearly in the silence.

"On behalf of the President of the United States, the National Park Service, and a grateful Nation, please accept this flag as a symbol of our appreciation for your loved one's honorable and faithful service."

Glen, a young man in his thirties, nodded as his face reddened and his eyes glazed with tears. His Adams apple bobbed. "Thank you."

Chloe barely heard the soft, trembling words. He lowered his gaze as his wife took his arm.

The sun had dropped below the horizon and darkness spread as the last rays lit the sky above the tree line. Stars twinkled above, joining the flickering lights around the cemetery. Fireworks began, showering an array of colors in the darkening sky, first to the north then to the west followed by others around the county.

"Company…dismissed." The bugler's voice rang out in the silence, and everyone began to break up and make their way toward the exit.

Blake turned to Chloe and squeezed her hand. "You okay?"

She heaved a sigh and nodded, peace filling her for the first time in a long while. "Yeah, I'm good. You?"

He reached for her hand and twined his fingers with hers. He grinned. "Yeah, I'm great. I'm here with you." Blake glanced toward Dan Fielding. Chloe followed his gaze. Her dad chatted with Chief Morton and a couple of other park personnel.

Blake removed his hat, then hers and dropped them onto the grass at their feet. He then slipped his arm around her waist and drew her close. "As I was saying, I'm gre—"

"Mommy, Mommy!" An excited Evie launched herself at them both, wrapping her arms around their legs. "Blake."

"Princess." Chloe took a step back from Blake's arms, an apology in her gaze, then bent to pick up Evie. "I'm so proud of you. You were so quiet during the ceremony." She dropped a kiss on the little girl's cheek. "How did you manage to stay so quiet?"

Evie twisted her fingers together and smiled. "Aunt Charlene pwomised me ice cweme if I didn't make a sound."

The promiser stepped up and grinned. "Yes, I did. I must admit I'm not above bribery when the occasion calls for it."

Chloe laughed at the comical expression stamped on Aunt Charlene's features. "Well, it worked, and under normal circumstances I might be upset, but these weren't normal circumstances." Chloe kissed Evie's nose. "You were great, so I think ice cream is okay."

Her daughter scrunched her shoulders and smiled with excitement, then she turned to Blake. "You gonna be my daddy?"

Chloe gasped. “Evie!”

Blake let out a loud laugh and rubbed the back of his neck. “What makes you ask that?”

“You like Mommy, don’t you? You had your arms ‘wound her just now. So you have to marry her.” Evie spread her hands and rolled her eyes. “Evwybody knows dat.”

Aunt Charlene clamped a hand over her mouth, but it didn’t hide the shaking of her body. From the warmth that rolled over her, Chloe was certain her face must be beet-red. She evaded Blake’s gaze but was drawn there nonetheless. Her fist clamped over her own lips.

Blake was struggling to control his own laughter. He coughed a couple times, but a smile broke out on his handsome lips.

“Ahem. Yes, well, Evie. I tell you what. Why don’t you run along with your Aunt Char, and I’ll discuss things with your mommy? We’ll see if we can come to an agreement. How about that?”

Evie’s brow puckered as her thee-year-old brain contemplated Blake’s words. Then she nodded once and turned to Chloe, framing her mom’s cheeks. Her words came out in a loud whisper. “Mommy, I weally like him. A lot. I want him for my daddy, so listen to him, okay?”

The laughter faded from Chloe as she met her daughter’s dark eyes, so like her father’s. This little girl had never known him, yet she wanted a daddy. She wanted one with her whole heart, and she’d picked Blake Hunter to be that man. Chloe’s gaze shifted to Blake’s. The humor had left it. The sheen of tears indicated his understanding of what her daughter was asking. He blinked several times then gave Chloe a crooked smile and a wink.

Chloe smiled at her daughter, dropping a kiss on her cheek. “I love you, princess, and I’ll listen to what Blake has to say. I promise.”

“I love you, Mommy.”

“Hey princess, let’s find Grandpa and go get that ice cream. What do you say?” Aunt Charlene reached for her and set her on the ground taking her hand.

“I say, let’s go.” And off they went to find Grandpa.

“Ever heard the word ‘precocious’?” Chloe shook her head as they walked away.

Blake took Chloe's hand and pulled her close. "Yeah, and I bet she's just like her mom when she was that age."

"Now what makes you say that?" Chloe placed her other hand on his chest, her smile meeting his.

"It's gotta be in the DNA." He clasped both hands against his chest as he pulled her closer. "She's a pretty smart kid, you know."

"Yeah, I know." Chloe let out a soft laugh. "Must have been the way you were holding me."

Blake's low chuckle rumbled in his chest beneath her hands. "Well, now you have to listen to me. Evie's orders."

"I'm all ears." Chloe took a risk and, reaching up on tiptoe, placed a tender kiss on Blake's cheek.

His breath caught, his gaze roaming over her features and landing on her lips. His breathing became ragged, and no words came.

"You were saying?" Chloe took pleasure in knowing she could cause such a reaction.

"Uh, yeah." Blake shifted his feet. "Listen to me. Like Evie said."

Chloe shrugged and gave a nod. "Any time."

"Well, doggone it, you're distracting me, Chloe Rogers. Stop it."

Chloe tried to hide the grin, but Blake lowered a brow at her. Wrapping an arm around her back, he tugged her to him, his lips meeting hers. He was gentle yet seeking, and Chloe returned his kiss, meeting his passion.

After several moments, he lifted his head a few inches and rested his forehead against hers. Chloe opened her eyes and met the flame in his gaze.

"Ready to listen now?" A crooked grin played about his lips.

"Oh, yes. I have been since Evie left, you know." Chloe quirked a brow at him, her own grin teasing.

All humor left Blake's features, and he twined his fingers with hers, bringing them to his lips. "Will you marry me, Chloe? I love you more than you can know."

She gave him another quick kiss. "I think I know, and yes, I'll marry you, Blake Hunter. I love you. You've filled that void Josh left behind. And you never have to worry that I'll compare the two of you. You're two completely different men with different personalities, different dreams and different plans for your lives." Chloe ran the tip of her finger down his cheek and smiled. "There's only one other thing to settle. Evie wants you for her daddy in the worst way. Are you willing to be that for her?"

Blake tenderly shoved a stand of hair behind Chloe's ear. "I'll treat her like my own child, Chloe, and when we have our own children, no one will ever know she's not mine. Even before ours come along, she'll be like my own." He held her away a bit. "I'm looking forward to that, you know."

"What?" Chloe already knew what he was going to say.

"To having kids with you." He waggled his eyebrows suggestively.

She gave him a gentle shove. "Behave yourself."

"Oh, I am." He lowered his head. "Get used to it. Marry me soon?"

She nodded as he laid his lips once again on hers.

They were so wrapped up in one another they didn't realize they were the only ones left in the cemetery except the folks closing Sergeant Edwards grave. Fireworks of every color continued to burst in glorious flares across the inky sky, yet Chloe and Blake were oblivious. Theirs was a love both deep and secure held with the promise of a future without deceit.

The End

Keep reading for a sample of Courage on the Run

Author's Notes

~

I'm fortunate to live only an hour and a half from Gettysburg, PA. I've been to the battlefield several times, the first when I went with my parents as a child. However, I must say my most enjoyable visit was when I did my research for this novel. Having driven through the battlefield many times, we've never taken any type of tour. This time we bought a recorded CD audio tour with a book of maps and pictures, and we did it right. My mother-in-law came with my husband and me, and we took our time at every stop, listening and learning so much. It was fascinating.

We drove our RV to a campground and spent several days there, taking in the sights and visiting museums and learning more than I've ever learned in all my previous visits put together.

As with the rest of my park novels, I try to base them in historical fact while the story is fiction. *Battlefield of Deceit* is the last in the *Faith in the Park* series, and readers from the North and the South I hope have found that I tried to stay neutral in this novel. I picked an actual division to stay true to history, but Col. Edgar William Mayfield is a fictious character from my imagination. If there was a real person with that name, I have no knowledge of it. The same goes for Sgt. Timothy Edwards and Maj. Gen Archibald McAdams. The dates and all other information concerning the Civil War are correct to the best of my knowledge except for the skirmish between First Squad and the southern troops. That was writer's license.

As to the subject of ghosts. That is a personal opinion that varies from one person to another and a topic of discussion since time immemorial. My father was an old-fashioned Baptist preacher who believed he saw something with his own eyes on more than one occasion, yet he believed in 2 Corinthians 5:8 "We are confident, I say, and willing rather to be absent from the body, and to be present with the Lord." As Christians, we can be confident in our destination when we die.

There are those who refuse to believe, and there are those who are adamant. I didn't write this book to convince or to deter anyone. I simply added it to increase the tension and interest in the story. Gettysburg is supposed to be one of the most haunted towns in our nation due to the horrific violence that the town and surrounding area endured those days of the war. You can walk into any gift shop or museum in town and find a variety of ghost books on sale, all telling stories related to the Civil War.

Having said that, I've had my share of experiences as far as hearing some strange things and seeing evidence of things being moved, etc. but I had never seen a ghost. Until last year when I was at my mother's home helping to prepare it to sell. The house across the road had been purported to be haunted for years. Every time I took my dog, Holly, out, she would always stop and look across the road at the house. Without fail. I never saw anything. Until one night last year when I was there by myself. I took Holly out and was waiting for her to do her thing. I always looked at the house across the road out of habit, and this time there was something different. A white figure paced back and forth on the front porch. I did a double take. Then a third one. I stared. Looked away. Then back. It was still there. Pacing. It was the first time in my life I'd ever seen one. I'd heard sounds in my childhood and seen evidence. But there, across the road. There was a ghost in front of me. My father's accounts from his past were true.

I don't understand all the strange things that go on in this world, but I know our God is in control, and as Blake said in the story, there is a spiritual world we cannot see. Spiritual warfare is fought around us every day. We are vulnerable if we don't put our trust in the One Who is all powerful, and Who can protect us. That's not fiction. That's straight from the Bible. Keep your eyes on Him. And if you've never accepted Christ as your Savior, today is the day of salvation. John 3:16 says, "For God so loved the world that he gave his only begotten Son, that whosoever believeth in him should not perish, but have everlasting life." Wont you trust Him today?

If you have any questions or would like to contact me to tell me you've put your trust in Him, you can email me at carol.nemeth.cn@gmail.com.

*What is 'Stolen Valor?
by
thomasr@stripes.osd.mil Thomas Ruyle
    June 16, 2010 Stolen Valor - The phenomenon of people falsely claiming military awards or medals they did not earn, service they did not perform, Prisoner of War experiences that never happened, and other tales of miliary actions that exist only in their minds.

Dear Reader,

If you enjoyed reading this book and want to help me to continue writing and publishing more books for your enjoyment, please take a moment to leave a review. They are very important to authors. We depend on them to let other readers know what they think about our books so they in turn will know whether or not to purchase and read them. Should you not care for it, I would appreciate an email to me rather than a negative review. And remember, the author has no control over prices, so please keep that in mind if you're not happy with the cost.

You can find me at Amazon, Goodreads and BookBub should you choose to leave a review.

Thank you again for reading my story. I hope you enjoyed it.

For His glory,

J. Carol Nemeth

Sign up for my newsletter and receive a free short story.

Courage on the Run

J. Carol Nemeth

Chapter One

"You have the grocery list?" Casey Hartman called to her Aunt Nora as the older woman slipped out the kitchen door heading to her car. Casey suppressed a chuckle at her aunt's disgruntled expression when she reentered the kitchen. Aunt Nora snatched the offending list from the kitchen counter where she'd left it.

"I'll try this again." Aunt Nora grumbled as she headed for the door, her loose auburn bun bobbing on the back of her head.

"You have the check book, right?" Casey tossed over her shoulder as she strolled toward the laundry room at the back of the bed and breakfast she and Aunt Nora ran together.

"Yes, I have the checkbook." Aunt Nora's clipped tones grew fainter as she climbed into her car and drove toward town.

Casey wasn't worried about her aunt's memory. She had done the same thing herself but had actually gotten to the store before realizing it. There was just so much to do in running Belmont Inn. When something slipped, it wasn't surprising. Casey pulled tablecloths and napkins from the dryer and began folding them. Aunt Nora would be gone for a while, and Casey had a list of things to do while she was gone.

The front buzzer rang indicating someone had entered the front door. Casey tossed the unfolded linens back in the dryer and restarted it on tumble. No way would she leave them to wrinkle. Ironing would not be added to her list today.

Casey hurried to the front of the inn and found a tall, dark-haired young man standing by the counter. She slipped behind it.

"Hi. Can I help you?" She put on her most welcoming smile.

Turning his gaze from the high ceiling and antique furniture to Casey, a grin lifted the corners of his lips. "Hi. I have a reservation for the next few days. I'm Will Kerns."

"All right. Let me take a look." Casey turned to the laptop beneath the counter and typed in his name. Within seconds she retrieved his information. "Yes, here it is."

She checked him in then reached into a box on the wall and retrieved a key. She walked around the counter. "If you'll follow me, I'll show you to your room, Mr. Kerns."

Casey led him up a wide, straight staircase with a mahogany banister. Thick burgundy carpet on the stair treads silenced their footsteps. Several old portraits graced the walls along the staircase with lighted crystal sconces casting a bright glow.

"Welcome to Belmont Inn, Mr. Kerns." Casey glanced over her shoulder at the young man following her up the stairs. "You may already know that our inn is an original Civil War home, and many of the antiques and portraits you see are from the family who originally lived here. There was a lot of history that took place here and in the town of Belmont."

"That's interesting. Was it your family?"

They reached the landing and Casey stopped and turned to him. "Actually, it was. This home has been in my family since the early 1800s. My great, great, great-grandfather built it."

His eyebrows shot upward. "That's pretty cool. Not many people can say they still live in their ancestral home."

Casey smiled and waved him on. "No, I suppose not."

At the end of the short hallway, she stopped before a tall, wide door, and using the key, unlocked it and swung it open. Stepping back, Casey allowed Mr. Kerns to enter first.

"General Stonewall Jackson, General J.E.B. Stuart, General Ulysses S. Grant, and General Orville Babcock all stayed here. Not all at the same time obviously." Casey released a chuckle. "The town and the house were occupied by both southern and northern armies at various times."

Mr. Kerns dropped his duffle bag on the suitcase stand at the foot of the canopy bed and gazed around the room. "This is quite something."

Casey was proud of the decor in the inn. In this room, the canopy was natural-colored, knotted rope with tassels stretched over the canopy frame. A quilt of the most amazing fall colors covered the bed, while a collection of throw pillows in the same colors were stacked at the head. The burnished oak bed itself was an antique as were the dresser, washstand, and nightstand.

"Don't worry. You won't have to fetch water to use in the washstand." Casey chuckled as she approached a door on a side wall. "Here's a bathroom for your use. Every room has been retrofitted with a bathroom, complete with toilet and shower. Originally, it was the staircase for the servants to access the room."

She stepped over to another tall, wide door and swung it open for his inspection. "Sadly, we don't have regular closets. In the old days they used pegs to hang their clothes on. As you can see, we still do. The closet is long and narrow. There are hangers for you to hang your clothes on the pegs, however, unlike what our ancestors used to do."

"Interesting. I'll make it work."

Casey held out the room key and when he held out his hand, she dropped it in it. "There you go. I hope you enjoy your stay, and if you need anything, don't hesitate to let us know. Breakfast is from 6 a.m. until 8:30 a.m. If you're here for a vacation, I'll be happy to recommend lots of things to see and do in the area. As I mentioned before, we're a historical town so there's lots to check out."

"Thank you. I may take you up on that."

"I lock the doors at 11 p.m. but you have a front door key on your keyring. We understand some guests do stray far from the fold and may come in later. That's why we provide a key. If you come in after hours, please make sure the front door is locked behind you."

"I'll do that." Mr. Kerns held up the keyring and nodded.

~

Casey and Aunt Nora lived at the rear of the inn in a small apartment with two bedrooms, a living room, small kitchen and a bathroom. It was nine o'clock and Aunt Nora was firmly planted before the flat screen TV in the small living room, a bowl of popcorn in her hand.

Casey dropped onto the edge of the overstuffed armchair and shoved her foot into a tennis shoe. "I'm heading out for my evening walk, Aunt Nora."

"Be careful, sweets. I wish you'd walk earlier. It's starting to get cooler these fall evenings. You're going to catch your death, you know." Nora's eyes never left the TV.

"I'd love to, but you know it's hard to do when we have guests. This is when I finally have the time. I'd prefer walking in the morning, but with breakfast prep, that's not going to happen."

"I know."

Casey finished tying her second shoe and stood to her feet. Leaning over the side of Nora's chair, she planted a kiss on her cheek.

Nora's gaze moved to her niece's face. "Love you, kiddo. Be careful. Got your pepper spray?"

Casey held up the palm-sized tube she always carried just in case. "Right here. I'll be back in a while. Love you too."

Casey headed out the front door and across the street where she headed further into town. Of course, in the little town they lived in, everything except a few restaurants were closed. Tugging up the zipper of her jogging jacket against the cool fall air, she power walked past the pre-Civil War era courthouse. She loved the stores and restaurants in Belmont, some of which were built before the Civil War and others which came along in the 1930s when the town expanded a bit. It hadn't changed much since. There were a few other people out walking, and she waved as she passed. Casey never felt fear when she was walking through Belmont. She always felt safe in her town. She carried the pepper spray to please Aunt Nora.

Casey usually took a shortcut down an alley that led to another street where she walked by the old cemetery. There were graves that were dated before the Civil War, and most of her ancestors were buried there as well as her parents. Most people thought she was crazy for walking by there at night, but she wasn't afraid. Yeah, she heard some things that sounded…well, strange. But she didn't go *into* the cemetery. Just along the edge of it. She never saw anything.

Her friend, Jennifer's, Aunt May led a ghost tour in Belmont from May through Halloween and one of the stops led through the cemetery. Supposedly she had lots of stories to tell. Aunt May had been after her for years to come on the tour, but Casey had no desire to creep through the alleyways and the cemetery of Belmont looking for ghosts. It just wasn't her thing.

Casey turned up the alley where her rubber-soled tennis shoes were silent on the concrete pavement. A light shone behind the building on her right at the end of the alley. Strange. There had never been a light on there before. She had always come out at the end of the alley behind the building and into a small empty parking lot onto another street.

Why was there a light on in the parking lot? It wasn't a bright light, but why was it there? Casey crept on silent feet along the side of the building until she got to the end, then she peeked around the corner.

Four men stood with their backs to her a few feet from where she stood. One man held another man close against him with a knife to his neck, and without warning, slid the knife across the man's neck. Blood spurted even as the man with the knife released him. The man slid to the ground facing in Casey's direction.

Casey released a gasp before she could slap a hand over her mouth. The other three men turned in her direction. Yanking back behind the corner into the shadows, Casey found her feet moving of their own volition as she headed back down the alley.

"Go get her and bring her back here."

The words assaulted Casey's ears even as she rounded the end of the alley and headed down the sidewalk toward Belmont Inn. They would be on her in seconds if she stayed on the sidewalk. She had to find a hiding place until they got past her then she'd wind her way home in the dark evading them. It was the only way to stay alive until she could get back and call the police.

Lord, help me! Hide me from those evil men. Don't let them find me.

Casey ducked into Mrs. O'Conner's yard and stuck to the grass where her footsteps were soundless as she headed for the elderly lady's garden shed. Was the backyard protected by a motion sensor light? Casey couldn't remember and sure hoped it wasn't. She made it to the shed in time to drop behind it just as she heard heavy footsteps run past on the sidewalk in front of the house. Casey's heart hammered so hard she hoped she hadn't mistaken it for the footsteps.

Surely the thugs wouldn't start searching through neighborhood yards. Guessing they most likely would, Casey couldn't take that chance. She had to get to the inn fast. After a few minutes, she crept from behind the shed and across the yard toward the next one. Keeping her head on a swivel and ears on alert for any sound, Casey made her way through the next five yards to a street. Two more yards after that and she'd be home.

Casey paused at the edge of the street behind a tree and waited for a car to pass. Heart hammering and breath pumping, she bent at the waist, her hands resting on her knees. Dogs lived at some of the houses where she'd come through the yards, but the Lord had cleared those hurdles. They'd all been inside. *Thank you, Lord.*

Glancing both ways, she stepped out, caution vibrating through every nerve. Here she'd be the most vulnerable as she crossed the street. The thugs could come from nowhere and grab her.

Casey started to step into the street when a hand came around her mouth and she was pulled against a hard chest. Her hands flew to the hand covering her mouth, and she struggled to pull it away.

"Don't scream. I'll pull my hand away, but I just didn't want you to scream. It's okay. Promise you won't scream?"

Casey stilled as she recognized a familiar voice. She nodded and turned as the hand dropped from her mouth.

"Will Kerns? What are you doing out here, and why are you scaring me to death?" Casey's voice was a mere whisper as her hand flew to her chest over her heart.

Will shrugged as he propped his hands on his hips. "I could ask you the same thing. Why are you sculking through your neighbor's backyards?"

Casey glanced over her shoulders and grabbed his hand, pulling him across the street into the next neighbor's backyard. "Ask me again when we get inside the inn. Just help me get there safely."

Author Bio

A native North Carolinian, J. Carol Nemeth has always loved reading and enjoyed making up stories ever since junior high school, most based in the places she has lived or traveled to. She worked in the National Park Service as a Park Aid and served in the US Army where she was stationed in Italy, traveling to over thirteen countries while there. She met the love of her life, Mark Nemeth, also an Army veteran, while stationed in Italy. After they married, they lived in various locations, including North Yorkshire, England. They now live in West Virginia, where, in their spare time, Carol and Mark enjoy RVing, sightseeing and are active in their church. They have a son, Matt, who serves active duty in the Army and a daughter, Jennifer, her husband Flint, who serves active duty in the Air Force, and their three grandchildren, Martin, Ava and Gage. Their four-footed kid Holly, a black Lab, is pretty special too. Mark and Carol love traveling in their RV, and when they pack up to go, Holly is waiting inside for them to head out. Carol, a multi-published author, is a member of ACFW, and is an Amazon bestselling author. She loves traveling to research for her books and Mark chauffeurs her in the RV wherever they go.

Connect with me on FaceBook

Twitter

Follow me on Amazon

Goodreads And Bookbub

Enjoy other books by J. Carol Nemeth

Yorkshire Lass

Faith in the Park Series

Dedication to Love: Prequel to Mountain of Peril

Mountain of Peril, Faith in the Parks Book 1

Canyon of Death, Faith in the Parks Book 2

A Beacon of Love, Prequel to Ocean of Fear

Ocean of Fear, Faith in the Parks Book 3

Glacier of Secrets, Faith in the Parks Book 4

Battlefield of Deceit, Faith in the Parks Book 5

Christmas Novella

Parade of Hearts

Collections

The Peaceful Valley Wounded Soldiers Anthology

Collections with Other Authors

Little Bits

Romancing the Roaring Twenties

Romancing the Flying Forties

Christmas Lights and Loves

Hearts of the Manhattan Project Short Stories

The Secretary

The Nurse

Made in the USA
Middletown, DE
02 July 2022

68210505R00156